FLOOD TIDE

DEVOTION SERIES - BOOK #2

TRACEY JERALD

Let the flood in.
xoxo,
Tracey Jerald

ISBN: 978-1-7358129-7-7 (eBook)
ISBN: 978-1-7358129-8-4 (Paperback)
Library of Congress Number, Pending

Tracey Jerald
Flood Tide
101 Marketside Avenue, Suite 404-205,
Ponte Vedra, FL, 32081

Editor: Missy Borucki
Editor: Happily Editing Anns
Proof Edits: Comma Sutra Editorial (https://www.facebook.com/CommaSutraEditorial)
Cover Design by Tugboat Design (https://www.tugboatdesign.net/)

DEDICATION

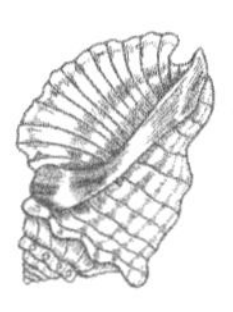

To the people I work with day in and day out. Balancing two worlds would never be possible without you.

Or, as Iris and Sam might say it:

Je vous aime mes amis, toujours.

01001001 00100000 01101100 01101111 01110110 01100101
00100000 01111001 01101111 01110101 00100000 01100110
01110010 01101001 01100101 01101110 01100100 01110011
00101100 00100000 01100001 01101100 01110111 01100001
01111001 01110011 00101110

Team Alpha Foxtrot Sierra

FLOOD Tide

TRACEY JERALD

ALSO BY TRACEY JERALD

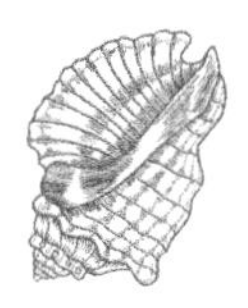

Devotion Series

Ripple Effect

Flood Tide

MIDAS SERIES

Perfect Proposal

Perfect Assumption

Perfect Composition

Perfect Order

Perfect Satisfaction (Fall 2022)

Amaryllis Series

Free to Dream

Free to Run

Free to Rejoice

Free to Breathe

Free to Believe

Free to Live

Free to Dance

Free to Wish

Free to Protect

Free to Reunite (Summer 2022)

GLACIER ADVENTURE SERIES

Return by Air

Return by Land

Return by Sea

STANDALONES

Close Match

Unconditionally With Me – A With Me in Seattle Novella

GO TO HTTPS://WWW.TRACEYJERALD.COM/ for all buy links!

PLAYLIST

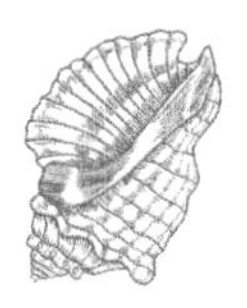

The Goo Goo Dolls: "*Iris*"
The Killers: "*West Hills*"
7kingZ: "*Born for This*"
Robin Loxley, Oliver Jackson: "*Be What You Want*"
The Well Pennies: "*The Wedding Song*"
Delta Rae: "*No Peace In Quiet*"
Ed Sheeran: "*Castle On The Hill*"
Maren Morris: "*Better Than We Found It*"
Lindsey Stirling, Christina Perri: "*Brave Enough*"
Jennifer Hudson, Tori Kelly: "*Hallelujah*"
Imagine Dragons: "*Bad Liar*"
Nickleback: "*Far Away*"
Imagine Dragons: "*Wrecked*"
Zayde Wølf: "*Born Ready*"

The single biggest problem in communication is the illusion that it has taken place.

GEORGE BERNARD SHAW

PROLOGUE
IRIS

Present DAY

I'M EMOTIONALLY EXHAUSTED.

Over the last twelve months, I've spent so much time rising above accusations cast upon me for crimes I never committed when the ones I was forced to relive in mind were worse. Far worse.

I've learned when the people you have to cross are faceless, it matters far less than if you know their names, let alone if you're directly connected to their hearts and souls. And this makes the second time I've withstood this type of inquisition.

A piece of my long curl escapes the clip I twisted my mass of hair into before we left our home this morning, but before I can reach up to shove it back, his fingers are there gently tucking the wayward curl behind my ear. Like he's done countless times.

Sam trails his fingers down my cheek before running them down my arm. Intuitively, our fingers tangle together as we wait to be called back. Silently, I study them as they interlock tightly at the webbing. Since the morning I woke up in a strange hospital, he's always held my hand like this—fiercely. As if he was afraid someone would try to rip my hand from his grasp before he had a chance to tether me to him.

I study his hands not without the same awe I always feel. Sam's hands have brought me incomparable pleasure, and yet they've been used as a tool for undeniable destruction. I apply pressure so he feels the pinch of my wedding ring, a reminder of the vows we took together all those years ago.

And have held steadfast to.

A near-constant pain lanced through me as I endured allegations of breaking apart our family, piercing more than my mind, more than my voice, doing its best to shred my very core. I shake my head, even now fervently denying the charges. Not true in any manner, but to right the wrongs inadvertently committed to the people I love before God and country, I agreed to take this step.

My husband did as well.

Because before our own comfort, someone else's needs come first. Peace of mind, putting some closure on this part of her—our—past is long overdue.

His lips brush against the back of my fingers when he lifts my hand to his lips. "It's graduation day."

"You hope," I retort. But I can't prevent the curve of my lips because I know he's right.

"I can't believe we made it this far without you cursing more."

"Sam," I warn him, but I can't contradict him. Reliving over twenty years of our past—when we could share it—has been incredibly emotional.

"Especially in Russian and French. You seem to enjoy the punch in those words," he teases.

I sniff but don't bother with a verbal retort. After all, how am I supposed to argue when this man knows me like no other person? We fell in love, created a family, and have faced death together. And that's only what's happened so far. Knowing we cast our future in a world that's murky at best, we relish every moment on our island of solace with each other. And along the way, hurt caused against our loved ones has caused our own marital struggles.

But like most others, we hung on past the rough seas into smooth sailing.

I lay my head on Sam's shoulder and bring him back to his original statement. "You hope it's our graduation day."

"I'm highly optimistic. Rachel asked me to help plan something," he murmurs, keeping his voice low in deference to the other people milling about the large waiting room.

I roll my eyes. "Just tell me it doesn't involve her cooking." One skill our daughter didn't inherit from her maternal great-grandmother was her ability to devastate the senses with food. *No, Rachel is absolutely mine and Sam's,* I admit silently. In fact, I'd do anything for my family, just short of murder. After all, if I was willing to give myself over to this torture, I'm willing to do anything to purge the demons that have plagued our family for far too long.

Demons everyone was certain we'd slain until . . .

Sam's always been able to calculate where my mind wanders to. "What she asked us to do just made us stronger, Iris."

Ignoring any eyes that may be trained on us—either the human or electronic kind— I tip my head back and press my lips to my husband's. Like the first time, the flash of heat leaps between us. Despite our rather auspicious surroundings, it makes me want to sink my fingers deep into his sable-colored hair to deepen this kiss. Hell, any kiss so long as it's Sam's lips touching mine.

Judging by the sparkle in his eyes as he pulls away, he knows it. "Later," he mouths.

I pout, pretending an insult I don't feel. Because, like so many things in our marriage, he's right. Now isn't the time to lose ourselves in one another.

I twirl a lock of my still dark waves around my finger as I contemplate what will be said in just a few moments. Sam may be right, but so many times he was wrong, refusing to listen to important things.

Things that have come back to haunt us.

The door swings open. A young man wearing a buttoned vest steps out holding a thick teal folder. Every time I see it, I'm reminded of the waters in the Cooper River when the sunlight hits it just so as it passes Sam's family home—Akin Hill. "Mr. and Mrs. Akin? Are you ready?"

We both stand, still holding onto one another's hands. Our future is just a few hours ahead. We've paid our penance, made our apologies. I can't deny when Sam's hand releases mine to drop to the small of my back to guide me through the door to greet the person on the other side, I'm bolstered by the support it provides me.

"IF I NARROW MY EYES, it would be so easy to imagine you the first time I saw you," Sam declares outrageously from where he's sprawled across the leather Chesterfield. His arm is draped casually across the back as if this isn't the most important meeting of our lives.

Which it is.

I remind him, "You ignored me for the better part of three years before you acknowledged my existence."

"I wouldn't say that."

"You're right." I agree immediately. His face morphs into a look of shock over my admission before I continue, "You treated me exactly like Libby. I had all these overwhelming emotions for you, and you kept petting me on the head. Proverbially, of course."

He scowls. "I didn't treat you like Libby." Libby is Sam's first cousin and was my college roommate for four years. She was, and still is today, my best friend. The two of us are closer than many of the biological relationships I've had a bird's eye to in the Akin family.

"Of course, that's the point you fixate on, Samuel." I roll my eyes skyward.

That's when he throws out, "Maybe you should have tried harder, Iris." His green eyes, eyes our daughter inherited, sparkle at me outrageously.

I scream incoherently. In all the trips we've made to this very office, I've never been so grateful for the soundproofing as I am at this one singular moment. After I finish with the primal shriek, I realize the pressure valve has loosened. Sam grins at me. "Feel better?"

"Strangely, yes." I drop down onto the sofa. His arm immediately curls around me, like it had merely been waiting to curl me into his side.

"Your ancestors—both sides— used to let loose some of those war cries before they'd go into battle."

"Like I'm not aware of that?"

But suddenly, I'm giggling.

"What's so funny?" he asks.

"You just reminded me of something I once said to Libby before we ever got together."

"What was it?"

I glance at the door behind the desk. Since it hasn't opened, I begin to tell him.

1
TWENTY-SEVEN YEARS AGO FROM PRESENT DAY

Iris

"THE BLOOD of warriors flows through my veins, and yet I'm a complete chicken shit," I declare to my best friend.

Libby Akin, quite used to me after four years of living together at the University of Georgia, merely quirks a brow before asking, "Didn't manage to work up the nerve to ask my cousin out? Again?"

Despite the fact her words are spoken in her native Charleston accent, they grate like nails on a chalkboard. I glare at her. "It's not fair. Why does he have to be the one man . . ."

"What? Whom you can't wrap around your finger, Iris?" If it wasn't for the wicked amusement dancing in her deep-green eyes, the same eyes I took one look at three-and-a-half years ago and lost my ability to speak when I saw them over a rock-solid jaw and chiseled lips, I'd probably be throwing a fit. But this is Libby, my best friend. She's someone I'd die for without a second thought.

Samuel Winston Akin. We've known each other since the day we all were required to move into the dorms, our first year of school. After moving in his own stuff, he graciously helped Libby and her parents move her bags and boxes into our room.

Reflecting back, maybe I didn't fall head over heels the moment I met him. It likely occurred the moment our fingers clasped together during our very first handshake, and an arc of awareness spiked between us. But now, all these years later, I'm completely bewildered by the fact Sam hasn't picked up on the same feelings between us. Well into our senior year, and nada. Squat.

I've spent an incredible amount of time studying the gorgeous senior. Up until recently, I would have said he had a pathological obsession about only three things: everything related to computers, dating every attractive girl on campus except me, and his family—which honestly makes my heart quiver even more whenever I am in his presence. But lately, something has shifted. It started when we bumped into each other after he returned from his time abroad. Then I thought he was giving me the high sign when he once murmured to me haltingly, "*Wǒ háishì jìxù shǒu zhū dài tù ma?*"

Since studying Mandarin is a part of my course of study, my heart skipped a beat when I translated his words to be, "Should I continue waiting around for something to happen?" Assuming he meant between us, I was immediately about to act upon my long-standing crush. In the very next breath, he shoved to his feet before calling to Libby he had to leave because he had a date, unwittingly crushing my heart yet again.

I shoved that night aside assuming he screwed up his nouns since Mandarin is one of the hardest languages to learn. Muttering to myself that night, I forced myself to tell my image, "He must have meant to say, 'The only thing I do is wait around for things to happen.'"

Deciding at that point to stick to my plan of ignoring my feelings for Sam, I went back to throwing myself into my studies and my social life. That is until recently when a small shift began to happen during our weekly dinners at the apartment I share with Libby.

The intensity of his smile when I tell a funny story. The casual mocking amusement whenever I get so frustrated at him, I begin to curse in another language. The lazy perusal of his eyes.

He's actively trying to both captivate and torment me, and I'm still not certain if I want to jump or hit him. *Damn you, Sam Akin.*

I toss my hair over my shoulder before addressing Libby. "I have never wanted a man I can wrap around my finger, Libs."

"Then what do you want?"

I drop down on the edge of her bed and reach for one of the throw pillows she shifted to the side earlier. Thoughtfully, I consider aloud, "I want a man who isn't afraid of a brain."

"That's reasonable considering the size of yours," Libby agrees.

"And yours," I toss back at her.

Libby rolls her eyes but doesn't contradict me. Most men judge by her princess-like appearance. Between her long glossy hair that hangs down her back and her sweetly accented voice, they dismiss her as nothing more than arm candy. *Certainly the men she's dated here have,* I think silently.

Like me, she has a secret crush she's been harboring for some time. Also, like me, she's been passing time dating men who have absolutely no chance of touching the core of her heart. Wryly, I consider our situations. If my feelings for Sam are out in left field, hers for Calhoun Sullivan—the man posing as an international political science instructor but who is so much more—are in a completely different ballpark. The man is a complete dick wrapped in a package—even I have to admit—was built for sin. As one of the few who are aware of the glib lies that constantly fall from his lips, I just wish I could get Libby to see that side of him. But much like she tells me horrid stories of Sam when he was little and tugging her braids as they ran around their home at Akin Hill—in an effort to stifle my wild imaginings of tackling her gorgeous cousin, her face turns dreamy at the first mention of Calhoun's name.

We're both lost causes for men who have absolutely no interest in us.

She yanks me from my musings. "What else?"

"What else, what?" I ask, confused.

She taps her pen on my purple notebook and smirks. "I'm adding a list of your perfect man attributes to your journal. Then I'm going to compare the *real* Sam Akin next to it. Later, when you're in bed, you can study the two. Maybe if you understand he's not all that and a potential miracle orgasm, you'll get over this obsession for him." She wrinkles her nose. "Remember, I grew up with him. I know what he smells like when he comes home from the gym."

"*Potselui mou zhopy*!" I fling the pillow at her head as I tell her to kiss my ass. Great. Now I have the image of Sam all hot and sweaty in my head and an excellent fantasy of how I could get him that way.

Libby grins at me, offended not in the least. "I love how your brain automatically flips to curse in—what was that, Russian?" At my nod, she concludes. "This way you don't sound like a complete gutter mouth."

I burst out laughing. "Your grandmother said pretty much the same thing the last time we were at Akin Hill."

Libby's eyes sparkle at the mention of her beloved relative. Dahlia Akin, the matriarch of the Akin family and of its holdings that include the lucrative Akin Timbers located on the outskirts of Charleston, South Carolina, can only be described as a *grande dame*. "She called earlier."

"What did she want?"

"To ask if I was coming home for spring break. As well as to determine whether I was, 'bringing that noxious man-boy with me. Really, Libby, you can do so much better than him.'"

I howl. "I wish I was here. I got stuck with a pop quiz during poli-sci. Cal has his dick in a complete twist. He needs . . ." My words trail off when I notice the way Libby's fingers clench around her pen. I clear my throat. "Anyway, what did you tell her about spring break?"

Libby relaxes slightly. "Well, I have a few interviews I need to take in Charleston for post-grad. I might as well head home."

I flop over onto my stomach, burying my head in my arms. I mumble, "Want company?"

Her eyes widen. "You know you're welcome at the farm any time. You don't have to ask. But don't you have to do the same?"

"Not for a few more weeks. I won't hear about that extended study program until then." I can't look Libby in the eye as I lie to her, not for the first time in the course of our friendship. Kristin Mansfield, the woman Cal Sullivan directed me to train with while still a student, said I may have additional requirements that she's checking into. Kristin used to work for the government contractor that has been pressing my application through for entry into an elite linguistics training facility. At our last meeting, she warned me of the need for absolute secrecy. "Your background is already being investigated, Ms. Cunningham. It would behoove you to continue to act in a fitting manner."

"Right, so that's settled," I answer both to Libby and to the cautionary voice in my head.

Libby, pleased, picks up the receiver by her bedside. "I'll just call Nonna back."

I flip to my back. "Will we stay with her or with your parents?"

Libby turns thoughtful. "Does it matter?"

My lips curve into a wicked smile. "Only with regard to the gifts we bring."

At that, we both burst into gales of laughter before declaring in unison, "Nonna."

WEEKS LATER, we're happily ensconced at Nonna's house for spring break. As expected, Nonna hooted like one of the owls that swoop freely near the river rushing outside over the bags of roadside jerky we proudly presented to her upon arrival.

Libby and I took every single backroad we could find, avoiding the interstate altogether, stopping off at every homemade lemonade, honey, and homemade jerky stand we could find. We didn't care we easily doubled our four-and-a-half-hour drive from Athens, Georgia to the outskirts of Charleston, South Carolina. We had so many stories to share with Nonna ranging from how we parked our car and went shopping in Augusta, where I had to drag Libby out of yet another art gallery, to the incredible people in Summerville who let us cast a few lines over a small bridge to try to catch some dinner. She roared with laughter when we admitted we paid a little girl selling lemonade twenty dollars each after she got permission from her parents to let us jump on her trampoline. Gasping, she manages, "Please tell me someone got a photo of that."

Libby holds up her camera. "There's not that many pictures left, Nonna. We have to use the rest of the roll tonight so I can drop it off to be developed."

Dahlia dabs her lips with her napkin. "Well, let's finish supper, child. Then I can take a few of you and Iris by the fireplace."

I'm already shaking my head. "Oh, no, Nonna. You have to be in them."

Dahlia frowns at Libby, who is already a mass of giggles. "Child, do you have a timer on that thing?"

"No, Nonna."

"They're the best kind of pictures," I assure her.

"Awful ones?" Dahlia exclaims.

Libby giggles and races over to flick on the radio. Dahlia places her hand on her chest when I climb on top of my chair and begin singing aloud to the music. I can't hear the shutter moving up and down, but I'm certain it is as I belt out Avril Lavigne. When the song ends, I explain to a shocked Dahlia what I said to Libby years ago. "You never know what you're going to find when you develop those photos, Nonna. It's a complete surprise."

"Or a god-awful shock," she retorts.

I shoot her a lazy grin. "You know, sometimes you just have to shake your hips and cut loose." My hips move of their own accord to the music only I can hear lingering in my head.

"Oh, I think you're going to be shocked," she utters faintly.

A chill races through me at her words. My eyes meet Libby's. Her lips form the words I absolutely did not want to hear at this moment. "Hey, Sam. What are you doing here? I thought you were going away for spring break."

"Plans changed at the last minute. Thought I'd come by to say hey since Aunt Natalie mentioned you were staying with Nonna." There's a pregnant pause before he drawls, "Hey, Iris."

I'm frozen on the chair. I'm unable to face him, nor can I speak. Sam steps around the chair until he's standing in front of me. He suggests sardonically, "You look a little stiff. Perhaps I should put on some music?"

That manages to get my limbs working. I leap down and land directly in front of him. Poking him in the chest, I rasp out, "*Zasranec*!" before I drag my chair back in place at the table and plop my rear into it.

Completely mortified I just called the man I've been aching for over four years an asshole, and that's the only thing I've managed to say to him, I shove an enormous bite of Nonna's coconut cake in my mouth to keep it busy for the next several moments so I can't embarrass myself any further.

2

TWENTY-SEVEN YEARS AGO FROM PRESENT DAY

SAMUEL

"WHAT ARE you *really* doing here, Sam?" Libby demands exasperatedly after Iris leaves the room hurriedly with a stack full of plates. Before I can come up with any excuse that she might find plausible, she drawls sweetly, "I'd have expected you to be trolling every bar in Athens searching for your woman du jour with your new best buddy, Cal."

My shoulders shake at my Libby's poorly suppressed aggravation when she associates Calhoun Sullivan with other women. I feel so much pity for Cal, who took one look at my ridiculously pretty cousin and lost his head. He can't have her name mentioned without biting mine off. I was unaware at the time he was only temporarily assigned to teach when I had approached him after the second class last semester. I'd felt myself being appraised in less than two seconds. I can easily recall the way his chin jerked up before he asked me what my major was. "Dual major in Computer Science and Computer Systems Engineering."

"You're taking this course, why?" He'd asked me disbelievingly.

I shrugged at the time. "I needed the credit to graduate. Besides, after the stint I did for my IT study abroad in China, I find international politics interesting."

Cal had barked out, "You studied in China? For how long?"

Exasperated, I answered, "How long is a semester, Professor?"

That's when Cal whispered sinisterly, "I'm no more a professor than you're meant to sit behind a desk, Sam." Those words hung heavily between us when he suggested, "Why don't we go get a cup of coffee and talk about your plans for after you graduate?"

Dumbly, I'd nodded. Cal strode ahead of me as we departed his classroom. That's when I noticed he did so with a limp. I'd followed close behind. After closing the door behind me, I turned to find Iris leaning up against the wall from one of her multitude of linguistics classes. It must have just been let out and she was standing in the corridor still. Just waiting.

Something inside of me twisted because I knew she was waiting for me.

In a second of intuition, I had to make a choice—either follow my professor blindly or stay behind for the woman. Either path was paved with both rewards and hell, but at that moment in time I wanted one more than the other. Instead of acknowledging her presence, I'd caught up with Cal and picked up our conversation. "Where's this opportunity located?"

He pursed his lips. "The company I'm thinking you might be interested in is based out of Charleston, South Carolina."

I had relaxed marginally and followed him into the unknown. But ever since that afternoon, a part of me has always wondered what could have happened if I'd stopped for just a moment to speak with the woman who has been in the background of my life for years. The same one who tonight who stood on a chair at Nonna's dining room table with her curly black hair streaming down to her waist as she swayed back and forth, lighting up the room with her laughter.

The sensuous siren who invades my dreams with such a frequent regularity, I'm beginning to wonder whether half the conversations I've had with her are a figment of my imagination.

"Sam!" Libby snaps, dragging my attention back to her. "Again, what are you doing here?"

"Do I need a reason to come home?" I punch back.

"Well, no. Of course not." Her eyes flit to the door as if she expects it to fly open any second.

"Cal's not with me despite the fact he was invited," I crush her hopes brutally. The fact is, Cal's likely at his apartment preparing for my formal job interview this week. *Which,* I think ruefully, *is what I should be doing instead of lingering over dessert.*

Libby's lower lip trembles slightly before she controls it. She smiles sweetly. "Well, after you get bored here, be sure to pass along my greetings when you see him after you head back." After she delivers that cut, she rises from her seat and joins Iris in the kitchen.

The door has barely swooshed behind her when Nonna scolds me. "I didn't raise you to be so rude, Samuel."

My head falls into my hands. "You don't understand, Nonna."

She scoffs. "I don't understand? What? Dense men or how they act when they see something they want but they won't touch it for whatever imbecilic reason they've derived?"

My head rears back. "Excuse me?"

She flaps her hand at me. "All three of you here at my home when you should be out living. My Libby wearing her heart on her sleeve for a man I've heard plenty about but I'm not entirely certain is good for her. . ."

"He is," I cut off my grandmother to interject. She skewers me with her green eyes, eyes which Libby, I, and a host of our cousins have inherited. "Cal's a good man, Nonna. He just has things he needs to keep private." *Like his past, his job, and the fact he'd likely shoot someone who would dare to do Libby harm despite the fact he won't admit to it.*

"There should be no secrets in between people who are to become lovers, Samuel." I'm certain my jaw bounces several times off the table handcrafted from the trees that surround her property. She sends me a menacing look. "Please, boy. Grow up. You think you're the first young man to sit at that table to feel the stirring of lust for a woman who challenged his every emotion? Think again. Your Poppa . . ."

"Stop. This conversation has to end," I plead just as Iris emerges from the kitchen with the coffee pot. My heart shrivels in my chest a bit when I realize she won't meet my eyes when she asks, "More coffee, Nonna?"

"No, thank you, sweetheart." Nonna stands. Lifting her cheek for a kiss, Iris immediately leans down and presses her lips to the soft, smooth skin I know she feels beneath her lips. Nonna reaches up and tucks a piece of hair behind Iris's ear.

My heart swells inside my chest at the sight. It's a gesture Nonna reserves for only those she considers members of the family. *She's already accepted the woman you want. What are you waiting for, you dumb ass?* Then I recall the real reason I'm in Charleston this week. I deliberately turn from the sight. "Well, I'm going to head back to Mom and Dad's. Thanks for dinner, Nonna."

"Thank your cousin. She's the one who cooked. Her and this lovely girl," she taunts, nudging me again in the not so subtle way of hers.

My temper flares at Nonna's continuous pushing of the attraction between me and Iris. I'm a grown man. *If, when, I decide to make this move, it will be mine,* I think furiously. Right now, with the job Cal's dangling in front of me, I'm terrified the choices I'm going to make may chew her up and spit her out. A low growl emits from my throat.

Nonna just smiles in her Sphinx-like manner.

Iris's hazel eyes widen. "Is there a problem here?"

"Nothing that concerns you," I snap, my eyes not leaving my grandmother's.

She backs away from the tension, clearly enunciating, "*Jsi blázen,*" before she whirls away calling out, "Libby, Sam's leaving!"

"On my way," can be heard faintly over the running water over the sink. As the two women pass, Iris says something to Libby, just nods in understanding.

As she approaches, Libby doesn't beat around the bush. She translates, "You're a fool, Sam. That's what she said to you."

As my grandmother walks me to the door, I think truer words could not be spoken—regardless of what language they were said in. If fortune shines on me, I'll know in a few days whether or not I can have it all—the job as well as the chance with the woman it took me years to wake up and notice.

Ah, Iris. You have no idea how correct you pegged it. I am a fool, but I'm a hopeful one.

3

SAMUEL

Present DAY

I murmur to Iris. "I remember that night so clearly. I was an ass."

My wife flashes me a look of mock consternation. "No! Not you, Sam."

"I hope I've made up for it."

She rests back against me. Her ringed hand rests on my thigh. "Am I counting the time after graduation when I was first at DLI?"

I groan. "You are never going to let me forget that, are you?"

"Talking, Sam." She flips her hand around the room. "Look what happens when that small chore fails."

Just then, the door opens, and Dr. Erika Ferguson enters the room from a door that hides behind her massive desk. "Mr. and Mrs. Akin. A pleasure to see you both again."

My fearless Iris stands and steps forward to shake her hand. "And you, Doctor."

She chides my wife, not for the first time. "Erika, remember? It's our last meeting. It's a day of celebration."

I stand as well before speaking up. "We both believe it will be."

Erika gestures for us to resume our seats. "That's because both of you have been incredibly open about your personal lives despite the limitations your careers present."

"We had to be. We had no idea of what happened . . ."

"Until it did," I pick up where Iris trailed off. We're going over old ground while we wait for one final person to enter the room. She's the reason why we went through a year of therapy, to begin with. I drape my arm over Iris's shoulders again and begin tangling my fingers in the few strands that have managed to spring free.

With a sigh, Iris unclips her hair. "Will this help make you feel better?"

I grin. "Immensely. You know, one thing I've learned through all this is playing with your hair clears my thoughts."

Iris merely pins me with her gaze before leaning over to attach her hair clip to the handle of her handbag so she doesn't lose it. The violet cloisonné iris was a gift from our daughter on her birthday years ago.

"Do you have something on your mind, Sam?" Erika inquires.

I hesitate before voicing, "Despite our careers, we've always tried to live quiet lives. But even before things fell apart, that wasn't always possible."

Now it's Iris who picks up where I've left off. "What Sam's saying is between what happened to our family receiving so much news coverage after everything that happened to Libby, then Sam's being asked back into the field after we began working here in New York, there have been times where we've been shoved back into the media's notice. In today's day and age, we're not certain what they'll uncover. Is she going to be able to handle it if she's faced with the notoriety that may follow us now that she knows the truth?"

Just as the question comes out, the door behind us opens and we hear a breathless voice respond, "Completely. Because you're right, Mama. I know the truth."

Hearing our daughter's voice, Iris stands, immediately opening her arms. It's a measure of how far she's come since we started therapy that Rachel immediately rushes into them. It chokes me up to see their dark curls tangle together as Rachel holds Iris as much as my wife clutches our daughter to her. *God, they're both so beautiful.* I'm as stupefied now as I was the first day

I spied Iris at Alliance, just before she tossed her recruiter on their ass at the training facility.

It was the day I felt the first stirrings of possessiveness turn to something more when it came to my wife. Never before had I experienced such jealousy surging through me as when I'd realized I might have a shot at having it all if I really worked for it—the life I coveted and the woman I always secretly yearned for—and she might not want it, want me. I might have botched the whole thing before we ever got off the ground. The idea of it over twenty years later still makes me shudder.

I'm just grateful my wife has a huge capacity for forgiveness because I needed to ask for it over and over until we finally were able to lay all our cards on the table with nothing between us.

And that took years.

4

TWENTY-SEVEN YEARS AGO FROM PRESENT DAY

SAMUEL

THE AVERAGE PASSERBY would drive by the Alliance compound in Charleston without a second glance. It isn't until the imposing gate guards stop my vehicle on my way to drive up to the seven-story building that I realize there's much more behind the ten-foot fences than meets the eye. I roll down my window and clear my throat. "Sam—Samuel Akin. I have an interview."

"ID please?" The heavily armed guard demands.

I slide my hand into my back pocket and pull out my wallet to display my driver's license. Without a word, he returns to the hut he emerged from to run it—to run me—judging by the way he holds it up to compare the image that was taken just before my seventeenth birthday to me now. *Shit, do I smile to match the picture? Not appear serious? What should I do?* They do *not* cover job interviews with companies like this during interview preparation courses.

The reality is, what I really feel like doing is vomiting, though that's probably a bad idea. Likely the guard is already on the radio calling up to Cal's office to let him know of my arrival, as well as informing him of my mental state. *If I'm right, Cal's probably up in his office laughing his ass off if the guard happened to notice the trickle of sweat falling down the right side of my face. I suspect these guys don't miss much,* I think dourly as the guard approaches. "Here you go, Mr. Akin. Let me do a quick walk around to get your tag information and then you'll be all set."

After I slip my wallet away, I place my hands back in the ten and two position on the steering wheel. "You're clear to head to the training center located in building bravo. Did Mr. Sullivan provide you with directions?"

I shake my head. The guard points behind him. "The main offices are located in building alpha. Drive past the visitor parking. Keep following the road about two klicks—that's two kilometers for you non-military folk. Bravo will be located on your left. Parking is across the road on the right. Keep this displayed in your window."

"Thanks," I manage to drawl as I put my car back in gear.

He raps on the hood of my car as he says, "Good luck."

Wryly, I admit, "I have a feeling I'm going to need it."

That's when the gates open and I'm granted entry into a whole different world—one I've touched with my fingers through a keyboard as I've hacked my way through firewalls, but never seen with my own eyes.

The afternoon Cal and I went off campus to talk, he asked me a million and one questions. I was allowed to ask one. "Why are you so curious about all of this information about me, Mr. Sullivan?"

"Make it 'Cal,'" he informed me, before lifting his coffee to his lips.

I nodded, but don't repeat the question.

He stood and held out his hand. "Give me a few days and I'll answer any question you want, Sam. Including that one."

Cal held me back after class two days later. "Come for a run with me tonight."

I think about the plans I made with Libby and Iris to go to dinner. "I'd like to, but . . ."

"No buts, Sam. This is your shot to do more than sit behind a desk and fix someone's blue screen of death. Do you want it?" Cal demanded.

"Yes." The word escaped me so quickly, I wasn't even aware it was waiting on the tip of my tongue.

Cal jerks up his chin. "Break the plans. I'll meet you at your apartment at six. Once we're done, we'll grab something to eat."

I begin to gather my stuff and head to the door. "And that's when you'll explain?"

"As much as I can."

That night, he did. Cal explained about Alliance and how they needed a computer security expert with my skills to round out their team. I leaned back in my chair, sore and aching from the five-mile trail run Cal dragged me on, and countered, "And what makes this job so damn special? I've had half a dozen offers just like it in the last month."

Cal slapped a newspaper down next to my plate. Without losing eye contact, he murmured, "Will those other companies make the front page?"

My adrenaline spiking, I picked up the paper and read the article. It was almost unbelievable, the stuff of movies. A black-ops mission conducted by the US Navy with the assistance of a covert government contract agency run by retired Rear Admiral Richard Yarborough. My head snaps up. "That's the one thing you told me the other night. You work for a man named Rick Yarborough."

"That's one of the things I like about you, Akin. You listen," Cal drawls. He leans over before his lips curve upward. "Now, listen. Tonight's run was a preliminary test. You passed. If you're interested, there are others who want the chance to meet you."

"When?" I barely breathe the question.

"Spring break. Charleston." He rattles off an address I immediately commit to memory. "I'll be working with you before then to prepare you."

"What does that entail?"

As I drive, I reminisce over the number of mornings Cal's had me out running, and the number of nights he's had me out at bars trying to spot threats. I try to recall the number of databases I've hacked into in the weeks since he approached me to prepare for what I think they might require of me today. "This better work out. Otherwise next spring, I'll be begging Libby to bake me a cake to bring me at Leavenworth," I mutter as I park across from building Bravo.

Suddenly all the breath leaves my body as a vision in a trim, purple suit checks both ways before she crosses the street on impossibly high heels. "No. It's not possible." I slam my hand on the steering wheel in frustration as I slam my car into park and jump out. I quickly grab my gym bag from the backseat. "Goddamnit! Fucking Cal, he couldn't tell me he was recruiting Iris as well?"

Of course not. Nor would she have shared even a hint of that information if Cal showed her even a bit of the same intimidation he showed me. Carelessly, I jog across the street in my wingtips just in time to reach the door at the same moment she does. "Let me get that for you," I offer.

"Thank you, Sam," Iris replies automatically. Her whole body jerks before she twists her face up to mine. Instead of saying anything—not a single fucking word—she just studies me for a moment with her iridescent hazel eyes before walking beneath my arm and into Alliance as if she owns the place.

What the hell was that? Anger surges through me as Iris smiles pleasantly at the man behind the desk. "Hello, Karl. Good to see you again."

"Ms. Cunningham. Good to see you as well. You remember the protocol from yesterday?" Iris nods. He hands her a badge which she slips over her neck. "Very well. If you'll take a seat, I'll get someone to escort you."

"Thank you." Still blatantly ignoring my presence, Iris makes her way over to the small waiting area and sinks into one of the wingback chairs strategically placed to overlook the street. My eyes narrow on the way she perches on the edge of her chair, crosses her legs at the ankle, and calmly waits.

The man across from me nods his approval before he picks up a phone, presses a few numbers, and hangs it up without saying a word. When he turns to me, I catch a look of severe disapproval over my obvious interest in Iris. But I can't help it. The woman sitting with her hands folded so demurely isn't the Iris Cunningham I know. That woman would spit in my eye, curse me with ancient words from countries centuries older than our own. She isn't a serene garden flower to be pampered. She's a hothouse bloom waiting to explode when the right mixture sets her off.

So what the hell is she doing here?

"I said, may I help you sir?" The beleaguered man prompts me again.

"Sam Akin. Here to see Cal Sullivan," I mutter.

Unholy amusement passes behind his eyes briefly before it's subdued. He stands, extending his hand. "A pleasure to meet you, Sam. I'm Karl. We've spoken on the phone. I'm responsible for your temporary clearance to gain access to certain areas of the Alliance compound."

I take his in a firm shake. "You as well."

"I need to review the protocol with you." Karl begins running through a litany of items with me that basically lets me know I can't be unescorted anywhere inside the building, including to take a piss. When he winds down, he gestures to where Iris is sitting. "Please take a seat in the waiting area. Your contact should be with you shortly to go over your schedule."

Nothing Karl's said so far has startled me so far except that. "My schedule? I thought I was here for an interview?"

My comment causes a broad smile to crease his face. "Well, that's one way of putting it, I guess. Let me guess, Cal just gave you a date and time to show up?"

I nod brusquely. He barks out a laugh. "Just because his own recruitment . . . well, you'll learn soon enough. Take a seat, Sam."

With nothing else left to do, I make my way over to where Iris is sitting. As I pass by, I unintentionally brush a hand against her arm. Her eyes flick to the side but she doesn't say a word.

"Why, hello, Sam. How lovely to see you." I pitch my voice higher. Then in my native drawl, I answer myself, "And you, Iris. What a surprise to meet you here."

Holding the same serene expression, she mutters, "Shut up."

"Excuse me?" I demand indignantly.

"They're watching. Are you—Mr. Computer Jock—really that obtuse?" she hisses. That's when she turns her face slightly from the parking lot and I get blasted by the impact of her eyes. "Or did Cal not give you that little nugget of inside info before you got onsite?"

I begin to swear ripely. Iris arches a perfectly groomed brow before sniffing and stating, "It sounds better when I do it."

I try to crack her veneer by coming back with, "Everything sounds better when you do it."

It's then I start to sweat inside my suit because Iris uncrosses ankles, almost daring me to run my eyes up her body. When I manage to drag my eyes back to her face, wisps of her long hair have fallen next to her eyes, which have taken on a wicked cast. Her plump lips curve in a sexy smile. She leans forward to barely breathe the words, "Wouldn't you like to find out?" seconds before she stands and holds out her hand to a tall blonde woman I vaguely recognize as one of the professors I've seen on campus talking with Cal.

My heart is still trying to regain its normal speed twenty minutes later when Cal himself comes bounding over to me. "Glad you made it. We've got some work for you to do."

Suspicious, I follow him. "I have some questions."

"I'm sure you do. I, uh, saw you ran into Iris Cunningham. Is that going to be a problem?"

So, the little minx was right. We were being watched. Resolutely, I declare, "No, it isn't. Are we competing for the same role?"

Cal snorts. "Hell, no."

I let out a small breath I didn't realize I'd been holding. "I wasn't aware there was more than one position you were recruiting for."

Cal shrugs as we walk down a long corridor. "She has a unique skill set, just like you, Sam. We're not about to pass it up."

I feel like smacking myself in the forehead. *Of course. Her language capability.* Every company on the planet is likely vying to entice someone of Iris's skills through their doors. Of course, an institution like Alliance would be as well. But I jerk to a stop as we pass by the windows overlooking a gym. Down below, Iris is defending herself against the blonde from earlier.

"Are you fucking crazy? She's about to get her ass kicked," I bark at Cal.

He pauses for a moment next to me just as Iris goes flying across the mat. "Don't be so sure" is his only reply.

Iris is tenacious. She leaps to a crouch before sweeping out the legs of the other woman, throwing her off balance and diving for something I hadn't spotted. Something dark and small that had fallen out of their circle of reach.

When she next gets to her feet, she's pointing it at her opponent. She verbally spits something at the other woman, who grins before getting to her feet. Iris lowers the practice weapon as the blonde walks over to her and clasps Iris on the shoulder.

Cal shrugs nonchalantly. "She won that round against Kristin. I'd say she's going to be just fine." As he begins walking away, he calls over his shoulder, "The person you should be worried about is yourself."

Fuck. With a last furtive glance at Iris, I pick up my pace and hurry after Cal. Karl's words begin to send a chill up my spine. What the hell does Cal have planned for me?

More importantly, will I make it out of here in one piece?

5

IRIS

"I WAS livid seeing your mother there," Sam recalls with a laugh.

"About what?" I counter. "Do you even remember now?"

"Yeah, Dad. What were you so mad about? You were interviewing for a job the same way Mama was," Rachel argues on my behalf. I reach over and squeeze her hand in gratitude.

Before Sam can answer, Erika's phone on her desk rings. She frowns before picking it up. "I'm with . . . I see. I'll be right there." Throwing the three of us an apologetic glance, she excuses herself somewhat frantically. "I'm sorry. I know this time is reserved for your graduation day, but . . ."

Judging the terror in her eyes appropriately, I encourage her to hurry. "Go. We're fine here together."

Nodding her appreciation, she scurries out the door as fast as she can on her heels, closing it firmly behind her. Once the latch is in place, Rachel turns on her father like fresh meat.

"There were things I never asked during our sessions," Rachel looks pointedly at the camera pointing toward us in the corner.

"Sam," I encourage.

He pulls out his laptop from my bag and proceeds to melt my insides as his fingers dance across the keys. Even after all these years, I can't fully explain the feeling it evokes deep inside as I watch my husband glide his fingers over a keyboard like a treasured lover. Like it's my own skin he's manipulating to the heights of pleasure instead of bits and bytes bending to his will.

The dot on the camera flickers to red and back to green. "We're good. I checked the settings. We're in video mode only."

My shoulders relax imperceptibly. Even though we agreed to Erika's rules, she also agreed to ours. No audio recording. No permanent record of us in her office. She could take notes about the emotional connections between us, but not around the circumstances that caused them. I hug Rachel around the shoulders. "What did you want to know, Rach?"

"How did you know it was love?" The words tumble from her mouth like they've been waiting for just the right moment to escape.

Sam and I exchange smiles wrought with memories. I speak first. "I fell with a single look."

"That's all it took?" She asks, not without some incredulity.

I nod. "After that, there was no one who could fill my heart the way your father did. For me, it was forever."

Sam leans forward, setting his laptop on the table. He captures Rachel's hand between his, rubbing it between his before answering, "It was different for me."

I barely refrain from spitting out something snarky as I recall the years of frustration I endured from the first moment I laid eyes on Sam. I drawl, "What your father is trying to say is while neither of us wasted our time at college pining for the other, there wasn't a time I wasn't aware of exactly what he was doing." *Or whom*, I add silently, unable to withhold my smirk.

Sam winks at me before agreeing, "What your mother said."

"Dad, that's such a cop out," Rachel groans.

He leans back and crosses his ankles. "Then how about this; I was always aware of your mother. She was, and is, the most beautiful woman I've ever laid eyes on. But until I knew how strong she was, I was afraid she would end up hurt."

"Hurt? Mama? How?" Rachel barks out a short laugh.

"Much like your Aunt Libby was. Like you were." I tread carefully so I don't bring up any emotional potholes without Erika here to steer us around them.

"Oh," Rachel whispers. Her lashes flutter as she contemplates our words and adds them to the months of therapy we've endured to be at a place where we can talk so openly.

Sam's brow furrows as he worries. I'm transported back to the days he wore that look often around me.

It goes as far back as the day we were notified we had both been accepted as the newest recruits for Alliance.

6

TWENTY-SEVEN YEARS AGO FROM PRESENT DAY

Iris

AFTER COMPLETING my objectives at Alliance, Kristin and I sat down to discuss my scores. As Kristin organizes the papers on the table, she flips me a quick smile. "Before we start, I have to say thank you."

"For what?" I ask in surprise.

Kristin sits back with a reminiscent smile. "It's been years since I've been back in the Alliance building. Because of the fact Cal spotted not one but two people to recruit, the admiral temporarily reinstated me to train you. For me, it's been a taste of the old life without the dangers I used to experience."

A surge of adrenaline pulses through my veins at Kristin's very telling words. "Oh?"

She clears her throat before directing her attention to the files in front of her. "I'll need just one more moment and we'll be ready."

"Take your time." It gives me a moment to calm my eagerness at this possibility waiting for me.

In addition to every Fortune 500 corporation, I've been recruited by all the agencies that have an alphabet acronym in the US federal government. The problem is, each and every one of them want to shove me behind a desk with "the rare, but very necessary and distinguished business trips overseas,

Ms. Cunningham. You would be considered a premier translator in some exclusive meetings around the globe."

Blah. Blah. Blah.

Nothing but lip service.

I was indignant none of them saw beyond my looks to recognize who and what I really am—a fighter. I was never the girl who drew pretty little pictures in the sky with hearts and flowers. I've craved action since childhood—a two-wheeler, a skateboard, roller-blades. I was all-state track in high school and while I wasn't quite good enough to make the team in college, still maintain my rigorous workout schedule.

My love of languages was a gift from my mother's family—a native speaking Lakota grandmother and an Irish grandfather. After my dad walked out on my mother when I was not more than a few months old, she moved us to where they lived—about a hundred miles from Pine Ridge Indian Reservation. My grandparents, more in love the day they died than the day they married, perished in a South Dakota blizzard where their car collided and lost against a semitruck.

While Mom spent years recovering from her devastation with other men, I buried my pain in my studies. I was constantly reading, becoming engrossed in books. My need to learn became obsessive. I craved more than just the small town I lived in and I knew the only way I could get it was through an education. While we're not close, more like sisters than mother and daughter, I hold no bitterness toward her. She was too young to have me, but she did the best she could. Now, we both acknowledge the people who loved and raised both of us died long ago. We're both happier with the limited communication we exchange. Presently living in my hometown as a hairdresser, my mom recently married a computer salesman. She's happy; that's all that matters.

As for me, I needed to get out, to explore the world outside of the vast plains that surrounded me. I knew if I didn't leave, I'd never escape the restlessness that had grown inside of me since I was a child. My mind was a million miles away, looking for a place I could fit in with the languages I picked up with such ease. Now that I know there is more out there, I want— no need— to experience it all. I refuse to settle for less. I worked my ass off for it, and no one is going to tell me I can't have it because they want to typecast me in some role they believe I fit into.

It was Kristin, my sociolinguistics and language variation instructor, who first approached me in the fall semester of my senior year. "I recognize something in you I saw in myself, Iris. The very last thing you want to be doing is reading someone else's calendars or emails to determine if there's anything that could help someone in the field."

I snorted. "You're right about that."

"Yet, when the agencies come knocking at your door—Oh, don't look so shocked. I'm neither a fool nor foolish. We both know they will."

I ceded the point with a nod.

"That's all you'll be doing despite their grand offers of travel." Her voice held a note of bitterness.

"Sounds like experience talking," I observed quietly.

"Can't hide that, can I? Listen, I have some thoughts. Why don't you come talk with me at my office next Wednesday at six?"

That was months ago. I was shocked not only to find Kristin waiting, but the new international poli-sci professor Calhoun Sullivan there as well. Their proposition was well worth listening to.

Now, as Kristin and I sit in a conference room at Alliance, I wait for something to happen to ruin this chance. Well, other than what happened this morning.

Damn, Sam.

I can only hope my reaction—likely filmed—would demonstrate I had the aplomb not to react to unexpected twists in a manner that would jeopardize a mission. Because from what Kristin was telling me, Alliance has a need for someone like me. And it's not behind a desk.

I try to keep my expression neutral as Kristin slides the final file to the side. "I have good news and I have other news."

Be cool, Iris, I warn myself. "That sounds concerning."

Her brow furrows. "Actually, for you, it's all good news. The other news is just . . . interesting. Are you ready to hear it?"

I clasp my hands together to prevent my sweaty palms from staining the silk of the suit I borrowed from Libby. "Yes, of course."

"Before graduation, you're to work with the campus Army recruiter, who has been briefed to expedite your application. Once you graduate, you'll be sent to Fort Benning, Georgia to attend Officer Training School and complete a twelve-week program. Due to the training we've accomplished together, and the physical tests you passed in the last two days, the ten-week Army Basic Combat Training has been waived with the admiral's sign off."

"I guess all those mornings I spent with you instead of my pillow were worth it," I drawl sardonically. Then I ask out of curiosity, "What happens if I don't complete Officer Training School?"

"Focus on completing it. But I'll warn you, Iris, the twelve weeks is no joke. Enlisted and Army Reserve candidates will have already completed Basic Combat Training. If I hadn't pushed you, you would be entering at a severe disadvantage," Kristin cautions.

"Will I get to pick any job I want after?" In my mind I keep whispering to myself, *Monterey. Monterey.*

"Combined with your Defense Language Aptitude Battery, the scores of which I have here, the better you score at OTS, the better your chances are to get the duty station you need for your permanent assignment." Kristin clears her throat. "That means your first duty assignment after OTS should be orders sending you to the Defense Linguistics Institute Foreign Language Center in Monterey, California. All of this," she voices sternly at my war whoop, "is to be kept under the strictest of confidence, Iris. Your time in Monterey will be a commitment of a minimum of forty-eight weeks, possibly as many as sixty-four, depending on which language is selected for you."

"I did it? It's actually happening?" My hands flatten against the table to steady myself as Kristin drops her cool demeanor and actually smiles.

"You sure as hell did. The admiral was impressed by your interview."

I replay her words in my head right before I jump to my feet and fist pump the air.

Then Kristin dumps a bucket of water on my joy. "Now, for the other news. Let's talk about Samuel Akin."

I almost trip over my heels as I stumble back to my chair. "What about him?"

"He's your roommate's cousin? I had no idea Cal was recruiting him as well, though it's not a surprise considering the skills he could bring to Alliance. However, this puts us in a very precarious situation, Iris. Elizabeth Akin is a civilian. She can't be informed about the recruitment process. If you find out that Sam has discussed Alliance with his family without authorization, we need to know." Her expression turns shrewd. "The same will be expected for him of you."

I manage to warble out, "Sam will be going to DLI?" I honestly don't think I can deal with another year or more of seeing Sam day in and day out. At least not with things as they are.

She scoffs. "He managed to hack into and secure an area of the Department of Defense in under sixty seconds today. No, there are other plans for him."

My heart swells with pride over his accomplishment, knowing how difficult my own tasks were. "Am I allowed to offer him congratulations for being accepted here?"

She lets out a beleaguered sigh. "It's preferable you didn't discuss the individual tasks. But yes, if you must congratulate one another, that is acceptable."

I nod as another wide idea flies into my head. No, I'm not going to ask about that. No. Nope.

"What?" Kristin snaps, clearly reading the indecision on my face.

" I feel my cheeks burning with embarrassment. Deciding to couch it as a general question might be a better idea. "Are there any kind of policies I should know about in advance?"

"Like what?"

Like . . . oh, fuck it. I blurt out, "What is the fraternization policy at Alliance?"

Kristin's eyes drop to her pile of files before she begins to stack and gather them. Lifting them, she heads to a door on the far end of the room without answering my question. *Crap. Such an amateurish question, Iris,* I berate myself. She pauses with her hand on the doorknob before turning and winking at me. "Alliance, as a company, has had several successful— and some completely abominable relationships— within team members. The rule— at least when I worked here full-time—was don't let it interfere with the mission." She opens the door. "Congratulations, Iris. I'll see you back on campus next week. We still have a lot of work still to do. You and your pillow won't see each other for quite a while still."

She closes the door, leaving me alone except for all the cameras observing my every movement, listening to my every sound. "Yeah, see you then."

I sit for a few moments alone to gather my thoughts before I leave the building. Then I drive back to Akin Hill with only the news I've made my decision, which is really not a decision at all. It's a life-altering mission.

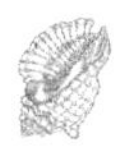

"SO, you spoke to the recruiter again?"

"Yes. I made my choice."

"I think it is a good decision for you, Iris. The Army will build upon your structure, strength, and fortitude," Nonna says approvingly.

Libby's biting her lip so hard in concern, likely imagining me in the worst combat theaters in the world. Maybe? I don't know. I'll go where Alliance sends me. But to reassure my best friend, I toss out a cavalier, "Come on, Libs. Once the Army's decided to have its way with me, you know I'll probably be stuck behind a desk somewhere. This just gives me a little more to beef up my resume before I get paid nothing to do the same thing by some big name corporation." I roll my eyes dramatically to punctuate my point.

"Iris, does no one else in the world but me realize you have the ability to become a badass? I know you down to your soul. You're joining the military hoping someone will sit up, take notice, and drop you in the middle of a room to unleash all the power you're withholding. You don't need my blessing, but please be careful," Libby begs.

My lips part in surprise. Just the fact she knows me down to my soul, knows I'm disenchanted with what was awaiting me, is enough. I lean forward and hug her tightly.

"I love you," she whispers.

Before I can reply in kind, a dark honeyed voice interrupts us. "Do you mind if I borrow Iris for a few moments, y'all?"

I break apart from Libby only to practically trip over Sam. He's a tower of teeming fury, green eyes glittering.

What the hell is his problem?

Fortunately Nonna declares, "After we eat. Go get yourself a plate, Samuel."

And just like that, my appetite—so healthy from the workout I was put through earlier—evaporates.

7
TWENTY SEVEN YEARS AGO FROM PRESENT DAY

SAMUEL

After an interminable dinner where my temper does nothing but simmer, I manage to get Iris alone out near the river where she wandered to.

I take a moment and breathe in the magic of the air that feeds Akin Hill. The rushing water of the Cooper River that races around the edges of the estate flows through my blood. Still a working plantation, the majestic trees blowing in the cool night breeze are prized not only for timber milling but for exquisitely handcrafted furniture sought after all over the world. Presently run by Nonna, future generations of Akins will never have to be afraid of bankruptcy due to the way she diversified and established a board of trustees. I cringe recalling the way my ancestors almost brought the mill to its knees as a result of gambling and stealing. Then there was my great-aunt who turned and walked away without a word. I've heard the story so many times over the years, I've become jaded about relationships.

Add to the fact I've heard the rumors on campus about a few of my supposed relationships, and plenty about Iris's as well, and I don't know what to think. I'm not the Lothario girls on campus make me out to be, but how much about her is real? Sure, I've dated some, but to be honest, the women on campus scare the hell out of me. But Iris? How much do I really know about her other than the fact that just seeing her face drives me wild?

Right now, she looks nothing like the sexy woman I ran into earlier today wearing the tight-fitting suit nor the aggressive defender I spied tossing her opponent in the gym. No, by the river in jeans and a hoodie, she's just Iris—my cousin's roommate. The girl I've spent way too many nights thinking about while I've been tinkering on my computers. Somehow, that fuels my anger further, making me believe I've never really known her at all. I demand, "You're in?"

Iris beams at me, quickly scrambling to her feet. "So are you, I hear. I'm so excited!"

I take a step back. "Why?"

Confusion mars her exquisite face. "Why what?"

"Why are you doing this? What the hell do you gain out of it? I have so many questions, I don't know where to start," I growl.

She sighs. "I don't expect you to understand."

"Try me," I challenge her.

Wrapping her arms around herself, she turns slightly so she's looking out over the rushing water of the river. "One time, when Libby and I came to visit, Nonna told me about a moment where the tide hovers between its lowest and highest."

"A flood tide," I interject when she doesn't continue. "What does that have to do with you taking a job at Alliance?"

Rattled, she faces me, "If you give me a moment, I'll explain."

I hold out my hand for her to continue. She begins to pace back and forth. "I've been recruited by— at a guess— some of the same corporations and agencies you have. I have zero interest in sitting behind a desk. I need to be doing. Life isn't about the high or low tides. It's made up of moments of the flood—the transitions in between. That's why I'm choosing Alliance. Because I can have it all—the overflow of emotions that happen every day whether I'm in the field, behind a desk, even the moments where I'm just me." Finished, she waits for my reaction.

Disturbed because Iris summed up exactly what I've been feeling so eloquently, and not only about Alliance, I drawl, "I don't buy it."

"What is your problem, Sam?" She demands.

"My problem is you," I taunt, just to gauge her reaction. I'd planned to follow it up with a declaration of how insane Iris has been driving me for years, but she recoils as if I slapped her. Immediately, I wish the words back as her pale skin turns chalky.

"Well, I guess it's good to get that out." Her voice shakes.

Hastily, I rush out with, "Iris, no. That's not . . ."

". . .what you meant to say?" She chokes off a laugh. "Of course it is, Sam. Deep down somewhere. Maybe that's why I never got up the courage to ask you out."

Iris lacking courage to ask me out? The concept of that blows all my circuits. I'm so stunned by her words, I can't speak. But I take too long to get my wits together. When her own laughter comes, it's hollow. "Yeah, that's what I thought." She takes off at a sprint back to the house.

"Iris!" I bellow, but it's useless. She just runs faster.

Away from me.

I drop to the ground in the exact spot I found her and spend the next hour thinking about how I'm going to apologize to her the next time I see her.

"SHIT."

"Samuel Winston Akin, I taught you to use better language than that," Nonna scolds me severely the next morning.

"Sorry, Nonna." *Fuck*, I think to myself as I mentally kick myself in the ass for being so stupid not to anticipate this.

Iris and Libby headed back to campus early, citing they needed to go grocery shopping and get some studying done before their Monday morning classes. They snuck off the estate before I made it over to Nonna's in time for breakfast. "I can't say I blame them," I mumble.

"What did you do this time?" She demands.

"What makes you think it was me?"

"Because you're a male. Therefore you already have two strikes against you," Nonna declares without hesitation.

I smile wanly because I've heard her scolding my father with that very statement almost my entire life.

"I'm tired of waiting for you to grow up, Sam."

I choke on my next inhale due to the slice of pain her words incite. "You've never said something like that before."

Her eyes, my eyes, glisten with tears. "You didn't hear that poor girl sobbing last night. If you don't feel the same way, you could have let her down differently. That's what a man in this family would do."

"I wasn't trying to let her down," I protest. My heart feels like someone has sunk a blade right through it knowing Iris shed tears for me. *Me*? I want to give chase and explain how confused I am about what she makes me feel when Nonna's words stop me from racing out the door.

She flings up her hands. "Then what were you trying to do? Iris is family."

Automatically, I protest, "No, she isn't." I don't have a single familial feeling for her running through my body.

Nonna studies me in silence. Then she laughs softly. "Just like your grandfather. Almost exactly like Bernard."

"I am? How?" I ask wildly. This declaration could either be very good or very bad depending on Nonna's mood.

A knowing smile spreads across her face. "You have no idea what you're feeling. I wish you luck, Sam. You're going to need it." She pushes to her feet and makes her way to her office.

I yelp, "Luck? Luck with what?"

"Iris," comes her answer just before she closes the door. Like the supposedly intelligent man I was raised to be, I don't go in and demand what she means. That's because I already know.

It's going to take a miracle to get Iris to talk to me, I think glumly.

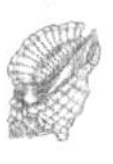

I HATE BEING RIGHT.

Libby steps out onto the porch of the small house she and Iris rent off campus. "I'm sorry, Sam. You can't come in."

I ask a question I'm certain I know the answer to, "Why?" God, I seem to be asking that a lot in the last twenty-four hours.

"Because right now, I feel the need to protect my best friend's heart from you." Libby's eyes blaze up at me.

I open my mouth to speak when she pokes me in the chest. "Don't speak. You said everything you needed to last night when you told Iris she was your problem. Fine. Go back to the little harem of brainless bimbos you've been dating and miss out on the best thing that could ever happen to you." Libby turns to make her way back into her house.

I fling up my hands in exasperation. "You and Iris. What makes you both think I'm dating half of the school?"

My cousin whirls around, mouth agape. "Are you joking? You think they don't come up to the two of us asking about you? Bragging about your prowess in bed?" Libby's lip curls in distaste. "I swear that's their Litmus test to ensure we truly are related. Seriously disgusting."

My stomach churns. "You're joking."

"Not even close."

"Why didn't you say something?" I demand.

She sniffs. "Because some of us have a little more discretion than to flaunt—"

I cut her off, "Libby, I haven't been with a third, no likely a quarter . . ."

Dryly, she wonders aloud, "I wonder if I should be impressed by your stamina. They compare you to Cal, you know?"

I blink a few times to make sure I'm hearing her right. Then I whisper, "Holy shit, that many?"

Her face closes up before she nods. I scrub my hand over my head, "Christ, Libs. I didn't mean that."

"Whatever. It doesn't matter," she lies with a straight face, breaking my heart further. We both know damn well it does matter, and it really makes me want to go hunt down Cal and throw a few punches to burn off this frustration for hurting Libby even if they, too, have never been anything more than friends. "Just, let her be, Sam. There's only a few weeks until graduation. Then we can all get on with our lives."

Except Iris and I will be working for the same company as Cal, and Libby doesn't know it. Mutely, I nod before turning on my heel and stalking away. Somehow, I've got to try to find a way to apologize to Iris, to explain how I feel. Somehow, before she's tired of waiting for me to wake up and is so far out of my reach I never have a chance with her.

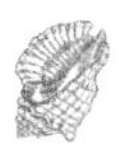

8

IRIS

"WHY WERE YOU SO PISSED, DAD?" Rachel asks incredulously.

He shoots me a lopsided grin that never fails to set my heart careening against my rib cage. Then Sam admits something he's never confessed before, even to me. "I was mad as hell because during my offer, your Uncle Cal let it slip that your mother asked her trainer about fraternization policies. I was so jealous; I could barely see straight. Even though we hadn't kissed, hadn't had our first date . . ."

"Sam, you hadn't even admitted to me you were interested!" I screech.

He waves his hand as if that doesn't mean a thing. "I thought she was planning to date other men at Alliance. We hadn't even started working there and she was already planning to get involved with someone else when I'd just admitted to myself how I really felt about her."

"That's the reason you were a jackass that night by the river?"

"Yes."

"I tried to congratulate you . . ." Words fail me.

"I know." He rubs his hand up my back, but I shrug him away. I don't want to be soothed; I want to strangle him. Reaching up, I measure his neck with my hands, sending our daughter into hysterical laughter. Wisely, she informs me, "Now I get it, Mama."

Knowing she's remembering all the times I referred to Nonna's wisdom about Sam being male and therefore having two strikes against him, I immediately lose my irritation with my husband and redirect my attention to Rachel. I'm grateful there's another woman in the room who appreciates my need to suffocate my husband—even if he is her father. "Right?"

Sam immediately begins to panic. "What just happened here?"

At the exact same time, we both reply, "Nothing."

"No. Something just happened. Something that just shifted Rachel's allegiance one hundred percent to your side. All during our talks, she wondered why it took us so long to finally get together," Sam argues, afraid our child who spent her life openly worshiping him is going to stop doing so.

My temper is already fraying. "Right here is the problem. There were no rights or wrongs for us. There was only one thing we *did* wrong and looking back, we both discussed how we should have stopped it long before it blew up in our faces. It almost destroyed everything."

He lets out a slow breath. "You're right. You were right all those years ago when you pressured everyone to just open up and talk. The only thing anyone ever needed was love and communication. Instead, miscommunication and lies nearly ended everything in a far too permanent manner."

I close my eyes, grateful to finally hear him admit that. Even though his heroism is remarkable, his true legacy will be defined by the choices he made. Not with the world at large, but with the people who matter most to him—his family.

"Mama, what made you finally give Daddy a chance after he was such an arrogant snot?"

I burst into laughter at our daughter's description while an equally loud groan escapes from Sam. When I finally get my laughter under control, I can't prevent the wicked smile from crossing my face. "Well, it was the night of my twenty-second birthday. Plus your father was utterly miserable."

"Don't remind me. I called Cal a sadist that morning," Sam grumbles.

I can't quite choke back the laugh that escapes. "Did you really?" Not that the sentiment didn't apply to so many missions later in our careers, but back then?

"He had me running in wingtips," Sam bemoans an incident that occurred almost twenty-two years ago.

There's complete silence in the room for a heartbeat, but Rachel breaks it by snorting out a laugh. "Yeah, that sounds like Uncle Cal. Aunt Libby says he's a madman, running around barefoot. Supposedly, it helps with balance and coordination."

"Around DC? Does she make him hose off before coming into the house?" Sam howls.

"Likely with chlorine bleach," Rachel agrees. The two of them share a good chortle over Cal's present-day antics but Sam's words trigger a memory.

"Now I know why he's the one who paid for my birthday flowers," I say softly, recalling Sam's adamance over an incident that almost beached our relationship right before I went to linguistics school.

Sam drops his lips to my ear and murmurs, "I was hobbling bowlegged with blisters in between my toes. You're lucky I was upright on the balcony when I first kissed you."

I tip my head back and my lips curve with the knowledge I've never shared with anyone, not even Libby. "It was a great way to convince me you were serious about giving us a chance."

"After the way I behaved? It was the only way I knew to show you I was all in." He leans down and touches his lips against mine. Even such a small brush has us lingering as we pull back.

Rachel just sighs, her satisfaction evident.

When I manage to escape the hypnotic promise of Sam's eyes, he proceeds to tell Rachel about the day he went running with Cal. I'm enthralled since I've never heard this story. Seconds after he starts, I'm giggling because Sam doesn't tell Rachel about running. Oh, no. First he tells her about the bar the night before. I, of course, yank my phone out of my purse and text Libby two words, *Emo bookends.*

Her reply text is a bunch of laughing emojis. Since she knows exactly where I am and what I'm doing, her questions don't surprise me in the slightest. *Who's telling the story? You or Sam?*

Sam. I add a rolling eyes emoji.

We'll have to tell Rachel the full story later. Love you. XOXO

I love you too. Dropping my phone back into my bag, I realize the room has become quiet. Sam's glaring at me. "Are you and Libby done laughing?"

I grin. "Never. But, Rach? Come to your aunt and me later when you want the real story."

She tucks her legs beneath her and agrees. "Come on, Dad. I'm waiting and I have more questions."

Sam lets out a beleaguered sigh. "Your mother and your aunt were sitting in a booth. Most of the men in the bar were watching them."

I interject sweetly, "How could you tell with the harem surrounding you and Cal?"

Rachel snickers as Sam places his fingers over my lips. "Who is telling this story?"

I wink at Rachel before mumbling, "You are."

Sam begins again. I sit back and listen to the past being told from his perspective. One thing that happens as he tells it, he keeps me close to his side.

Just like he did that night.

9

TWENTY-SEVEN YEARS AGO FROMPRESENT DAY

SAMUEL

"WHAT ARE we doing on this side of the bar when the women we really want are over there?" I mutter to Cal as I fend off the advances of yet another underage coed who somehow managed to get her hands on a fake ID.

Cal just blasts me with a frosty glare. He doesn't like being reminded by me how much his infatuation with Libby has grown into something he can't easily ignore. In order to wrangle my way to get past guard-dog Libby to begin repairing my relationship with Iris, I've needed his help. So, I casually mentioned Cal had two extra tickets to a Dave Matthews concert to my cousin. I was thrilled after I politely asked her "Would you and a friend like to join us?" Unsurprisingly, she dragged Iris along.

Although Iris never spoke a word to me that night, she eventually began to thaw. Thank God because I'm certain I gave myself food poisoning off my own cooking. Libby reinstated my invitation to dinners at their place—and of course, "Cal is invited too." Not being a fool, he joined me every single time once he tasted Libby's cooking.

Much to my frustration, Iris has completely placed me in the friend corner. I'm more frustrated than ever, especially the night when she disappeared after dinner to get dressed for a date to a theater production on campus. Mentally, I relished her date being so awful because she was back before I finished drying the last of the dishes Libby washed.

Cal stills next to me when Libby's laughter floats over the annoying whine of the woman who is trying to climb him like a tree. "Sam, let's go," he barks.

"Thank fuck," I mutter, shaking the hand of the grasping sophomore off me. "Listen, don't try this with someone else. You're completely drunk. It could end badly," I warn her.

"But . . . ," she slurs.

I catch the eye of the bouncer as I follow Cal across the room. He tips his chin, indicating he'll handle it. Mentally I wonder, *Is this what makes everyone think I've got some sort of harem going? Because I try not to be a dick?* Deciding to ask Libby later, I catch the tail end of Cal shocks Libby as he slides in next to her.

Iris is joking with Cal to give Libby time to recover. "Well, you know us, Cal. We know how to enjoy ourselves." As soon as the words pass her lips, I slide in next to her so our bodies are touching from ankle to hip. Her scent gets lost somewhere in the mealy smell of the bar. It's the closest I've been to her in forever, but I don't have much time left. We three graduate in just a few weeks.

Giving Iris a wink, I smile at Libby before asking, "Cousin, do you know what to do with the trouble sitting next to you?"

She retorts, "Who says I plan on doing anything?"

Iris and I begin laughing. My cock eagerly begins to press up against the zipper of my jeans when she collapses on me in her mirth. Our mutual hilarity has her unable to stay upright, which I have absolutely no problem taking advantage of. My hand drops down and squeezes her hip. Realizing she's now pressed completely up against me, her head snaps up. Our eyes meet just before she begins to shift away. I smile down at her and whisper, "Don't."

"But . . ."

"I'm about to tell her about the job. Cal said it was all right." I whisper. For the last few weeks, I told Libby my attitude problem over spring break had to do primarily with a job interview I really wanted.

"Oh." I absorb her soft puff of breath against my lips but it's not close enough. Not nearly.

Straightening, I announce, "I have big news."

"Oh, what's that?" Libby leans forward eagerly.

"I got a job," I announce proudly. Unobtrusively, my hand slides across Iris's thigh and seeks the warmth of her hand beneath the table. When I find it, I give it a squeeze. I hope she understands what I'm trying to communicate—that I know she was the first one to congratulate me weeks ago. I know I fucked the whole thing up.

Libby reacts much like I anticipated she would. She gasps excitedly before shoving at Cal like he's blocking her from crossing the line first for a million dollars. "Get out of my way. I need to congratulate him."

Cal's expression is bemused. "Don't you want to hear what it is?"

"It doesn't matter. Look at him. He's so happy right now, he's lighting up the room." Libby beams.

Cal mutters something only Libby can hear before he slides out of the booth. I stand just in time to catch her close for a hug. She begins swaying us back and forth as she murmurs in my ear, "I am so, so proud of you. Was it that government contractor you were telling me about? The one with offices overseas? Confederation?"

I chuckle as I squeeze the breath out of her. "Alliance and yes. That's the one."

"When will you tell the family?" I let her go and she returns to her side of the booth. I sit back down next to Iris, closer than before. Her chest is moving up and down at an accelerated pace. I draw on the leg of her jeans, *O-K-?*

She writes back on mine, *F-I-N-E*.

I manage to ask Libby if she's still planning to head back to Charleston after graduation. She reminds me how she's been waiting for this opportunity since she was six, before Cal captures her attention and I turn mine to Iris.

"God, I hate that word—fine. It could mean anything from 'Fuck you, Sam' to 'I finally forgive you for being a douche, Sam.'" I wait with bated breath to determine which it could be.

Iris eyes me critically before she lifts her beer to her lips. "The second."

I sag in my seat.

"But we will talk about it, Sam. I firmly believe talking can either make or break a relationship," she warns.

"I fully agree with that."

She hums. "Yet you're so terrible at it."

I bark out a laugh. "Pathetic, isn't it?"

Cal interrupts us to ask if we want another drink. Iris orders a second beer, and I indicate I'm driving before I give my attention back to the woman next to me. "Do you have plans for tomorrow?"

She bites her lip before admitting, "Yes."

"Concrete?"

"Yes."

Disappointment shoots through me. "I see."

She opens her mouth, but I just squeeze her leg. Iris doesn't have to explain anything. It's me who has to make up for all the harsh words between us.

That starts right now.

10

TWENTY SEVEN YEARS PRESENT DAY

SAMUEL

"You're a sadistic bitch, Cal." I pant next to him the next morning, barely after the sun's risen. The wingtips he insisted I wear are causing so much chaffing there's either sweat or blood dripping inside of the dress socks on my feet. I whine a bit when we approach another hill. I'd scream, but no one is up this early to hear my cries of agony.

Next to me, the cold son of a bitch makes me feel ridiculously out of shape with his level breathing. "What if you had to run for your life, Sam? You're not always going to be in running sneakers and compression socks."

"That's not why you suck," I mutter, glaring at him with as much force as I can as we approach the hill.

He appears unperturbed by my irritation. His words give credence to that. "Not that I care, but curiosity has me now. Why am I a sadist?"

"A sadistic bitch," I correct. I blink in shock. That sounded fairly normal. Huh. Maybe these crazy-ass workouts in the humidity are doing some good, not that I'd ever admit that to Cal. Continuing with my griping, I admit, "It's because you make this look so easy."

Cal jolts to a stop, so I take the opportunity to do the same. "Sam," he says patiently. "I've been doing this for seven years, three of those in the military. You're coming straight into Alliance because you're a fucking genius with a computer. We just don't want you to end up dead in the process of working out in the field."

"I know. That would piss Libby and our family off to no end."

Wrong move. Cal shakes his head and starts running again. "You're the oddest person I've ever recruited."

"Yeah, but I bet I'm the only one who has a family member you've got the hots for," I taunt cheerfully.

My day is made when Cal trips. He growls, "Jesus Christ."

I laugh at him. "So, what are you going to do about it?"

"Nothing."

My face contorts, thinking of how disappointed I'd be if Iris wouldn't give me a second chance. "Why not?"

He glares at me. "Because it's not a good decision."

I stretch my arms over my head. "Hmm."

A long period of silence extends between us before Cal snaps, "What?"

I don't know what makes me say it, but I throw out offhandedly, "I never took you for a coward."

Like a flick of a switch, Cal turns from an affable pain in the ass to the badass I'm certain could kill in a heartbeat—someone I know I don't stand a chance against. "Excuse me?"

Shit. "Now Cal, I just meant in terms of matters of this. You're a badass."

"Better run, Sam. If I catch up, there's going to be hell to pay." I'm warned.

I take off in a sprint. For the rest of the workout, Cal torments me by playing cat and mouse. Damn him, I can barely remember my own name by the time he drops me off at my apartment.

Hobbling over to my bed, I flop down face first and curse myself for trying to interfere in Cal's life, swearing I'll never do it again.

IT MIGHT BE MINUTES, it might be days later, but my phone is ringing. I groan when I see it's Cal calling. "Didn't you torture me enough this morning?" I growl.

No hi or hello from him. He launches in with, "Is it a special occasion for Libby?"

"Not that I know of." But I glance at my watch to double-check the date. Something niggles at the back of my pain-ladened mind.

"Birthday? Anniversary of an important date? I can find out, but I'd prefer you think."

Impatiently, I snap, "It's not her birthday, Cal. That's October first."

"Then why is she carrying a cake, a bouquet of flowers, and . . ."

Dread seeps through me. It's late April. There's only one birthday I know of that Libby would go all out for. Still, I yelp, "What kind of flowers?

"I don't know. Purple."

Mentally I slap myself on the forehead. "They were irises, Cal. It's Iris's birthday! Shit, I can't walk, and I need to go to her birthday dinner at Libby's."

"Go take a shower. I'll pick up some flowers for you to bring to her and drop them by with some tiger balm."

I let out a relieved sigh. I didn't screw this up. Maybe tonight's the chance I've been waiting for with Iris.

Cal probes, "Are you going to be able to let her go?" Meaning Iris. I'm startled by his insight but I guess I shouldn't be. He's a formidable figure with keen perception.

"Let her go? I don't have to. You all tagged her to be recruited as well. Remember? One of your colleagues is training her?" With that, I hang up the phone and shove myself into a prone position, recalling the conversation between Cal and myself that drew all my feelings about Iris to the forefront.

"Well, Sam. I'm impressed. So's the Admiral." Cal props his hip on the desk as he reads from a file.

"It wasn't that hard, Cal," I begin to protest until he pins me with a stare.

"You blew past multiple firewalls without setting off any alarms and captured the data we wanted in forty-two seconds. That's quite possibly the fastest anyone's ever managed it. Now, tell me why you want to work for us instead of some company that could pay you much more than we can."

I explain how I've spent my whole life wanting what I do to mean something instead of being used for it. Cal smirks, "We're going to use you, Sam."

"But the reason is important. It's to help protect people, this country. Right?" I question.

"Without question. There might be a few gray areas, but that is one thing that is an absolute."

"What do you mean, gray areas?"

He shrugged. "As an example, we don't have a no-fraternization policy. Many companies do."

I frowned. "Why are you bringing that up?"

"One of the other recruits who was here today asked about it." Even as my temper began to boil knowing Cal was referring to Iris, he continued, "I was asked to remind you of that. None of us care what you do in your personal life so long as it doesn't affect any of our missions."

Tightly, I responded, "Understood. Now, what other reasons would I want to join Alliance?"

Cal began to give me the details of some of his missions, information he'd left out before. I listened with only half an ear. I was too stuck on the fact Iris was interested in the dating policy at the company.

I was outrageously jealous then. Not now.

Now, I have the chance to make this burning longing a reality if Iris feels the same way. If I didn't ruin it.

11

TWENTY-SEVEN YEARS AGO FROM PRESENT DAY

Iris

"Not bad," Kristin remarks.

Critically, I examine the target that's floating toward us on a wire. My Glock, warm from the number of rounds I fired, is held empty next to my thigh in a much-practiced downed position. I take all the safety protocols that have been drilled into me seriously, despite knowing the clip was fully expended into the silhouette target moments before to find some sense of calm amid my confusion. I criticize myself as the blasts through the paper become more apparent. "Not great, either."

When the target is in her reach, Kristin jabs her finger through each hole. As she reaches the space where a human's eyes should be, she wiggles her fingers causing me to snort. "You'll find moments of levity in morbidity, Iris. Otherwise, you won't be able to survive this job for long," Kristin informs me wisely.

Mentally, I file her words away as she counts aloud, " . . . seven, eight, nine? You consider nine head shots not great, Iris? When you had never picked up a weapon before last fall?"

"No, what I consider a problem is I only see fourteen holes. What could have happened that I missed the target?" I gnaw on my lower lip wondering if this is a sign. Can one missed shot, one missed warning, change the course of everything? The lives of people I don't know but will be responsible for rescuing?

Before I can voice these concerns to Kristin, she contemplates,. "It is possible you put two through the same hole."

"Not likely."

Her voice holds remorse. "No. It takes someone with expert-level marksmanship to accomplish that. While you're good, you have a long way to go. You're going to need to be diligent about practicing."

I nod, accepting her criticism and filing it away. "Thank you."

"For what?"

"Explaining to me how I'm lacking in a respectful manner." My head jerks down to study the target. I swallow hard. "I don't mind being told I'm not perfect but being provided with tangible feedback I can work with is good."

"Iris?" My head jerks toward my trainer because at that moment she's not speaking to me in an instructional manner. Her voice is concerned, like that of a friend.

I shake my head. "It's not a problem." *You're the problem*! Sam's words echo again through my head. I can't escape them no matter how much I try.

She gives me an odd look before redirecting her attention to the task at hand. "How did you get so good at languages?"

"At first, they came easily to me—as simple as breathing." I frown, thinking about my struggles with Mandarin. "Then I came up against one that required me to put in the time to study, breaking down the basics."

While I've been speaking, the two of us begin examining the paper closer. It's Kristin who finds the small mark in the upper right corner. "Here's number fifteen."

My lips form a moue of disgust. She shakes her head before informing me, "You're not going to be perfect at everything. Sometimes, you're going to screw up. Accept it. Move on."

"That's unacceptable."

"Why?"

"Because what if someone was being held hostage? What if number fifteen went into them by mistake?" I counter.

A brief smile touches Kristin's lips. She attaches a new target to the wire clip and sends it back with a punch of a button. "Then we'll keep going."

I begin to shove bullets into my empty clip, knowing if this were a real life scenario, I might not have a second chance.

HOURS LATER, the smell of cordite has burned away the capability to appreciate the floral scents permeating the Athens air as Kristin and I step into it. "Hey, come by my car for a second." Kristin gestures me in the direction of her SUV.

I follow behind her, swinging the strap of my duffle over my shoulder. The request isn't unusual; I typically dump my duffle carrying the weapon I've been training with into the trunk of her vehicle so it can be secured out of sight of my home with Libby. Kristin has already hoisted her bag inside the trunk and is reaching for something when I make my way there.

My bag falls out of my hands when I recognize what she's holding.

A cupcake.

Specifically, a birthday cupcake with a candle sticking out of the top.

"You didn't say anything," she accuses gently.

My bag slides from my shoulder even as my eyes are transfixed by the flickering flame. My voice comes out hoarse when I say, "It's not a big deal."

Kristin extends the small cake in my direction. "Speaking as someone who has made it through to the other side of the madness you're about to begin, start celebrating your life. You never know what might happen to it from one day to the next."

I close my eyes and make a wish. *Guide me to the place I'm supposed to be with Sam.* If that means friendship, so be it. But this constant turmoil has something churning inside of me I can't live with.

"Serious wish?" Kristin teases.

Shaking myself from my reverie, I blow out the candle before taking a swipe of the delicious buttercream frosting with my tongue. "Aren't all wishes serious?"

Kristin's words reverberate in my mind long after I'm back at my place. *"They should be."*

12

TWENTY-SEVEN YEARS AGO FROM PRESENT DAY

Iris

"YOU'RE the best friend ever, Libby Akin." After she gives me her traditional bouquet of irises, I read the card from her and throw myself into my best friend's arms.

She hugs me back fiercely. "Love you."

"Love you more." I wipe my eyes. Only Libby would have the foresight to write me a birthday card that promises me she'll stand by my side no matter where in the world life might take me. I have to get my mind away from what she wrote or I'm going to be a blubbering mess and blurt out every one of my plans. "Now, are you going to tell me who you've been cooking for all day?" The scent of the food she's been evoking from our microscopic kitchen is destroying my willpower not to knock her over and eat it all for myself, especially after the rigorous workout I was put through this morning by Kristin.

She shakes her head no. "Do you want me to put your flowers in water?"

Knowing if I try to do it, she'll just stomp her foot and order me to relax because it's my birthday, I give in. "Yes. Just tell me this—do I need to change?"

She gives a critical once-over of the backless T-shirt and ripped jeans I'm wearing. After shrugging, she declares, "You look hot."

"As in I need to go slap on some deodorant or I'm going to knock some gorgeous man on his ass, Libs? Cut me some slack; it's my birthday."

Just as she's about to respond, the doorbell rings. "That must be our surprise guest."

"You're such a brat," I accuse from my place on the couch.

She calls over her shoulder, "You've lived with me for four years and you're just now getting that idea?" Her startled gasp almost has me leaping to my feet. That is until both Sam and Cal step into our living room. Libby's complexion is pale as she graciously welcomes them into our home as I stew from my place on the sofa. "Come on in, gentlemen. I hope you both like shrimp and grits." She waits for Sam's kiss on the cheek.

Despite the détente we had last night—something that kept me up thinking about him well past the sun rose—the last few weeks have been difficult with Sam around. We've only spoken to one another when we've been in Libby's presence. I'm so disenchanted with the man I thought he was. Over and over I hear his voice shouting at me, "*My problem is you!*"

I've stared at my face in the mirror and debated what I can change about myself that he'd find unacceptable. Is it my hair? Maybe I should dye it to the light-ash color of the women that fight to wrap themselves in his muscular arms. There's nothing I can do about my eyes, but I could make more of an attempt with makeup. Unless it's my brain or worse yet, my courage. Maybe he believes me incapable of successfully supporting the mission at Alliance. Lacking in valor?

Imperceptibly I shake my head. If that's the case, then I've misjudged Sam for far too many years and it's better he exit my life now before my heart has no chance to recover from the wounds it's already sustained.

As he breaks away from Libby, I let my thoughts drift to the options I've been debating—namely whether to take the sixty-four week class once I'm in Monterey. *Hell, what would it matter if I was done sixteen weeks sooner? Who but Libby would care if I was gone that long?* I think bleakly to myself as he approaches. *This way, Sam will be doing whatever Sam will be doing when I get to the office and I'll be completely out of his way.*

That's when I realize he's holding a beautiful bouquet in his arms. Hesitantly, he holds it out to me. "Happy birthday, Iris. I hope it's been a memorable one."

Automatically, I lift my cheek to accept his kiss before he lays the flowers in my arms. I lift them and inhale the delicate scent that wafts over me. My eyes lift to his and I see swirls of regret mixed with apology. "Thank you." My arms drop the flowers into my lap and automatically, like I have for each birthday we've celebrated together, I entwine my arms around his neck, giving him a fierce hug.

He crushes my body against his, lifting me from my seated position. I'm certain my beautiful flowers are being massacred between us, but I don't care. I'd rather the recollection of them so long as I can bank one more happy memory with him to accompany them. He lowers me back in place. I pick them up from where they carelessly fell and begin to stroke them, as if my touch will give them staying power.

Sam drops onto the couch next to me, capturing my hand in between his. "Can we talk later?"

The mature woman who confronted him weeks ago in Charleston must have been left in my bedroom while I was getting dressed tonight. "I . . . uh . . . what?"

"Talk. You, me. Later?" Just as I'm about to ask him what about, he smiles that damn panty-dropping smile that makes my insides quiver. "I'd say, let's bail on dinner but Libby cooked."

Just then, his stomach growls and I burst out laughing. He tangles his fingers in the ends of my curls before admitting, "I missed that sound."

"I've laughed recently."

"Not at me. Not with me," he counters roughly.

I get the difference. I really do. Because regardless if Sam's about to tell me we can be nothing more than friends, we were actually more than that. We're a part of Libby's family. Even before I nod, I brace myself. I have to make things right, not just for me, but for my best friend. I can't keep up this eternal estrangement from someone who's such a huge part of her life.

I can't forget he's been such an enormous part of mine these last few years despite our falling out. Especially when it's possible I'll have to trust my life to him at some point in the near future.

HOURS LATER, Libby shoos me out of the way as I try to help her clear the table. Cal and Sam are lingering at the table, so I slip outside trying to give myself a moment of silence. I need to order my thoughts so when Sam finally approaches me to talk, I can clearly articulate why I've been so upset.

No matter how hard I try to be reasonable, I keep returning to the incensed expression on his face as he taunted, "*My problem is you!*" "How am I supposed to forget he said that?" I wrap my arms around myself protectively.

The door closes behind me, startling me. Sam steps out onto the minuscule porch with me. "I'm not sure. I've been trying to forget I said it. It wasn't meant to come out like that."

I laugh bitterly. "Is there a better way to say it?"

"Yes." His voice is firm.

"How?"

"I lost my mind when I saw you at Alliance."

I scoff. "That much is obvious."

He steps closer and brushes a curl that's fallen away from my updo. "Give me a chance to explain. Please?"

Since my breath escaped me the moment his fingers tangled in my hair, I merely nod. Sam continues, "I felt something for you the first moment I saw you."

"Stop, Sam. I don't need pretty little lies." I step back. Much to my surprise, his fingers are still entwined in my hair. It's another connection between us, as if the one he has on my heart isn't strong enough.

"It isn't a lie, Iris." His eyes bore into mine

I want to believe him, I really do. But the number of times his words have echoed in my mind have me hesitating. "So, explain what spring break was about then. What did I do to earn such antagonism from you?"

Much to my surprise, his lips kick up on one side. "Again, I didn't lie. You were becoming a serious problem long before that day. I was just forced to confront it."

"What do you mean?" I practically shout.

He leans forward and snatches me around the waist, yanking me to him. "You haven't figured it out yet?"

I'm ready to blast him when Sam lays a finger across my lips and proceeds to blow my protests to smithereens with his self-deprecation. "In the span of a few short hours, you showed me everything I knew deep down that you were, Iris. A beautiful, brilliant woman who has the confidence and strength to take on the world. What on earth would you want with a guy who is more comfortable with computers than people?"

My mouth opens and closes a few times. I'm certain I'm doing a memorable impression of a fish when Sam drags his finger down my cheek. "Over and over I keep replaying your words."

"From that night?" I croak.

He shakes his head. "From every night. Do you remember when Libby got sick with the flu last year and we went and had dinner anyway since it took us forever to get reservations at that new Italian place?"

"Yes." Immediately, I begin flipping through my brain trying to recall everything that happened that night.

"You said, '*Non, tu m'as dit qu'il n'y avait personne d'autre avec qui tu préférerais être*' when I asked you if you wanted to use the reservation yourself. You told me there was no one else you'd rather be with."

"How on earth do you remember that?" I ignore the complete butchering of his pronunciation of the French language as he gives my words back to me.

"Because you wouldn't have said it in a foreign language if you didn't mean it. I know you well enough to know you say all the important words first in another language so no one can hold them against you. I committed those to memory and translated it after I dropped you off." He lifts my chin. "I feel the same way, Iris. And I don't mean for a single night."

My lips part in surprise. "Then why did you say what you did at Akin Hill?"

"Because I thought I finally had a chance to have everything I ever wanted and then had it pulled from under me," he admits obliquely.

"Sam?" I'm still confused.

"Can we leave it as, I was a complete idiot who misunderstood simple English when I should have been paying attention to the language expert?" he asks me patiently.

I break away from his hold and put my hands on the balustrade, giving his ask serious contemplation. Finally, I relent, "It was out of character for you."

Then he warns me, "This might be as well, but I hope it helps my case."

I whirl around to find him directly behind me. His long muscular body presses mine against the wrought-iron railing. "Sam?"

"Let's go out on our second date tomorrow night," he murmurs as he drops his forehead against mine.

"Second? When did we have our first?" I squawk.

"A year ago. I'm just the bonehead who didn't recognize it for what it was."

My lips curve upward. Sam's head tips to the side. "Are you agreeing to my being a bonehead or the date?"

Deciding to take a leap of faith into unchartered waters, I say flippantly, "Both."

One sinewy arm slips around my waist. "Thank God." That's the last coherent thought I have as his other hand sinks around the back of my neck tugging me up to meet his lips as they descend.

I catapult myself upward, a need born of endless nights imagining this very moment propelling me tighter against his body. My arms slide over his muscular chest, over his broad shoulders, until all I can do is relish the moment when the impact of his breath mingles with my own.

The second our lips touch it's a point of no return. I'm certain my heart must be falling out of my chest and landing at Sam's feet but I can't register it. Anything beyond the feel of his desire crashing over me has been forgotten lest it interrupts what I've dreamed of since I met this man.

Even as a groan works its way up from the depths of his chest, his tongue slips past my lips. My head falls back in supplication as my mouth falls powerless to his will. All I can taste is this man as I try to inhale the sweet spring night air so I never have to lift my lips from his ever again.

This kiss is everything I ever imagined it could be. It tastes of dark and light, of smoky wine and birthday cake. His kiss is a reflection of the man himself. It says so much I'm not certain he realizes he meant to share.

With our mouths touching, Sam pours out his need, desire, and something elusive I can't quite put my finger on. I just know it has something to do with him, me, us.

For now, that's enough for us to give this a try.

Slowly, he draws back before burying his head in the curve of my neck. "Whoa."

Panting, I have to agree once I can speak. "Whoa, is right."

He runs his fingers up and down my exposed back while pressing electrifying little kisses against my neck. "Iris, I'm sorry."

I pull back to force him to lift his head for this. He obliges. "Truly sorry. I never meant to hurt you that day at Akin Hill. I . . ."

"Why Sam?" I push because I need to know why I hurt for so many weeks.

He pushes back a curl from my face before admitting, "Too often, I can't think clearly around you. I fumble what I do, what I'm supposed to say."

"Sam," I start to release the hurt feelings I've been holding onto in the warm Georgia air.

"I need you to forgive me," he concludes.

Wrapped in Sam's arms, I feel them tremble as he holds me close. "This means something to you."

"This—you—mean a lot more than something to me. I just don't know what that is yet."

I trail my fingers over his cheek before I give myself permission to enjoy the decision that really had no other choice. "Then why don't we see where this leads tomorrow."

His breath rushes out right before he tightens his arms around me. "Tomorrow."

13

TWENTY-SEVEN YEARS AGO FROM PRESENT DAY

Iris

I WIPE the towel across the mirror in the small bathroom attached to my bedroom and whisper, "I shouldn't feel guilty."

But I do. There's nothing I can do to stop the sound of Libby's tears from penetrating through the thin walls of our house. I really want to take some of the lessons Kristin's been teaching me and use them on Cal, but not only would that likely screw with my grade point average, he likely knows all the moves to block them.

Dick.

As much as I didn't want to overhear what happened, Cal just came over and broke the date with Libby he made with her last night that had us both jumping up and down in excitement when I admitted Sam finally asked me out. At the time, I wasn't certain who I was more excited for, but now I can't bring myself to feel joy for either of us. "How am I supposed to get all dressed up to go out with Sam when Libby feels like this?"

"You've got to be kidding me, right?" Her voice causes me to whip my wet hair around, slapping me in the face. "You have been waiting for this night for almost four years, Iris."

"Libs," I start to protest.

"No. We're not thinking about me. I'm going to help you get dressed so you can finally explore who you are with Sam. Besides, there's always hope. He said he'd write to me."

There must have been doubt on my face because she digs in stubbornly. "He did, Iris. He told me he's a part of the National Guard and he was called up. He's not even staying to finish teaching your class. He's leaving this weekend."

It's a good thing he won't be around, I think angrily. Because if I had to face Cal Sullivan after the pack of lies he just shoved at Libby to escape their date, I likely would put my future at Alliance at risk. I mutter, "I wouldn't care."

"What was that?"

"I was just thinking about how I likely wouldn't graduate if I had to see his homely face in class because I'd leap across the desks to whack him in the head with a sharp object," I lie. Great, now Cal and his shenanigans have me lying to Libby.

She steps forward and wraps her arms around my towel-clad body. "I love you, Iris."

I hug her back just as fiercely. "I love you, too, Libs. Sam won't mind if I postpone."

Her laughter might not be as bright as normal, but at least she's doing it. "Right. Now, did he mention where you were going?"

I pale. "Oh, God. No, he didn't and I forgot to ask."

She spins me around, ordering, "Do your hair and makeup. I'll find out."

Panicking, I unzip my small bag of makeup and immediately drop the contents in my sink. I shriek. "*Opezdol!*"

"Yelling 'Idiot' in Russian isn't going to help. Get yourself under control while I get some insider information."

Knowing she's likely falling to pieces on the inside, I yell, "What did I do to deserve you?"

I hear Libby's voice float into the bathroom as she leaves my room. "Nothing. That's why you're going to name a kid after me."

Thinking about what I'm about to do over the course of the next few years as a job, I burst into gales of laughter. Children? As I grab my moisturizer, I whisper, "We need to find you a decent guy who treats you like a queen, Libs. Then once he's proven he's the one, you can let him get you pregnant." Even though she's going through so much pain right now, I have severe doubts that guy is Cal.

I'm in the process of defusing my hair when Libby comes back in, a bemused expression on her face. "You need to borrow my eggplant slip dress."

My brows lower into a V. "But I have plenty of dresses."

A smile hovers on her lips. "Sam wouldn't tell me where you were going. Only that it had to be perfect, thus the dress."

I rack my brain trying to figure it out when everything clicks into place. Our second date is going to be a redo of our first because this time we're both cognizant of the meaning behind it. I lean against the vanity. "I always knew he was charming, but I didn't realize he could be romantic. Did you?"

She shakes her head. "But when it came to you I had high hopes. I'll be right back with the dress." She turns to leave the bathroom

Alone again, the talons of fear grip my heart. In that instant, I completely understand the exaggerations Libby's been building up in her head about Cal because, "What if I've been doing the same about Sam?" No one likes to believe the feelings they have are one-sided. What if last night's kiss and tonight's dinner are just a way to ease me into becoming Sam's coworker?

I slide to the floor and wrap my arms around my legs, pulling them up to my chest. "What do I do then?"

"I have it right here. I'll just leave it on the back of your . . . Iris? What's wrong?" Libby cries.

I can't reply; I'm too busy trying to deep breathe through the panic sweeping through every cell of my body. "I feel like I'm standing on a bridge waiting to be rescued from my own thoughts."

"Talk to me."

I lift my head and meet her jewel-colored eyes, now swimming not with angst, but fear. I take a deep breath and try to reassure her. "I've wanted this for so damned long. What if he doesn't mean it?"

Her hands fold over mine. Wryly, she voices, "Like me and Cal?"

Immediately, I'm contrite. I didn't mean to go there. "No, Libby. You're different."

"You're right. It is different. Now I can tell you what happened the night we got back from Charleston. Sam came here. He wanted to see you, to apologize. He knew he screwed up within hours of saying something so stupid to you. We will see about . . ." Her eyes take on a faraway cast as her words trail off. She jolts herself back to the here and now. Her hands apply pressure to mine. "Don't borrow trouble. This is the night you've been waiting for. He has a lot to make up for but give him the chance."

My breath evens out. The anxiety recedes. "Okay."

"All right? Then let's get you ready. He'll be here soon."

Both of us scramble off the floor before entering my bedroom. Hanging on the back of the door is the slip dress I wore to the Italian restaurant the night Libby got ill. She stands by me before musing aloud, "You know, I really hoped faking being ill that night would be a beginning."

I gawk for a second before I throw my head back and laugh. "You set us up?"

She shrugs. "I tried."

I wrap my arms around her again. "There is nothing I wouldn't do for you."

She squeezes me back. "I know." With that, she lets go of me to finish getting ready.

After I slip into the dress and a pair of silver strappy heels, I twirl in front of the mirror giving myself a pep talk. That is, until the doorbell rings. Immediately, my hand flies to my stomach and I press in. Hard. "Oh, God. I might be sick."

Libby overhears me as she makes her way down the hall. "Can't do that. I am not your backup date."

I can barely manage a growl because just as I'm about to drop a multitude of curses in Russian, I hear Sam's deep baritone asking, "Hi Libs. Is Iris ready?"

"Just about. Come on in and wait while she finishes up."

"I heard what happened. Are you okay?" Sam's voice is laced with worry.

"I don't want to talk about it."

"Libs," he begins.

"It was just a date, Sam. I'll get over it," she protests.

I can tell from the sound of Sam's voice that he's clearly seeing past the words she's saying to the hurt that lies beneath. "Right."

That's when I decide to rescue Libby. Opening the door to my room, I take two steps and barely refrain from tripping over my own heart since it just fell at my feet. Sam's taken his handkerchief out of his pocket and is dabbing at the tears dripping down Libby's face. "I'm certain Iris won't mind if I rearrange our plans. She wants to be there for you as much as I want to be."

Libby shakes her head adamantly. "No."

I add my voice to the conversation. "Libby, Sam's right. We're good just staying in."

"I appreciate that but I need to be alone." If it wasn't for the fact that she manages a smile despite the wreckage Cal left her heart in, I'd cancel my dream date with Sam with him standing right in front of me. "Go. Please. Don't worry about me."

I stride forward and wrap my arms around her. "Call me if you need me. I don't care where we are, we'll come back to be with you."

Slightly reassured by the smile I feel against my cheek, I feel even more so when she whispers, "I know. Now, go."

I pull back to finally get my first real look at Sam. The waves in my stomach begin churning like the moon and the sun are spinning around in fierce competition. He's gorgeous in the same charcoal suit and black shirt he wore the last night we were alone together. Just like it has from the moment I met him, an unexplainable gravity pulls me in his direction. This time, I don't forcibly stop my feet from moving and instead give them the free will to do as they please. "Sam," I greet him softly.

"Iris." When I'm close enough for him to capture my hand, he does. He lifts it to his mouth for the barest touch in an almost extinct southern courtship ritual. The chills that run up my arm end up arcing my body involuntarily toward his. I stumble slightly on my heels and his other arm is quick to catch me around the waist. In a heartbeat, his eyes plumb the depths of mine. Whatever he finds must please him because his lips curve in a purely masculine smile. "Are you ready?"

My heart, yes. My mind, no. I feel like I've been wishing and hoping for this moment for so long, I don't know how to respond. Sam patiently waits until I finally manage to say, "Of course."

I'm rewarded by the brilliance of his smile and the sparkle of his eyes. "Then let's head out." He holds out his arm for me to tuck my hand into.

Just as we reach the door, my heads whips back to search Libby's face. What I find makes my heart sigh in relief. There's still sadness from what happened earlier, but there's also an overwhelming joy lighting her features from within—for me. I toss her an "Oh my, God. Is this really happening?" look over my shoulder which causes her to giggle uncontrollably before I pass through the door Sam's holding open for me.

After the door closes behind us, he immediately presses me back up against it. "Thank you."

"For what?"

"For loving her the way you do." Leaning close, he breathes into my ear, "Cal was called back to Alliance today. He's not coming back."

"Libby?" I ask quietly.

His breath explodes against my neck. "I don't know."

I will myself not to fling open the door behind me and expose everything about Cal to Libby but I know I can't. It would hurt not just Libby, but the Alliance team which soon will include Sam and later, me. I grip Sam's jacket and hold on, transferring my anger so I can be there for my best friend the only way I'm allowed to be.

He smooths a hand up and down my back until I physically relax. Pulling back, he whispers, "Better?"

"Nothing makes her hurt better, but I'm not going to go off and hunt him down out of vengeance, Sam."

He brushes his lips against mine. "Good. Now, let's go stuff ourselves full of Italian."

As he begins escorting me to the passenger side of his car, I run my tongue around my lips capturing Sam's taste as well as anticipating the delicacies of *Le Stagioni*. "Recreating our not first date? How very charming of you."

Sam returns, "Well, not exactly."

"What do you mean?" But my question is cut off by Sam closing the car door.

I study him with narrowed eyes as he jogs around the front of the car with a fluid grace. I cross my legs to ease the shattering throb between them that matches the pounding of my heart as I enjoy the pure masculine beauty of Sam Akin. Although I'd have no problem slipping a blade through his ribs at this very moment, Cal's rigorous workouts with Sam have caused his shoulders to broaden, his waist to flatten, his rear to be cupped more lovingly by the dress slacks he's wearing since he last wore the outfit in question. And I'd know; I checked him out just as thoroughly that night as well.

Sam slips beneath the wheel before admitting, "Well, I tried to get a reservation at *Le Stagioni*."

This doesn't sound good. "What happened?"

He tosses me a chagrined look. "Before or after they laughed at my begging? Let me sum it up by saying I was called foolish and they hung up on me."

"Want me to try?" I offer lamely.

He drapes an arm over the back of my seat. "Iris, I bought two Stouffer's lasagnas so we can eat back at my place."

"Sam, knowing our cooking skills, we'll likely have the fire department at your door."

"Does that matter as long as we're together?"

My head swivels from side to side, never losing eye contact with him. "No. Besides, I want to see the inside of your place." Sam moved when he came back from China and I've been dying to get my hands on some of his souvenirs.

He slides his hand around the nape of my neck. "You, me? Alone together. You're good with that?"

I think about it for a moment before nodding.

He releases a slow breath. "You're a tempting woman, Iris Cunningham."

Helplessly, I lose myself in the admiration swirling in the jewels staring down at me. "You're just starting to notice that?"

"No." His reply disconcerts me because he doesn't elaborate on it. Instead he slides away from me with a mysterious curve to his lips. "Buckle up."

"Right." Instead of trying to figure out what just happened, I focus on the menial task of latching my seat belt so we can be on our way and I can determine if I've wasted years of emotions on a man who doesn't return them.

14

TWENTY-SEVENYEARS AGO FROM PRESENT DAY

SAMUEL

Iris is relaxing on my couch with a glass of wine while I pull our slightly charred lasagna out of the oven. Even with my back to her, I can feel the appraising head-to-toe perusal she gives me. I can't say I don't appreciate her frankness when it comes to admiring me, as I've long admired her tall, trim form.

We've been talking for the last hour about everything from classes to trips overseas—my recent one to China and hers with Libby to Mexico. When we finally touched on the subject of work, all the pieces finally clicked into place: her skill with languages, her keen sense of situational awareness, her combat training at Alliance.

They're training her to become a field operative.

My head whirls around at the sound of her musical laughter as she snorts into her wine over some personal amusement. Her long black curls fall effortlessly down her narrow back and a thought whip through me that I didn't put together before now. *God, if something happens to her, what will I do?*

While I've been adjusting to the idea of an us, dreaming of her being with me, she's been preparing for a life away from everything either of us has ever known. *You're such a fool, Sam,* I berate myself. I believed I had one chance to make up for my mistakes, to become a part of her life. But the reality is I might not even have that. *Too late.* The words whisper through my mind.

That's when I feel the delicate touch of her hand on my arm. "Sam? Is there a problem?" Her hazel eyes stare up at me with concern.

As I meet her stare head-on, a seismic shift happens inside of me I'm completely unprepared for. An overwhelming urge to clasp Iris to me and never let her go rushes through me. I want to wrap her in as many layers of protection as I can, but I know she'd resent me if I tried. So, even though I'm going to have to let her go to soar as high as she can, I will do my damnedest to pinpoint all of the hunters who will be trying to shoot her down and destroy them the only way I can.

I slip my arms around her and brush my nose against hers before urging her, "Tell me more about the trip to Mexico."

"Libby wanted to spend all her time in museums. If it wasn't for the pact we made never to leave one another alone, I'd have abandoned her for the beach."

"Come on, you can do better than that."

Her shoulders shake. "Just that I'm certain I must have scared off half the hotel staff."

"Why's that?"

Iris blushes fiercely. "Because I might have told them a teensy lie."

I rock her back and forth. "Spill it."

"They assumed I couldn't understand them. I corrected their misconception after overhearing two of the men say they wanted to approach me and Libby. I told them, in no uncertain terms, I was desperate to be with my lover but had just gotten my cycle. Then I described her. Her eyes are a remarkably similar shade to yours."

Her sweetness and light tone doesn't fool me a bit. My shoulder's shake. "What did Libby have to say about it?"

"'Isn't that special.'" Her drawl that's an almost perfect impression has me in stitches.

"You realize I'm going to have to call my grandmother and break her heart," I lament.

"Non . . . Nonna?" she stammers. "Why?"

I lean down and press my lips directly next to her ear before I whisper, "Because she'll be devastated you chose Libby over me."

Iris's reaction is everything I hoped it would be. Her laughter illuminates the walls of my apartment, brightening the space. Her reaction reminds me of her uninhibitedness the night when we went to the Italian restaurant. It prompts me to ask, "By the way, when did Libby admit to you she faked being sick the night of our first date?"

Iris jerks her head back just far enough so our lips are in perfect alignment. "Tonight when I was getting ready. How did you know when I just found out?"

"Because I was raised with her. She's practically my twin. When she's sick or injured, she moans for Nonna's bread pudding. It's her biggest tell."

Iris softens against me so I can feel the press of her breasts against my shirt. I hold her tighter when she says wistfully, "That's lovely."

"Hmm, except when she butts her nose into my business." Iris's eyes narrow on me. I just laugh before pressing a kiss to her forehead. "One of the things I've always admired is how ferociously protective you are of Libby, Iris. You don't have any siblings?"

She shakes her head. "I was adopted by Libby and the rest of your family."

"She loves you."

"I'm grateful to hear that."

I get up and drag Iris into the kitchen with me, unwilling to waste a single precious moment with her. I give my next words some thought, not thinking before I reach out to touch the lasagna dish . Quickly, I rip my hand away. *Too hot.* There's no way we can eat that. I continue as I shuffle Iris back into the living room, "To be honest, I know and love Libby probably more than my older sisters because I know her better. Evie and Lisa are so much older than I am. In a lot of ways, I grew up feeling like I had three mothers instead of one. The difference being that instead of the constant love and support Mom provided, they would challenge my decisions, my path forward. It was almost freeing to spend a semester abroad."

"Tell me about China," she urges.

"Well, the first thing I learned very quickly was to pack an extra pair of shoes if I was going somewhere outside of a major city, because I was easily the tallest person there and footwear was at a premium."

"Good to know."

I spare a glance down at her delicately shod feet. "If you're ever there, you might want to consider the same. I'm fairly certain women's shoes don't run that large either."

"Oh, you . . ." Iris goes to step on my foot, but I shuffle mine back. She falls off balance but I catch her.

"I suppose we should eat," I murmur reluctantly.

"I guess so."

I guide Iris to her seat, then move quickly back to the kitchen to cut into our dinner. That's when disaster strikes. I frown. "It was in the right amount of time."

"What's wrong?" Iris calls.

I don't answer. Instead, I take one of the forks I laid on the counter and jab it into the center of the half-frozen mess, lifting it clear from the container.

Iris roars with laughter before standing and making her way back to the kitchen. She takes my hand. My heart beats triple time. I clear my throat before asking, "Well, now that dinner's ruined, what should we do? I'm certain I have peanut butter and jelly around here."

Iris rises to the balls of her feet and murmurs, "I have a better idea."

I clear my throat. "What's that?"

"Chinese takeout. Maybe it will get you in the mood to tell me about your trip and how you managed to survive without cooking." Her voice is filled with amusement.

I leave the mess on the counter for later and decide to give in gracefully. "That question is easy."

Her forehead scrunches as she arches both brows, waiting for my answer.

"I ate out a lot."

Iris grins.

I snatch up my keys. "Come on. The least we can do is eat at the restaurant."

MUCH LAUGHTER and several hours later, Iris and I put away enough food to make us both groan. Unwilling to end our date, I pull up to the park where I did a significant amount of my training with Cal. "Are you up for a walk with me in those shoes? There's a special place I want to share with you."

Wordlessly, Iris slips off her seatbelt. Quickly, I undo mine and leap out of the car. Racing around the other side, I catch the door just as she's opened the latch. Holding out my hand, she slips hers into it so I can help her from the vehicle. We walk in silence down the stone path until she says, "Give me a moment to get out of these shoes, Sam. I don't want to twist anything."

At that point, I swoop down and catch her behind the knees. "Let me."

"Sam," she gasps as I lift her higher against my chest and begin down the dark path. "You can't carry me!"

I brush my lips against hers. "Will you trust me that I won't hurt you?" It's a question that's been burning deep inside me. Before I screwed things up between us, I'd have laid odds on Iris's answer being yes. But now? I find myself holding my breath.

The patch of moonlight that shines off her face allows me to see her nod. Relief surges through me. My forehead crashes down on hers. "Thank you."

"Sam." There's still hesitancy in her voice that I know I put there.

"Iris, listen." We both still so she can hear the rush of water. She gasps. "It's just up ahead. That's where we're going to talk."

I begin walking in the direction of the water and the green knoll that leads down to it. Once I reach it, I slide Iris down the front of my body. Hearing her breath catch makes me want to hold onto her and never let go.

But I have to.

I clasp her delicate hand in my larger one before I guide her to stand in front of me. I release a rush of air that rustles the curls on the top of her head. "Maybe Cal had the right idea."

"Excuse me?" It erupts from her with so much fury, I can't help but smile before pressing my lips against her crown.

I continue, my tone almost conversational, "Maybe it will hurt less since he never started anything with Libby, because after the last two days, I wish I could just stop time. I'm kicking myself in so many different ways for not realizing what everyone else saw long before I did."

Iris stops struggling and becomes a statue. "Sam?" My name comes off her lips as a question and a plea.

I spin her around gently, cognizant of the heels she's wearing sinking into the soft earth. My arms slip around her waist as I draw her up against my body. "I never thought I'd run out of time. Maybe it was a ridiculous arrogance assuming you'd be waiting for my heart and my head to catch up with one another. But the reality we both face is time's passing us by too quickly to start what we both want."

Tears begin to slowly drip down her face. I bend slightly and begin to kiss them away. "It hurts my soul to know I'm the reason you're crying, Iris."

"You've made me cry before, Sam." I feel that shot directly to my heart when she keeps going. "But for the first time, they're tears of joy."

"You're happy?"

She nods and a smile I've never witnessed spreads across her face as she slides her fingers up my chest.

I stumble trying to give my thoughts voice. "I figured you'd be infuriated."

"Because you're putting us on hold? Again?"

I bob my head in ascent.

Iris clasps her hands around my neck. "Tell me why."

"Why what?"

"Why are you stepping back, Sam? Is it because you don't want me, us?"

"Hell no!" I shout. Then my voice drops to a husky shell of its normal self. "The idea of being with you isn't something I take lightly. I've dreamed of it so often."

"Then talk to me, Sam. I can guess, but I need the words. Remember, communication?"

I clasp her to me as tightly as I can. My lips search hers out to find them eagerly waiting. In the moonlit night, no one can see us, except for maybe the gods I'll begin praying to the moment I get home for this beautiful woman's safety as she embarks on a journey that will possibly take her to places where mistakes could kill her. For long moments, there are no actual words. The only things we say to one another are through our hearts and communicated with our lips and darting tongues as we memorize the taste and feel of each other.

Finally, I draw us out of the kiss, breathing heavily. Iris snuggles up against my heart, making it almost impossible for me to turn this moment of love away, knowing it may be our only chance. But I need to let her go until Fate decides whether it's meant for us to be together again. I set her back just a bit so I can see her face. "I realized tonight you're in training to be a field operative, aren't you?"

Her lashes lower to hide her translucent eyes. For long moments, she doesn't respond. The only sound that pounds through my ears is the rushing water from the Middle Oconee River, a sound that once comforted me as it used to signal the end of Cal tormenting me at the end of a run.

Now, the rushing water signifies the beginning of something I have no control over. That's only amplified when Iris flicks her gaze up at me and mouths, "Yes."

My next words are ripped from my soul. "I don't want to let you go, Iris, but I have to."

"You don't," she protests.

"I do." I stop her next words by laying a finger on her lips. "I'll never lose you in my heart. Nothing, no matter what, could cause me to do that. But you need to be focusing all of your energy on what you're about to learn so I know when you're"—I swallow hard to keep the bile down—"out there, I know you're as safe as you can be."

Her body trembles against mine in the cooling night air. I wrap her tighter against me. That's when I hear her whisper, "I thought this was going to be one of those in-between moments, Sam. The ones between the highs and lows. Do you remember?"

"You said they're the kind you wanted to live," I manage.

She shakes her head so her fragrant hair brushes beneath my chin. "They're not supposed to hurt like this. I dreamed they would be filled with moments of us curled in front of a television, cuddled beneath a blanket." Her wet eyes lift to mine. "The in-between wasn't supposed to hurt like this."

I pull her head against me as tight as I can. "Then call this a low and pray this is the worst hurt we ever feel, sweetheart."

She wraps her arms around my waist and squeezes. "Sounds perfect."

15

TWENTY-SEVEN YEARS AGO FROM PRESENT DAY

SAMUEL

"HELLO?" I answer my call without checking the caller ID. I assume it's likely my mother pestering me again for more graduation tickets.

"Sam? It's Cal." His voice is tough, not at all like I remember it the last time I saw him at Libby's.

I almost drop my cordless handset, I'm so floored. "What the fuck, man? You left without a word!"

"Get used to it," is Cal's brutal reply. "You're going to find yourself in the same position soon, Sam."

Before I can spit out my frustration at him with the way he handled the situation with Libby, Cal demands, "Where's your laptop?"

"Where the hell do you think it is?" I drawl.

"I need you to access some data," he begins.

Disgust crawls up my spine. "No 'Hey!' 'How you doin'?' 'How's training, buddy?' Just get me the information I want?"

"Preferably without the damn attitude, yes."

"Up yours, Cal." I'm about to disconnect the call when his words stop me cold.

"Wait, Sam! Don't you fucking hang up! I can't get through to the team at Alliance; none of us can. For some reason, our calls aren't being relayed through our satellite uplink. Right now, there's no time to waste fuckin' with a game of telephone. I have a kid who's in trouble."

"What kind of trouble?" I ask, but I'm already reaching for my laptop knowing I'm going to help. My fingers begin tapping on the keys after the terminal window opens up the basic scripts I wrote in preparation for my interview at Alliance.

"Aarushi was kidnapped by radicals in Kashmir who object to political change in the region. They're demanding the release of militants belonging to the Harakat ul-Ansar in exchange for her release."

"She's not the only one," I hazard a wild guess.

"She's the only one I give a damn about." Cal's voice is controlled but I hear something beneath it.

Worry.

"I'm not sanctioned by Alliance for any of the actions I'm about to take," I remind him.

"Kidnapped children trumps your authorization, Akin."

Ethically, I agree with him, but I still hesitate. "Cal . . ."

"For shit's sake, Sam!" Cal shouts. I rip the phone away from my ear to save the drum. He roars, "I lost eyes in that compound twenty minutes ago. I need to know where that little girl is before she's killed—or worse."

I can hear my heart thumping against my chest even as I decide to side with doing what's right over what might be legal. "What do you need me to do?"

As Cal begins rattling off orders, I'd be lying to myself if I didn't feel equal measures of anger, excitement, and fear over what my future holds.

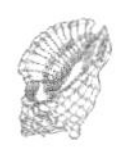

Later that week, I'm frustrated. I save my work before leaning my chair back and glare at the laptop in front of me. "Why is condensing the purpose of this software so impossible?" I growl. My capstone is due in a few days.

This paper is ninety-eight percent complete. This final part—the top sheet introduction—should be a breeze in comparison to the coursework I've already completed in preparation for it. Simple, provide an overview of the purpose of the software development process I designed from initial concept to prototype to its final implementation. With the number of papers I've written to earn my degree, I ought to be able to write this one in my sleep but these last few nights my dreams are spent replaying every moment of the date I had with Iris. "Why can't I get her out of my head?"

"Are either of these rhetorical questions or do you want to talk to someone?" A feminine voice breaks into my thoughts. I recognize the woman as the one who Iris threw during her 'interview.' Brazenly, she plunks a bag of food on the table of the fast food joint I retreated to in order to get an escape from campus.

I frown at her. "Can I help you with something?"

"Kristin Mansfield." She holds out her hand to shake, which I do. Her explanation comes on the heels of it. "Cal asked me to keep an eye on you, Sam. Although it's just a few weeks until you join the team at your new job, he wanted to make certain you had somewhere you could turn to if you had any questions."

I pointedly comment as she slides into the booth across from me, "I was looking for some peace and quiet so I can finish my paper."

She snorts as she unwraps a cheeseburger. "Obviously working. Talk to me. Tell me what's on your mind."

I open my mouth to tell Kristin to kiss my ass, but I find myself confiding in her about my past with Iris, the change over time of our feelings, especially my getting my head out of my ass recently after I saw her at Alliance. I miserably conclude, "As much as I want our time to be now, it can't be. I need her to focus on her training so I know she's safe more than I want there to be an us. She has to be safe beyond everything else."

Kristin is quiet during the entire spiel. Not once during the entire recital did her facial expression change but it does now, softening in a way that reminds me far too much of the woman that's been invading my thoughts. "Does she know how deeply you're in love with her?"

I jerk back so hard, my shoulders hit the back of the plastic booth. Shock flows straight from my heart to my mouth. "We've been on two dates."

Kristin calmly crumples the paper of her sandwich before tossing it into the bag. "From what I was told, you studied abroad for computer science." At my nod, she continues. "While you were in China, I don't suppose you took any other classes?"

"No time."

Standing, she grabs her handbag before she declares, "*Yǒu yuán qiān lǐ lái xiāng huì.*"

While I'm certain Iris could translate this woman's words in her sleep. I shake my head with a complete lack of comprehension. "Sorry. The most I learned overseas was 'Where is the library?'" *Then there's what I tried to say to Iris when I first got back*, I amend silently

Kristin's lips curve. "It means 'Fate brings together those that are a thousand miles apart.' Eventually, when your hearts are meant to be together, it will happen."

I'm mulling that over when Kristin leans down and murmurs, "Sam? Letting her go so she can be trained is an incredibly beautiful gift. Right now, you may be questioning your decision but don't. In the long run, it may be what guarantees you that future you're hoping for." Standing back to her full height, she offers, "Now, do you need any assistance with your paper?"

"No. You gave me a lot to think about." *Including a focus for finishing this assignment*, I realize suddenly.

"Then I'm glad I stopped by." She pulls out a card and lays it on the table. "Feel free to reach out if you need a touchpoint since Cal isn't available."

I immediately slide the card into the pocket of my jeans and stand. Holding out my hand, I say honestly, "I will."

She gives me a once-over before shaking my hand and giving me a final piece of advice. "Each day, the job you're taking will require you to embark on a new adventure. It's easy to lose yourself in the emotions of work. Don't let that happen. Find your tie to reality and hold onto it."

"Is that what you did?" I ask.

She shakes her head. "It caused me to almost lost it all." With that oblique response, Kristin drops my hand and walks away.

After she leaves, I spend quite a while thinking about what she said and didn't. I recall Iris's words from the night she tried to congratulate me at Akin Hill. *"That's why I'm choosing Alliance. Because I can have it all—the overflow of emotions that happen every day whether I'm in the field, behind a desk, even the moments where I'm just me."*

Finally, I drag my laptop back in front of me.

Maybe I didn't know it at the time, but the purpose of the software I developed crystalizes in my mind. Tool names like Python, Frama C, and Cnerator all make their way into the software reference. But it's the introduction that's been holding me tied to this place, afraid if I write these words, the future I imagined for myself will be completely unrecoverable

I made my choices. Now I need to finish this so I can move forward into the future I never knew I wanted with the only woman I can picture by my side.

My fingers tap away as I wrap up almost four years of work on machine learning and mining software repositories, knowing it won't be published in the traditional sense after it's graded. Its implications are too far-reaching not to be immediately classified by the US government.

After I type the last word, I save the document when the realization hits me and I begin to laugh softly. "I guess you were on my mind much longer than I realized, sweetheart."

My eyes sweep over the title of my assignment—Interactive Response for Intelligence Sorting. IRIS. "Maybe there was a part of me that knew I was going to do my damnedest to keep you safe and happy, wherever you are." Closing the lid of my computer, I drop it into my backpack and clear the table of the cups and wrappers strewn about.

Then, I head back to campus to face graduation and whatever the future may hold.

16
SAMUEL

Rachel reaches for a tissue and wipes her eyes. Her first question is to Iris. "How did you stand it, Mama? Being in love with Dad for so long and then knowing nothing was going to happen because of your career choice?" She shoots me an astounded look over her shoulder.

"Somehow in the retelling of how you and I managed to get together, you've lost some of the gleam on that suit of armor, my love."

"Apparently," I reply dryly.

"No, Dad. I didn't mean it to come out like that," Rachel is quick to correct herself.

I laugh and pull Iris back against my chest. I press a kiss to her temple before explaining, "Honey, we were just a few years older than you are right now. Your mama was being deployed to the Army for twelve weeks and then to California for over a year. I had orders to return to Charleston and was promptly sent on assignments all over the world."

"But what did that have to do with how you felt about one another?" Rachel demands.

Iris scoots forward and clasps Rachel's hand in between her own on her lap. "Not. One. Thing. I might have been young, but I knew my heart, Rach. Your father was it for me. But realistically, it would have been relationship suicide to have started something when we hardly knew each other."

Rachel scoffs. "You already had known each other for years."

I jump back in. "It's different, being friends with someone versus trusting them enough to unlock the deepest parts of your heart. There's a shift in the vulnerability you're exposing yourself to."

"Then how did you manage it?"

Iris stands and pretends to hobble like an old woman. With a creaky voice, she says, "Well, you see, lassie. There's an invention called letters."

"You sent Dad snail mail?" Rachel is astounded.

Iris cocks a brow. "Your father and Uncle Cal raised you better than that."

Dawning comprehension crosses her face. "You and Dad talked via secure email."

"Almost every single day," I confirm. *After a while,* I amend silently.

Iris sends me a surreptitious wink.

"You didn't get busted for using company resources for personal reasons? Didn't you and Uncle Cal also teach me not to do that?" Rachel taunts.

I pretend to choke her from behind, setting her off into gales of laughter. Then I catch the expression on Iris's face, who's smiling with so much love, I'm immediately transported to that night we stood by the river in Athens. *God, how did I not recognize the love glowing on her face back then?* Cursing my hesitation and the time we wasted, I direct my question to my wife, "Do you think we trained her too well?"

"Clearly not or she'd have figured out who the admin of the network was, which is how we didn't get caught," Iris states pointedly.

"Dad? They trusted you to admin a classified network?" Rachel is guffawing with laughter.

Only moderately offended, I inform her, "At twenty-two, kiddo. I was doing it before your Mama graduated from Fort Benning."

"He wrapped up my new email address as a gift," Iris said dreamily.

"Wait, Dad. You went to Mama's graduation from Officer Training School?" Rachel straightens.

My eyes meet Iris's and I inform both of the women in my life, "I wouldn't have missed it for the world."

CHAPTER 16

17

TWENTY-SIX YEARS AGO FROM PRESENT DAY

Iris

Twelve weeks of physical and mental tests that designed to keep me alive in the field are over Finally, I cross the stage after its announced proudly, "First Lieutenant Cunningham, Military Intelligence."

Returning to my seat, I catch a glimpse of an ostentatious green hat in the audience and try to squint to see who might be wearing it. Even though Libby told me that she, Sam, and Nonna would be at my graduation ceremony, I never caught a glimpse of them before I focused on the general's words congratulating the newly commissioned second lieutenants.

The haze caused by the summer humidity in Fort Benning doesn't even cause me to blink as I'm attired in my dress blues. *They're not as bad as day-to-day wear,* I think ruefully. Wearing my cargos and combat boots in this heat took some adjustment. Then again, nothing was as awful as rucking almost twenty klicks with a backpack on to graduate. I curl my toes inside my dress shoes just to make certain I still have feeling in them. *Praise the lord, I have a few weeks off before reporting to Monterey so I can recover. Then, it's back to training.*

I received a packet via FedEx this morning from the team at Alliance. They told me I'd be contacted by an Alliance liaison about my next steps some time today in person. My eyes scan the plethora of officers wondering which one is going to approach me with the parameters of my next assignment. I feel more ready than ever to head out west.

Particularly since I haven't heard from Sam since graduation day in Athens.

My heart jolts when I realize the ceremony is over. You did it, Iris. No matter what you will face in the future, what will attempt to break you, you accomplished this all on your own. That's when I finally feel an enormous smile break free across my face.

We fall out in the same processional we entered. I try one more time to spy them in the crowd. I almost fall out of formation when I realize the garish hat belongs to Nonna. On either side of her are Libby and Sam. Each of their faces are lit with a different emotion—pride, love, and regret. I focus on the fierce pride emanating from Nonna's as I disappear from view.

Because if I focus on the regret on Sam's, it will sour this incredible moment I've worked so hard for.

"IRIS!" Libby's practically climbing on her chair the minute she spots me to wave me over at the restaurant I agreed to meet the three of them at after the ceremony was over.

I flick my hand in awareness while waiting for the hostess to seat the couple in front of me. Just as it's my turn to step up to the hostess station, Sam steps into the lobby. His smile broadens. "Iris."

Just my name. It sounds so sweet on his lips. I want to turn and run from the feelings he causes inside of me, but I refuse to run away. "Samuel."

His gem-colored eyes narrow on my face with intent as he tries to discern my mood. I'm not fired up. Inside, my emotions are a wreck. I'm on the brink of the edge, but in uniform and having not been contacted by Alliance yet, I'm hesitant to cause a scene. "Should we head to the table? I'm certain everyone must be hungry."

He holds out an arm.

With a smile, I shake my head no, gesturing to my uniform with my hand.

Sam gestures for me to precede him into the dining room. "Then if you would be so kind as to join us, Lieutenant Cunningham."

I lift my chin high as I pass by him.

Sam follows hot on my heels. "We need to find time to talk."

"What's so important now that you couldn't say it for the last twelve weeks?"

"Iris," he groans.

"Not a word, Sam. Three months. What happened to not letting me go?" I hiss almost soundlessly.

"I haven't been in the country for most of it," he admits.

"Bully for you. There's this invention you were a big fan of in school. It's called email."

He scoots around so he's facing me. "That's why we need to talk."

My eyebrows form a V. "What do you mean?"

His eyes dart to the side. "Later." Stepping to the side, he announces to Libby and Nonna, "And here's our guest of honor. She was waiting patiently in the lobby despite your display, Libs."

Libby sighs. "You called it, Sam."

Nonna just nods her head, a smile playing about her lips.

I take a seat, frowning. "What do you mean, Sam called it?"

"Poppa was in the Army. He used to do the very same thing."

"Libs, remember how many times he'd take us out for pancakes as kids and he'd let families go ahead of us at restaurants? We'd be the last ones seated because he had to make certain everyone was taken care of before us." Sam remembers his grandfather fondly as he reaches for the breadbasket and hands it to me.

I pause in the act of taking a roll before addressing the table at large. "I never knew he was in the Army. Is that why you supported me joining, Nonna?"

Nonna nods her head. "Oh yes. When Bernard served, he was also in military intelligence. He'd be proud of your accomplishments, Iris."

I'm grateful I haven't taken a bite of food as tears well up and threaten to choke me. "Thank you, Nonna."

Libby asks, "Did you hear from your mother?"

I nod, grateful for the emotional lifeboat. "I did. She and Arnold sent me a card this week. They're happy for me. Neither understand my choices, but that's okay."

"Arnold?" Sam questions.

"My stepfather. Solid guy for Mom. They met just before I went to college."

"Do you and your mother get along?" Sam prods.

I take a long drink of water, thinking about the question before answering truthfully. "Yes? I love her, but she is more like my sister. I've never doubted she loved me, gave up a lot to have me, but we are mismatched as parent and child. We both freely admit my grandparents were the ones who truly raised me. They were adamant about pushing my boundaries and encouraging me to absorb knowledge like a sponge."

"Kind of like you, Nonna," Libby pipes up.

I wink at Libby and Sam's grandmother. "I always knew I liked you for a reason."

She sends me a wink back before pushing to her feet. "Libby, would you be a dear and help me to the restroom? I remember that chicken place we ate at in Jacksonville—"

"Beach Road Chicken Dinner?" Sam pipes up.

I can't restrain my chuckle at the look of complete avarice on his face when Nonna confirms the restaurant name. "Yes, Samuel. Now, Libby, your grandmother does not need to flip head over heels on a grease-laden carpet again. Iris, when we get back, I want to know where you're going next."

Stifling her mirth, Libby agrees. After the two women leave the table, I'm again left alone with Sam. This time, I do have something to ask about. "Did I miss something?"

He frowns, as he reaches inside his jacket. "Miss what?"

"Did I just join the Army or did something happen with my Alliance liaison? They haven't made contact today."

"Ah, about that." Sam pulls out an envelope and hands it to me. "You might want to take a glance at that before Nonna gets back."

"What?" I tear into the tamper-evident envelope and scan the document inside quickly. It's my orders to report to the Defense Language Institute Foreign Language Center. *Please report to the center two weeks from Monday 1200 PST unless counter orders are received during that time.* Beneath it is a phone number where I need to report my whereabouts during my two-week break. I clutch the paper to my chest before whispering, "I did it." I unbutton my shirt pocket and slip the orders inside.

Then it hits me; Sam's the liaison. My head snaps up. "It's you?"

"They knew I was invited to attend your ceremony because I requested the time off. Admiral Yarborough asked if I would have a problem delivering that to you. As you can imagine, I didn't. You killed it, Iris. Everyone at Alliance knows it."

The pride in Sam's voice seeps through every barrier I've tried to hold erect between us. It also allows all the hurt to come rushing in with the lack of contact in the last twelve weeks. "Why, Sam? Why didn't you contact me?"

His harsh groan rumbles up from his chest. "I couldn't. Not until I was able to hand you this as well." Reaching back into his pocket, he draws out a long white box tied with a lilac bow.

Frowning, I inform him, "I don't need gifts, Sam. I need answers."

His lips curve. "This is both."

I reach for the box hesitantly. The electric arc that springs between us as our fingers touch almost causes me to jump back. Sam doesn't let go. My eyes fly up to his and I'm shocked to find his are shining with moisture. "You have no idea how hard it was not to respond to your public email. At one point, I almost said fuck it. That's when Cal took my computer away for both our sakes."

I mutter something in French about Cal's parentage. Sam chuckles, letting go of the box. "Although I have no idea about what you said, that's likely true. I found out in the last few weeks some stuff about Cal I'll share with you later."

I frown as I slip the bow off. Inside is a folded piece of paper. At the top, it has a set of instructions on how to access a secure email server. At the bottom is a purple sticky note. I lift it, and my heart starts pounding madly. "Isn't this a little premature?" My Alliance email address is staring up at me.

Sam shakes his head. "No. All the responses to your emails are waiting for you the minute you log in."

My voice shakes when I say his name, "Sam." He didn't just give me a graduation present, he gave me the knowledge he's been supporting me the whole time even if I didn't know it.

Leaning forward, his lips brush my ear when he whispers, "Password is your birthday—all numeric in the form of month, month, day, day, year, year, ampersand, capital A-T-H-E-N-S" He sits back slightly and explains, "The system will force you to change it the first time logging in."

I swallow repeatedly staring down at the box I'm clutching harder than I did my DLIFLC orders before I can whisper, "I really want to hug you right now."

He sighs in relief.

"But let me tell you, Samuel Winston Akin, there had better be something good waiting for me in my email or I'm going to be really upset," I warn him.

"How about we save the really good stuff for the time we have together before you fly to California?" He wags his eyebrows suggestively.

I'm about to slap down that suggestion when fortunately Nonna and Libby return. Libby, noticing the open gift, asks excitedly, "Oh you opened it! What did Sam get you?"

Before Sam can answer, I pipe up with, "A way to talk to me while I'm away."

Even as Libby groans, "Boring," I'm contradicting her in my mind. The fact I have a way to speak with Sam at all during the time I'm isolated in Monterey is a gift I never expected.

18

TWENTY-SIX YEARS AGO FROM PRESENT DAY

Iris

I'm lying by the banks of the Cooper River in complete heaven. Sam's head is propped on my stomach. My fingers comb through the mink-colored strands, offering them up to the sun for them to be kissed. His head turns in my direction. When he smiles, my ribs actually ache with the way my heart knocks against them. "It's a perfect day," I say softly.

He nods before capturing my hand in his on the next pass. He brings it to his lips, nuzzling the palm. "Then again, we could be in a hurricane and as long as we were just like this, we'd be perfect."

Before I can curl myself upright to reward that comment with a kiss, Libby's voice drawls, "That's so sweet I might be stickier from more than just the humidity."

Immediately, I start laughing because now that she mentions it my top is clinging to my stomach like it's a damp bathing suit instead of cotton. Sam scowls. "There isn't a single place on this property a man can have any privacy."

I'm about to smack him for being so rude but I don't have to bother. Libby merely ignores him, plopping down next to me. "Then don't choose my spot to escape to."

"It was my spot before it was yours," he argues.

"Was not."

"Was too."

Libby's about to open her mouth to contradict him, but I slap one of my hands across each of their mouths. "We can share." I lift my hands.

Sam grumbles, "She doesn't get to take all the credit for finding this spot."

Libby declares, "Of course I do. I'm the one who escaped out of Nonna's house and found it."

He retorts, "I found you."

Just as they're about to get into it again, I play peacemaker. "Now we're all here. Together." What's left unsaid is *for a few more days.* The hands of the clock are spinning round and round so fast, one moon barely has a chance to disappear before the next one starts to rise. Like I've experienced before, that's summer in the South. I only have a few days left of my break before I'm due to report in Monterey.

That means leaving Sam. Again.

Shoving the thought aside for the moment, I catch the glare of the sun off a lens as Libby snaps a picture of me and Sam. I shove my hand through the weight of my curls. "Talk about candid photos."

"The best ones," she agrees. Then she does something unprecedented. "Get together with Sam, Iris. I'll actually take a couple of pictures of the two of you."

I scooch around the blanket until Sam—who has curled up from his reclined position—can wrap his arms around me. After Libby has taken an umpteen number of photos, I joke, "Watch. Those will be the worst ones. I'll likely have my eyes closed or something."

Sam brushes a soft kiss across my lips. "It wasn't you with your eyes closed for so long; it was me. The pictures are going to be perfect. Just like you."

For a brief moment, I wonder what it would be like if I suggested not going to Monterey and just staying here in his arms. Then I realize Sam has feelings for me because of who I am, not because of who he wants me to be.

THREE DAYS LATER, I'm not so sure.

"Sam, they're beautiful, but I can't bring them with me." My hands touch a velvety petal of the irises he gave me a few days ago that are still in perfect condition.

He frowns. "Why not?"

"Well, first of all, they'll be dead by the time I make it to Monterey. I want to remember them like this." *I need to remember every memory exactly the way it is during the long weeks we're apart.* Including the way Sam would sneak into my room at night and drive me mad with drugging kisses that almost had me ripping off both our clothes so we could solidify our relationship in the most intimate way possible before we lose the opportunity to.

Before I can give my words voice, Sam snipes at me, "You kept the first ones."

"I pressed a single flower from them, Sam. One. They were the first flowers you ever gave me."

"Then why won't you do that with these? They're nicer," he argues.

"Forgive me for being sentimental enough to do that. They were the *first*, Sam," I emphasize. "It means something."

"So only firsts count? Lasts don't matter?"

I get a chill when I realize we're no longer talking about flowers but have moved into very dangerous territory for both of us. Carefully, I begin, "I haven't asked you certain questions."

"You should feel you have the right to; you should know everything about who I am."

"I know, but we agreed we weren't there yet." Two nights ago when our touching and tasting got out of control, Sam was the one to pull back. "Not now, not in secret. Not where we can't explore everything about each other. I've been dreaming about you for far too long to rush this," he panted hotly in my ear, his fingers tracing around my nipple.

"We're not." Suddenly Sam's voice is suddenly as cautious as mine.

"Then why would you pick a fight with me about my past when we're not? When we have so little time left together?"

"I'm not. I just don't understand why they don't matter." Sam's ire explodes again.

"Everything about you matters to me. No, don't give me that look," I argue when his jaw firms up. I insist. "Everything, Sam."

He begins pacing back and forth, like a tiger on the prowl. His agitation is obvious, but so is my confusion.

"If you wanted the flowers to last, why didn't you give them to me sooner?" I ask.

The stubborn mule insists, "Because I thought you would keep them, just like the first ones."

"Sam, I kept the first one because it was the first time you gave me flowers," I say, exasperated."

"If I asked you to throw it out, would you? Keep these instead?"

"What is it with you and the flowers?" I explode, unable to rein in my temper.

"Iris, if they're just flowers take them with you," he shouts back.

"Sam, fine. I have a perfect solution. I'll send you flowers. Bring them with you to Alliance," I counter.

His eyes go wide. "I can't do that. It would be—" He cuts himself off before he says something asinine that will make me hurt him.

"Foolish? Showing up at your new job with a vase of flowers from your girl-friend? What? Don't want the people on the drive through the parking lot to make comments?" I rub my fingers over my eyes, wondering why in the hell we're having such a stupid argument in the first place. "Is this due to flowers or the fact I'm packing to leave?"

Sheepishly, he admits, "Both? I really want you to take the flowers."

"Sam," I warn him.

He holds up his hands, and I pray it's in surrender. Suddenly, his phone rings. Slipping it from his pocket, he answers it. "Yeah?" His eyes go cool and flat. "Already? I thought . . . okay. I'm on my way."

He flips it closed before he slides it back into his jeans. "I have to go."

"Go? What do you mean?" I demand frantically.

His eyes are distant when he approaches me. "It's time for me to go to work."

"Sam." I know he's likely already getting into the Alliance headspace, but I don't know who this man is and I need to. He was right. I have a right to know every aspect of him, every inch of his soul. He's supposed to know all of mine.

It's not supposed to be over like this.

Sam's face lowers until his lips hover just over mine. "I'll be in touch as soon as I can, Iris."

I feel like my heart is bleeding from a gushing wound as his arms slide around my back to tug me closer. I feel like we're both disconnected from this kiss as we never have been. This may go down in history as the worst kiss between us because my soul is breaking knowing there's a good chance I won't see this man for close to two years. *What will happen to me? To him? To us?*

This is the moment we've both been waiting for, but I'm not ready. We've just spent the last twenty minutes arguing about flowers.

"Sam." I try one more time to stop him, to get him to reengage with me but we've barely learned how to say hello to each other properly. How could we be any good at saying goodbye?

He pours everything he's feeling into one last kiss before setting me aside. "Be safe. Write when you can."

That's how he walks out the door.

Long minutes later, Libby enters. "I've been knocking for close to ten minutes."

I don't respond as I'm motionless, staring out the window. From here, I can see the spot where just days ago, we laid on the grass. "Everything was perfect," I say aloud.

"It will be again. He had an unplanned business trip and you're heading back to school in a few days." Her simple explanation jars me the way nothing else can.

"God bless it, Libby. I wasn't ready."

"Would you have been ready to say goodbye the day after tomorrow?" she asks me wisely.

"No." I catch sight of the irises and want to hurl them into the nearest wastebasket. "We were arguing when the call came in. I didn't get to say goodbye the way I wanted to."

She plops down on the bed, at ease here as she was in our home in Athens. "What was the argument about?"

I fill her in. She frowns over his adamancy about my taking the flowers. "Sam's not like that. Maybe he was feeling the pressure of your separation too."

Fear begins to trickle in, knowing what I do and she doesn't. Can't. Maybe what he doesn't need anymore is me. "Or it's something more. Everyone thinks they want someone who is strong in their life until that person fights back."

Libby rises gracefully before joining me at the window. "Well, it's a good thing that's not the kind of man Sam is."

God, I hope so. Before I can express any of the fears trickling through my heart, she washes them all away. "Because the important thing is you'll always fight for Sam as much as you might fight with him."

I cock my head and ask, "What makes you so sure?" Not that she's wrong, but how does Libby get it?

"Remember your purple notebook?" Libby drawls.

"My journal?"

She nods happily. "That's the one. You listed everything you wanted in Sam. I'm the one who said he smelled, remember."

I groan. "It's also the same one where I wrote a dissertation bashing all of the trollops Sam dated. We should burn it."

"That's not all you wrote in there, Mrs. Samuel Winston Akin," Libby singsongs.

"Definitely burning it. What did you do with it?"

"Me? What did you do with it?" Libby asks straight-faced.

I shake my head. "The last time I saw it, we'd finished several bottles of wine . . ."

"After returning home from spring break. Think Iris. What did you do with it?"

I completely blank. "Libs, I have no idea what happened to it."

She hooks her arm into mine. "Well, now that you're not glued to my cousin we'll spend your last few nights trying to solve that very thing. If I find it . . ."

"You'll burn it." Then I stop. "You really don't mind about me and Sam?

"Don't be stupid." But being the best friend she is, Libby drags me from the room with the lingering memory of my fight with Sam, punctuated by the scent of flowers that carry my name.

19

TWENTY-SIX YEARS AGO FROM PRESENT DAY

Iris

THE FIRST MONTH in Monterey was nothing I expected and everything I dreamed of.

Dear Libby,

I quickly learned the balmy idea I had in my mind about being stationed in California was complete propaganda. For someone who grew up in South Dakota, I'm embarrassed to admit my years in Georgia may have thinned my blood because it's cold!

After telling her what else I could in the hastily scribbled note—and forcing myself to think in English to write it—I dropped it in the mail. A week later, I got her response— telling me she put pen to paper just as quickly. *What happened to California's glorious sunshine and beaches?*

I replied the same night. *I haven't stepped a foot off base since I arrived; it's been so crazy.* I can't disclose to my best friend how all newbies are prohibited from leaving the base for the first month, that we're only permitted to wear our uniforms or our gym clothes when we're outside of our rooms. Nor do I share the sheer volume of work I'm expected to complete five days a week with assignments on the weekends. It's one of the many reasons I'm presently curled up in my room beneath an oversize college sweatshirt and a pair of leggings with multiple laptops open, working on the five hours of homework I need to have completed by 0800 tomorrow.

But while all this is true, I'm just lonely.

I set up my Alliance email and have read, and reread, the messages Sam replied to while I was at Fort Benning until I have them memorized. Knowing Sam would have factored in the protocols about email monitoring, I access the Alliance email server and begin to reread his last message to me.

Iris,

It's daylight where I'm at and I feel like we're separated by more than miles. I hate having to make you wait for the responses to your messages, but this is the only way for me to let you know how much I miss you.

You've been a constant in my life since the day we met and now that you're not here, there's something wrong. Every moment of every day, I wait for you to respond, but I know I have to be patient just as you were for me.

I will be as long as I know you and me is still what you want.
I wish this could be longer, but I have to head out. I just dug up some information that might have us heading back Stateside sooner than we expected.

Just a few more weeks until I can wrap my arms around you and congratulate you.

Sam

I contemplate where to start as the misty rain beats against my window. Hesitantly, my fingers begin to type but soon, all my emotions begin pouring out.

Sam,

I really don't know what to say. It's been more than a month and we haven't exchanged a word. Is it because of the flowers? Is an apology what you want? If so, fine. I'm sorry for hurting your feelings but not for the decision I made.

You were so angry about why I was leaving the irises you gave me in Charleston but what was I supposed to do? Show up at my post clutching a bouquet—no matter how beautiful they were? How much they meant to me?

God, Sam, things here are difficult enough as it is. You would think people wouldn't pick on me because we're all here for one goal, right? Try again.

After I arrived, I attended a Joint Service In-Process Brief that first Tuesday. That might not mean much to you, but it included an intake process that ran the gauntlet of reviewing my medical records for the umpteenth time, morale training, recreation guidelines, safety briefings, antiterrorism and force protection briefings, as well as a thorough legal assistance discussion. I know I'm forgetting at least half of it.
To say this program is intense is a wild understatement.

A day here is like two weeks back in Athens academically. We're in class six hours a day with a minimum of two hours of homework a night. But if you're only doing two hours of homework, you're only squeaking by. Each day, the work is becoming tougher because by the time I (hopefully) graduate, I'll have the equivalent of five years of college-level training enhancing one of my six languages. No, I can't tell you which one it is.

For the first month I was here, I had to wear my uniform (or military workout gear) even after duty hours. That included any time I left my room, even if it was just to dash across to the commissary or to grab my mail. It's like this green neon light flashing my new DLI status. If I wanted to go grab a bottle of water or a cup of coffee, I had to be in full dress. Officer or not, I'm constantly being heckled by the second and third semester students. For Christ's sake, they ran out of some very important things the other day and I couldn't even leave the base to go buy tampons from the local pharmacy. TMI? Sorry. Fortunately, Libby overnighted me a massive care package to get me through—which, again, I had to wear my uniform to go pick up.

I constantly feel on guard except when I'm in my room. This is definitely not the same experience I had in college. It's scary to admit I was less on guard in Officer Training School. I feel like there's no place on base to just be, and I've barely had time to step off since I've finally been granted the privilege to do so. I'm planning to spread my wings a bit and make my way to the local drugstore to stock my room with things I can't get at the commissary.

I'm not sure if it was luck of the draw or if Alliance pulled some strings, but I am one of the few first semester students with a single room. Either way, I'm grateful. I'm beginning to think in the language I'm studying, which is the point I guess. But somewhere along the way, I don't want to lose who I am, because that's important too.

I miss you, Sam. I keep dreaming of your arms around me, the way your lips feel against mine. Knowing you were hurt by my actions has weighed down on me. Again, I'm so sorry. I hope you found it in your heart to understand.

I'll look forward to hearing from you. Also, can you confirm if the email is being scrambled so DLI can't read it?

I miss you.
Iris.

I check it to make certain I don't sound too lonely—even though I am. Then, without giving myself too much time to think, I hit Send before turning back to my assignments.

Maybe an hour later, I get a message back. Eagerly, I click on it. It takes me less than a minute to scan it.

Iris,

Email is secure. Will talk later.

Sam

With a heavy heart, I close my personal laptop. "He's not why you were joining Alliance, Iris. Work hard and you can forget all about Sam Akin," I coach myself aloud.

Deciding I've had enough of studying modern Arabic dialects for the night, I lower the lid of my Army-issued laptop as well. Without stripping off my clothes, I crawl beneath the covers and roll to my side. Taped to the cinderblock is a picture Libby sent me when she mailed me the necessary feminine products—one of me and Sam sitting on the edge of the Akin property watching the tides of the river change.

Staring at it, I whisper, "I think you know I didn't mean to hurt you."

When I reach to pluck it off the wall before tossing it onto my desk in my cramped quarters, tears start falling from my eyes. I fall asleep with the pillow soaked with them.

"LIEUTENANT CUNNINGHAM, please stay behind for a moment," Commander Agha, my lead Arabic instructor, respectfully asks me. It's the end of the following week with no further word from Sam. All I want to do is to slip out of my uniform and into my running gear so I can forget the emotions I've been hauling around as I run for miles to burn off these feelings threatening to overflow inside of me.

After the last student leaves, he hitches on the corner of the desk before asking me if I'm all right in Italian—a language I haven't spoken since I arrived at DLI. Concern penetrates his voice. "*Va tutto bene,* Iris?"

"I'm fine, sir," I reply in Arabic, refusing to slip out of the full immersion I'm supposed to be living in.

He shakes his head kindly before continuing in Italian. "I used to work for the admiral when he was in active duty, Iris. It is an honor to know I'll be helping to provide a level of protection to one of his agents in the future, especially one as talented with languages as you are. But I can sense there is something troubling you."

"Has my work suffered?" I continue in Arabic, not acknowledging anything about my future or my mental welfare.

"*No, forse il tuo spirito però.*" No, but perhaps my spirit. *Of course it has, Commander,* I think morosely. While part of me is grateful that someone in this place has taken notice of a behavioral concern, particularly after the incident earlier this week where a second semester committed suicide, the last person I want them to be focusing on is me. I can't bend. Not here. Sure as the devil, the minute I do, I'll break.

Then, I'll really have lost everything and for what?

Getting to my feet, I gather my computer and slide it into my briefcase. Still in Arabic, I declare flatly, "Quite simply, it's been a difficult week for us all with everything that's happened, but I thank you for your kind concern."

Making my way to the door, I place my hand on the handle just as Commander Agha calls out, this time in English. "Will you go home during the break, Lieutenant? Plans to visit family or friends?"

I thought I had. That is until I'd received Sam's curt reply. Up until that point, I'd always believed that despite the way we'd ended things in

Charleston, I'd end up asking either him, Libby, or maybe both to come see me in Monterey. Now, I couldn't bear to face either of them. Still holding to Arabic, I give him my response. "No. I'll stay here on base. Is there anything else you require, Commander?"

He shakes his head. "No. Thank you, Lieutenant."

I incline my head before escaping as fast as my heels will let me.

Thirty minutes later, I've dumped my bag, stripped out of my uniform, and am running full-out through the cool mountain air.

I spend the first few miles clearing my mind. Around mile three, I feel like I can take a breath without agony weighing it down. This was what I needed —alone time to clear my mind. *Plus permission to do so while thinking in English.* I can't prevent the quick curve of my lips that quickly disappears as I push myself harder. While I do, I think about Commander Agha's words. *So, he knows the admiral?* The illustrious admiral is a man I've yet to meet but one who exudes a great deal of control over my life. That reminds me of the picture of Sam I removed from my wall earlier in the week.

Not long after Libby took that shot, Nonna had approached us, interrupting our interlude. After apologizing, which we all waived away, she explained it was her favorite time of day to spend by the water. The wild wind whipped across her face. "Even the flood tide threatens to crash over the meadow of flowers."

"What?" Sam exclaimed.

"It no longer takes a hurricane, Sam. It can get so bad now that floodin' from a strong storm combined with the high tide will do it. Essentially, the whim of Fate and the mercy of man it seems."

"Too much is at the mercy of man, in my opinion," Libby muttered beneath her breath as she dropped down next to us all at the tail end of Nonna's remark.

"I happen to agree, darling. But if the man is strong enough, he'll hold on through the storms to the other side."

I was fascinated by the way the ageless woman strode to the edge of the land and the sea, challenging the water levels to rise, daring the land her family stood upon for ages to crumble. Now, as I reach the summit and stare out at the Pacific Ocean, part of me just wishes the water would come sweep the ache inside of me away once and for all.

After all, it was a man who created the crevice for the water to fill.

20
TWENTY-SIX YEARS AGO FROM PRESENT DAY

SAMUEL

SITTING outside the small tent I had to carry along with all the electronics to the pickup spot, located in a country we're finally considered safe in, I give a longing glance toward my computer. I want nothing more than to log in to see what Iris wrote back since I said the server was secure, but I have to wait one more night.

Well, one more day and one more day. Cal's already laid down the law about comms while we're still hot. "Absolutely not, Sam. We're in enough danger as it is. Our job is to help get the injured out, not to help facilitate your love life."

When I grumbled that I could have done both, he shot me a lethal look. "If we didn't need that fucking equipment to get out of here, I swear to all that's holy, I'd dump it into the fire."

That's when I got into his face. "Then you could expect the admiral to dock your pay because that's what he said he'd do if I lost any of these babies after what they cost him."

Cal paled before he scooted to the other side of our small camp. While it felt good to shove his shit right back at him, it still didn't take away the yearning to quickly log in and do a burst transmission to download our messages like I've been doing for the last three weeks. That being said, I understand Cal's reasoning: why give away our location when we're being airlifted out of here in just a few hours?

In just a few hours, I'll be able to absorb every nuance of what she wrote back.

AFTER WE DROPPED off the wounded at Ramstein, the team and I were ordered to board a series of private jets to get us back Stateside. It ended up being a dash and nap situation as we all were running through foreign airports trying to connect to our flights. Finally, on the last flight carrying us across the Atlantic, I have a moment to take the time to secure a connection and pull up my email at Alliance.

Only to find nothing from Iris.

I'm devastated. I hit Refresh muttering, "I told her the connection was secure."

Cal flips his head toward mine, grumbling, "This, right here, is why I will do everything in my power to prevent the two of you from being on the same missions."

I flip him the bird before I do a system check from 30,000 feet to ensure my email went through. It shows she read it over a week ago. "Then why didn't she respond?"

Cal sighs before involving himself in something that he has no business in. In a sotto voice, he asks, "What happened?"

Too wrapped up trying to figure it out myself, I begin talking aloud. "It was the first message I'd received from her since Charleston. Iris was telling me what life was like at DLI—especially how difficult the first month was."

Cal nods. "I've heard that from a number of people. Go on. What else did she say?"

I feel heat rise in my cheeks. "I gave her flowers when we were in Charleston and threw a fit when she decided not to take them with her. It was a stupid, immature decision."

Cal frowns. "Based on what?"

"Based on the fact she kept one of the flowers *you* bought for her birthday. She pressed it in between some of her books." I scrub my hand through my hair. "It caused a fight between us and then I left to head out of the country with you."

"In other words, you were an idiot," Cal summarizes.

"Pretty much. Wait, what?" I can't believe he's taking Iris's side.

"Sam, I bought the flowers and you paid me back about six seconds after you saw me the night of Iris's birthday. You're the one who gave them to her. Do you think if I'd laid that bouquet in her arms, she'd have had half the reaction she did? Likely she would have spit on them before she crushed them into the ground," Cal explains patiently.

It amuses me to imagine that, because considering the way Iris feels about Cal, he's probably spot-on. But to spare his feelings, I reply, "I never thought of it in those terms, no."

"So, you're an idiot."

"Okay, fine. I'm an idiot about the flowers. Then help me explain this?" I flip my monitor around to show him the email chain. Aggrieved, I moan, "What did I do wrong?"

Cal reads the message and simply shakes his head. He simply asks me, "Change the name on the emails, Sam. What would you do if you'd written to Iris and received that back from her?"

I do that and my heart clenches when I see what Cal did. "She thought I was blowing her off."

"Yes."

The idea I've added to Iris's burden makes me feel like a complete ass, but I can't stop myself from prodding at him, "So, have you written back to Libby yet?" I know for a damn fact Libby's sent Cal at least one email since we graduated, as I had it forwarded from his UGA account to his Alliance email.

His face closes up. "No. Not yet. Now, figure out the rest of your love life on your own. Some of us need to get some rest." He turns in his chair and proceeds to close me out, much like he's done to my cousin.

I start and stop an email over and over until I decide this isn't going to work. There's only one way to fix things with Iris and that's face-to-face.

IT TAKES days to debrief the FUBAR of a mission. Admiral Yarborough is less than thrilled American soldiers were injured on our watch when our sole function was to provide comms support. "You were sent in for tech," he hurled at us, standing to his full height.

Even Bruce, Dawn, and Cal, who are rarely intimidated by the man's temper, seem to shrink back against the walls of the only secured room we're able to talk openly in—the underground SCIF.

"None of you had better be off in any way during the next assignment."

"Which is when?" Cal was brave enough to ask.

"You fly out in the morning." I set my teeth at the news but don't voice my frustration. I don't dare. Yarborough bellows, "I don't want any more American lives threatened. Is that understood?"

"Yes, sir," we all mumble.

Karl pipes in at that point. "One hour downtime and then mission briefing. Wheels up an hour after the briefing is over, children."

"Shit. One hour? That's barely enough time to wash." I groan.

"I'd shower with your clothes on," Cal suggests. "Saves time in washing them before you have to pack them up again."

"Hardy, har, har. Funny."

Cal tips his head in the direction of Bruce and Dawn who are scrambling to yank out all their undergarments as fast as they can. "Nothing will cause blisters worse than wet socks, Sam."

"Hold up. He was serious about that timeline?"

"As a heart attack." Cal turns away and begins digging in his own bag for the necessities he needs to clean.

"What if we need something we don't have? What if something exploded on it? Or there's blood on it?"

"Then I suggest you hurry, Sam. This isn't a trip to Disney. The plane is wheels up an hour after the briefing is over." Cal strides away with his arms ladened with clothes.

"Shit." Quickly, I unzip my noxious duffle and begin sorting through it for socks, underwear, and T-shirts I can throw into the wash. "Everything else will take too long to dry."

Racing down the hall, I manage to shove my stuff in the last available washer before I jump into the first real shower I've had in three weeks so I can luxuriate in it. I try to compose an apology letter to Iris in my head, but far too soon Cal's shouting, "Get your asses in gear, boys and girls. Admiral's waiting. Ten minutes to dress and switch clothes."

And with that shout, the whirlwind starts all over again. I've barely caught my breath after almost slamming my hand in the dryer door before Karl begins briefing us on a SEAL team needing comms assistance in the middle of the Indian Ocean. Karl sends a wicked smile in Cal's direction before announcing, "It's Thorn's team."

Bruce and Dawn begin catcalling insults to Cal about being reunited with his best friend, but I'm confused. "Who's Thorn?"

Cal presses the heels of his hands against his eyes. "A pain in the ass, know it all. Don't say I didn't warn you, Sam. This is a punishment from the admiral, pure and simple. Likely Thorn doesn't even know we're coming."

Karl slaps a folder against Cal's chest. "Have fun, buddy."

"Kiss my ass. You know this is going to be a train wreck."

"Yeah, but it's going to be really fun to watch from the ops center here." Karl grins, showing off rows of exceptionally white teeth.

Right now, after weeks spent in the jungle, I feel like punching them both. Even though I'm frustrated in a completely different way than Cal is, I find no humor in our situation. I need just five minutes alone to send Iris an email before we're wheels up.

But somehow time flies faster than a hummingbird's wings. Between repacking my bag and ensuring I have the right equipment, I barely have enough time to grab a private moment to use a bathroom where I'm not being accosted by some kind of varmint threatening to poison me by taking a bite out of my dick before we're scrambling for the airfield. Again.

I send a prayer to the heavens as we shoot up into the clouds that Iris has the capacity to forgive me for bad timing on top of being completely obtuse. Lord knows, she's had to do it before.

CHAPTER 20

21

TWENTY-FIVE YEARS AGO FROM PRESENT DAY

Iris

Tonight, I celebrate. The first of three semesters is over and I'm still going strong at the top of my class.

Even though I don't have the time to go back to Charleston—not that I would anyway because that would mean I'd chance running into Sam—I let Libby convince me to treat myself to some time away from my studies. The words of her letter resonate with me. *You need to take some time to recharge, Iris. You're the one who said to me it gets harder from here. Just go somewhere and disconnect your brain from everything for a few days. I wish I could get off work to be there with you.*

As much as I miss my best friend, part of me is glad she couldn't join me at the spa I decided to go just a short taxi ride away from the base in downtown Monterey. Set in the historic heritage district, Casa Munras gives me everything I want for my three-day getaway—excellent access to shopping, dining, and beaches. I couldn't ask for anything more.

Well, yes I could. But I refuse to think about Sam any more than I already have.

It's been close to six weeks since he sent me his one-line response. In my world, where every day is equivalent to two weeks in college life, Sam's made his opinion about my apology clear. "My life's feels like it's been edging on two years since we spoke. I get the point, Sam. I really do," I announce to the air as I flip my weekender onto the bed and begin unpacking.

Quickly, I shed my uniform and slip into jeans and a violet button-down. I tug on a pair of boots before standing and slipping a butterfly knife into my pocket. Quickly, I tie my hair back before wrapping it with a scarf and hurrying out the door.

I have an important date in just a few minutes.

"HOW ARE YOU DOING, IRIS?" The redheaded giant who introduced himself to me as Gillyard sits back to stretch. He wipes a cloth over the spot beneath my arm he's been meticulously sticking a needle into repeatedly for the last hour. "No pain?"

"Surprisingly, no. It doesn't hurt that much. Just when you hit that one spot with the black."

"Yeah, black is always the worst." Critically he examines his work. Shaking his head, he says, "This might be the most unusual design I've ever done, little lady."

"I'm fairly unusual," I reply, not at all offended.

"Can you really speak all these languages?" he wonders aloud.

I think about the list that's now permanently inked on the underside of my arm in a variety of symbols before I answer honestly, "All but one of them, fluently. The one I just know a few words in." *But they're the most important words a person can ever say*. I keep that thought to myself.

"You ready for me to get started again, lass?" After I slide back into place, he pushes my arm back before the gun starts buzzing. "Never got more than a secondary myself, but I meet all kinds of interesting people like yourself in the chair. What book do you recommend a git like me read as one of the most influential of today?"

My reply is immediate. "Do you want to understand the past, forget the present, or change the future?"

He lifts the tattoo gun away from my skin. "That's an interesting question. Give me some examples."

For the rest of the appointment, we challenge each other by tossing out books we've each read. At one point I ask Gilly—as he's demanded I call him—to pause so I can reach for the notepad I always keep in my handbag. Using my right hand while he tattoos my left arm, I write down lists for both of us involving biographies of world leaders, fiction, and non-fiction. "I swear, some of these are hysterical. My college roommate was obsessed with interior design books."

Gilly grins. "M'wife will love them."

"I'm sure she will. How long have you been married?"

He nods toward the statuesque inked and pierced goddess who checked me in. "Ten years this spring. She's been going on about remodeling our place, making it look more like my family's home in Ireland."

"Libby would advise you to tackle one bathroom at a time," I caution him.

He arches my arm far back while he works on some fine detail that has me squinting my eyes closed as it's particularly close to my armpit. He mutters, "Good advice." Sitting back and setting down the gun, he swabs my arm again. "Want to see it?"

"We're done?" I start to sit up but feel a little bit light-headed.

"Whoa, *ceann beag*. Let's get you some juice before you keel over on me."

"Little one? Well, I supposed next to you, I am."

He makes a snort of derision before handing me a can of juice. "Drink that and we'll see what m'Norah thinks."

I pop the top and begin to guzzle the juice. Swiping the back of my hand across my lips, I nod at his wife. "Did you do her work?"

"Aye. Most of it. She came into the shop I owned in Dublin. I swear it was love at first sight. Do you believe in that?"

I think about the combination of 1s and 0s making up the stem of the iris. Then I shake my head. "I thought I did. Turns out I was wrong."

"This Sam did you wrong, then?"

My lips part in surprise. Then again, I don't know why I am. Gilly and I just spent the last few minutes discussing the masterminds behind the technology boom in America and how once again the Americans started out strong but seem to be dropping against international markets.

"Iris, binary code isn't that difficult to read once you know how." He lifts my arm and holds up a mirror. "Are you going to regret placing his name on your skin? We still have a few minutes; I can ink over it."

I stare at the ink that's exactly the way I envisioned it. An iris in the center with a symbol for each of the languages I speak plus the inverted triangles to represent my Lakota heritage. I bring the mirror closer to inspect the tiny numbers that make up the stalk of the iris before shaking my head. "No. It's perfect because regardless of what happened he taught me some important lessons—mostly about myself."

I don't leave myself open to answer what they are. I only have to answer them to myself. And I know the most important one.

Life didn't mean for Sam to fall in love with me. It meant for me to fall in love with myself. That's what this tattoo represents. It's a damn important lesson to remember.

AFTER I FINISH at the tattoo parlor, I decide to head back to my room and change before grabbing a quick bite at the hotel. Norah recommended it highly. "Great place if you like Spanish food, Iris."

"I like any food I don't have to cook. I'm certain I'll love it." I informed her much to her and Gilly's amusement. After paying them and leaving a hefty tip, I returned to the hotel and quickly showered, careful to keep my one arm out of the water, per Gilly's instructions.

I spend a few minutes studying my face in the mirror. "Is the heartache I'm left with so evident? First Commander Agha, then Gilly— a complete stranger. God, now I'm more grateful than ever I didn't try to squeeze in a trip home to Charleston. I'd have been humiliated the very moment you saw me, Sam." Lifting my arm, I ignore the slight swelling and admire the delicate lines and swirls that now are a part of me. "This is you, Iris. You're stronger than a man who gave you flowers, even if for a moment you thought he might make your dreams come true. That's impossible. Only you can be the one who will make your own dreams come true by working hard, being strong. No one, especially Sam, can take that away from you. Love has no place in that future."

At my fervent declaration, one symbol of my tattoo throbs more than others. I don't have to guess which one it is. I already know it's because my grandparents are suffering in the Spirit World due to my grief over Sam. "I know who I was meant to say the words to, Grandmother, Grandfather. Now, our family's traditions will stop with me." I remove the towel from my hair and finger the long locks. The last time I cut it was when they died. "Maybe it's time. It will be a new start."

A whip of wind bangs against my balcony doors answering me. I can picture the horror on my grandmother's face that I'm contemplating such a decision for one who isn't a part of the family. Tears prick my eyes. "What you don't understand is that in some way or another for the last five years, he has become a part of my heart. Doesn't that make him my family? Now, he's gone and it's my fault over something stupid as what? Flowers? I apologized. What more can I do but move on?"

I turn away from the mirror and drop the towel at my feet. I slip into a body-hugging black tank dress and heels. Due to the soreness of my arm, I'm grateful I remembered to pack my shawl which I wrap around my head to avoid knots to my hair and bare arms. *Well, one benefit to whacking off my hair, I won't have to deal with all the knots.* But as much as that's a perk, I'm already sick thinking of the long masses falling to the floor in a random salon chair. Refusing to think about it more tonight, I quickly add some silver jewelry, a touch of gloss and mascara, and head toward the door.

I fling it open and almost find my face filled with a man's fist. "What the hell?" I shout, not even realizing I'm doing it in Arabic.

The man steps back, stumbling over his words. "I . . . I'm so sorry. I thought this room belonged to . . . I'm sorry."

That's when I get my bearings and realize who almost rapped me repeatedly in the forehead. Certain I conjured him up, I double-check to make certain I'm not seeing anything. "Sam?"

His eyes go wide before his face sags in relief. "Iris." He reaches for me but I quickly step back. His face falls.

Suddenly, the last six weeks of hell I've lived through surge through me like a lightning bolt. Thrown off by seeing his handsome face appearing in my door, I revert immediately back to my behavior before he turned my heart upside down. I hurl, "*Zasranec*!" at him before I try to slam the door in his face.

Unfortunately for me, Sam likely anticipated such a move. He shoves his bag forward. "No. Sweetheart, we need to talk. I know you're angry, but I need to explain."

"Fine. Explain. Take all the time you need." I gesture him inside. He pushes his bag in and steps over the threshold and turns to face me. Stepping around him, I cross it and grab the doorknob. "But be gone by the time I get back."

Just as I'm about to turn and stalk away, he catches my arm. My scarf falls off my hair as I whip my head around, eyes blazing. But just as I'm about to let him have it, I deflate under the crushing defeat on his face. His voice holds the same when he begs, "Iris, please. Give me a few moments to explain. Then, if you still want me to leave, I'll go."

I feel myself being dragged under the waves by this simplest of touches. My skin vibrates where his fingers have circled my wrist. My heart, aching for so long with barely any contact from the people I love, begins to soften. Shaking my hand free, I whip the scarf from around my neck and storm back to the entryway to my room. "Fine. But we're not leaving this room until we get this settled once and for all."

As I sweep by him, I hear his muttered, "I'm barricading the door if that's the case."

The part of me that's ecstatic he's here tries to shove all my wariness aside. *No problem with that.* I can't deny there's a part of me that's thrilled he's finally right where I've always wanted him. But the wounded part of me needs an explanation why he's been absent for so long.

We will have words. It's time for me to see if Sam understood what I meant about communication because that email he sent me told me a lot.

Taken at face value, it's evident Sam doesn't want me.

22

IRIS

Rachel is practically ripping my jacket off me. Sam leans over to whisper, "I don't even think I was that eager to get your clothes off that night."

"Hush," I murmur to him. To our daughter, I restrain her so she doesn't rip off any buttons. "Give me a sec, Rach. I'll show you. Not that you haven't seen it a million times."

I unbutton my suit jacket and hand it to Sam before lifting my left arm and there it is twenty years later. As Rachel bends back my arm just a tad more than is comfortable, I address Sam, "I was so determined to believe I was inking you on my skin because I wasn't irrevocably in love with you—that I was teaching myself a lesson."

"You had every right to be pissed at me."

"Oh, I was that right up to the point you showed up at my hotel room. Then I was desperate to hold back the words I wanted to say more than anything.

"Which were?" But he already knows. Sam turns my face up toward his so he can watch my lips form the words he knows come from the depth of my soul.

"*Čhaŋtéčhičiye.*" The Lakota escapes my lips on a puff of air, absorbed by his. I watch as, just like the first time when I explained the words "I love you" also mean "my heart is inspired by you," his face shifts from disbelief, to pleasure, to a devotion so intense, my heart throbs in my chest. I know why my grandparents used to say that to one another instead of the more traditional, *Thečhíȟila*. It's because Sam's soul does inspire mine. His life is tied to mine. Over and over, he's given me the most important gifts to prove it—love, hope, and trust.

His face fills my vision as Rachel oohs and ahhs over my ink. His lips brush against mine gently. "Forever, Iris. Until the tide stops ebbing and flowing."

Since we both know that will continue last long past the time our bodies are bound to this plane, I know he means our love is for eternity. Still, I can't help but tease him, "It's a good thing you're such a smooth talker."

"No, I'm a fast one," he counters before lecturing our daughter. "Rachel, your mother is not a Barbie doll despite how flexible she's kept herself over the years. Give her joints a rest."

Immediately, Rachel lets my arm down. I almost clunk Sam with it; it's released so quickly. "Sorry, Mama. Will you tell me what Dad said?"

I blush. Rachel drawls, "Oh, so it was one of those kinds of conversations? The kind where I used to be shipped off to Nana's house when we still lived in Charleston?"

Sam guffaws before tweaking his daughter's nose. "No." Then he amends himself. "Not at first."

"Sam!" I screech.

"Do you want to tell it, or should I?"

"Oh, by all means, you." Standing, I shrug back into my jacket before sitting back down and waiting for my husband to throw himself under a bus, because there's no way he gets out of this conversation without admitting to our precocious daughter we had sex the first time that night.

None.

23

TWENTY-FIVE YEARS AGO FROM PRESENT DAY

SAMUEL

Iris is placing the phone back into the receiver once I've recovered enough to push my bag fully into the room. She barely spares me a glance as she announces, "I called down to the restaurant to cancel my reservation. If you give me a few moments to change, then we can talk." She turns to head into the bedroom part of her suite.

"I think you look lovely just as you are." My words cause her to trip on the lush carpet in her heels. I race forward and catch her under her arm to hold her steady, prompting another hiss of pain. That's when I notice the redness spreading out from the underside of her left arm. Frowning, I start to lift it. "Iris, what's wrong? Did something happen?"

She yanks her arm back. "Nothing. Well, something happened. I got a tattoo earlier today, but it's nothing."

Shock causes me to drop her arm. "Really? Can I see it?"

Her emphatic, "No!" makes me more curious than ever to see the design, but we have more important things to cover—such as months of constant silence broken by a single email.

Backing off, I drop into one of the plush couches facing the fireplace. "If you were going to eat, you must be hungry. Do you want me to order you anything from room service while you change?"

"What makes you believe I was going eat, Sam? This is the first time I've left base since I arrived. Perhaps I just wanted some company?" she offers suggestively.

For a moment, a roaring fury surges through me. I'm prepared to lash out until out of the corner of my eye, I catch sight of the vulnerable expression on hers. "I know the game you're playing." I push myself off the couch and begin to approach her.

"What game?" she bluffs.

"Doing your damnedest to use your words as swords to drive me away?" She begins to protest, but I lay a finger over her lips. "I royally screwed up, Iris. I behaved like a jackass in Charleston and then tossed off an email like I was responding to someone from work instead of dancing for joy—which is what I felt like doing when I saw your email come up in my box."

Her lips tremble beneath my finger before she firms them. "It doesn't matter, Sam."

"I think it very much matters." My fingers trail up and down her left arm. "Why don't you get changed into something you'll feel more comfortable talking in, and I'll order some food before we do just that?"

She deflates before me. Her eyes drift shut. "I came here to escape the pressure of everything. I just wanted a few days during the break to be me."

"I'm not going to stop you from that. I just want the chance to be with you, learn how this assignment has changed you. I want to get to know the woman you are."

"What if you don't like her?" Her words come out small.

My laugh is hollow. "I sincerely doubt that. The pull is still there between us. Can you deny that?"

Wordlessly, she shakes her head. The pressure releases from my chest just a bit.

I move closer. "God knows the work at Alliance has changed me. I need to tell you the things I would never be able to put in an email, regardless if it's secure or not. I just want to be with you, Iris. There's so much that's happened . . . wait. I forgot." I go to my bag and pull out a handheld device. Immediately, I start scanning the room, looking for bugs. Much to Iris's shock, I find two that I end up neutralizing by scrambling the signal. With a rueful smile, I inform her, "You would choose the one hotel certain officials are known for making its assignations."

She gapes at me like she doesn't recognize me. "Do I know you anymore?"

"Truth be told, after the last six months, I'm beginning not to recognize myself in the mirror either." I dare to cup her chin. I take heart in the fact she leans into my hand instead of away from it. "That's part of what we need to talk about, once I secure the room."

She nods, her hair brushing my arm as it flows unchecked. I shiver in response. Her eyes glow at my reaction. "Order what you want from room service, Sam. I want soda water with a twist of lime, nachos, and chocolate." She breaks our physical connection to turn toward the bedroom area of the suite. Just as she's about to pass through the door, she pauses. She pins me with her eyes before whispering, "I am glad you're here. You've been a part of my life for far too long to have you disappear without any explanation."

Then she slips inside, shutting the door firmly behind her.

Oh, Iris. If you think I'm letting you slip from my life, my heart, you have another thing coming. This isn't the end of us. We're only just getting started.

With that grim resolution, I reach for the phone to place our order. For the first time in a while, I'm ravenous. Just not for food.

IRIS IS NIBBLING on what remains of a mountain high plate of nachos. She finally pushes them away on the wrought iron table of the balcony, groaning, "I'm not certain I can eat whatever you ordered for dessert."

Having restrained myself to half of the seafood paella, I uncover the chocolate lava cake before adding the blood orange sherbet on top. "I guess I'll be forced to choke this down all on my own."

Iris's eyes dilate. "Give me a spoon."

I bait her waiving the spoon back and forth. "I thought you were too full."

She snatches it right out of my hand. "There's no way I'm too full for that; you know it."

I wait until the first bite passes her lips and she's groaned her appreciation for the luscious cake. "What I know, sweetheart, is you looked like you've lost weight. Am I wrong?"

Iris slips the spoon from her mouth, leaving a trace of chocolate on her full lips. I want to lean across the small table and kiss it off, but I don't. I'm jealous of her small tongue that darts out and flicks the dark cocoa away. "No, you're not. Eating isn't really a priority, my sanity is."

I hold out my hand, palm up. "Will you tell me about what your life is like here?"

Hesitantly, Iris slides her hand not holding the fork into mine. I clasp her fingers to give her strength as she begins to detail the days that begin early in the morning, the depth of the learning—not just the language but economics, politics, and current events. Worse yet, the solitude. "If I didn't occasionally hear from Libby, I might have gone mad. Especially the first month when I couldn't escape to try to reach yo . . . anyone," she quickly adapts her confession.

Guilt crashes over me. It's time for me to share what I really have been doing for Alliance. I jerk my head inside to the sofa. "Will you sit with me?"

Iris looks longingly at the cake. I burst into laughter. "Bring it with you, sweetheart. This story might take a while."

Iris snatches the plate with the rapidly melting sherbet and makes her way to the couch. Along the way, I grab our glasses and set them down before also flicking on the box that will repel any listening devices.

I intercept Iris's quizzical look before carefully choosing my words. "It's good up to fifty yards. It helped us out while we were in Africa about six weeks ago."

"Too bad I don't have one. The weekends can get kind of rowdy." I grab the plate that goes slack in her hands the moment my words penetrate. She asks, "Six weeks ago?"

After setting the cake aside, I grab her hands which have turned cold as ice. "Yes."

"Sam, six weeks ago in Africa, there was a bloodbath trying to help American soldiers escape. I presented on it for my class." Her voice is frantic.

This is where things get dicey. "I'm not a field agent, sweetheart, but there are times I need to be in the field to provide comms support." I pause to let her absorb my words.

Her indrawn breath doesn't release. I go on. "I'd just downloaded a burst transmission to determine our extraction coordinates when I got your email. God, Iris, I was overwhelmed with joy to hear from you."

She sucks in her breath even more, if that's possible. "You were?"

I twirl a strand of her long black hair around my finger. "I was. I was an idiot before you left Charleston."

"I knew the flowers meant a lot to you, Sam, but it just would have been awkward," she begins her apology.

I lift her hand to my lips. "I was jealous."

"Of what? Of whom?" she cries out.

"Of Cal," I admit. I hate myself for what I'm going to have to admit about the flowers.

She rears back in shock. "Calhoun Sullivan? The same sanctimonious shit who broke Libby's heart? For Pete's sake, why?"

A slow grin crosses my face when I realize Cal was right. Iris would sooner have spit on the flowers than accepted them from him. "It's not important." Iris obviously doesn't believe me by the squawk that emits from her mouth. "It was my own stupid male ego that couldn't handle something that happened before your birthday dinner back in Athens."

She gives it some thought before nodding. "I will agree with part of that statement."

Uh oh, that was too easy. I ask cautiously, "What parts?"

"Stupid. Male. Ego. Nothing about Cal should influence what happens between us." Even as she hostilely enunciates the words, she points back and forth between the two of us.

I take the verbal jab as my due, but there's more to tell her that will likely set her off, if I know Iris Cunningham the way I do. Fundamentally, she's been forged from a long line of fierce women whose foremost mission was to protect those they care for. Taking a deep breath, I go on, "When we were in Africa, I'd just downloaded your email and shot off a response. It was all the time I had when I was sending a burst message back up through the satellite . . ."

"What does that mean?" Her frustration is evident.

Here it comes, I think. But I give her the truth. "We were hiding from guerrillas. We had the American soldiers we'd been sent in to rescue with us in camp. I . . ." My voice trails off when Iris stands.

"We? What do you mean 'we,'" Sam?" Her voice is trembling, but not with upset. Her fury is shimmering off her in waves.

I stand as well and clasp both of her arms. She winces slightly but doesn't break my grasp. Recalling the tattoo she had done earlier, I relax my grip slightly. "I was there providing comms support, Iris. The Alliance team was in charge of helping extract American soldiers. I was careless, hurt you—us—because I ridiculously presumed you could read my mind. We didn't get to a safe spot for days. Then, I swear, I checked my email waiting for your next response. Only, there wasn't one."

Iris wrenches from my arms, shoulders heaving. I make a move to approach her, but her hand flies out. Heart shriveling inside my chest, I finish it. "I'd planned to come to you as soon as we were wheels down, but I couldn't."

"Why?" Her voice is raspy.

"After we got back, the Admiral was so pissed about the job being bungled, he sent the entire crew out on another assignment—primarily to punish Cal."

A rough chuckle escapes. Encouraged, I give her a bit of insider information. "He and this Navy SEAL do not get along. They bickered like an old married couple the entire time we were on board."

Her "Good" comes out forcefully. Then, "Why didn't you tell me you were working?"

"It's need to know, Iris," I remind her gently.

She whirls around, her long hair flying around her like an ebony cape. After it lands on her shoulders, she begins to strip off her overshirt as she spits out, "Then you'd better figure out a way to tell me things in the future without saying the words, Sam. After all, I just did."

That's when she raises her arm and I spy her tattoo.

After studying it for a moment, it only takes the space of seconds for me to cross the room for me to have my mouth crashing down on hers as I back her against the closest flat surface—the wall.

24

TWENTY-FIVE YEARS AGO FROM PRESENT DAY

Iris

Sam never lifts his lips from mine as he bends down and hooks his forearms around my thighs, boosting me so I can wrap my legs around his waist, which I do automatically. This hunger between us was what I wanted to revel in the first time Sam and I reconnected. Instead, from the moment I opened my hotel door and realized he was standing there, I've been on guard as we've spent the better part of the evening churning up even more emotional mayhem.

Wrapping my arms around his neck, I hold on to him like he's the buoy in a storm, the anchor to keep me grounded in the waves we're churning up between us as he rubs his body against mine. Without breaking our kiss, I attempt to slow down our pace by reassuring him without words, *I missed you. I need you. It's only you.*

But when Sam presses me deeper against the wall, his tongue begins battling against mine, lips sliding back and forth, forcing me to gulp down air, I realize his own emotions are pushed to the limits as well.

I just can't read them.

His strong, calloused hands make easy work lifting my camisole tank up until they close over my breasts. My nipples are already little stones when his palms graze over them. The second he captures one turgid point between his thumb and forefinger and rolls it back and forth, I tear my lips from his so I can swallow down the sea air in enormous gulps.

I'm drowning in everything that's Sam Akin and I don't want to be rescued.

Switching, he starts up again, never relenting in his ministrations. It may be minutes, it may be hours, but over and over, Sam lays siege to my mouth and heart ruthlessly. Then, he pulls back. For a moment there's a reprieve, but Sam drops his head and captures the sensitized tip of my breast in his mouth.

"Oh," I moan.

My fingers find their way into his thick hair, seeking purchase not to push him away but to pull him closer. A rough chuckle escapes his lips as he nips and sucks around the overly sensitive nerve endings until I'm dizzy from the highs he's driving me to.

I'm saturated. I stave to hold off my impending orgasm simply from him nipping and sucking on my breasts. My pussy is clenching every time he rolls the tip to the roof of his mouth before drawing deep. I'm afraid I'm going to crest before I have him inside me, but I don't want to. The emptiness in my soul is mirrored by the lack of his filling me.

I frantically protest, "Sam . . ."

His face is lined with perspiration when he draws back and smooths his body up against mine to pin me against the wall. "Tell me you want this. You want me?"

In the long months between the beginning of our intimacy in Charleston and now, I wasn't sure how I'd manage to go on without knowing the fulfillment of this between us. Now, I know I could, but I don't want to. I readily answer, "Yes."

A small smile plays on his lips when his words bring me back to the night he first asked me out. Sam's head cocks to the side. "Are you agreeing to wanting this or wanting me?"

Refusing to take the bait, I grab his head with both of my hands and stare deep into his eyes. "Both."

Sam drops my legs to the floor before he takes my hand and leads me into the bedroom.

Once we're next to the bed, he cups my face in his hands. "Be sure about this, Iris, because this might be the final line we cross together. You're all I can think about anymore. You're interfering where you haven't been yet."

Rising up on my toes, I wrap my arms around his neck and whisper into the solitude, "So are you. Now do something about it."

His hands make a slow journey down my back. I feel their roughness against my skin as he grazes them down my back, beneath my sleep shorts, over my buttocks, before dragging the shorts down over my thighs so they can fall unaided to the floor. Pulling my arms from around his neck, Sam steps back so he can quickly rip his polo over his head, toe off his shoes, shuck his own jeans and briefs—pausing to toss his wallet on the nightstand.

Suddenly, he's as bare before me as I am before him, and judging by the expression on his face, just as vulnerable. Then it becomes hunger filled as his eyes take a lingering journey of my body from tip to toe. His gaze rakes me as thoroughly as his fingers and lips did earlier when they land on my swollen breasts. I inhale sharply when it dips down to the notch between my legs. And lingers until he prowls forward like a panther guiding me backward toward the bed.

Despite my increased heart rate over the hunger in his eyes, I manage to take in his long limbs, his broad chest, and his fully engorged shaft pointing in my direction. It's hard not to when his fingers have dropped down to it and have begun stroking it as he makes his way to me.

Until the sensuality of that movement hits me, I thought I was prepared for the intimacy of this act between us. But realizing Sam's holding nothing back, I know I can do nothing but the same. With that realization comes fast on its heels the understanding that for me, this is going to be more than a merging of bodies, but a melding of my soul to his.

Scrambling to kneel on the bed, my hand reaches out for him. Together, we glide our hands over the length of his shaft—up, so I can feel the pre-cum dripping from him. Then down, so I can feel the length and girth that will be filling me. A simultaneous moan of pleasure escapes us both when his hand drops and returns to the tip of my nipple.

My body sways forward. I lick in between his pectorals. I feel a tug as one of his hands slips into my hair, tipping my head back just in time to capture his lips as they descend. Our lips duel as our bodies mold to one another. I rub against him, my fingernails scoring down his back as I give up the luxury of holding onto his shaft, knowing there's so much more I want to feel and taste this first time between us. I push him backward, fully determined to have my time to touch, to taste.

Sam must read the intention on my face because he promises, "Later," before he tackles me backward on the bed.

We roll over and over until Sam manages to pin me. He begins kissing his way down the center of my body, his intentions clear.

I'm shaking as he parts my thighs, pushing them wide before the first touch of his fingers brushes against the damp folds. Using his fingers to part the light dusting of curls, his thumb begins tracing circles around my clit right before he slides one finger inside.

Then a second.

I can't prevent the way my body rises as his fingers thrust inside me over and over, preparing me for him. Nor can I stop the way I demand more from him as he prepares me to take him. "More. Please. God, Sam." That's when he cocks his fingers forward toward the front wall.

I detonate, squeezing his fingers with my tight inner muscles. Sam keeps his fingers buried deep until the last spasm eases. Then he grinds out, "I can't wait a fucking second longer." His arm reaches past me for his wallet.

I watch as he flips it open and draws out a few condoms with quick ease. Ripping one off, he tosses the others aside before tearing into the packet. Carefully rolling on protection, he prowls over me. Lust fills every one of his features.

What wouldn't I give if it were love? The thought flies into my head and I shove it quickly aside. Opening my arms and the cradle of my legs, Sam nudges me with the thick head of his cock before it starts to penetrate me.

His head drops down, as if the weight of it is too much for his shoulders. He whispers, "Finally."

Then he begins to push inside me. It takes a few strokes for him to fully seat himself. By the time he does, my body is drawn tight once again, as if I never orgasmed just a few moments ago. My nipples are sharp daggers buried into his chest, my legs are wrapped around his hips.

Sam is filling my body

Sam, who my heart has ached for.

The ability to process this much emotion may exceed the overwhelming fortitude I believed myself capable of. Despite my uncertainty of survival if this doesn't work out, I lift my hips to encourage him.

Sam immediately takes up the hint and begins drawing back slowly, before pressing his thick flesh back inside. Each movement searing him more permanently on my soul than the ink that holds his name.

As if he can read my mind, Sam grips my wrists and pushes them above my head. His eyes flit away from my own and lock on the red underside of my arm as I take him deeper. Deeper. In both body and heart.

The heartache of the past few months rescinds as he drives for completion, taking me along with him. Each time his cock drags along my sensitive tissues, they flutter. His mouth drops down to my neck to suck lightly before capturing my lips in a kiss so powerful, it causes my toes to curl. He groans, "Fuck, Iris. I won't go over without you."

His declaration sends a rush of pleasure through me. I moan into his mouth as I feel the way my body tightens further around his. He grunts, "Yeah," before picking up the pace.

We're both shaking when Sam stills, fully lodged inside me, before popping his thumb in my mouth. I swirl my tongue around it briefly before he takes it out and wedges it between our bodies. Rubbing it over my distended clit, I begin to tremble uncontrollably.

Even the air around us is charged when Sam braces himself on one elbow and thrusts hard, hard, harder as his thumb continues to apply pressure to me. I score my nails down the bedsheets. The word is pulled from me in a gasp, "*Čhaŋtéčhičiye*!"

He grunts before I feel the throb of him as he releases inside the condom.

Then he wraps me in his arms before he takes us to our sides as the raging tide drags us both under.

WORDS OF LOVE, once spoken, can never be taken back, my grandmother used to tell me.

I lie curled up next to Sam as he plays with my hair—stretching and releasing the curls over and over, not saying a word for fear the Lakota will escape past my lips again. *Not that I regret saying it*, I tell myself firmly. But if I'm the only one who feels it, then Sam shouldn't be obligated by my emotions.

My heart desperately wishes he would be, could be. But if this is the closest to him I'll ever be, at least I'll have this incredible memory of us.

At least that's what I'm telling myself right now.

Sam presses a kiss to my forehead, murmuring, "I'll be right back."

I nod absentmindedly.

He chuckles when my arms don't loosen from around his waist. "Iris, that means you have to let me go."

My cheeks burn. I lift my head away from his chest and roll to the side. "Sorry about that."

He slips off the bed before informing me, "I'm not. Save my spot; I'll be right back."

I flop to my back while Sam heads to the *en suite*, not even noting when the door closes indicating Sam's back in the room. It isn't until I feel the bed depress that I'm jolted from my thoughts by the touch of his fingers on my arm. "What are you thinking so hard about?"

My deepest fears begin to surface. "If you're here out of guilt with the way we left things in Charleston, then leave. Just leave."

His entire body locks. "Excuse me?"

I fling my arm up over my head, exposing my new ink. "I don't expect anything, Sam, just because our emotions are lopsided."

"Maybe it's time you should," he semi-roars.

I'm shocked enough to twist my face in his direction. He's even more furious than he was the last time I saw him in Charleston. He flings himself back and gathers me in his arms. "I'm blindsided by what I feel for you."

I'm gobsmacked by this admission. "You are?"

His eyes narrow. "What? You're not?"

"No! I've felt so much for you since the moment we met." Uncertainty swamps me. "Are you certain? This is what you want?" *Me? I'm who you want?*

His fingers glide up my jaw as they tilt my head back. "I feel like I'm drowning in you and I don't want to be saved. Open your eyes, Iris. It's our time now."

I can't prevent the tear that slips from my eye at his words. Nor do I try to stop Sam as he lowers his head to take my lips in another kiss.

I'm too busy drowning myself.

25
IRIS

"Let me state for the record, you're not having sex until you're thirty-five."

"Dad!"

"Not negotiable." Sam declares resolutely.

"Mama!"

"Sam, a little realism, please?" My voice is dry as a bone.

"Fine. Her betrothal. Plus, it better be someone both me and Cal approve of, or he's going to die," Sam growls.

I sigh before tipping my head toward Rachel. "Your father is making this sound like seventeenth-century England."

She shakes hers sadly. "Do you think all the time in his server rooms has made him delusional to the passing of time?"

"It is not wrong to save yourself for marriage," Sam argues.

Both Rachel and I shoot him incredulous looks. I'd just finished explaining to our daughter about the first time her father and I made love together after we finally cleared the air between us. I certainly hadn't gone into the level of details that floated through my memory, but I need to remind him, "Sam, you are insane if you think we can pull the last few minutes back now. Not unless you built a time machine in the Hudson lab."

"Or you actually created the zappy rod from *Men in Black*," Rachel offers.

"True. It's portable and much more efficient for moments such as these," I agree. Both of us burst into a fit of giggles that remove more splinters that have been lodged in my heart since the phone call I received eighteen months ago.

Sam, not even moderately affronted since he's used to our teasing, joins in. "One of these days, I'm going to surprise you both by doing something completely unexpected."

His words cause me to shudder remembering the first time Sam *did* surprise me after that weekend in Monterey. It wasn't a surprise that ended well.

Rachel picks up on my physical cue. "Mama? What is it?"

But Sam knows. He reads me so easily after all the years of marriage, all the love and pain, the laughter and tears. His thumb weaves through the ends of my hair so it can run over the other tattoo of the scripted word *love* I had tattooed in Arabic I had done years later where my clavicle meets the ball of my shoulder. The burning sensation that churned in my stomach eases when he brushes my hair to the side and presses his lips to the very spot the bullet grazed me. "You're mother's thinking about Egypt."

"What about Egypt?"

God, what can we tell our daughter about Egypt? Frantically, I twist my head. Sam nuzzles my ear and whispers, "Start with why you were there. That part isn't classified."

Right. Taking a deep breath, I explain to Rachel, "If you're in the top fifteen percent of your class at DLI, you have the opportunity—depending on what school you're in—to be fully immersed in the country of the language you've been studying for a month. I was sent to Egypt to be fully immersed in the culture." *Never knowing my world was on the verge of collapse.* Nausea begins to churn in my stomach while excitement steals across Rachel's face.

"Mama, that's seriously cool. Did you get to see the pyramids?"

"Yes, I did." *That and so much more.* Sam squeezes my shoulder, giving me the strength to go on. "I'd been there almost my entire time and was ready to come home when I received a message from your father."

"What did you say, Dad?"

Sam's face turns grim. "That's the problem, baby. It wasn't from me."

Rachel's face goes slack. Weakly, she falls back against the couch. "What?"

I shoot my glance up to the video surveillance to ensure we're still reading green before I ask her, "Are you sure you want to hear this, Rach?"

Wordlessly, she nods.

Swallowing hard, I push out of Sam's arms and make my way over to the window. "It was a beautiful day in Cairo. Then again, most of them are. The sky is so blue it almost burns your eyes, especially when it bounces off the desert sand."

26

TWENTY-FOUR-AND-A-HALF YEARS AGO FROM PRESENT DAY

Iris

When I was informed I'd be going to Egypt for a month of complete immersion, I was overjoyed. I had so many questions Commander Agha finally ordered me to make a list, which he quickly forwarded to the protocol office. Instead of slaving away on my nightly assignment as devoutly as I had every other night I had during my time at DLI, I prepared pages of questions ranging from where would I be living to as a non-Muslim woman, do I need to cover my hair once I reach Cairo? What do I do with my room here at DLI? How do I keep up with my coursework?

It took them a few days, but I had my answers. Within two weeks, I was boarding a military transport with a number of other DLI students for their assignments in other locations— Hong Kong, Vietnam, a military base at an undisclosed location over the border from Russia, and finally Egypt.

I was pleasantly surprised to find the temperature similar to that of Monterey when I stepped off the plane. Recalling my integration briefing about blending in, I elected to pull my hair back in a braid and wrap the mass with a long shawl before I entered the main city. I was excited to reach the apartment procured for me off Nile Street in the Dokki. Although not luxurious by the standards I've been used to back home, the 120 square meter apartment is furnished and clean, which is all I can really ask for. As a bonus, it includes laundry, which is a luxury, as I quickly found out from my colleagues at my job as an assistant to a tour operator.

Every day, over and over, I spoke in Arabic to both locals and foreigners as we drove from downtown Cairo to the Sphinx and the Pyramids. By the end of the first week, my skin quickly acquired a lush tan that hailed me as a local instead of the paleness of a visitor. The fact I spoke the language as well as a native, not slipping once even when words were slurred together frantically by eager children or impatient adults, was a testament to the training I endured during the fifty-six weeks in Monterey.

Even my name helped me fit in as Iris was the wife to Osiris, god of the underworld. I made a joke out of it when I politely asked for tips at the end our journey indicating I was hoping to restore my headwear to that of a goddess since mine was now buried beneath masses of stone. Everyone chuckled and as they were generous with tips, I donated them to a local children's shelter.

The land I worked so hard in every day needed a reprieve.

Not that it was going to give me one.

I MANAGED to call Sam before boarding the plane three weeks ago. He warned me, "I'm probably going to be away with Cal while you're gone, sweetheart. Do you understand what I'm saying?"

I twisted a lock of hair around my finger and stretched it out to its full length before letting it go. "I do. Promise me you'll travel safely so Rick won't have the opportunity to cause a ruckus when you get back."

His laughter rang in my ears, causing my lips to curve. It was like he was in the next room instead of over three thousand miles away. "If Cal does so something on this 'software installation'"—his code word for mission when we are on an unsecure line— "To throw us that far off schedule, I'll be sure to find some way to let you know."

"I'll keep an eye out. Besides, who knows if your project will land you where I'm going. There are major corporations who need your expertise everywhere," I teased him.

"If that happened, I'd never get any work done, and you know the exact reason why."

My own laughter pealed out. "I can't wait to see you."

"Me neither."

"Sam?" The words of love I've been holding back because I want to see his face are desperate to burst out of me. Still, I hesitate.

"What is it, Iris?" His tone is husky.

I shake my head. We both need to have our heads in the game. "Nothing that can't wait. Stay safe."

"You too, sweetheart. You won't believe the plans I have for when you get home."

Dryly, I inform him, "If you can get past Libby. She's sent me an agenda about what we're going to do."

He promptly declares, "Burn it. I'm not letting you out of my bed for two, maybe three weeks."

I shake my head, but I can't stop the tingles running up and down my spine at his provocative words. "Go to work."

"I'm going. Hey Iris?"

I hold my breath. *Is he going to say it first*? My heart thumps against my ribs. "Yes?"

"I miss you."

My hopes deflate. "I miss you too. I'll talk to you when you can."

Now, eating my leftover *Ful Medames* with the side of *Ta'meya*, I plug into the local internet and access the Alliance network through the secure network, I realize I'm going to miss the fava beans prepared with oil and lemon juice as well as the Egyptian version of Falafel. "There's nothing in the States to match this," I mumble around a mouthful of food. "People need to give local cuisine a real shot when they travel overseas."

My food is forgotten when to my shock, there's an email from Sam dated today. The subject line reads, Cairo. Cursing, I dump my plate to the side before double clicking on the message. "Don't tell me I missed the chance to see him, even if it's just for a few hours."

The message pops up with a flicker I blame on the poor internet signal in the building and I read.

Iris,

I'm here in Cairo for the unforeseen future. There's nothing I wouldn't do to be able to see you.

Meet me at the address below after sundown.

Love,

Sam

I quickly recognize the address as one in the Sayeda Zeinab district. Although the district is defined by the glorious Al-Sayeda Zainab Mosque which is in the center of the square, the district also has a high number of crimes which I studied during international news. Being here up close, it's an area I try to avoid as a woman after dark. But if there's a reason Sam's asking for me, I have to trust him. I do trust him, with my whole heart.

Quickly, I scramble to shove my food into the small fridge before I shoot off a quick email to Commander Agha. Then I race into the bedroom to change my clothes. If there's nothing else I can do, I can be prepared.

I APPROACH THE ADDRESS WARILY. The whole street gives me the creeps, let alone the building where the Alliance team is waiting. Staring at the door, I glance up at the windows on the third floor and find the windows have been completely blacked out. There's nothing to indicate they're occupied. Then I shake myself internally. *You're a fool, Iris. This job is going to have you staying in a lot worse places than this. Open the damn door and go to Sam.*

But something still makes me slide the knife out of my bag and palm it. Call it an overabundance of precaution, call it nerves from the number of rodents I hear scurrying as I make my way up the stairs, but I'm comforted I have the blade in my hands when I approach the door. I softly knock.

A voice calls out in Arabic accented English, "Who is it?"

The accent is off. What's wrong? Then I hear a spate of Levantine that orders the man at the door to shoot whoever is there. I immediately throw myself to the side as the door is flung open and a man's head pokes out. But just as I'm about to slink away, my heart stops at the sight presented to me in the wedge of the door frame.

Sam is bruised and bloodied, with a gun pointed at his back as he types on his laptop. His eyes are lackluster, cheeks gaunt. God only knows how long they've had him, let alone the last time they let him eat.

I quickly survey the room. There's only the man at the door to get through. He calls back in the same dialect, still not Egyptian. "No one here. Maybe the knock was across the hall."

"Good. Shut the door. We'll use this American before we kill him tonight. If his lover shows up, then she's stupid. I'm certain we'll find a use for her." Both men laugh uproariously.

I hope they enjoy it. It's the last time they'll laugh before they have to face their maker.

Without hesitation, I spin back toward the door and use the element of surprise. Quickly I slash the blade across the larger man's neck before jabbing it deep into his trachea. Leaving the guard gurgling as air escapes in a bloody bubble, I quickly reach for the gun in his holster. Automatically, my body reacts to the training I received from Kristin, from the Army. Lifting the already cocked gun eye level, I order in Levantine, "Step back" to the man guarding Sam.

He grins malevolently before he takes aim, assuming I won't pull the trigger. I'm grateful I was trained better than that. There's no second chance when someone's life is on the line.

I meet Sam's eyes which are now blazing instead of being lackluster. It doesn't take a genius to realize he's ordering me to take the shot. Praying harder than I ever have, I pull the trigger just as Sam jerks his head to the side. The assailant pulls the trigger as his brains splatter behind him. The bullet, intended for the back of Sam's head, shoots through Sam's laptop, shattering through the screen.

I race over to Sam and press my lips to his cut and bruised ones. He shakes his head and motions to his legs tied to the chair. "Later, sweetheart. We have to go. Now." His voice is urgent.

"Why? Where is the team?"

"They don't know where I am. I was taken from Libya two weeks ago. But we have to get out of here. There's . . ." But Sam doesn't get to finish his sentence as another man pointing a gun kicks the man with the knife aside.

Sam jerks the gun from my frozen hands, leveling it at the intruder's heart. Viciously, he rasps, "It's over."

"If you say so, Mr. Akin." His smile is the pure essence of evil. In the time it takes Sam to pull off one round, the unknown assailant pulls off two. One aimed at me, which goes over my head. The other that doesn't miss. Especially because I shove Sam's chair over and leap into the path of the bullet.

I land with a grunt on top of Sam, our combined weight breaking the already rickety chair. Sam scrambles to his feet, dumping me to the side. He crawls around the desk, and I hear two more shots, one from Sam. Then blessed silence.

That's when I allow myself to feel the searing pain rippling through my shoulder. Barely able to focus, my lips part when Sam races back to my side to assess the damage. I don't feel anything but agony. It increases incrementally every second, even when Sam rips off my scarf and folds it into a square to apply pressure to stop the bleeding.

I manage to lift my eyes to focus on him. I wasted too much time. He needs to know how I feel. But just as I'm about to tell Sam how I really feel about him, I pass out.

27

TWENTY-FOUR-AND-A-HALF YEARS AGO FROM PRESENT DAY

SAMUEL

When I next lift my head from the side of Iris's bed, I'm aware of another presence in the room. I automatically reach for the gun tucked into the holster at my side through the haze of sleep when his voice penetrates. "Relax, Sam. I just flew over to see how she is."

Retired Admiral Richard Yarborough, the owner of Alliance, was and is not the kind of man to be stopped when he makes his mind up to do something. A former SEAL, he was taken out of the line of duty with a shot to the leg that shattered his kneecap. Unwilling to sit on the sidelines, he brought together a coalition of the best ex-military and civilians to operate with the permission of the government to go where they can't due to negotiated treaties and peace agreements. As Cal once laconically drawled, "Alliance has never been limited by such boundaries."

The fact he's here in Germany, in Iris's room, with us after we had her airlifted out of Cairo, is both comforting and terrifying. "Why are you here, sir?"

His eyes light on Iris's still form. He declares bluntly, "She took the bullet meant for you, Sam. I've seen the footage you managed to collect from the cameras they had in the room. They were aiming right for your heart when she knocked you over."

I duck my head to the side, eyes filling with unshed tears. I'm still unable to reconcile the depth of risk Iris took to protect me. "I know."

Iris's eyelashes begin to flutter. Her hands grasp at the blankets on the bed. Thinking she's agitated because I'm not in reach, I scoot closer to her. I'm not certain whether the admiral or I am more surprised when she manages to retrieve the pistol and point it at Rick. She demands gutturally, "Who are you? What business do you have here?"

Rick throws his head back and laughs uproariously. "Now, I know she's ready to become one of us. Iris, I'm sorry we haven't had the opportunity to meet before now. I'm Rick Yarborough."

"Sam?" Iris questions me, still holding the weapon aimed at Rick expertly, much to the other man's amusement.

I need my warrior to stand down, and there's only one way I can think she'll do that without injuring herself further. Reaching over, I chamber the bullet before flicking off the safety. "Shoot him if you want, but we'll lose a great leader in the process, sweetheart."

The admiration on Rick's face and the trust I have in her to do the right thing must penetrate through Iris. Shifting the weapon to her non-dominant hand, she flicks the safety back on before flipping the weapon around so it comes to me butt first. Then she speaks to Rick for the first time. "I apologize, Admiral, but I didn't save his life to let some yahoo sneak into my hospital room to take it."

Rick leans back against the wall, propping a booted foot against it. "For being such a delicate thing, you're a bulldog, Ms. Cunningham."

I smirk. "Well put."

Iris smacks me in the arm before wincing at the jostling movement. "The shot took off several layers of skin, but the doctors say it was a graze."

"One that's going to leave a scar," I mutter.

Iris continues to explain, "They're really keeping me due to the blood loss I sustained before the Alliance team could get to us." To prove her point, Iris slowly lifts her right arm almost perpendicular to the floor until the stitches begin pinching. Then she lowers it back in place.

Rick nods. "That's good to know. Then, how about another day in this lovely resort before we transport you back to Monterey?"

My heart sinks at Rick's words. Monterey, not Charleston.

He goes on. "You have some tests to prepare for, if I'm not mistaken."

Iris groans. "Yes, my OPI begins in about a week. Then I have two weeks to prepare for the DLPT after the OPIs."

Rick nods sagely, but I'm lost in a sea of acronyms. "English, please, sweetheart?" I implore her.

Iris relaxes back into her pillows and reaches for my hand. "The OPI, which stands for Oral Proficiency Interview, is to establish the graduation candidate's—er, my—proficiency in speaking the language or languages we've trained for."

Rick breaks in at that point. "The DLPTs are the Defense Language Proficiency Tests. They're used to test the skills of reading and listening. If they're anything like what they were when I was in school there, you're going to want that two week break to review your materials."

Iris's chin lifts arrogantly. "You think so?"

His gaze shifts to the thick padding beneath her shoulder before a smile crosses his face. "Perhaps you're right. If you hadn't been able to translate the Levantine dialect Sam's kidnappers were speaking so rapidly, there's no way he'd have come out alive." Rick clucks his tongue. "It's just too bad your shoulder is going to suffer a major setback shortly after your graduation."

Iris stills next to me. "It is? Why? Did the doctors tell you something I don't know?"

"Sadly, yes. You're going to need major rehabilitation in a facility I'm going to recommend near Charleston." Next to me, I hear Iris's sharply indrawn breath. Rick goes on, "Now, you're going to have to fulfill your National Guard duties to the best of your capability, Iris, but purely as a translator. Think you can withstand the urge to kick some ass if you're called up?"

"Unless we're faced with another life-or-death situation, I can."

He approaches the bed at that point, holding out his left hand for Iris to shake. His Academy ring on his right hand still manages to capture the light from the overhead fluorescent lights sending beams of rainbows around the room. "Then I look forward to getting to know you better back at the office."

"You as well, sir." Iris shakes his hand with her good one.

For a moment, Rick doesn't let go. Instead, he studies her face intently before addressing me. "Sam?"

"Yeah, Rick?"

"I hope you understand what you have here. It took me three times until I got it right." With that oblique statement Iris won't understand, he lets go of her hand. Touching his fingers briefly to his forehead in a salute, he leaves us alone in her hospital room for a brief reprieve from nurses, doctors, and visitors from the Alliance team.

In fact, it's the first thing she asks me about when the door closes behind him. "What is he talking about?"

"The Admiral is on his third marriage," I inform her.

Her eyes bug out. "There's no way. He's like forty."

I snort. "Try late sixties and you'd be closer to target."

Iris looks impressed. "Do you plan to look that good in our sixties?"

I'm not going to get a better opening. I slip from the bed and drop to my knees beside it. Pressing her good hand against my chest, I lay my head in her lap where she immediately begins tangling the fingers of her other hand in my hair. Stiltedly, I begin sharing my feelings I've been holding in through the long hours of the night. "I was terrified. You were just lying there bleeding. I had to stop holding the pressure on it long enough to contact the team; then it wouldn't clot. We decided to airlift you here."

Her hand clenches around mine before letting it go. Her other hand grips my hair firmly. I don't protest the pain because I'd rather the sharp tug against my scalp than to feel numb, which is exactly what the rest of my life would have been if Iris had died. Lifting my head, I find her eyes surging more bluish gray than green as the same anguish I suffered is written on her own face. "Don't you understand I felt the exact same way? There was nothing I wouldn't have done to save you, even taking the bullet directly into my heart."

It's at that moment I realize I'm not alone in what I feel. Right along with me, Iris's feelings for me have sucked her through the waves. We've ridden down through the trough and now are on top of the crest. It's fearful to be so high, to risk it all by saying three little words, but the last twenty-four hours have shown me I'm not guaranteed the time before the world can come crashing down. I shift to cage her body with my arms. "Before another minute passes, I need you to know something."

"Me too," she rasps.

Her good hand reaches for mine. When it does, her hospital robe falls back, exposing the ink she placed on her skin almost a year ago. A year since I first touched her skin, made her mine. Since I realized there would be no other woman for me in this life or any other. I lean down and brush my lips against the iris bound with binary code—Iris wrapping the core of herself in me. I shake my head ruefully and murmur, "I should have said it a year ago. I knew in my heart that first night we were together."

The steady beep of the machine monitoring Iris's heart rate begins to pick up. "What did you know?"

"That I love you." I await her reaction, prepared for a similar declaration or even tears.

What happens wasn't even on my radar. Her head turns away before she whispers, "You don't have to say that, Sam. What you're feeling could just be because of what happened yesterday."

I brush my lips on her cheek before nuzzling the soft tresses near her ear aside. "You're afraid to believe. Why?"

"Sam, you've never given any indication before now that's how you felt." I can tell Iris is striving for patience.

"Because maybe I hoped you'd see it. Maybe I thought it was a sign of complete forgiveness if you said it first," I counter.

She opens her mouth to say something and then quickly snaps it shut. A flush begins to ride her cheeks. "Ah, sweetheart. You sneaky little devil. You have been saying it, haven't you?"

"I refuse to answer on the grounds it might incriminate me," she huffs.

"*Čhaŋtéčhičiye*. What does it mean?" I slaughter the pronunciation.

"Damn you, Sam." Iris's eyes close in defeat.

"You know the man I am, Iris. Do you really believe I'd cast aside what we've created between us? Forsake it? Not when you've become everything to me, when I question every decision as if you were by my side."

Her eyelids flutter briefly before her eyes spring open and pin me in my place. "My grandparents said it to one another. They believed it held more depth than *Thečhíȟila*."

I lean forward again, my lips a hairbreadth from her own. "What does it mean?"

Her lips part and I can feel each and every touch against my own when she stalls, "Which word?"

"Iris." My voice is shaking with impatience only because everything I could want is three words away.

But Iris doesn't just give me more; she gives me everything. "*Čhaŋtéčhičiye*—literally translated—means 'my heart is inspired by you'. Since I've fallen in love with you, Sam, that's the truth. Everything about my life has been inspired by you." Tears she never shed, even after she took the bullet meant for me, trickle down her cheeks. I use my thumbs to brush them away while she chokes out, "I just never believed I'd have the opportunity to tell you."

Just before I lean over to kiss her, I make a vow—that there will never be a day Iris will ever question my devotion to her from this day forward. I will stand by her side supporting her whatever happens.

Without hesitation.

28

TWENTY-FOUR-AND-A-HALF YEARS AGO FROM PRESENT DAY

Iris

I slip into my dress uniform for only the second time, the second graduation. If the message I received via my Alliance email is to be believed, it may be the last time. After I do up the gold buttons on the front of the blue jacket, I pick up my matching dress blue hat with its gleaming insignia before moving to the window for a final glimpse of the view in private.

The Army has been my way of life for the last year and a half. Despite the adventure I'm about to embark on, there are things I'm going to miss about it —the camaraderie, the mission, the regulation. A soul as restless as mine never expected to fit in, but somehow eventually I did. Touching the scar on my right shoulder, I murmur, "Maybe it's because I know what they're about to face."

A sharp, "Cunningham," has me whirling and snapping into an immediate salute. "Sir. Yes, sir."

The Commandant of DLI stands in my open doorway, scowling. "Give me the word and I'll tell Yarborough to go kiss my ass."

I stare straight ahead and reply in Arabic, "Sir, I believe the Admiral would be displeased if such an occurrence would truly happen. However, if it makes you feel better you should say whatever makes you feel best." *Just leave me out of it.*

His teeth slash brightly across his dark-skinned face. "At ease, soldier."

I assume a command rest quickly as I'm supposed to be unable to bend my arm in such a position. He goes on, "I plan on stealing all your National Guard hours to bring you back to DLI; you make certain Rick knows that."

A little glow of happiness bursts inside of me. Still in Arabic, I ask, "Permission to speak freely and in English?"

"Permission granted."

Switching languages, I finally meet the Commandant's eyes. "It would be my honor, sir."

"No, the honor would be ours." He pauses, catching my attention again. "Iris?"

I reel at the shock of hearing him use my first name? "Sir?"

"You should have won an award today—several, in fact. But knowing what Rick's doing, the mission he's undertaken, I hope you understand why I'm awarding those honors to someone who will be remaining in service." His black eyes penetrate mine.

For just a moment I think about what it would have meant to have heard my name called in front of all those individuals and then I let it go. I don't need notoriety with what I'll be doing. "I do. I appreciate you letting me know."

He knocks on the doorframe as he exits the doorframe to head down the hall.

I return to my spot at the window and wonder where Sam's sitting amid the crowd of people. I know he arrived last night to speak with the Commandant, which is why neither the email or the conversation I just had surprised me. While my classmates have been packing up boxes to be shipped to their next duty station, mine were addressed for a 'rehab facility' which coincidently bears the address of the Alliance office in Charleston.

It's time for me to go home. I can hardly wait

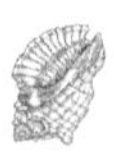

THE NEXT DAY, I'm out of uniform and in what Sam laid out for me after we crawled out of bed. Prior to that, after graduation, I spent the night wearing nothing but his skin sliding over mine—over and over. Amused, I glance down at my jeans, top, and well-worn Predator boots, something he told me not to bother packing with the boxes I was shipping back. He refuses to answer any questions about my unusual outfit as he drags me up the stairs of the jet waiting in a private hangar at Monterey Regional Airport. Laughing, I inform him, "If this is some kind of secret graduation getaway, I hope you packed something other than this."

Sam winces, but doesn't reply. Then again, I'm not certain if words are needed when I spy the cadre of people strapped in working on cleaning weapons or typing away on laptops. But it's Cal Sullivan who stands and approaches me. "Good. You both finally got your butts here." To everyone else, he calls, "Wheels up in fifteen."

Suddenly, there's a mad scramble by the men and other woman on board. Weapons begin being holstered in leg harnesses. Guns are quickly reassembled. Laptops are shut down and stowed. Sam doesn't make an attempt to move away from me. Jokingly, I ask, "Am I being kidnapped?"

Cal, who I haven't seen since before graduation, doesn't even crack a smile. "No. We got word late last night of a child kidnapped from the Saudi consulate in Italy. Our intel has us heading to Monte Carlo for a rescue. Do you think you can get the stick out of your ass so we can get to work?"

I hate this man. Suddenly I want to hurl the news I've been keeping to myself about Libby at him with such force I permanently wound him, but somehow I have a feeling it would just bounce off his impenetrable shell because he just never cared enough about her. Somehow she must have guessed that because she's moved on—in one hell of a huge way that not even Sam knows yet. Mildly, I state, "I wasn't aware I'd said or done anything."

He bites out, "That's the damn point. Don't," before stomping toward the back of the plane.

To Sam, I just smile with a patent sweetness before I take a step forward. He pulls me back against him. "I was banned from saying anything to warn you, Iris."

"Oh, I figured it was Captain Bligh's tactics. Do I at least get to contact Libby to let her know I won't be in tonight? I'm fairly certain she had something planned with Nonna," I remind him sweetly.

Sam's face falls. "Shit. I'll take care of it." He bounds off the plane.

"Where the fuck is Akin going?" Cal barks.

I storm up to him and jab my finger in his chest. "Cleaning up your mess already. If you'd let him give me half a clue, I could have canceled the plans we had waiting for us with his family back in Charleston with some, you know, grace."

Cal has the good sense to look abashed for half a second, most likely because he recalls who those plans will include. When thunderclouds start dropping down over his face, the desire to release all I know bubbles up inside of me again. Fortunately, Sam jogs back up the stairs. Judging by the poleaxed expression on his face, I'm guessing Libby just dropped her news. I turn my back to Cal and collide with him as he stalks up the aisle. "Nothing. Not a word," I warn him.

He looks at me like I've just sprouted horns. "How long have you known she's been dating this horse's ass?"

I frown. "What makes you think that about Kyle?" In her letters, Libby has been nothing but effervescent about how her fiancé swept her off her feet.

"Josh and I have known him for years. After I got off the phone with Libby, I called Josh to ask what he thought about her so-called engagement. He told me in no uncertain terms." Uh oh. If both Sam and Josh, Libby's older brother, dislike her fiancé so intently, then there must be something she hasn't shared or just doesn't know.

"He sounds great from everything Libs has said about him," I offer tentatively as I sit down in the seat he gestures to.

Sam snorts. "Sure. Looks pretty too. That's why he can't keep it zipped around one woman longer than two months, max."

"Libby doesn't know this?" I hiss, careful not to raise my voice so Cal can't hear me.

"Josh has tried talking with her until he's blue in the face. She thinks he's just being an overprotective big brother with the first guy she's been serious about. She's happy." Sam scrubs his hands up and down his face, his frustration evident.

I slide my fingers between his and he clenches my hand so tightly it's like he's trying to mold our hands together. Reassured for the moment that he's going to be okay, I drawl, "Let's focus on us. We're off on a grand adventure to celebrate my graduation. So nice of you to leave out the right clothes."

Just as Sam's about to say something ridiculous in return, Cal stomps past us. "Save it, Iris. The only time I want to hear your mouth running in the next few minutes is if you have something to contribute to the mission planning. We're wheels up in two minutes, boys and girls."

Shooting daggers at Cal's back, I mutter to Sam beneath my breath, "Really, Kyle can't be worse than that."

"Wanna bet?" He mumbles as he straps himself into his seat.

Well, crap. That really doesn't bode well for Libby.

29

TWENTY-FOUR-AND-A-HALF YEARS AGO FROM PRESENT DAY

Iris

My hips sway back and forth in the midnight-violet satin gown I wear with ease. The slit up to practically my hip shows a goodly length of leg as I saunter down the hallway of the infamous casino in Monte Carlo. My crystal-encrusted sandals catch the light from the overhead chandeliers and refract it all over the walls. Around my neck is a collar worth half-a-million dollars that Sam took a soldering device to earlier to tack a tiny blob of platinum. "It holds a tracking device. When you lose . . ."

"When I force myself to quit," I was quick to correct him.

His grin flashed quickly. "You say to-may-to, I say to-mah-to."

"No, I would normally tell you '*Potselui mou zhopy.*'"

"Kissing your ass is one of my favorite past times, sweetheart," Sam reminded me with a suggestive leer.

I rolled my eyes. "Stop making me hungrier, damn it."

My heart melted as he wove his fingers tightly to mine, so close the webbing felt like it was going to mesh. Gently, he urged me, "Eat something, sweetheart."

I blinked back tears. "I can't, Sam. I'm not certain I could hold it down."

He snagged the unopened bottle of protein-infused milk from the desk next to him. I managed to choke down a few sips before whispering, "What if they're not feeding him?"

He countered, "You won't do anyone any good if you pass out."

I was about to argue when there was a knock at the door and Cal poked his head in. "Showtime, Iris. Play kissy face on someone else's time."

I glared at him before I stood and faced my lover. His frown of concern sent a flurry of butterflies in my stomach. "Well, here goes nothing."

"Wrong," Sam countered. He rose and pulled me until our bodies were flush against one another.

I cocked my head to the side as he laid his lips gently against my ear. "When you walk out that door, you're taking everything I love with you. So, the correct thing to say would be 'Here goes everything.'"

Recalling Sam's words cause the corners of my ruby-painted lips to lift as I approach the well-guarded doors. Armed with the passphrase Alliance paid handsomely for—one which will either gain me access beyond the magnificently carved oak or possibly shot for the second time in as many months—I purr to one of the large men with a semi-automatic weapon nestled openly at his side, "*Où se trouve la banque?*" Imperceptibly, I hope that asking for directions to the bank won't lead me on a path to my death.

I have too much to live for.

Relief courses through me when the other burly man murmurs, "*Votre sac, mademoiselle?*"

Playing the role Cal briefed me on to the hilt, I hesitate before handing over the crystal clutch. I can hear his words in my head, "Show reluctance over the handbag, your shoes, anything but your choker. These guys aren't trained to look at anything beyond the obvious, Iris."

"You hope," I retorted.

"You have no idea."

As my purse is being inspected, I lift my leg to openly fiddle with the heel of my right sandal for just a second longer than necessary. The first guard coughs—loudly. The second glances back at him and notices his attention on my shoes. "*Droite ou gauche?*" Right or left?

Part of me wants to smile when my right heel is pointed at and subsequently inspected, but I refrain. *Save your charm for the man inside, Iris.* I caution myself. He's the one who knows where the boys are.

Finally, after long moments, the doors are swung open. In heavily accented English, the second guard gestures me inside. "Enjoy your evening, Mademoiselle LaFleur."

Internally, I trip at the sound of my cover name falling from his thick lips. *Christ, get it together before you get killed, Iris.* But anyone watching on the multitude of cameras strategically placed around the entrance—how I hope Sam is one of them now that he's had time to hack in—merely witnesses me regally incline my head as I step across the threshold.

And enter a world where children being sold to the highest bidder is as common as losing at the house tables downstairs in Baccarat.

A LITTLE MORE THAN an hour later, I've won close to a quarter million francs with the help of the inside Interpol agent doubling as a Baccarat dealer. I've had to trample my own personality down and adopt a laissez-faire attitude despite the heinous wrongdoings I've witnessed within these gilt walls while waiting for contact.

The dealer coughs imperceptibly as he slides a card across the felt.

Before I can casually turn around to scan the room, a man's fingers grip my upper arm. "Congratulations, Mademoiselle LaFleur. You appear to be doing well this evening."

I shift slightly in my evening gown. I can't prevent myself from blurting out my thoughts. "Your face—it looks just like the statue *David.*"

Although his eyes remain cold as the stone statue that rests in Rome, his lips curve ever so slightly. "Thank you for the compliment."

"You are?" I prod gently.

"Ah, my apologies, Violet—if I may be so bold? Jacques Delacourt."

My heart pounds in excitement. This is the man I'm supposed to contact, the one who will lead me to the missing child. But his next words turn my blood to ice. "If you're interested, you're certainly welcome to try your luck at a grander table than this. There are far more interesting items being played for tonight than money." He holds out his hand, assuming I'll accept it.

I do without hesitation, even as my heart stops in my chest in realization my contact is the one holding an unknown number of children hostage.

Even as I lightly touch my fingers to his to slide off the stool, I promise myself I'll do what I can to help them escape.

Or die trying.

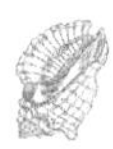

"WHEN I WAS WALKING AWAY, I heard sounds of their cries when they breathed fresh air for the first time in what? Days? Months?" I shudder as I lift the mug of coffee to my lips to try to warm myself from the inside out.

The moment I crossed the threshold into the suite the team commandeered for this mission, Sam ripped the duvet off our bed and wrapped me in it. Cal immediately congratulated me in front of the rest of the crew, having been witness to "Mademoiselle Violet LaFleur" turning over the Saudi prince's son to the French authorities waiting just beyond the perimeter of the warehouse Delacourt had them kept in before Interpol took her into custody.

And set her free.

"After losing all the money to Delacourt, it went just as we planned."

Cal drops into the chair across from where Sam's holding me. "Go on."

"Right before we sat down, he asked if I had any sort of 'special interests' he could accommodate." I shoot Cal a fulminating glare. "What the hell kind of background did you set me up with?"

"One that got the job done," Cal declares bluntly.

"He warned me, 'Too much greed may not gain you access to the sins you are aching to sink your teeth into.'" My voice loses its fire and drops back to monotone. "All through the ceaseless games of Baccarat, Delacourt kept making innuendos."

"Like what?" Sam murmurs. I know it galls him he couldn't manage to have eyes and ears inside the casino, but with Interpol covering me, it was a calculated risk.

One that paid off.

My laugh is bitter. "I'd be dealt a king and Delacourt would tsk before leaning over to whisper, 'I bet you wish it was a young jack in your hands, don't you, Violet.'" A shudder ripples through me despite the warmth of what I've consumed and the layers of love enveloping me. I tip my head back to meet Sam's eyes. "That man had no soul."

His arms crush me to his side. Muffled against his shoulder, I manage, "I'm so grateful you managed to create a cover so deep, so quickly."

"Sam's the best at what he does," Cal interjects.

For long moments, no one speaks as my eyes scan the room attempting to ground myself in my surroundings, trying to regain some semblance of myself. Finally feeling calmer, I hazard a glance in Cal's direction. "It went off just like you expected." I even manage a wan smile. "Unlike you, I had no problem with Interpol taking over once I was reassured Josef was safe. I owe you an apology."

His furious eyes meet mine. "For what?"

"I'm certain if it wasn't for my shock setting in, you would have stayed. I'm sorry."

His jaw clenches but he manages, "You did okay for your first time, Iris. You got your target out and didn't wind up dead. Don't worry about me."

Sam's arm tightens around my shoulders. He begins to rock me back and forth, whispering, "You were so brave."

My control flies out the balcony doors. Words coming out choked, I say thickly, "I don't feel that way, Sam. God, they were just helpless children—up to kids just a few years younger than we are."

"They'll go home now," he soothes me.

"If that's the best thing for them," Cal interjects.

Upon hearing that, I bury my head in Sam's chest, needing to inhale his clean, masculine scent generated from his goodness as much as his cologne. After being surrounded by the stench of virulent corruption earlier, it's the trigger that finally ends our conversation. I begin to shudder uncontrollably as salty tears roll down my face.

Cal stands. Slamming the chair forcefully away, he storms from the room.

Sam wraps me close, enveloping me in his warmth. I welcome the tightness of his arms around me, reminding me I'm not Mademoiselle Violet LaFleur. Thank heavens. His lips move against the crown of my hair. "I know how you feel. I felt the same sort of helplessness after my first mission."

"It's more than that, Sam. I feel weak and so angry. I want to go back and hurt everyone in that room." Leaning back, I whisper, "What kind of person does that make me?"

"Human," he declares bluntly.

"Sam?"

"Hmm?"

"The moment I stop feeling this way after a mission, I want out."

He rubs his hands up and down my back before murmuring, "You wouldn't be the woman I love if you didn't."

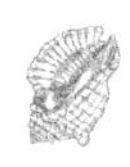

30

IRIS

I PASS my hand through my hair, unsurprised to find Sam's fingers threaded through the back, massaging my neck. "I became a field operative seeking something more. That's why your father and I both took jobs at Alliance. It isn't until you're in the field that you realize the job isn't about excitement. If you became an operative for that reason, it's the wrong one."

"What's the right one?" Rachel asks from where she's sitting across from us.

"People's lives depend on the decisions you make. Every second of the future changed by what I was doing in the present. That first mission fundamentally changed the woman I wanted to be."

Rachel tucks her legs beneath her. "What do you mean, Mama?"

"Rachel, when I came back from that mission, I made a vow that if I ever had children I'd never let them suffer. I would do everything within my power—cheat, steal, hell, even kill if I had to—to protect them."

"Even lie," Rachel draws her own conclusion.

"Whether directly or by omission, I wouldn't hesitate." I readily agree.

"Again."

My eyes meet hers. "Again."

Sam backs me up. "Wait until you have children of your own someday, Rachel. I hope you'll understand there's no hell we wouldn't walk through for you."

I want to sag in my chair in relief when she admits, "I understand that now." But I immediately tense when her next question is, "If you, Mama, and Uncle Cal were all working together, what was Aunt Libby doing? How did she handle it?"

Sam and I both wince.

31

TWENTY-FOUR YEARS AGO FROM PRESENT DAY

Iris

We knew we were going to be stateside for at least a month when we decided to meet Libby out for dinner to cheer her up after she decided to end her engagement to Kyle, "the *Zalupa konskaya.*" I had to explain to Sam the translation made me calling him an asshole all those times practically an endearment even though the literal translation in Russian meant horse pee hole.

He gave me a perusal worthy of Admiral Yarborough before he nodded in agreement. "Yep, that sounds like Kyle. You might need to teach that one to me and Josh."

As we wait for Libby to join us, we discuss in low voices our Alliance adventures. "After that first mission of becoming LaFleur, I had moments of hesitation if I could do this."

"I'm not surprised." His head is bowed close to mine. In this pose, we appear exactly as what we are to the rest of the world, lovers. We, along with a select few know we're also more. Because of it, the people who dine around the room might be able to sleep a little better at night.

My voice barely a whisper, I confess, "My guts were churning when we arrived back from Europe. Then Rick declared the mission a success."

Sam's lips curve against my cheek. "From what I've been told, so have the last nine months' worth. Even when I'm not with you."

I moan softly when his lips brush the side of my neck. "They're so much better when we're together. I hate that we're not always on the same assignments."

"I know. It drives me insane when I go to one part of the world and you another."

I pull my head back and clasp his cheeks. "Worse yet, when you're mere streets away and I have to pretend I don't know you."

He growls before brushing my lips lightly with his own. "You're still the one I turn to, Iris. No matter what happens."

"Same," I breathe against his mouth before I seal our lips together for an intimate exchange.

Sam and I have been on numerous assignments the last nine months—together and apart. Regardless of who I worked with, it's always Sam I reached out to when a mission ends. Just like that first night when I stepped into the role of Violet LaFleur, I need Sam to remind me of who I am, where I belong. A large part of who I am doesn't belong in a combat theater; it belongs in the arms of this man regardless of where we might be in the world.

Breathlessly, I pull away. "Tell me I'm not imagining it. We have a whole month where I can ignore the phone if Cal calls us?"

Sam's lips curve into an amused smile. "Yes. We can ignore the call from your boss when he tries to wake us up in the middle of the night to translate something."

I laugh delightedly before I pout. "Wait. Why is he suddenly *my* boss and not *our* boss?"

Sam pours a little champagne into my glass before handing it to me and filling his own. "I was going to wait for Libby to get here to share the news."

Suspiciously, I take it from him. "What news?"

He clinks his glass against mine before announcing, "I just received a promotion today. Rick called me into his office to let me know." Sam lifts the glass to his lips and waits for my reaction.

I take a quick sip and place my glass down so I can fling my arms around his neck. "Oh, Sam! That's incredible. You completely deserve it." Then I realize the repercussions of Sam being promoted and I start gasping for air. "Oh. My. God. It's official. That wretched . . ."

"Now, Iris," he warns.

"Excuse for a human is my boss?" I screech. I grab my glass and immediately drain the rest of it. "We can't wait for Libby; I need more drinks to drown the pain."

"Don't worry about me. I'm not really in the mood for alcohol anyway." Libby's voice approaches from our side. Her face is chalk white, which isn't unusual since she broke the engagement to Kyle. But her eyes, they appear even more vacant than normal. Still, she attempts to smile at both of us. "What are we celebrating?"

Sam stands and wraps his arms around his cousin. He's completely oblivious to the fact she barely touches him, but I'm not. Frantically, I go over what I shouted and sigh in relief. Cal's association with Alliance appears to still be under wraps, which is the way he wants it. I doubt she'd care very much, with the way she fell head over heels with Kyle, but who knows? I speak up with Sam's news. Proudly, I announce, "Sam just got promoted."

Her head tips in his direction. "Congratulations, Sam."

"Thanks Libby."

"Elizabeth," she corrects him softly. Sam looks like he's taken a full impact broadside when she does. "Libby, and everything she stood for, is gone. I'm not the same girl I was. Now, it's time for me to be proud of the woman I am."

"And that's Elizabeth?" he questions gruffly.

"Yes." Her voice is resolute. I may be the only one who can hear the sadness beneath it, but I'm not her family. I'm the person who held her the night she found out Kyle cheated on her with his new wife, her cousin Krysta. Her eyes meet mine and for just a moment I'm taken aback by the hostility in them. When I narrow my eyes to ask her non-verbally *What's wrong*? her face blanks as the sadness descends on it once again.

Sam, too busy filling a tiny amount of champagne in Libby's glass, completely misses the byplay. After he fills our glasses, he raises his again for a toast. "To Elizabeth. May your future bring you nothing but happiness and success in all of your endeavors."

Libby lightly touches her glasses to both of ours. "To you both for not saying 'I told you so.' For standing behind me. For loving me."

I tip my glass at her, and whisper, "You'll always be my Libby."

Her lids drop demurely. She takes a sip but doesn't respond.

She suspects something.

Damn these secrets. They're going to destroy us all but I chose my side when I decided to help save what I could of the world by supplying my talents. I'm proud of the work I do but I can't go back on my word, not unless I completely walk away.

For now, that's not an option.

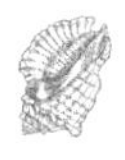

32
IRIS

I'M FACING the window overlooking the city below, lost in thought. "Up until that night with your Aunt Libby, much of it felt like I was living in some sort of a fantasy. Here we were bouncing from country to country, being sent on missions to lend our services where they were most needed. I was always certain we were leaving the world better for people. Now, I'm not so certain."

"Why, Mama?" Rachel questions quietly.

"When I signed up for Alliance, I had no real concept of what being a field agent meant. What it would do to your father, what I would do to protect him." I turn around and let Sam read the myriad of thoughts running through my mind—the apologies for the fear, the sleepless nights, grateful for the enduring love. God, I love this man so much. His slow smile beneath his neatly trimmed beard causes my mind to blank—just like it did the day we first met and he introduced himself to me as Libby's cousin. Refocusing my attention on our child, I continue, "Most importantly, what it would ultimately do to our family, to you."

"Mama, I wasn't even aware of what you used to do for a living until it was done," she protests.

"But it affected you in ways I never could have predicted. You'll find life is full of looking back, questioning whether you can turn back the wheels of time to see if you've taken the right path. But you'll also learn that to change one thing is to change them all. There were far too many things I had a chance to regret over the years." I'm haunted by what the small lies I told did to Libby, how some of the decisions I made in the field spilled into my personal life, hurting those I loved even as recently as a year ago. "Often I'd question what would have happened if I'd been the kind of woman who embraced the traditions of the Akin family? A stay at home—or on the plantation—mother. At the time I had you, that wasn't really who I was. Don't get me wrong, baby; I—we—wanted you more than you can ever know. But if I'd conformed to more of their image, would more than just your father have stood by my side?" Rachel is silent as the words rush out. I finally shake my head. "The question haunted me for years, especially during those long months when the entire family cast me out. Until they understood what your father and I gave up so they could rest easy amid the beauty of the Akin farm. But I'd like to think Nonna would have understood."

Sam tightens his arm around Rachel. "I, for one, wouldn't change a moment."

I arch a brow at him. "Wouldn't you?"

Rachel turns to face him. "Not a single one, Dad?"

Sam thinks for a moment. "Well, there might be a few but nothing about the woman your mother was."

My eyes mist with tears that spring up out of nowhere.

Rachel announces, "I never thought you would have changed a thing about Mama. The two of you still act like teenagers on your first date." The three of us burst into laughter but none of us deny her statement. "But what's something you regret?"

Bone-deep sadness wraps around Sam. "I wish you could have met Nonna, baby. That's all." He tightens his arm around Rachel, crushing her against his side.

She hugs him back just as hard. "Me too. Between the stories from you, Mama, Nana, Aunt Libby, Uncle Josh, well . . . everyone, I know I would have loved her."

Sam glances toward the ceiling to ward off his own tears after a quick nod.

"She would have loved you fiercely, Rachel. That's the kind of woman Dahlia Akin was," I manage to croak, still devastated after all these years I couldn't be there when they finally laid her to rest.

33

TWENTY-FOUR YEARS AGO FROM PRESENT DAY

SAMUEL

"SAM? Cal said to inform you there's a coded message waiting from Admiral Yarborough through the usual channels," Dawn informs me on the stairs of our warehouse in Munich.

I frown because I'm the one who usually passes along those kind of messages to the rest of the team. *What's going on that has Cal involved*? I eye Dawn with some suspicion. "When did it come in?"

"Just a few minutes ago." Dawn continues down the stairs, heading for the kitchen where Bruce is attempting to put some semblance of dinner together.

I vault the stairs two at a time to find Cal sitting, casual as you please, in front of my terminal. "What the hell do you think you're doing? No one accesses my equipment without my knowledge," I growl out. He'd better be logged into his own account, because if he's logged into mine, I'm going to lose my shit. There are emails I've saved from Iris in there, not to mention messages from Admiral Yarborough that are for my eyes only.

"Sam." That's all he says, but his voice has a note of helplessness in it that I recognize immediately.

Death. It's been years since I started playing this game and I've had to report too much of it back to headquarters not to recognize the wariness on Cal's face, the sorrow pinching the corners of his eyes. "Who?" *Please, God, don't let it be Iris.* I pray with all my might it's not going to be the woman I love.

"It's not Iris." Relief floods through me, but too soon. "Apparently . . ." Cal swallows hard, clearing his throat. "Apparently, Libby contacted your emergency number. I'm sorry to let you know your grandmother passed away."

I fall back against the door behind me, the strength in my limbs lost in an instant. I manage to croak, "Nonna?" That's impossible. I'd managed a phone call home to her just a few days ago from a pay phone a few miles from here.

Cal nods hesitantly. I shake my head in denial. "That's impossible. He must have got the message wrong." I stride over to my computer to contact the Admiral myself.

Cal reaches his hand out and grips my arm. "Sam, he didn't . . ."

"Get your fucking hand off me and let me check!" I shout. My voice cracks at the end of the sentence.

Cal's hand drops. "I'll be right outside."

I don't care where you go. Just as long as you're wrong about the message, I think brutally.

But ten minutes later, I have more than the admiral's confirmation, I have my father's. The admiral had me patched through immediately to my family. I beg, tears falling unchecked down my cheeks "Dad? Tell me it's not true."

Winston Akin, my father, the man I've spent my life loving even if I didn't want to follow in his footsteps to assume more responsibilities of Akin Timbers, sniffles in my ear. "I wish I could, Sam. I wish I could, buddy."

"I just talked to Nonna a few days ago," I manage.

"That's what Lib . . . Elizabeth said."

"Was she in the hospital?"

"No, son. Elizabeth went over to see her. She and Josh's daughter were supposed to spend the day with Nonna. When she tried calling a number of times, she went over. That's . . . well, she found she had already passed. It was easy like, Sam. She went in her sleep."

Ah, Christ. Libby. My heart shatters not only for the loss of the greatest woman among us all, but the fact it was my cousin who found her. "Evie and Lisa?"

"Everyone's coming home, Sam." He clears his throat. "The funeral's Saturday, son. I don't know if that gives you enough time to get here."

"I'll find a way," I declare grimly. Alliance can go to hell. I'm not missing the burial of the woman who was the bedrock of the family she left behind, and if my team can't live without me for a few days when we've been sitting here with no leads for weeks, then too bad.

He lets out a sigh of relief. "Good, that's real good. What about Iris?"

Christ, I have to get word to Iris. I want to throw up and pretend none of this is happening. Right now, she's gathering intel for Alliance on a different case in Helsinki.

Her last word murmured against my lips before she and I separated at the airport was *Čhaŋtéčhičiye.* I replied immediately, *I love you.* Then she darted down the terminal to make her flight, which was departing in just over an hour to work with another Alliance field team.

Now the first ones I'll have to say to her since that time three weeks ago are, *Nonna's gone.* My shoulders begin to shudder under the force of my grief. "I . . . I don't know, Dad. She's locked into the treaty negotiations." *Lies. Even now, when I want to be able to share the truth with you, I can't.* I sniffle, wiping the back of my hand beneath my nose.

"We understand, son. It's important work you both do. She should try to reach out to Lib . . . Elizabeth if she can."

"I'll let her know." Just as soon as I can get a hold of her.

"I have another call—it's your Aunt Natalie. Marcus is too devastated to talk."

Hearing my father admit how devastated his brother—Libby's father—is chokes me up further. I know what an effort it was for him to be the one to deliver this devastating blow. I don't hold back my sniffles when I say, "Give her my love. Tell her I'll be home."

"I will. Love you, Sam. Travel safely, son. Let me know when you'll be getting in." Before I can return the sentiment, my dad disconnects.

The moment he does, harsh sobs burst forth. I can't control them as flashes of my childhood come rushing as fast as the Cooper River runs around the plantation. For a long while, all I can think about is the number of times Nonna told me and Libby about how brave Poppa was serving in the military. Fishing along the bank while Libby read. Listening carefully when we both explained what we were going to school for. More importantly, respecting the fact neither of us had an interest in running the mill. The words well up out of nowhere, "I would have, Nonna. If it would have kept you alive, I'd have done anything."

A hand clasps down hard on my shoulder. I lift tortured eyes to find Cal searching my face, worried. "What do you need me to do? I'm here for whatever you need."

"Help me let Iris know. Help me get home," I rasp.

He nods. "Done."

Much to my surprise, Cal did it personally. First, he talked to Rick and explained our situation in Munich—how it was a complete dead end. "Respectfully, I think Cunningham is getting more intel on her side."

"Then shut it down and come home. There's no way Sam is missing this funeral," I hear his familiar boom through the computer.

"Then we'll keep Cunningham in place. I'll make certain Akin is back to the US in time." Cal winces when he realizes he's on speaker and how every word out of his mouth is yet another knife to my already pulverized heart.

Go back to Akin Hill without Iris? The thought has me rocking back and forth as I try to work up the strength. Then I recall something Nonna used to say all the time to me. I can even hear the amusement in her voice as it whispers through my head, *"Just like your grandfather."*

I am, Nonna. I bet you never realized just how much. Now that you know about me, Iris, and Cal, is your mind finally put to rest?

Unsurprisingly, I don't get a reply.

WE'VE PACKED up the warehouse and are boarding the flight when Cal's cell rings. His eyes drift in my direction. "I know. He is as well. No. Keep her in."

Iris. I can feel her trying to reach out even though I didn't get a chance to speak with her. The heart just knows what it wants and needs. Right now, mine is calling for the part of it that blooms to make it complete. I'm too emotionally weak to challenge Cal. Instead, I just confirm my suspicions.

He doesn't beat around the bush. "She wanted to break cover and come back with us. She's devastated, Sam. She also passed along something through her handler, but I can't even begin to translate it. Chan . . . Chunka"

I whisper, "Čhaŋtéčhičiye." I know, sweetheart. I love you, too.

"That was it." His eyes narrow questioningly.

I press my lips together firmly. Her words aren't for Cal to understand, but they do give me the strength to climb the short flight of steps to take me away from the continent Iris is on and fly back to Charleston.

The plane taxis down the runway a few minutes later. Numb, all I can do is stare blankly out the window as we take off, waiting for someone to tell me this is a mistake, that we're not flying into the evening sky just so I can go home to the worst kind of pain—the kind I'll never be able to recover from no matter how old I am.

I yank out my wallet and begin flipping through to the photo I have tucked away in the billfold. There's a picture Libby took of me, Iris, my parents, and Nonna all laughing behind Nonna's house. *Now, who will live there? Who will always be there with a welcome home? Who will remind me I need to be a better man?* Tears spring to my eyes.

I'm not sure how much time passes before Cal drops into the seat across from me. My hands are shaking from clutching the photo with such intensity. He reaches for the photo, asking, "Mind if I have a look?"

Wordlessly, I hand it over. Cal stares at it a few moments before surmising, "Your grandmother and parents?" He hands the photo back over.

I jerk up my chin in assent. "Taken the last time we were all home. I have a larger one printed out at my—our place," I correct myself. It's still hard to believe Iris's clothes hang next to mine in the small space for the times we're home. I trace my fingers over Iris's beaming face wishing with all my might it was her sitting across from me and not Cal, though I appreciate his being my friend and not my team lead right now. "Did I ever tell you about the spring break I came home for my interview with Alliance and I walked into Nonna's? There was Iris, dancing on her chair to some song as Libby took pictures while Nonna laughed. I thought my tongue was going to fall out."

Cal begins to choke on air. "You've got to be kidding."

I shake my head, a bemused smile on my face as I lovingly trace my finger over the image of my grandmother's face.

"What happened?"

"I made some stupid comment to cover the fact I was so off-kilter, and Iris called me an ass—in Russian, of course."

"Of course," Cal says wryly. He's been cursed out more than once by Iris, particularly in French, in the last year and a half since she officially joined Alliance. Iris admitted to me one night in bed, "My psyche chooses a language for someone and refuses to cuss them out in anything but that."

I laughed so hard I fell out of our bed. I'm not close to laughing now, even though I don't lose the smile thoughts of her bring to my face. "A few days later, I almost ruined us before we ever started getting jealous over you telling me she was asking about the no-fraternization policy." My thumb rubs over Iris's beloved face. I've seen it in so many different ways but so rarely is it ever this unguarded, carefree. It's my favorite expression of the myriad I've been exposed to. It reminds me of everything I help protect.

Cal's eyebrows wing upward. This time a small smile lifts the corners of my lips. "Did you really think I needed your help to get back in Libby's good graces? Let me guess; you thought I was bringing you around Libby so much to interfere."

"Frankly, yes."

I shake my head. "You made your feelings about her clear."

Cal glares at me. "You have no idea of what I felt or feel for Libby."

Those words draw me from my grief and bring my attention to the man across from me. He's strung tight as a bow, his hands gripping the armrests on either side of him. I blurt out, "You care about her."

Cal blasts me with a look so incendiary, I wonder if the phoenix is my spirit animal as I should be dead on the spot. "I always have. It's why I stayed away."

"Well, wasn't that stupid of you." For a brief moment, I feel like she's with me. I know I'll be okay. Not without some deep-seated pleasure, I mock Cal. "You know, Nonna always used to say we had two strikes against us because we're male."

His, "Smart lady" has me grinning.

I confide, "She was."

Then I begin to indulge Cal's need for family by telling him stories from Libby's and my childhood. An hour later, I realize I can't go home without a friend. If I can't have Iris by my side, I'll take Cal at my back.

34

TWENTY-FOUR YEARS AGO FROM PRESENT DAY

SAMUEL

I WAS DEBRIEFED FIRST so I could shower, shave, and make my way back to my apartment. For a moment, I hesitated on which car to bring before I decided, *Fuck it.* Just as I was leaving, I snagged the keys for the 'Vette off the rack instead of the truck I normally drive to and from Alliance. Due to the debrief running over, I'm already running late and I'm going to need all the horsepower I can get to make it on time.

It's not like Cal hasn't read the paperwork on me anyway.

Swinging through the employee entrance at Alliance, I find him waiting, dressed in a similar manner to the way I am—dark suit, light shirt, and tie. I call out, "Get in. We're running late."

He's barely slid in when I whip the wheel around and head out the way I came.

"Christ, Sam, if I knew you could maneuver a car like this I'd have let you drive," Cal's reaching for the 'oh shit' bar as he makes his declaration.

Grimly, I mutter, "The problem is I can't operate a computer and drive at the same time."

"Right. Forget I said anything."

I do for the next several minutes as I pass cars with inches to spare. I ignore the blaring of horns as I drive in ways that would have my license revoked if a police officer happened to pull me over until I manage to get to the fringes of the city. Then I just drop the gear and floor it.

Every second water rushes past us is another second lost in my race to make it on time to walk in with my family. I keep checking the clock as I increase our speed on the straightaways, pushing my car to its limits. Finally, the stone and timber fencing comes into view and I begin to slow. Unsurprisingly, there's an officer directing traffic. I roll down my window and flash my license. He nods, offering only a quick, "I'm sorry for your loss" before I'm rolling it back up.

The officer stops the oncoming traffic. I take advantage of it, once again slamming my foot down on the pedal—sending my tires squealing. Cal, who somehow managed to get a bouquet of sunflowers brought to him at Alliance while he was being debriefed, finally demands, "What the hell are we doing, Sam? Don't we have a funeral to go to?"

"We are. I'm going to be royally fucked because I'm late."

"Dude, where the hell do you plan on putting someone else in this car? The trunk?"

For long moments, I don't say a word. My jaw aches from clenching it under the strain of withholding my emotions, of trying to get here. I inform Cal, "We're not picking up anyone. Nonna's being buried here." I drop the gear and press the pedal again racing the water of the Cooper River, trying to outrun the emotions choking me as much as the tie strangling my throat.

Soon, Nonna's home rises in the distance as well as the sea of cars. I let out a shaky breath. *I made it home, Nonna.* Tears burn in my eyes. Then Cal catches me off guard when he blurts out, "Holy crap!"

"And that's just the main house. Wait till you see the rest of the homes on the property." I slam on the brake, which flings both of us forward. I twist the wheel to park the car beneath an empty spot near a tree, shutting off the engine.

"Sam?" Cal starts to ask as we alight from the car. But he doesn't get to finish as one of my youngest cousins comes racing towards us—Libby's brother's daughter, Sydney. In her hands, she's carrying the ugliest monstrosity of a hat from Nonna's collection.

"Sam! This is the last one left!" She flaps the hat at me. I scoop her up in my arms and twirl her around for a moment before burying my face deep into her neck. "I told Nanny it wasn't your color."

"What did she say to that?" I blow a raspberry into her neck, making Sydney giggle.

Cal stands apart, obviously not wanting to intrude. Sydney, for the moment, ignores him. "Nanny said you should have been here on time, and then you could have worn . . ." Then she freezes spying the stranger. Scooching against my legs, she offers a polite, "Hello."

I smooth a hand over her hair, so like Libby's. "Sydney, I want you to meet my friend, Calhoun."

Cal crouches down to her level and holds out a hand. "Hello, Sydney. My friends call me Cal."

Her eyes widen comically as she edges forward. "You know my Aunt Libby, too."

Cal drops his hand. He shoots me a questioning look. I shrug in return, having no idea how Sydney would know this. Cal gives her the truth. "I do."

Sydney studies Cal for a moment, inspecting him from head to toe. Hesitantly, his uncertainty with children showing, he levers to his feet just in time because my darling cousin stomps on the instep of his foot. Hard.

Cal yelps in surprise, almost dropping the flowers he brought to lay on Nonna's grave.

I yell, "Sydney Elizabeth! What was that for?"

"Boys aren't supposed to make you cry. You taught me that, Sam," Sydney accuses. Stomping in my direction, she shoves the grotesque hat into my hands. "Here. We're in the back waiting on you."

The moment Sydney is out of earshot, Cal hisses, "Care to explain?"

I sigh before slipping the hat on my hair. "I honestly have no idea. But right now, I have to say goodbye to the woman who taught us everything."

The combination of humiliation and irritation slip from Cal's face. He nods. He clasps my shoulder as we make off in two separate directions—me to my family and he to those who came to pay their last respects to the late, great Dahlia Akin.

AS I WAIT SOMEWHAT IMPATIENTLY for two pieces of coconut pecan cake to be handed to me from the dessert line attendants, I reacquaint myself with the miracle of the land I was blessed to be raised on. Years ago, during the "War of Northern Aggression," as the preacher joked during Nonna's eulogy, my ancestors staked their claim on Akin Hill. There's a contrast between the acres of dark majestic trees which reach for the clear blue skies that never fails to ground me.

Except today. All it does is make me wish I could bound up the steps to Nonna's house and walk in, assured of the welcome I've received since I was a little boy. Finally getting cake, I make my way back to where Cal and I put forth a good effort to decimate the low country boil dumped on our table earlier.

Dropping the plate unceremoniously in front of him, I take the seat across from him and dive in without a word. Then as the flavor erupts on my tongue, a whole new host of memories I'll never be ready to let go of flood my mind—afternoons studying at Nonna's counter, birthdays blowing out candles, or celebrations of an infinite quantity. Barely even done with my first bite, I'm shoving in the second when Cal exclaims, "Jesus Christ, this is good."

I nod, while resuming my rapid consumption. "That's why I ran when they said dessert was ready. Libby made it. It was Nonna's specialty; no one can make it like either of them."

Cal forks off another piece and lifts it up to the air, inspecting it before shoving it past his lips. "What's in this exactly?"

One ingredient pops into my mind. "Butter." Then I grin at the exasperated expression on his face.

"And now I know why you're not our cook when we're deployed."

"I'm not kidding, Cal. Nonna used to say her coconut pecan cake has a 'Southern amount of butter.'"

"How much is that exactly?"

"Don't ask. Just eat it and accept you'll work it off later."

Cal obviously decides not to question my sage advice. After the two of us moan our way through at least half of our enormous slices, Cal surprises me by asking, "What made you join us, Sam?"

I think back to the woman I love. No amount of money could have compared to the opportunity to have shared the experiences we have with no encumbrance between us. My answer flows freely out of me. "I knew you were recruiting Iris."

Judging from the look of incredulousness on his face, that wasn't the answer he was expecting. "You're kidding!"

He shakes his head, lost in his own thoughts for a moment. I drag him back by kicking him under the table. "Even though I wish she was here, I'm glad you are."

I've obviously pressed an emotional button. Cal's voice is choked up when he says, "Thanks, Sam."

Deciding to lighten the mood just a bit before we become as maudlin as some of the aging well-wishers meandering around the yard, I joke, "You know, Iris is so much like you, it's scary. If it weren't for the fact you have a dick, I'm not sure which one of you I'd have fallen for."

Cal laughs. "You're such a douche." Then his face pales when a woman I'd know on my deathbed chides from behind him, "You're only just recognizing this? Tsk, tsk. Here I thought Sam presented those traits much earlier than now. Maybe around birth?"

My heart, feeling light for just a moment, sinks back down into the murky abyss. Libby's face is closed off like it has been since that dinner with Iris and me when I announced I was being promoted. Only today, the mask has definite cracks of agony as she, too, is suffering Nonna's death.

Cal, not reading her 'Stay Away' warning, touches her arm. "I'm so sorry for your loss. I'm here for anything you need. Anything."

Libby steps back so his hand drops. Her arctic voice informs him, "Don't say something unless you mean it, Cal. I'm all too familiar with men saying pretty words and then not following through on them."

In profile, I can read the shock on Cal's face as he whispers her name. "Libby."

She turns towards me, tuning him out. "Your parents are wondering if you plan on mingling with any of the family. Your friend is certainly welcome to join you." Without a further word to either of us, Libby glides away. All the laughter that used to live in her face has been drained, replaced by a woman so untouchable even I can't reach her.

Cal mutters something beneath his breath that I don't catch. Absentmindedly, I prompt him, "What?"

"Libby looks . . . haunted."

I'm stunned speechless for a moment before I recall Cal wasn't around when our teammates Dawn and Bruce listened to Iris and me unload our concerns about Libby. Sagely they advised us to stay out of it. "Healing from pain is a personal journey. No one can give you a timeline. Just keep letting her know you're there for her," Dawn let us know one night while we were in Barcelona waiting for our transport home the next morning.

When I made it out to Akin Hill, I was disappointed to see the whole family there but not Libby. Nonna had told me, "She's at the gallery, Sam." Then she chided me, "Surely you don't expect her to put the rest of her life on hold? She's stronger than that."

Now that I realize that Libby's been coping, I reluctantly share, "Cal, I don't know how to tell you this."

Frowning, he gives me his whole attention. "Tell me what?"

"That *is* Libby. Or should I say, Elizabeth." For the first time I understand why my sweet cousin decided to use her formal name. If this helps her to move past the agony she suffered, I'll honor it. "No one but her parents or Iris get away with calling her Libby anymore. Not even me. The girl you knew as a college student is long gone. Over the last few years, she's closed up. One time I was home in between missions. She wasn't supposed to tell me, but Iris said Mom and Aunt Natalie speculated if it was because of her engagement gone bad."

Stunned, Cal manages, "She was engaged?"

I sneer, unable to prevent my lip curling. "Yes. For a few months. Her brother and I hated him from the minute we first met him. Turns out we had reason to."

"What happened to him?"

I use the fork I'm still holding to gesture to the man Libby's passing. His arm is wrapped around another woman—our cousin Krysta. "He works for Akin Timbers. The woman he cheated on her with is a cousin. It's only at events like this she acknowledges either of them."

Cal's face takes on a feral cast. "Let me kill him."

"If I thought it would bring our Libby back, I would. She's so closed up, the only person she ever really talked to about it all was Nonna. I thought I was closer to Libby than anyone—even Josh— but I haven't been able to figure it out. She's shut me out."

Cal's contemplative for long moments, his fingers stroking his jaw. His very appearance is exactly like when he plans an op. I begin to worry. *Don't tell me we have to leave so quickly*. But the next words out of his mouth are almost worse. "I think I know how to fix this."

I gape at him. The man is certifiably insane. When our backs are in a corner and he makes this exact same statement, it's normally a fifty-fifty chance we're not going to end up being shot at. "You do realize I've tried everything to break through to her, right? That I love her more than I love my own sisters?" Realizing how loud that came out, I curse. "Shit, I need to be careful about saying crap like that here. Sure as hell, it will get back to them." Evie and Lisa will do something to make life miserable while I'm stateside.

Like show up.

Cal's stony face is resolute. "I need to find time to talk with Libby."

For the first time, I actually laugh. "Good luck with that. Every time your name has come up, she's . . ." It finally dawns on me Libby's recent reticence might not have anything to do with Kyle and everything to do with the man across from me. "Son of a bitch, what did you do to hurt her?"

"Nothing. And that's the problem. I made a promise and then stupidly broke it."

My protective instincts kick in. I want to tackle Cal into the green grass and pound the answer out of him, but this is Nonna's funeral. While she might appreciate the way I'm trying to protect Libby, the rest of the family would be in shock. Menacingly, I probe, "What kind of promise?"

He lets out a measured breath. "To talk to her. All she wanted me to do was talk to her."

I slam my fork down and am about to say something scathing—about all the times I reminded him to answer his damn email—when we're interrupted by Sydney's crying out. Just as I'm about to go see if either of my cousins need my help, I glance at Cal's face.

He's riveted by the sight in front of him—of Libby caring for our young cousin—just as enraptured by her as he was when we were back in Athens.

As I stride forward to ask Libby what I can do to help, all I can think is, *Here we go again.*

35

TWENTY-FOUR YEARS AGO FROM PRESENT DAY

Iris

It's been three weeks since Nonna died and the circling of the jet around the Alliance airstrip has me snarking, "We've been circling for twenty minutes. Why can't we land?"

"You have to pee or just have a burr up your ass, Cunningham?" Comes Pete's laconic drawl. When I'm not working with Sam and Cal's team, my other team gives me a lot more ribbing which I normally take in good fun.

Today's not the day for it. I'm aching to wrap my arms around Sam and let loose the emotions that have bound me up inside while I played the part of a waitress in Helsinki in order to overhear a conversation between members of the *Bratva* confirming what we suspected—they were going to try to intercept the American soldiers' caravan as it passed near the border.

After we passed along the intelligence through to our Army contacts—one whom I graduated from DLI with, bringing back a host of memories—we began the process of extracting ourselves so we didn't arouse suspicion. Then we finally boarded flights that had us crisscrossing the globe for days before we boarded the final one in Las Vegas this morning to carry us back to Charleston.

Even though I've been able to email him, I need to stare into Sam's face to ascertain how he is. He informed me he had "Huge news. The kind you're never going to believe," he wrote. Ever since I received that email a few days after Nonna's funeral, there's been a lead ball bouncing around the gut of my belly waiting to explode. But no matter how many times I demanded a hint, he wouldn't give it to me.

The pilot announces, "We're beginning our descent. If you're not already buckled up, please do so at this time."

"About frigging time," I gripe.

Pete just laughs in my face as the plane circles once more before the altitude changes. As we bank, I can see the Cooper River Bridge in the distance. My heart begins to pound in anticipation. I spy the lush green intermingled with low country flats flash by as we begin our approach. Mere minutes later, the wheels lock into place and we're falling through the air in feet per second. Soon, the flaps go up as we bounce on the tarmac. That's when I see him in the distance. Waiting.

"Welcome back, team." The pilot drones on, but I barely listen because as soon as the door's unlatched, I'm racing off the plane.

I call over my shoulder, "I'll be back for my bag," before tearing down the steps and running through the humid Charleston air until I'm swept up in Sam's arms. The moment I feel his arms clasp around me, I let go of all the pent-up emotions I've been suppressing to get through my mission—to stay alive for just this moment. Tears begin falling in earnest. After long moments, I sniffle. "I'm so sorry, my love. I'm supposed to be comforting you."

He tips my head back and smiles down at me gently. "Do you think this isn't? I know how much you loved Nonna, sweetheart. She loved you."

His words cause the waterworks to begin again. Suddenly, something bumps hard against my back. I whirl around, fury rising at our moment being spoiled. I find Pete holding my backpack. "Here, Iris. There's no need for you to come back. Get debriefed and go home."

"Thanks man." Sam holds out a hand to shake.

Pete's face is filled with sympathy when he holds out a hand to Sam. "She's been a complete bitch to work with. I'm just grateful to get rid of her."

"Pete!" I shout, but Sam just laughs.

"Don't worry. I'm about to give her a target to take it out on."

My head whirls in Sam's direction. His face holds both unholy amusement and underlying anger. Suddenly my eyes narrow. "Why are you so upset?"

He lopes an arm around my shoulder. "Why don't you debrief with Cal first. Then the three of us will talk about it."

My mind whirls but I'm so overwhelmed by Sam's nearness, I can't reason it out.

I'VE JUST SPENT two hours in debrief and am ready to tell Cal to kiss my ass when he clears his throat anxiously.

Cal? Anxious? I sit up and pay more attention. Casually, I ask, "What's on your mind?"

He picks up his phone and presses a few numbers. "I think Sam should be here for this."

Uh oh. That lead ball that's been bouncing around my stomach slips free and lodges firmly where it can do the most damage—my heart. Sam opens the door without knocking. "Since the soundproofing hasn't broken, I assume you haven't told her."

Cal scowls. "Funny Sam." He gestures for him to take a seat.

Sam plants himself right behind me, dropping his hands firmly on my shoulders. "You probably want me right where I am, Cal."

He opens his mouth to argue before his face cedes the point. He begins with, "I went with Sam to the funeral."

Immediately my body stiffens. With just that one line, I know this isn't about me or Sam. There's only one person this could be about—Libby. Hotly, I fling out, "I refuse to give you any information about her."

Cal's voice takes on an amused note. "What makes you think I'm going to ask you and not Libby herself?"

Wait, what? My confusion must be clearly readable on my face because Sam leans down and whispers, "Brace."

I sit back in my chair and cross both my arms and legs.

"Sam has already expressed his concern," Cal begins.

"I believe my exact words were 'Don't start something with her unless you're in it for the long haul.'" Sam's voice is so hard I twist my head to see his face. He's clearly pissed at Cal judging by the way his eyes are narrowed at the older man.

Cal tries to portray the soul of patience. "I explained to you, Sam. I thought she'd move on to someone better suited to her life. That's why I never replied to her emails over the years. I was willing to turn my back on her to give her that chance at a happily ever after with a white picket fence. But the minute I saw her again, I realized it was completely futile. The pull is just as strong between us."

Sam struggles to hold me back, but I break free. Leaning over Cal's desk, I plant my hands smack dab in the middle of the file he's taken meticulous notes in. "Are you telling me the reason my best friend has become a shell of herself is because of *you*?" I spit the words into his face.

Cal winces but doesn't deny it. "I made her a promise and broke it."

I snort. "What a shock that is."

Cal surges to his feet. "I thought I was doing what was best for her."

"How about letting her make that decision? She is a grown woman!" I yell.

Undistinguishable sounds come out of my mouth over the satisfied grin suddenly gracing Cal's face. Unable to restrain my temper any longer, I shout, "*Vas tu future!*"

"Calling your boss a fuck isn't the way to earn a good performance bonus," Cal replies calmly.

"I don't give a shit, Cal. She's my best friend, and you're part of the reason she went from being . . . Libby to miserable. If I'd have known that, I'd have . . ." I can practically feel the spittle flying from my mouth as I try to form a complete sentence. I'm incoherent with rage.

"What?" he demands. "Shot me?"

"I'd have considered it," I retort. Unable to handle this without making any more threats, I fling a look of fury at him before storming out of his office. Just for good measure, I slam the door behind me.

A few minutes later, Sam emerges. He's unsmiling until he spies me down the hall practicing deep breathing exercises. Then a small smile lifts the corners of his lips, transforming his handsome face. Forcing sarcasm into my voice because I can't resist Sam at any time, let alone when he's smiling, I demand, "Is that what you had to tell me?"

"Only part of it. Libby's already different."

I bend at the waist and let my hair form a curtain around my face. "God, Sam. It's Cal? After all this time?"

He rubs my back comfortingly. "I know. What you said in there is a portion of the things I said to him in private before you came home."

Suddenly straightening with a snap, I question, "Is he going to tell her?"

"Tell her what?"

I wave a hand around. "About all of this? About Alliance. What the three of us really do?"

He frowns. "I don't know. I imagine he will if they end up going the distance. I can't imagine he'd keep that from someone he's in love with. Do you?"

Sam doesn't really want to hear my opinion about Calhoun Sullivan right now. I restrain myself by replying, "I pray he does."

Those words are the truest ones I've ever spoken because if he doesn't tell Libby, then their whole relationship will be built on a lie. *What will she do if she finds out?*

36

IRIS

"UNCLE CAL WAS an ass to put you both in that position," Rachel declares.

I burst into laughter but quickly tamp it down at Sam's disapproving look. I clear my throat and try to stand up for a man I wanted to shoot for more years than I can count on two hands. "Cal had a rough childhood, Rach. You've been told about this." After she reluctantly nods, I go on. "He thought he was protecting Libby by keeping her away from the life we led at Alliance. He wanted to create a world for her that was better than anything she ever knew but not let her know how it was happening. He thought it might make her think less of him."

"Does it make you think less of Dad? Dad, you of Mama?" Rachel asks with keen intuition.

Sam jumps in before I can formulate my answer. "Not a chance. Your mother was, is, a hero. She did things that, had she remained in the Army, she would have been decorated for time and time again. She put her life on the line in situations you can't possibly fathom."

"So did you," I say softly.

Sam shakes his head adamantly. "Maybe a few times, but it was different. Usually, I was blocks away tinkering with computers to make certain we didn't lose contact with our field agents, hacking into some system, generally supporting the people who needed knowledge fast."

"As time went on and we proved how strong we were together, more often than not, that became your father supporting me."

"Your mother persistently confronted our enemies face-to-face. With the amount I prayed, I'm certain I'm probably earned a doctoral degree in religious studies from some university along the way."

That breaks the tension in the room and the three of us lose ourselves in a moment of hilarity. Our laughter evaporates as Erika comes rushing back in, the anxiety having amped up further in her eyes. "I'm terribly sorry to do this, but I'm not certain how much longer I'm going to be."

This time it's Rachel who waves her off. "If you don't mind us using your office, Erika, we'll be right here. We're just talking, filling in some missing pieces."

A look of pleasure eclipses the strain for just a moment. "Take your time. There's refreshments in the refrigerator. You all know where the bathroom is." Then she darts out the door again, her stride purposeful.

Rachel looks thoughtful. "I'd like to do something for her. Like you both, she's an unsung hero."

Sam nudges me. I ask, "Not that we disagree, but what makes you say that?"

"How many lives has she saved that no one has acknowledged? It's just like you did, Mama. And like you, Dad." Rachel walks over to us both and gives us both hugs before she moves over to the wet bar. With her back turned, I'm given precious seconds to lay my head down on Sam's chest. He strokes his hand over my hair. Hearing that from our daughter after everything we've been through makes all the pain that fractured our family worth it.

Because what we built out of the pieces of the life we had before is forged together out of the strongest steel. It's something even Trident himself could feel the power surging through.

37

TWENTY-ONE-AND-A-HALF YEARS AGO FROM PRESENT DAY

Iris

"I'm afraid to curse it if I say it aloud," I admit to Sam. We're lying behind Nonna's house on the banks of the river staring up at the blue sky.

"What? Test Fate for once." He dares me as he tangles his fingers in mine, being careful when he adds the extra pressure to them. After all, just a few moments ago, he slipped a diamond on my finger that I won't take off unless I'm working—something we both know will happen often enough so I'll be damned if I remove it right now.

"In all our years together, today may be the most perfect day of them all," I say softly. I lift our joined hands to my lips and press his fingers against my lips.

He tugs me to him so I'm sprawling across his broad chest. "It will be the first of many, Iris. That's a vow I intend to keep."

I take my free hand and cup his cheek, loving the stubble of his beard against my fingers. "Ask me again," I beg hoarsely.

Sam, understanding immediately, rolls me to my back. He teases, "Aren't you glad I spent a week memorizing what I was going to say?"

"I don't really care what you said, Sam. It's the fact you asked."

He brushes his lips against mine before he whispers the words against my lips that set my heart soaring as high as the birds in the blue sky over his shoulder. "Wherever we are, you are my home. It doesn't matter if we're here at Akin Hill or in the middle of a desert somewhere. As long as I'm with you, my heart is settled knowing it's where it's supposed to be. We've done everything together and come out the other side even more in love."

"Like what?" I whisper the same question I did the first time he spoke the words.

Where the first list was all about romance, this time his answers cause me to grin. "We've danced next to a ring of fire beneath the stars with catcalls from our colleagues. Then there was the time Cal had to bail us out when you broke cover because you couldn't keep your hands off me. . ."

"Hey, it's not my fault. I forgot how gorgeous you are in a tux," I protest.

"Hmm. Then there was that interesting ride in the car back to base in Italy. Honest to God, Iris, I thought you might be pregnant."

Staring up into his eyes, I admit my most secret wish. "One day I'd love to carry your baby."

That earns me a blistering kiss that lasts for a blissful eternity communicating his agreement. Long moments later, he lifts his head. "Back to what I was saying, I want a life with you. If that life includes us holding hands or hurling through the same sky, you know we'll be creating memories so precious they'll last forever. Can you give me that? Your forevers?"

I choke up hearing the words now, just as I did the first time he asked. "They're yours."

He twiddles with the ring. "Will you marry me, Iris Cunningham?"

I surge upward and press my lips to his. Amid the tears again falling, I cry out, "Yes!"

That's when Sam rolls me to my back and proves to me how thrilled he is with my answer—both times he received it.

THE SUN IS SETTING behind us as we make our way, hand in hand, down to his parents' home. We keep stopping to pepper kisses all over each other, so the fifteen-minute walk is taking closer to thirty. By the time we get to the front door, the driveway is littered with cars—including I note with interest, Cal's and Libby's.

Cocking a brow at my fiancé, I question, "You were that certain of my response?"

He immediately looks horrified. "Hell no. I figured if you said no I'd need some people to drown my sorrows with. If you find the ratio of men to women off, that's why."

I let loose a carefree laugh, certain nothing could mar the perfection of today. "I love you, Sam."

His arm tightens around me. "And I you. Now, are you ready to see your family?"

I reach for the knob and open the door to a bunch of cheers. Dryly, I start, "You mean your . . ." But my words fade when I spy my mother and Arnold. My jaw hits the floor. "Mom? Arnie?" I break away from Sam and run toward them, arms open.

My mother catches me, falling back a step as I hit her full speed. Arnold wraps his arms around us both. I sob, "What are you doing here?"

"Surprise, *mičhúŋkši*. When Sam contacted us, we were thrilled to come share in your joy." My mother pushes my hair back from my face to study me. "The joy in your eyes would tell me what you answered even if the ring on your finger did not."

"Congratulations *mitȟáwaǧaŋ*." Hearing the word for stepdaughter be mangled coming from Arnold's lips causes me to grin as it always does. He tries so hard and he loves my mother so much.

I hug him fiercely before whispering, "Thanks. Thank you for loving Mom as much you do."

I can tell I've shocked him. None of our relationships have been particularly close ones, but no one is to blame. By the time we could have become close, I was already a grown adult, ready to spread my wings and fly. It was my mother's time to soar then, just like it's my time now with Sam at my side. Speaking of Sam, I turn and find him leaning against a wall waiting patiently. The expression on his face, the love in his eyes, causes me to jolt because it's always been there, even as far back as our time at UGA. I just didn't recognize it for what it was when it started to change.

I soak it in for half a beat before I hold out my hand. He saunters forward and I formally introduce him. "Sam, this is my mother and stepfather.

Mom, Arnie, I'd like you to meet the man I plan on spending the rest of my life with."

Sam clasps Arnold's hand and then my mother's. Then he shocks the hell out of me when he welcomes them both in Lakota. "*Wíyuškiŋyaŋ waŋčhíŋyaŋke ló.*"

"Do you speak Lakota, Sam? I must say I'm surprised. Even Iris only knows a few words." My mother is clearly impressed.

He grins charmingly. "No. It took me weeks to practice how to say that correctly. The languages I speak fluently involve computers."

Arnold, a computer salesman, slaps Sam on the back. "We'll have a lot to talk about."

"I look forward to it. I'm afraid I have to bring Iris around to say hello to a few people, but we'll be back," Sam promises.

I call over my shoulder, "Mom, my college roommate's here somewhere! I'll be back with her."

She just flaps her hand at me, beaming.

For the next hour, Sam and I move in between his relatives, accepting well wishes. When we finally come upon Cal and Libby, we halt some feet away. I murmur to Sam, "Trouble in paradise?"

"I'm guessing so," he responds just as low.

Libby's face lights up as she catches sight of me. She immediately reaches for my hand. "Oh, I'm so happy for you both." Her arms wrap around me tightly.

I hug her back warmly. "Is everything okay?"

A burst of air blows through my hair. "It's fine. It's nothing. Cal just has a business trip tomorrow." Her voice turns sorrowful. "I know he wants to move up in the firm, but I miss him when he's gone running these projects."

My eyes cut over Libby's shoulder to skewer Cal. He still hasn't told her. If it wasn't my engagement party, I'd be hard-pressed not to choke the crap out of him. She forces a smile to her face before demanding, "Now tell me everything about how Sam proposed."

"No!" I reply just as quickly. There's no way I'm going to tell her about the tender way he made love to me either time he spoke such tender words of love.

A knowing look enters her eyes before it's replaced by a revolted one. "Yeah. I don't ever want those kinds of details."

"I didn't think you did." We fall onto each other snickering, much like the way we did in college. I spy my mother across the room smiling indulgently at us both, and I begin dragging Libby by the arm. "Oh, snap. Did you know Sam brought my mother here? You have to meet her."

"You don't need to rip my arm out by its socket." A horrified look crosses her face. "Did you tell *her* the details about how Sam proposed?"

My face must reflect such distaste of that idea that Libby immediately breaks into gales of laughter. Just like old times, we leave Sam and Cal bewildered while we walk away holding each other up as our guffaws can be heard around the room filled with well-wishers.

I hope it will never be any different.

38

TWENTY-ONE YEARS AGO FROM PRESENT DAY

SAMUEL

We're at an undisclosed airfield, and our bird is down due to mechanical failure. Cal is cursing a blue streak at whoever is suffering the razor's edge of his tongue lashing while the rest of us review and re-review the plans we've been going over to locate the cache of missing weapons stolen from a military base.

Rarely are Iris and I used on the same mission, but Cal insisted upon it for once to Rick. "Akin's hacking skills and Cunningham's linguistics may be the only shot we have within the timeline before those weapons are moved."

The admiral shook his head. "It's your decision, Cal. You're the one who keeps them apart instead of unifying their strengths."

I sat in the briefing room waiting for my colleague's response. His disgruntled, "Christ, do I look insane? The two of them would focus more on each other than the mission," was barely out of his mouth before Iris leapt to her feet.

"I resent that, Admiral."

Rick stood slowly. "I do as well. Cal, you never made such an egregious statement when you worked with Dawn and Bruce."

Cal opened his mouth and quickly pointed out, "They were married."

My brow cocked before I drawled, "We're engaged. Is there something about slipping the second ring on Iris's finger that's supposed to turn us into . . ."

"Into what, Sam?" Cal challenged.

It's Iris who smiled sweetly, even though her eyes were shooting daggers at her boss. "Into you, Cal. After all, you're such a model for domestic bliss."

Cal's mouth gaped before he managed to shut it and glare back at Iris with equal animosity. "My marriage isn't up for discussion."

She uncurled herself from her chair like a cat ready to strike. "Then this conversation shouldn't be occurring. You're not thinking correctly. These flimsy excuses for continuing to divide your strongest resources are pathetic. If you don't like being reminded of your own problems, then fix them."

Cal reacted as if Iris had actually scratched him. He actually fell back a few steps. Glaring at me, as if it's my fault for Iris defending her best friend's welfare, he turned and called over his shoulder, "We're wheels up in three hours. That includes you, Iris. I don't care what you have to pack to be ready."

The glass embedded in the admiral's door almost shattered as he slammed it. After the tension lifted, Rick asked the two of us, "Is there something I need to be aware of?"

I spoke before Iris could. "It's Cal's business."

He just nodded. "You'll let me know if I need to intervene, Sam?"

My fiancée was ready to explode. I had to get her out of his office before she detonated. Standing, I grabbed her hand. She squeezed mine back with all the strength in her delicate fingers. I winced. "I'll do that. If you'll excuse us, we have to pack."

"Good luck."

I nodded before dragging Iris in my wake out of the admiral's office. We barely cleared listening range when she starts to simmer over. "Cal has problems, Sam."

I sighed. "It's not for us to interfere, sweetheart."

Her face flushed. I knew Mount Iris, as Cal calls her, was about to erupt with full force, so I shoved her through the closest door, which fortunately happened to be the empty conference room. The minute the door closed, she shouted, "Not for us to interfere? He's lying to his wife—your cousin, my best friend."

"That's his choice."

Iris began wearing tracks into the plush carpet beneath her feet. "Nothing is like I thought it would be, Sam."

I stiffened. "What do you mean?"

"I mean for Libby. I know her, Sam. There's no way she's as happy as she's claiming to be—as we are—no matter what she says."

I frowned. "You think she suspects?" If she does, I need to report it immediately.

She flung her hands into the air, easily interpreting the look on my face. "Who the hell cares if she does? Christ, I'd be happy if she did. I'd also be grateful if I didn't see her die a little inside every time she lets me know Cal told her he had to go out of town for a 'business trip.'"

I dared to approach her and wrapped my arms around her. "I know it hurts you because you love her. I do too, but there's only one person who can fix it."

Her eyes narrowed. "Yeah. I see him racing to do that. Let me tell you, Sam. If I was Libby, and I was being fed the load of bull Cal shoves at her, I'd swear you were having an affair."

I was shell-shocked at the condemnation. "Not with the way he loves her."

Iris shook her head sadly. "Love has nothing to do with it. Fears do."

Just then, the conference room door flung open and Cal stood in the doorway sneering. "Are you two going to bother getting packed? Our timeline has shifted. We're wheels up in ninety minutes."

Iris threw me a withering glance before she walked past Cal without saying a word.

In fact, she didn't say a word to him during the four hour and forty-five minute trip west. It wasn't until we touched down a few minutes ago to refuel, learned our plane was unable to lift off again, and Cal began cursing that Iris drawled, "Do I have time to get off the plane now to pee, oh great and wondrous Oz?"

I had to physically block Cal from leaping for Iris's throat while she saunters down the stairs, across the tarmac, and into the Quonset hut behind the hangar.

The sound of metal tools clanking against the tarmac accompanies Cal tossing his phone across the inside of the plane. Luckily, Iris has great reflexes as she ducks so it doesn't hit her in the head as she ascends the steps. The phone bounces harmlessly down the stairs.

Cal, diverted from his missing phone momentarily, stares at her incredulously as she drops her purse in her seat. "You went to change?"

Even I'm surprised. I pass my hand over her now neatly tied back hair. "Sweetheart?"

She answers me, not Cal. "I was on my way to the bathroom when I overheard them ordering a part for our plane. It won't be in until tomorrow. Since we're going to be stuck in this heat, I decided to be comfortable. Is that such a crime?"

"So instead of coming out to tell me this, you decided to primp?" bellows Cal.

Iris, able to give as good as she gets, informs him, "I figured you were getting all that intel from your phone calls and would come off your high horse long enough to let us in on what was actually happening when you saw fit. In the meantime, I had an opportunity to adapt to my environment and I took it."

A faint ringing can be heard—it's coming from Cal's cell that he hurled off the plane. His voice is lethal. "We will be discussing mission parameters when we get back." He bounds down the steps of the plane and snaps, "Sullivan," into the phone to answer it.

Blissfully, Iris stretches her arms over her head. "I feel much better now."

"Why?"

"I just transferred all my annoyance to Cal. I'm ready for anything."

I can't prevent the chuckle that escapes my lips. Pressing them against hers in the lightest of touches, I pull back before asking, "Did you really overhear them ordering parts for the plane?"

She nods emphatically. "Honestly, Sam, the real people Cal should be chewing out is whoever prepped this transpo back in Charleston. The mechanic said we should never have been cleared to fly."

Fear crawls insidiously up my spine. The job we do has us putting ourselves in harm's way far too often—especially Iris. She's already taken a bullet meant for me. *What happens if we lose one another before our lives are so entwined they can't be undone?* With that thought pulsing through me, I surge from my seat and hold out my hand. "Come on."

Without hesitation, she places hers in mine. "Where are we going?"

"We're getting out of here for a little while."

AN HOUR after we've left an infuriated Cal standing by the plane and borrowed a truck from the mechanic—with a hefty monetary incentive—I pull up to The Little White Wedding Chapel.

Iris's eyes light speculatively. "What are we doing here?"

I lift her left hand and press it to my lips. "I think we should get married. Tonight."

"What?" she squawks. "Sam, your mother and my mother are planning an enormous wedding at Akin Hill for next summer."

Ruthlessly, I declare, "So, let them plan it or make it our first anniversary party."

Iris lifts her right hand and lays it over my heart. "You're serious about this."

I nod, emotion welling up.

"Can you tell me why?"

A car swerves behind us to take our place in line. "You said it yourself. The mechanic said our plane should never have been cleared to fly. What would have happened to me if you were on that bird and it crashed? To you if it was me?"

She warns me, "If this is about money, your inheritance, you know I don't care about that, Sam."

I thread my fingers through the loose curls that have escaped her braid. "Don't you think I know that by now? But what I want you to have is my family. If something happens to either of us, I want to be lying next to you for eternity at Akin Hill."

Her swiftly indrawn breath tells me she hadn't thought about that. I pull her close. "I want to chase the clouds around the world while holding your hand. We'll live all the highs, lows, and in-betweens together but when I finally get to sleep—wherever that might be—I need to know I'm doing it with my wife curled next to my heart."

"That's what I want too," she whispers. Then she tacks on a caveat, "But you have to explain this to your mother."

I agree swiftly. "Deal. Now, the biggest decision; do we park the car and rent a pink Cadillac with an Elvis impersonator to marry us through the drive thru?"

She shakes her head, her lips curling up in a smile. "That's not living in the moment, Sam. Years from now, that's what I want to be able to say to our children—that we were so excited to get married we couldn't wait."

I lean over and capture her smile against my lips. "It's the truth."

Then I put the car in drive and get into the lane so less than thirty minutes later Iris Cunningham officially becomes Iris Akin.

My wife.

39

SAMUEL

"Is THIS YOUR SAME RING, MAMA?" Rachel is fiddling around with the gold band on Iris's finger.

"That it is. Your father's is as well. He offered to replace it at least a hundred times, but I wouldn't let him." The look Iris sends me is filled with such devotion it makes me want to scoop her up and fly to Vegas just to marry her again.

"Dad, women are sentimental about things like this," Rachel scolds me.

"Some women are, Rach," I correct her. "There are circumstances where maybe a couple can't afford engagement rings and make promises to get them at a later date or upgrade bands due to wealth. Maybe they have a tradition to pass along rings when children reach a certain age. Case in point, the engagement ring your mother wears is one of Nonna's. When Bishop gets old enough to propose to someone, your mother will give it to him."

Rachel is horrified the diamond she's only seen grace her mother's hand will be passed along to her younger brother when he's ready to marry. Iris's laughter fills the room. "Darling, he's seven years younger than you. I don't think you have to worry for quite some time to come."

"But Mama, what will you wear?"

Iris works the diamond off her finger and holds up the gold band. "If for the rest of my life I only had this to wear, it would be enough because this is the symbol of the words your father spoke to me promising to love me forever."

Rachel's eyes fill with tears. I blink my own rapidly to stop the burn from forming into something more. To alleviate the emotion, I promise, "Don't worry, Rachel. When the time comes, I'll take you shopping with me."

Immediately, the emotional wreckage evaporates as intrigue replaces it. "That's a deal, Dad. Maybe we can go to Europe to shop?"

I pretend to consider the option even though I have ideas of my own in mind. Still, I wouldn't give up any shot to be with my daughter. "Maybe."

Iris, groans, pressing her fingers to her temples. She begins rubbing them in circles muttering, "I have years. No need to get worked up now."

"What's Mama upset about, Dad?" Rachel directs at me.

Iris lifts her head and in her eyes, I find the bittersweet memories of giving birth first to Rachel and then years later to Bishop. I pull Iris to me and she burrows into my shoulder murmuring, "I'm not ready for them to grow up."

"Neither am I, sweetheart. But together we can handle anything."

She lifts her head and reaches for my hand. Our fingers squeeze. "You said that when you found out I was pregnant with Rachel."

"It was true then; it's true now."

"What are you two talking about?" Rachel asks.

"Your mama is just wishing you and your brother weren't growing up so fast." Iris nods earnestly agreeing with me.

Rachel's face softens. "Mama."

Disentangling herself, Iris straightens her skirt. "Let's talk about something else before I completely break down."

Knowing she isn't kidding, because her children are one of the few things that can make my wife a complete watering pot, I change the subject back to our wedding in Vegas. "Right after, we drove back to the hangar and your Uncle Cal almost took our heads off."

"Why?" Rachel's hanging on my words.

Iris laughs. "Because now he couldn't object to keeping us apart on missions."

Rachel growls. "Uncle Cal was really an idiot in the early days y'all knew him, wasn't he?"

I pin Iris with a look. She feigns innocence. "No more so than the rest of the family."

"Isn't that the truth," Iris mutters.

"Why? What did the family do? Did they say something about the two of you already being married?" Rachel demands.

"What didn't they say is probably a far better question," Iris says wryly. "They were furious."

"They wrongfully blamed your mother," I tack on grimly.

"What? But Dad, it was your idea!"

"Which I explained to them several times." I recall the way the family was so cool to Iris after we announced we were married—with the exception of Libby and Cal, of course. "But none of them believed that, baby."

"Well, why not?" Rachel's infuriated.

I open my mouth to explain, but Iris cuts to the chase. "Rachel, you've grown up with all the traditions of being an Akin. You've heard—short of school or work—the discussions around the table if a family member misses a holiday."

Our little girl's face transforms to one of outrage. "It was like that?"

I shake my head. "It was worse. It was to our faces, or worse yet, directly to your mother. We'd done something that hadn't been done since the time of your great-great-grandparents—married without family present."

"But it was because you were so worried about Mama! How could they judge . . . ?" Rachel's words trail off. "No one knew."

Iris's voice is poignant. "No. It would be years before they found out. How they found out made things so much worse."

40

TWENTY-ONE YEARS AGO FROM PRESENT DAY

SAMUEL

Iris is nowhere to be found in my parents' house. I'm stomping through it like an enraged bull when Libby catches my arm. She hisses, "Come with me."

"I'm trying to find my wife."

"That's what I want to talk with you about." She shoves me into my father's study before closing the door.

Impatiently, I wait for her to lambast me like the others but the first words out of her mouth are, "I'm so thrilled for both of you, Sam."

Taken aback after all the snide comments we've endured today, I fumble, "Excuse me?"

Libby crosses her arms across her chest. "You heard me. Life has enough complications; hold your happiness close. If that means you and Iris chose to elope instead of enduring the never-ending weeks out here at the farm planning a fairytale night where inevitably the real world breaks through, then good for you."

Relief surges through me. I step forward and wrap my arms around Libby. "Thank you."

Muffled, she informs me, "I said something similar to Iris before she left."

My body stiffens. "She left?"

Libby pulls back. "Just for a walk, Sam. I told her to go. After what I overheard, I knew she needed some air before facing the family again."

Grimly I ask, "What did you overhear?"

She shakes her head. "That's for you to find out from your wife." Then a smile lights her pale face. "It feels good to say that, you know?"

I'm making my way to my father's study but pause to look at Libby. "What?"

Libby makes her way next to me and squeezes my arm. "Calling Iris your wife. Now, go find her. She was headed toward Nonna's."

I lean down to press a kiss on each of her dimples that ride close to the side of her lips like I've done since we were toddlers. I love how she still calls Nonna's house 'Nonna's' though since the estate was settled Libby technically owns it. "I know where she's headed."

"Good. I'll save the serving of cake until the both of you get back." Libby returns the kiss on my own dimples before shoving me out of the study toward the front door. I hear the clatter of the coffee service being prepared in the background.

I wink at her. "If we don't come back, save the whole cake for us."

She purses her lips. "I could be convinced of that."

I open the door and dash out into the drizzling rain after my wife.

The warm rain begins to melt the misery that's been suffocating me since the moment I stood to toast my new bride. That's when the veiled comments began.

"Did you have time to sign a prenup, son?" From my father.

"Oh, did you find yourself expecting, Iris?" My mother, Lukie, dropped in that little gem.

Libby's forceful, "Good. Maybe now when they travel they'll have an opportunity to be together" caused Iris to turn tear-filled eyes and her only smile on her best friend.

After that it was a damn free-for-all with our extended family either saying nothing or sticking their noses in where they didn't belong. Iris excused herself after the meal was over under the guise of freshening up. The moment she left the room, the comments became more pointed.

"Sam, I can't believe you'd let your mother down like this," my dad said.

"We had everything planned. An announcement was made in the paper," my mother wailed.

"Don't worry, Lukie. Everyone will understand. Children today," soothed my Aunt Natalie.

That's when I stood and proclaimed to the room, "Neither Iris nor I is a child. What we are is in love. The fact my plane had mechanical failure when I was flying on it gave me a bit of perspective. I thought, foolishly it seems, that Iris would benefit from having this family behind her should something happen to me. I was obviously wrong."

I stormed out of the room to horrified gasps and demands for my return.

Now, I'm terrified someone either didn't hear what I declared to my family or they still said something to estrange my wife further. Either way, I just want to take Iris in my arms so she's wrapped tightly against the one place she's loved for exactly who she is—my heart.

I crest the hill and see her exactly where I expected to find her; the place where I proposed. I purposefully make noise as I come down so I don't startle her. Her hair, which had been up before, is down, wildly twisting in the mist and wind. I plop down next to her, immediately reaching for her hand. The pinch of her wedding band is the sweetest feeling as she clutches my hand as tightly as I do hers. In front of us, the river's rising high, the crest of the waves causing white caps against the rocks.

After a few minutes, she says, "This one's a low if you were wondering."

Thinking she means the tide, I correct her. "Have your tides mixed up?"

Her shoulders shake. "I meant my emotions, Sam. Not the actual tides."

I scoot closer, encouraging her to lean against me to unload her burden. "What happened?"

She's silent for a moment before asking, "Why didn't you tell me the last woman who wore that diamond before Nonna was your great-great-aunt? The one who left her family?"

I frown, my mind spiraling through the plethora of family history. "Likely because I didn't remember it before you told me. Why are you bringing that up?"

For far too long she's silent. "She didn't have a proper wedding either, I was told."

A chill races through me. "Who told you that?" I lift Iris's hand to find Nonna's diamond missing. "Where's your ring?" I bite out harshly.

Iris shakes her head, yanking her hand away from mine. "I don't need it. I don't want any of your money, Sam. I'm perfectly happy with this," she says, clutching her hand with the ring I slipped on her finger close to her heart.

"Who said those things to you?" I bite out.

She shakes her head, refusing to answer.

"The moment I find out who has your ring, I'll know," I warn.

"No you won't, because I gave it to Libby to put back at Nonna's, where it belongs," Iris concludes sadly.

"Libby was there?" I keep my tone calm while inside I'm raging at the nerve of my pretentious relatives. "This is your last chance before I call Libby to ask."

"Sam, please don't," Iris begs with tears in her eyes.

"They hurt you and tried to drive a wedge between us. Nothing and no one will be able to do that. I love you, Iris. Do you believe that?"

"Yes."

"Then tell me who it was," I encourage her.

Her head drops before she utters a name I'm not surprised by but still feels like a blow. "It was your sister Lisa."

I stand and reach for my wife's hand. "We have a stop to make, then it's time to go home."

She takes it unhesitatingly. "Where are we going?"

I pull her flush up against me. "We're going to pick up the cake Libby baked for us." *And your ring.*

"WE'RE HAPPY, Sam. Aren't the others around us supposed to be? Shouldn't we help them get to that place? I mean, I really don't mind signing a postnup if it makes your father happy." Iris shoves a bite of the wedding cake Libby lovingly baked for us into her own mouth before feeding me the last bite in bed. She sets the plate aside before declaring, "I'm going to have to bring some of that to the office so it doesn't spoil. There's no way we can eat a cake that big, even if we do save the top layer."

I was pissed enough not to let anyone else have a single bite before we headed to our home in downtown Charleston. From the moment we entered the door, I spent an exceedingly long period of time reminding her it was she who I love. I scoff, "Bring the cake in, yes. As for the other, you don't need to do anything of the sort."

She frowns. "Why not? The way your father put it, it's a fairly common occurrence within your family."

"For douches like Kyle, sure. Krysta's mother—my Aunt Nancy—wanted him to sign a document even back while they were dating. But sweetheart, Aunt Natalie and Uncle Marcus respected Libby's decision to never ask Cal for one. And I refuse to ask you for one."

Her eyes hold mine. "Sam, if it helps your family accept me after we eloped, I'd be willing to."

I roll her over to her back and smooth my hands up her arms, pinning her with my weight. My cock nudges her opening but I make no move to enter her. "Iris, this has nothing to do with accepting you. They've loved you for far longer than we've been together. I guarantee this has to do with my sisters bringing up old family lore. Rabble-rousing. Provoking trouble. I just need to figure out why."

Her eyes narrow as they trace my features. "You think something's wrong."

"Damn straight I do." I intend to use all my talents to find out exactly what it is before I confront my family. This time I enter her partially, causing her breath to catch. Growling, I bite out, "They don't get to threaten me and mine without repercussions."

"You're positive it's not just the elopement?" Iris questions vulnerably.

I brace on my elbows so I can cup her chin. My lips form words in a language I've only become fluent in because Iris's heart taught it to mine—love. "It isn't. Trust me."

"I do," she breathes, wiggling as she tries to lift her hips to get closer.

"We didn't do anything wrong, Iris. To say that implies we don't know our hearts and what was happening in that moment. We did. No one else does but us."

But . . ." She struggles with what she wants to say.

"What is it?" My hand slides down over the curve of her hip to curl around it, preparing for that moment when I thrust inside her fully.

"But they're your family!" She finally blurts out.

I shake my head as I push my way fully inside. "When it comes to the love we share, they're no one."

Then I once again demonstrate the truth to my words.

41

TWENTY-ONE YEARS AGO FROM PRESENT DAY

SAMUEL

I LET OUT A BELEAGUERED SIGH. "Lisa better be grateful I found this out. She wasn't just teetering on bankruptcy. She was halfway over the edge, praying for a miracle she wouldn't drown in it."

Rick agrees as he watches my fingers fly across the keyboard as I systematically strip the evidence of my brother-in-law's gambling debt from a mob syndicate's hidden system. "She may not realize it, but you may be the only thing standing between her and potentially her and her husband's death." His face hardens. "I hope you plan on making that very clear to her."

"I'm going to say something that I hope you take in context."

"Go ahead."

My fingers stop moving as I eliminate hundreds of thousands of dollars of horse racing debt her husband racked up. Finally, I admit, "It's a heady feeling to know I hold the keys to my sister's downfall, to know she'll have to beg for mercy depending on what path I select in the next few moments. Do I send this evidence to the board of trustees? Do I eliminate it?"

Rick doesn't deny what I'm saying. "What's holding you back from doing either?"

"Iris." Her name comes out like a benediction. "She was willing to humble herself to accede to their requests, to make me happy. I took a vow to do the same for her for the rest of my life."

"You also took an oath," Rick reminds me.

"I did, we did. That plays a huge part in what I'm about to do." With that, I finish executing the series of commands under Rick's watchful eye. If it wasn't for the fact we've been recording my session so it could be used in the event law enforcement needs more proof than is available to take down the syndicate, I'd worry about the potential of tampering with evidence. But there's only one thought on my mind. Iris. The actions I'm taking now are only to keep her—my true family—safe. It's just a boon I'll get to use it when I confront Lisa.

Within minutes, there's no more evidence Aaron Jorgenson's life was being threatened to pay his gambling threats. A small part of me, the part of me that held a fondness for my sister, feels empathy for the desperation of my sister's situation. Then when I remember the way she tried to drive a wedge between my new bride and our family, that feeling evaporates until all I'm left with is a desire for revenge.

While Iris couldn't care less, each of Nonna's descendants was left with a sizable fortune managed by the board of trustees. Lisa is apparently in such a hole that if she were to approach the board to remove her funds she would never fully recover. At least that's what she thinks.

I'm about to tell her differently.

Fortunately for my older sister, I have my own reasons for ensuring her husband's gambling debts were quietly dismissed, but I'm not so altruistic that I'm not going to enjoy her squirming like a fish on a hook before I set her free.

Carefully backing out of the tunnel, I stop the recording. With Rick's approval, I make a copy of the few pages I need— showing only the debt Aaron owed to the crime syndicate. After I carefully fold the paper in thirds and slip it into my jacket, I stand and hold out a hand to Rick. "Wish me luck."

He accepts it, declaring, "You don't need it. You already have a win at your back."

"I do?" I don't know how I've managed to win with my family still in turmoil over mine and Iris's elopement, but I'm curious about Rick's train of thought.

"Love, son. Sometimes it takes a few tries to get it right. But you managed it the first time." Rick pumps my hand up and down before dropping it and striding for the door.

I wait until he's left before I choke on my laughter. It's not over the avowals of love because Rick's right. With Iris standing by my side, there's nothing we won't be able to conquer together.

Now, I have to get a move on if I want to make it to the restaurant before my sister.

AS I SIP my club soda, I debate the wisdom of meeting my sister in person or whether to cancel the meeting again. Running my finger lightly along the rim of the glass, I muse, "It might be simpler to go directly to the board of trustees."

That's when I hear her patronizing drawl. "Marry in haste, repent in leisure. Isn't that the old adage, Samuel?" Lisa stands at the side of the table waiting for me to be a true southern gentleman and stand to greet her. She'll have to wait for hell to freeze over first.

Mentally apologizing to Nonna for deliberately ignoring all my upbringing, I nod at my sister. "Lisa."

Her chin lifts in a challenge of the blatant disrespect I'm showing her. After long moments where I don't twitch a muscle, she huffs as she lowers her body into the chair across from mine. Dropping her purse to the floor, she snatches up her menu before sniping, "Well, I hope you had the good manners to order me my drink."

As my sister has drunk nothing but sauvignon blanc in the early afternoon since I can remember, I know exactly what she's asking me. I lift my own drink to my lips before relishing in responding, "No."

Her eyes narrow to slits. "What has put you into a mood, Samuel?"

You have, you bitch. But the words don't pass my lips as our waiter appears at the table. "Ma'am? May I get a beverage for you?"

Lisa orders the most expensive bottle of her favorite wine on the menu. Just as the waiter's about to depart, I remind him, "Separate checks."

While his murmured, "Of course, sir," is only noticed by the two of us, her shrill response to my request may be heard in the next county. "What is your problem, Samuel? This isn't how you were raised. I should know more than anyone."

This is the opening I was waiting for. I slip the papers from my pocket and drop them on the silver charger plate in front of me.

Lisa's eyes land on them hungrily. "Are those what I think they are?"

I challenge her. "That would be?"

"A postnuptial agreement."

"Why would you think these would be them?" I stroke the papers with just the tip of my finger, luring my prey to take the bait.

Lisa's eyes are fixated on the movement. "Because there are assets which we need to ensure always remain in Akin family hands. Papers like that mean you appreciate that, Samuel."

I don't respond at first, letting the ping of silverware on china act as background noise while I stare into my sister's earnest face. Then I flatten my hands on the linen tablecloth and lean forward. "I would rather every asset of the Akin family holdings fall into Iris's hands than yours."

Her gasp is loud enough to attract the attention of other patrons. She assumes a similar position, hissing, "How dare you, Samuel?"

I begin ticking off the names and amounts I found so easily. "Actona, $250,000. Dalio, $460,000. Duffield, $1.6 million. Aishwarya, $2.3 million. Then there's the worst of the bunch, Han Fu. Your idiotic husband owes him close to five million dollars because he has a gambling addiction."

Lisa begins shaking her head back and forth frantically as if in denial. My lips curl in a sneer before I toss the packet of papers onto her plate. "It's all there in black and white, Lisa. You can't escape this by ignoring it with social platitudes."

"How did you find out?" she whispers frantically, glancing around to make certain I wasn't overheard.

I want to roll my eyes at her concern her precious social status might be marred, but the potential of losing either her own life or Aaron's hasn't occurred to her. "It wasn't hard."

Her hand forms a fist on top of the table. "You and that computer hacking. One day, someone isn't going to thank you for it. Mark my words." She tries to stand.

I lay my palm over her fist and rise to tower over her. Breathing into her ear, I murmur, "You will. You very much will after you sit your ass down and listen."

A fine tremble courses through my sister all the way to the hand beneath my own. She does what I've said without an argument—a first. I might have smiled at that if it weren't for the fact all this is coming about because she made Iris feel like an outsider. The thought of that curdles my stomach. To keep the bile down, I take another sip of club soda. "You made my wife feel unwelcome when I was the one who insisted we should get married."

"Mother was outraged, Samuel. You know what she had already planned for your wedding," she insists as if I committed some grievous sin.

"I wasn't joking about the plane we were on being unsafe to fly—the mechanics on the ground said we should never have been allowed to board it."

True regret washes over her face. "I imagine an experience like that would make a person want to ensure their loved ones were taken care of."

I jerk up my chin. "It did."

For just a moment, my sister becomes the woman I wished I'd had in my life growing up. Her fingers pick at the edges of the papers I tossed at her. Her face becomes haggard. She laughs bitterly. "It likely hasn't escaped your notice how much of the family is built on impressions."

"Nonna wasn't like that," I declare with conviction.

A true smile lights her face, making Lisa beautiful. "No, she wasn't. She never was. I wish I had the time with her you did, Sam. She was still very much a part of Akin Timber when I was growing up."

Curiosity has me asking, "Did you resent her for it?"

"Resent Nonna?" I nod. "No. Never. If I resented anything, it was the expectations for being an Akin."

"Expectations?"

Lisa waves her hand encompassing the ambiance of the restaurant. "We had, have," she corrects herself, "an image to uphold. A reputation."

Suddenly the events over the last few days become clearer in my mind. "That's why they flipped out about the wedding."

Lisa leans forward and smiles sadly. "Iris is loved by the family, Sam. Never doubt that. There have been plenty of times over the years I've wondered if Aunt Natalie loved her more than me and Evie."

My lips curve slightly.

"That being said, she's no longer a friend of the family; she's your wife. That holds a whole different set of responsibilities that she has to live up to. Frankly, it's time you accept them too. You're old enough to deal with the fact you're an Akin and not run away from it—whether our history is good or bad, it's ours. Now, it's Iris's."

I nod, finally understanding Lisa's motives weren't completely malicious. Then again, after the hellacious welcome to the family she suffered, I'm not surprised Iris placed a negative connotation on Lisa confronting her. It would have been too much for anyone. "The family should have stood behind my wife. That's something I can't quite forgive just yet."

Wearily, Lisa points out, "You know how the family can be, Sam. They're overprotective. After Nonna and Poppa rebuilt our legacy, they feel there are certain traditions which should be upheld if for no other reason than to demonstrate we've learned from the past." She lifts the packet of papers I flipped at her earlier. "Now I'll have to explain to the family—and the board—why I need half of my inheritance. At least you won't be on the hot seat."

Unless they find out about what we really do for a living. The thought whispers through my mind. The ball of lies that would unravel if the truth were exposed would be catastrophic.

Not just for me and Iris.

Scraping my chair back, I walk around the table. Lisa appears years older than when she first sauntered in on the stacked wood heels she prefers. I bend next to her ear to whisper, "I fixed it."

Looking ahead, she asks, "Excuse me?"

"The last page has the name of a top-notch gambling rehabilitation center. I'll approach the board with you if you need me to for the money to be released." I stand to my full height and am about to move away when Lisa grabs my hand.

"Sam." Just my name but it's laden with gratitude and apology.

I shake my sister's hand off. I don't want to feel either emotion. "I didn't do this for me, nor for you."

"Then who? The family?"

"No. I did it so I could guarantee someone else would be in Iris's corner other than Libby." With that parting shot, I stalk away from the table.

42

SAMUEL

Present Day

Rachel is stalking around the office growling. Iris is trying to placate her, "Calm down, darling."

"Dad, I'm sorry, but Aunt Lisa learned nothing from the lesson you tried to teach her. To this day, she's a roaring bitch," she bites out.

Iris looks at me helplessly, wordlessly wondering if we should control our daughter's fury, but what am I supposed to do? Argue with my daughter's very astute assessment of my older sister? Not long after that day at the restaurant, she got her husband into therapy and then they quietly divorced so I wouldn't have anything to hold over her head. Her truce with Iris would have ended the day the ink was dried on her divorce papers, but by then, Rachel was born. "I suspect your mother would like you to use your vocabulary to choose different words about a member of the family."

"Sam!" Iris snaps. She slaps her hand down on the couch, the lights glimmering off her diamond—Nonna's diamond.

"Oh, Mama, give it a rest."

Iris's head whips in the direction of our child.

I frown. "You'll watch your tone around your mother, young lady. We didn't just go through a year of therapy for you to disrespect her."

Rachel winces. "Sorry, Mama. I'm just worked up. How dare Aunt Lisa play judge and jury to what makes you happy, Dad?"

I reach out and clasp her hand on her next pass. "I don't know, Rachel. It's just who she is."

"It doesn't mean I have to like it," Rachel declares, calming enough to sit between me and Iris.

Listening to our daughter defend our love so fervently when it wasn't that long ago she would have cast it—and us—aside chokes me up. Iris, understanding that, jumps in. "There are so many emotions a human can go through in the blink of an eye: devastation, fury, jealousy, and love. Sometimes we're wise enough to be able to understand what motivates them."

"But Aunt Lisa?"

"I've never been able to understand her," I admit. I jiggle my leg in agitation. "Maybe it was because our parents had me when she and Evie were already in college, but I've never been able to connect with them. That being said, the moment you were born, Rachel, you were a bridge between us and them. Both of your aunts—"

"All your aunts," Iris corrects me with a smile, reminding me that although Libby is my cousin, she was raised as if she were my sister.

"Right. All your aunts love you unconditionally."

"I feel that when I'm with Aunt Libby, but I feel different when I'm with Aunt Evie and Aunt Lisa."

"Like what?" Iris probes.

"Like they've been holding onto this secret they've been wanting to share . . ." Rachel's voice trickles off and her lips form a perfect O. "They have been, haven't they?"

I nod slowly. "It never been anybody's business but ours, but yes. Likely they're waiting to hold your mother emotionally hostage over what happened to between her, Uncle Cal, Aunt Libby, and me."

"Again," Iris agrees, grimly.

Rachel's eyes flit back and forth between the two of us before she declares, "I don't want to fall in love unless it's strong enough to handle the storms you've endured."

Iris leans over to kiss her on top of the head. "That's all I pray for both my children—that you both find a love like the kind I'll always have for your father. One that's blossomed to include each of you."

I can't keep my eyes off my daughter as she leans into Iris. Rachel asks, "What was it like when you found out you were pregnant with me, Mama?"

Iris chuckles. "Do you want the truth? I was terrified."

"You? Terrified? Of what?"

"For so many reasons, darling. Remember, I was still working for Alliance at the time."

"So work changed, I guess."

"*That* wasn't the problem. Telling your Aunt Libby was. She was utterly devastated at the time, even though she didn't let it show."

Rachel's face turns to one of immediate understanding. "Wait, let me guess, Aunt Libby pretended to be happy for you?"

Sadness crosses Iris's face. "Do you want to guess or do you want me to tell you?"

Rachel's whispered, "Tell me," may end up breaking my wife's heart because I know where this is leading even if she doesn't.

I can only hope Erika comes back into the room before we get to the point of no return.

43

TWENTY YEARS AGO FROM PRESENT DAY

Iris

"Damn it, Libby, pick up the phone," I mutter. I'm pacing back and forth at the house Sam and I bought not far from the home Libby and Cal own. And I feel like puking. Again. That is when I'm not curled into a ball wondering what on earth I'm going to do.

How am I supposed to tell him our life is changing so soon?

At first I thought it was the food I ate on our last trip to Berlin. I would have sworn the street chicken was raw, but I was the only one who got sick. Then Sydney—Josh and his wife Bailey's daughter—brought home the flu from school the weekend we went out to the farm. Since Libby's and Sam's mothers, Libby, Krysta, Lisa, and I took turns amusing the patient while the men went out on ATVs around the property, and we all were vomiting within days of the visit, I again pushed my nausea out of my mind.

That is until mine continued, and I began counting.

My hands quickly slapped over my lower stomach and my mouth simultaneously as I raced again for the toilet. Grateful I told Sam to head to Alliance without me this morning, I called and made an appointment with my OB-GYN.

The results are conclusive. I'm carrying Sam's baby.

I want to cry I'm so ecstatic, but how am I supposed to do this? How am I supposed to be the field agent who slips into dark corners and eavesdrops on conversations in the field while I'm carrying the most precious miracle in the world under my heart? Just as I'm about to burst into tears at the idea of something happening to destroy the world or some child unable to be reunited with its parents because I can't translate the intel, Libby picks up. There's noise as she dumps a variety of items on her desk. "Hey, babe. What's up?"

My voice is faint with shock. "I just came from the doctor. Libs . . ."

Hers is frantic. "Iris, what is it?"

"I've been sitting here for thirty minutes trying to figure out who to call first. I . . . I don't know what to do."

"What's wrong?" she shouts. "Spit it out!"

I finally manage to whisper, "I'm pregnant, Libs. Sam and I are having a baby."

There's a long pause after my announcement. But instead of voicing one of the million questions that have been flying through my own head—like how am I going to raise a baby when I travel so much—Libby asks the most basic one of them all. "Are you happy?"

"I . . . Libs, I never thought about it. I always assumed you'd be the one with a houseful of kids, not me." Christ, is pregnancy brain already starting? I begin cursing myself for blurting out something so potentially hurtful. It wasn't more than a year and a half ago, Libby's marriage hit a rocky patch when she debated walking out because Cal was unable to be reached after she was in a serious car wreck. *All because of his damn stubbornness to admit to her what we really do.* I restrain myself from cursing him out in Libby's hearing vicinity, a real test with pregnancy hormones surging through me.

Even after giving her a tour of the Alliance facility, he still hasn't shared what it is that we do. Sam was certain he would after that day, but still, nothing. She's as in the dark now as she was the day she said 'I do' to the bastard. Murderous rage surges through me but I mask it as Libby pulls me back to our conversation. "Iris, maybe the time isn't what you were prepared for, but you and Sam? You were made to raise a child."

I sniff, my gratitude for her support overwhelming my ability to keep my tears at bay. "You think?"

"Absolutely. Just think of the amazing support system you have backing you up."

My voice warbles as I manage, "Aunt Libby. I'm going to have a baby. And it's going to be able to call you that."

Her voice is firm. "Damn straight, they will. How are you going to tell Sam?"

I begin to feel anxious for a different reason—excitement. Sam is going to lose his mind with overwhelming joy; I just know it. "Oh, God. I didn't even think about it."

I can practically imagine the smirk on her face as she laughs at my panic. I begin to relax as we fall into the banter that's been a part of our friendship for the last eleven years. I'm floating in a haze of bliss imagining Sam's kisses when she asks, "What made you think you were pregnant?"

Now cheerful, I inform her, "I didn't. I thought I got some bug from the crap I ate in Germany."

There's a pause, then she declares flatly, "You were on the last trip with Cal."

My bubble is popped and my mind scrambles. "Well, yeah. It's a part of my job, Libby." Lame, completely lame. I don't add anything to it, nor does she. The silence expands between us.

My urge to hunt down her husband and gut him from neck to navel expands exponentially. *I despise you and everything you're doing to Libby, Cal.*

Every time Sam or I suggest bringing Libby into the loop because of the strain it's causing on us— having to hide our jobs from her—he continually insists, "She's not strong enough to handle what we do. I refuse to place this burden on my wife." Or, worse yet, "I'm doing this because I love her, not because I don't."

It's like every other ass wipe she dated; they loved the image of her but not the woman inside. After all, who but a woman of incredible strength could breach silence to say, "Well, you'll have to let me know what you end up deciding."

"Libby," I start, but I can't go on. The tears clogging my voice prevent me from saying what I want to which is a good thing because the words that would slip from my mouth would include how much I hate what her husband is doing to her.

She feebly jokes, "I'm going to have to fight Aunt Lukie over throwing your shower, aren't I?"

I let out a shaky laugh. The idea of telling Sam's mother about being pregnant is almost as terrifying as having this baby. "Oh, undoubtedly. The first grandchild on her side of the family—despite Sam's sisters being so much older? If the estate wasn't thirty minutes away and we didn't spend so much time out of the country, it wouldn't surprise me to find out she was poking holes in Sam's condoms."

Instead of chortling, like she normally would, Libby assumes her professional demeanor. "Honey, I hate to cut this short, but I have a call with a client in just a few."

Disappointment laces my voice. "Oh, I didn't realize."

"We'll have to make plans to talk more when there's more time."

That's when I drop the second bomb of the morning. Hesitantly, I inform her, "Well, we're wheels up in a few hours. That's why I wanted you to know."

Libby Akin Sullivan has a spine of pure steel and I'd love to use it to beat her husband over the head. Instead of hanging up on me, she worries, "Is it safe for you to travel?"

"For now. We'll discuss it again at my next appointment."

"Well, you be safe anyway. That's my future niece or nephew you're carrying," she chides lovingly.

I swallow the lump in my throat. Her godchild. Not that I've told Sam, but I doubt he'll protest. "Absolutely. I'll call you when we're home. Have a good call, Libs. Kick some design ass."

After she disconnects, I race for the bathroom to vomit one last time in the peace of my own home before I take one of the anti-nausea pills the doctor assured me were safe. "With luck, they'll knock me out on the flight so I don't give in to the temptation to slit Cal's throat."

LANDING IN PARIS WAS A MIRACLE. I slipped into the uniform supplied to me prior to deplaning without a word of protest. Cal kept giving me funny looks after he alighted from the plane with Sam, but I ignored him. I was already in work mode.

When the customs agents approached us, I shouted, "*Mien! Reculer!*" so they would back away. Though the only thing I would ever claim in totality as mine is Sam, the last thing any of us need is foreign officials inspecting the cache of computers and weapons we have stashed in various areas of our cargo hold.

Sam slips his passport into my hands, murmuring, "Nicely done, sweetheart."

Keeping a straight face until he manages to loop the cameras, I breathe, "Thanks. How much time do you need?"

"Two minutes. Check everyone's documentation." Sam passes by and ducks under the plane out of sight.

Cal approaches me next. Without hesitation, he hisses, "Do you know what's wrong with Libby?"

I make a big deal about inspecting his passport, holding it up close to his face. His brown eyes shoot daggers at me. His lips barely move when he utters, "Cute, Iris."

I slap the passport back into his hands with a snap. "*Bienvenue à Paris, monsieur.*" He starts to move away and I mutter, "*Vas tu future*, Cal."

He whips around and glares at me. Good, I hope Sam got that on loop so his fury at a "customs agent" appears over and over. Pete, our site logistics specialist, caustically hands me his passport. "*Bonjour.*"

"*Bonsoir,*" I correct him, nodding to the pitch black sky. We flew in under the cover of darkness so anyone approaching would have to be on top of me to notice the plastic holders on my chest hold no credentials. "*Bienvenue à Paris, monsieur.*"

Pete nods in return. I give his passport barely a glance as out of the corner of my eye, I spot my husband scooting from beneath the plane. "We're good, Iris."

I hand Pete his doctored passport back. Cal yells, "Let's move it, people. We still have a long ride to get where we need to go."

I'd argue for the sake of arguing, but he's right. Besides, I'd like to be safely checked into our hotel before this little one tucked inside turns me into a vomiting wreck again.

I'd really like the opportunity to tell his or her father before I declare it to the entire Alliance team.

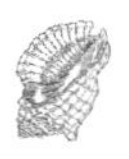

44

TWENTY YEARS AGO FROM PRESENT DAY

SAMUEL

"Ohhh, that's the spot," Iris moans. She's practically panting as I drag my nails up and down her back because she says her skin won't stop itching.

"Sweetheart, if I go any harder, I'm afraid your skin is going to have welts."

She purrs from where she's sitting between my legs. "I'll deal with it."

"Worse yet, what if you start to bleed. I'm going at you pretty hard here." I start to drag my nails on another voyage over my wife's skin, but she stills before leaping from the bed and racing for the bathroom like the hounds of hell are chasing after her.

Just as the door slams, I hear her begin to retch. "Iris? Are you all right?" I shout as I fling my legs over the side of the bed in the junior suite we're sharing in Barcelona.

There's a pause before she begins to cough and more ungodly sounds come up. "Fine. Can you get me some water?"

"Not until I see you," I demand.

"Get the water, Sam. I'm not going anywhere," she replies weakly.

Hastily, I snag a bottle of the complimentary water from the bar before hurrying back to the door. "I have the water and I'm coming in."

"I'm fine, Sam. Just pass the water in."

"Yeah, not happening." I fling open the door and find Iris lying with her head against the bowl of the toilet, one hand holding her stomach while the other pulls her long hair back so it doesn't dip into the contents of her stomach she just expunged. Her coloring is non-existent, but it's the terrified expression on her face that holds me captive. Dropping to my knees, I plead, "Iris, sweetheart, what is it?"

"I'm a wreck, Sam."

"Whatever it is, we'll get through it together."

A spark of her fierceness lights her eyes before fatigue glasses them over. "Damn straight, we will." She presses her hand against her lower stomach again, bringing me to the brink of the edge of terror while clinging to the side of a toilet seat in a foreign country.

"Iris, just tell me," I plead, a note of desperation entering my voice.

"Everything is changing, Sam. Everything. I was hoping to wait until we got home. I wanted to bring you to Akin Hill to the spot where you proposed."

"If you don't get on with it, you might have to share your toilet with me," I warn her.

"Anxious?" My frantic nod causes a glimmer of the smile I love to tip the edges of her lips. "Then imagine how you'll feel when this little one arrives in about seven months." She reaches over and presses my hand against her abdomen to the exact spot she's been holding.

My jaw unhinges and I gape at Iris. Her buoyant laughter over my reaction causes her stomach to unsettle again.

That's when I get my first lesson in fatherhood—the importance of taking care of expectant mothers. I spend the next few moments kneeling behind Iris, holding her hair back, as she upends her dinner from last night. Then I carry her back to bed and order dry toast from room service.

She protests, "We're supposed to meet Cal and the team in thirty."

"They can wait or they can do it on their own. My primary objective just became the welfare and safety of you and this little one." I lean down and press my lips to the space between her hips that holds our child.

Her hands thread through my hair. "*Čhaŋtéčhičiye,* Sam. You and this little one are my world."

I lift my lips from her soft skin and give her the same words. "I love you too, sweetheart. Both of you. Now, get some rest. I'll deal with Cal."

LATER THAT NIGHT, Pete teases Iris about training the baby while in the womb. "Think about it? If your kid becomes one of us, there would be one less future team member to train. Do they make earwigs in baby size?"

She punches him in the arm before I wrap my arms around her and say, "You have to knock that shit off, babe. Someone's going to hit back and then I'm going to have to ask someone to kill them."

Cal muses, "Just think, we have a designated driver for the next however many months."

Iris sends Cal a glare that could fry an egg, but doesn't dispute his claim as she sips on sparkling water while the rest of us indulge in Coke and red wine—a favorite of hers.

"You know if you'd have ordered it, faked it. Sam could have drank it for you. Then we still wouldn't know," Pete points out as he pours more of the local favorite.

Iris curls into my arm draped over her chair. Then she drawls, "Pete, your problem is you'll accept a woman who will fake things. Sam takes better care of me than that."

The group howls with laughter when Pete turns as red as the can he's just used to top off his glass.

Cal voices a question, "So, what does this mean going forward for work?"

Iris gives him the same information she told me earlier. "I'll find out at my next checkup. For now, nothing changes."

I glare down at her. "Oh, things are going to change. No more crazy ass stunts until our child is born."

Cal lifts his glass. "I second that."

Iris appears moderately frustrated and appears to debate protesting until I press a kiss against the top of her head and dare her in my best evil villain voice, "Come. Join me in communications." Reverting to my own voice, I add, "We serve cookies."

"Plus he has access to real bathrooms most of the time," Pete tacks on. We all turn incredulous eyes in his direction. "What? Isn't that something a pregnant woman might want to know about?"

Iris leans forward and squeezes his hand. "It absolutely is. Thanks for looking out for me, Pete."

When she does, I catch sight of Cal's face. There's a yearning on it that's hard to miss. He's mentioned to me privately on different occasions he's uncertain about where Libby now stands with her desire to have a family. It's plain as day that Cal still wants one. I make a mental note to have a conversation with him about it later in the week.

But those plans are thwarted when Cal announces the mission is terminating early. "We have no new leads."

Iris lets out a frustrated hiss. I jerk my head before saying, "What she didn't say."

Everyone chuckles. My comment even elicits a brief smile from Cal. "On a good note, I've arranged transportation to get us home by 1600 tomorrow. Debrief should be fairly short with the help of God"

I ask the question everyone else wonders. "Big plans?"

Cal shoots me a disbelieving look. "The Akin ball? It's tomorrow night."

Iris flaps her hand. "Yeah, we figured the job would go long. We RSVP'd before we left we wouldn't be able to make it." I make a sound of agreement.

Cal doesn't bother to acknowledge our response as he pushes to his feet. "Wheels up at 0600." With that news, he strides away.

Pete shoves to his feet, sucking down the rest of his drink. "I'll see you guys on the plane. If this is our last night, I plan on making it a memorable one." He scurries away, leaving just me and Iris at the table.

She trails her fingers up my arm. "What do you want to do on our last night here in Barcelona?"

I cup her cheek and smile down into her glowing eyes. "I want to spend time with my wife getting to know every change in her body—intimately."

Her voice drops to a purr. "How intimate do you intend on getting?"

"The kind where we'll both be grateful we're not going to that damn ball tomorrow night."

Iris skates her fingers up the inside of my leg. "Then what are we still doing here?"

I shove my chair back and reach for my wife's hand. "We're leaving."

45

NINETEEN YEARS AGO FROM PRESENT DAY

SAMUEL

I BATHE my wife's forehead with a damp cloth right before another contraction hits. She grips my wrist hard enough to snap the bones before wailing, "*Zasranec*!" at the top of her lungs. On the downside of the contraction, she pants, "Why did you put this thing inside me?"

I open my mouth to respond before she jerks my head down for a kiss. "Oh, God, Sam. We're going to be parents soon. What the hell do we—do I?—know about that?"

Pushing back sweaty ringlets of hair that keep managing to escape the band across her head, I remind her of the same thing I've said over and over the last six hours. "It doesn't matter what we know or don't know—we'll learn together."

Her eyes glow and her mouth opens just before another keening wail escapes. The contractions are practically on top of one another. I rub my free hand, the one with feeling still circulating through it, over the mound of our child. "Soon we'll get to meet you, little one." Neither of us wanted to find out if we were having a daughter or son. I recall the conversation so clearly. "So much of our lives revolves around ferreting out information, Sam. Can't we just have one secret? Keep this little one tucked away as our own just for a while longer?" Iris begged me plaintively on the day of the sonogram. We'd asked the technician to step out of the room briefly so we could have this discussion privately.

We decided together we wouldn't find out until this moment. Our now.

Iris pants maniacally before reminding me, "Rachel Elizabeth for a girl. Bishop Calhoun for a boy."

I brace myself for wounds that might require my own hospital stay in the event I can't pull back before another contraction comes on before daring to press my lips against my wife's. "I've got it, sweetheart."

She growls. "That's why I refused the drugs, Sam. You're getting this right."

I chuckle before reminding her, "You're better at target practice than I am. Do you think I was going to risk you getting even if I slipped a 'Lukie' or 'Winston' in there?"

Iris visibly shudders right before another contraction hits. Her voice wails, "Saaaaaaaammmmmm!" Her body arches forward before she flops back on the bed. She begins panting differently. "I have to push."

Just then, the door swings open and Iris's OB-GYN strolls in. "I heard that, Iris. And you're right. It's time to push." As if conjured by air, the room is suddenly filled with people circling the once magical bubble that seemed to encapsulate me and my wife. Screens are erected, a nurse with a sympathetic smile moves to Iris's left side, and I remain on her right.

Despite the long hours we've been at the hospital, once my determined wife decided it was time to push, it takes five attempts before Rachel Elizabeth is born. I don't even have time to cry until she's laid in my arms for the first time, wailing away. Then, after I lay her on her mother's breast, a crest of emotions drags me under as I witness the perfect beauty of her face nestled next to her mother's.

"The only two women I'll ever love," I manage, as I fling the wetness from my eyes. A drop lands on Iris's cheek but it's mingled with so many of her own I doubt she notices. But I do.

It's a memory I swear I'll never take for granted because everything I could ever want is right here in my arms.

With that, I bury my head on the side of Iris's bed and weep. I don't race out of the room to tell the members of our family there's a new Akin to celebrate. Let them wait.

I need a moment with my whole world.

46

NINETEEN YEARS AGO FROM PRESENT DAY

SAMUEL

My head is throbbing so badly, it feels like it's going to explode. I've been up half the night trying to prevent an attack on the Alliance network, but Iris doesn't seem to realize that or care. I can't be certain which.

She's fussing as she paces back and forth with Rachel in her arms. "I can't stand this, Sam. She won't stop crying."

Wearily, I ask, "Did my mother say anything when she dropped her off?"

"Nothing. This came up overnight and the pediatrician said she can only see her at three."

That gets my attention. "Three? We're supposed to be wheels up at two!"

She shoots me a fulminating glare. "No kidding, Sam. Are you even listening to what I'm saying?"

"I am. Our daughter is sick and you're not going to be able to go on the mission," I summarize.

There's a deadly silence broken by only Rachel's soft cries as she nestles in her mother's arms. Without raising her voice, Iris questions, "Me? Why not you?"

Exhaustion permeates every pore of my body, so I don't think before I open my mouth. "Because you're her mother, and she wants you."

"Because you—her father—haven't once left your cave to see if she's all right, Sam! Rachel is running a 102.4 fever, for Christ's sake. Don't you care?" Mount Iris is on the verge of erupting.

My head pounds harder, causing the leash on my own temper to slip. "I never expected it would be like this." The words escape unbidden. Ever since we had the baby, there have been endless nights of no sleep, missing my wife when she's lying in bed next to me, and frantic moments interspersed with overwhelming relief—many of which we're not around for.

Even the bouncing of our daughter stills as Iris pins me with a glare. "What? Being a father or our marriage?"

I'm so deep in my thoughts I don't consider my response or how Iris will take it. "Yes."

Iris absorbs the blow much like I've seen her do in training. Reaching into her back pocket, she whips out her cell phone and dials a number. I have no idea who she's calling until she speaks. "I can't go. No, I'm fine; it's Rachel who's ill." She turns her back on me to mutter, "Why don't you ask him all the details when you're together, Cal? I'm certain you'll enjoy having company while you lie to your wife about where you are and what you're doing for the next several weeks."

Once she disconnects the call, she slips the phone into her pocket. Without a word, she makes her way out of the kitchen, giving me no chance to apologize for my inconsiderate and completely out-of-line comment. I'm certain the reason Iris hasn't erupted into her famous temper is because of the precious life she's holding as she storms away.

But it's obvious she's more than furious with me; she's devastatingly hurt. I caused it. Just like I've been picking more and more of our arguments lately. I bury my fingers into my hair and rock my head back and forth. "What's happening to us?"

Is it Rachel? Immediately, I dismiss the idea. Our little girl unlocked the key to why we've been fighting for so many years to rescue children who have been kidnapped. She's the reason we fight for justice. One night by the fire, Iris confessed, "She's the reason I want to leave the world a better place, Sam. If I know one day she'll look back on the things I did, we did, with pride, then the sacrifices we're making while she's young are worth it." She's the center of our universe, the star in our sky.

I know it's not my feelings for my wife or hers for me. My heart still thumps crazily when she presses her lips to mine. It stirs my soul when her eyes flutter open as I drag my finger over the side of her cheek to wake her up when she's fallen asleep on the couch. I feel like I've won Husband of the Year when I surprise her with coffee in some godforsaken hell hole. No, it isn't us. As sure as I know my own name, I know Iris was meant to live on earth at the same time I do just so we could walk side by side. Partners in every way.

I'd be lying to myself if I didn't admit the primary source of Iris's frustration. Libby. Iris is sick and tired of watching Cal blossom in the field while Libby retreats into her shell. Every time we're Stateside, we spend time with the other couple. Between the avarice in Libby's eyes when she holds Rachel or the way she dismisses Cal's attempts to understand her business growth, my cousin has shut out everyone from her life.

But Iris sees through the crap and is constantly pestering me to reason with my friend. Two weeks ago it was, "Talk with Cal, Sam. He's going to lose her."

"They love each other too much." But that sounded lame to my own ears.

Iris scoffed. "Love will only carry you so far. Remember when we got home the other night and Libby wasn't home?"

"Of course I do."

Iris plowed on. "She was in Atlanta on a job."

I frowned. "Really? That's great."

"Cal didn't know it." Iris dropped that bomb.

"That's not possible," I argued.

Iris flung up her hands in exasperation. "This is exactly my point. What do we talk about at home?"

"Rachel, the family, our work, and our hopes for the future." I rattle off the top of our dinner table conversation list immediately.

"Think about what you just said."

Now, I am. Frantically. When I circle back to the words I flung at Iris carelessly, I panic. I race out of the kitchen to overhear her on the phone with my mother. "No, Lukie. I won't be going on this trip; just Sam. I guess they don't need a translator." There's a pause before she says, "If the doctor says it's nothing more serious than an ear infection, we'd love to. Maybe we can talk Libby into it as well. Great, I'll let you know."

After she hangs up, she shoots me a glare hot enough to fry an egg. "You have sixty minutes until you're expected at the office. I'd appreciate you spending a few of them with your daughter while I take a quick shower."

Spinning on her heel, my wife storms away from me, unwilling to forgive just yet that I displayed even a moment's doubt—even for a second—about her and the miracle we created between us. Heading down the hall to Rachel's nursery, I pause at the door. Looking back over my shoulder, I get a glimpse inside the double doors ajar to our master bedroom to find my wife crumpled on her knees silently weeping.

And I damn well know if I were to walk in there to try to make up for my stupid mistake right now, she'd rebuff me. *Rightfully so, asshole. You just told her you regret her and your daughter.* Vowing to make up for the wrong I just caused her, I slide inside the nursery to spend time with my little girl before I need to go pack.

FIFTY-FIVE MINUTES LATER, Iris waits by the door as I haul my duffle to the garage. "Be safe." It's the first words she's spoken to me of her own will since my outburst earlier.

In the last hour, my heart's been decimated like a disk thrown into an industrial shredder. The cool one word responses Iris has been treating me to are eerily familiar because they're the same way Libby acts when she's around the three of us when we return from one of our assignments. Suddenly, Iris's reminders for open communication between the two of us mean more than any sworn oath we've taken. Because the alternative strikes fear in my chest. *What if your marriage was as cold and empty as today has been? Is that what you want?*

I drop the bag to the side and yank my wife into my arms. "I'm sorry."

She struggles to free herself, but I capture her face between my hands. Tipping her head back, I see the wounds I've inflicted in her eyes. "I never meant for it to come out like that."

"Sam, you don't have time," she begins.

"They can wait for me or they can find someone else. This, you, us, is more important."

Her breath shudders out. "It can wait. The team can't. They need you."

"I need you, Iris. I miss you." I struggle to find the words.

Confused, she frowns. "I haven't gone anywhere."

I shake my head. "We both have. Rachel, work—we've been putting other things first and sacrificing ourselves. This morning, I reacted to that. I need you to know how much I love you, sweetheart." When she doesn't respond, I press my lips against her forehead. "Please believe me, Iris. I don't regret us. How could I when you're everything to me?"

She melts slightly in my arms for just a moment before pushing back. "You have to go."

My heart begins a free-fall. "Iris."

She leans forward and presses her lips over my heart before murmuring, "*Čhaŋtéčhičiye*, my love. Now, you're going to be late. We both know Cal's a little bitch when people are late."

"Well, if I'm going to be screamed at anyway . . ." I pull Iris to me and put every emotion—love, devotion, apology—into the kiss I give her. That's when I determine eternity isn't long enough because when our lips finally part, I say, "I never want to be far enough away from you where I can't do that."

She steps to the side so I can kick my bag through. Cupping my chin, she murmurs, "Then come home to us safely." Without waiting for my response, she closes the door between us because we know that's not up to us.

It never is.

47
IRIS

Sam is squeezing my hand so tightly that I know he can't go on.

Those particular memories are the worst he's held onto for the duration of our marriage. He's beaten himself up over and over again for giving me a shadow of a doubt that I, we, weren't where his heart was. Sharing them with our daughter brings up the shame that's riddled him for far too long—particularly in the immediate months after he returned from that mission. A mission, it turned out, where his computer skills helped crack the code to allow the Alliance team to rescue some Americans who were being unwillingly detained by ISIS.

I confide to Rachel, "If our relationship didn't have the foundation it did, the rise of the tides life was throwing at us might have knocked us to the ground. As it was, it was a test."

"Because you knew Dad didn't mean it?"

"Because I knew he meant every word," I correct my daughter. Despite her gasp, my eyes don't stray from my husband's devastated ones. "Rachel, when your life constantly fluctuates between living on the edge and maintaining a foothold in the 'real world,'"—I air quote—"those lines can blur. The longer we lived the life we swore to uphold, the more estranged we became from each other, our loved ones, even you. We couldn't turn to anyone else but each other to fix it."

"Even with each other, we had to work for it," Sam says quietly.

"Explain, Dad," Rachel demands point blank.

Sam gives up my eyes to seek out his daughter's. "The life we were leading was meant for people who had nothing to live for when we had everything to die for. For your mother first, and me, not long after, it became harder to dedicate ourselves to strangers when the people we were meant to protect were breathing beneath our roof."

Her face softens. "You mean me."

Sam nods. "And each other."

It's time to stop dancing around the subject. "Unfortunately, not everyone agreed with us." *Not then*, I add silently.

My words penetrate and Rachel slowly stutters, "You always said . . . said that, 'Life's biggest regret isn't the words failed to be spoken; it's the ones you willingly don't speak.'"

"That's the truth, darling. Whether it's with a professor, an employer, or a lover." I ignore my husband's growl. "Speak. Don't let words fester inside. Doing that can cause a meltdown that can change your whole life."

"Or cause the ruin of someone else's." Sam sighs.

"Exactly." Rachel eyes me thoughtfully as my words begin to penetrate. "It took a few precious seconds for years' worth of communication failures to surface, almost leading an entire family to certain tragedy."

"Do you think about it often?" Rachel probes.

"Which part? The fight your father and I had?" Rachel nods. "Absolutely. I wouldn't be human if I didn't."

"You hold it against him?" Rachel is shocked.

"Not at all. But I appreciate the fact that at that moment—in our own way—we reached our own precipice. So easily, we could have fallen over the cliff and never returned if we hadn't recalled the pillars of our marriage."

"Love and communication," Rachel murmurs.

"Exactly. So yes, I will never forget it. To forget is to dishonor everything that happened before and since. I remember every time I see you, your father, and Bishop smile. Every moment we laugh as a family."

"I thank God every time your mother kisses me, every time she tells me she loves me," Sam declares without missing a beat.

My own smile creases my face when he reaches up and brushes his lips against mine. "The idea is to learn as much from the times that we're ashamed of as much as we do from the moments we're proud. Both teach us valuable lessons."

Rachel contemplates our words for long moments without saying anything. "What made you both give it up?"

I leap off the arm of the couch and drop down next to my firstborn child. "That's easy. You."

"What? Me?"

I nod before giving her my own guilty truth. "You were starting to beg me not to leave every time I packed to go. One day, I decided I couldn't do it anymore."

Stunned, Rachel leans forward and asks Sam, "Dad? What did you have to say about it?"

"I was all for it."

My daughter's nose scrunches. "Because you didn't want Mama in danger any longer?"

"In part," he admits freely. "But this was her decision, Rach."

"I just wish it had happened a few weeks sooner."

"Why?"

Why indeed. Sam's hand is suddenly covering my own. The door behind us remains stubbornly closed. I say a quick prayer that the patient Erika's with is safe because we're about to enter shark-infested waters with my own child.

And there's no life raft for her in the room.

48

EIGHTEEN YEARS AGO FROM PRESENT DAY

Iris

"MAMA, don't go! You always go away!"

My heart aches at her little girl plea, but I have to go. There's another child out there who needs my skills and the decisions I've made haven't been fully discussed with the powers that be. *Though that's coming*, I vow. To my daughter, I say simply, "I have to."

Petulantly, she demands, "No. Let Daddy go. You stay here with me. I miss you too much." Then she rattles off in perfect Russian, "I don't like it when you both go."

Taken aback, I grin at her incredible language skills before the heartache on her little face causes my smile to evaporate. The pain in my own chest almost does me in as I drop to my knees in front of the little girl Sam and I created. On the outside, she has my perfect black ringlets, but her skin and eyes are pure Sam. Her spirit is a combination of both of ours—cautious like him, daring like me. I love her more than I ever could love a single human being, with perhaps the exception of her father.

I tug one of her curls perfectly straight, extending it all the way down to her little waist. "It's only supposed to be a week, love bug. You won't have time to miss me. Besides, you'll be staying with Nana."

She scrunches her nose with its dusting of freckles. "I'm not a bug, Mama. And Nana isn't you."

I ignore the guilt each word of Rachel's causes because I'll never get on the plane this afternoon otherwise. Instead, I tap each of her perfect tiny freckles and whisper, "I think we were both kissed by them."

"Eww! That's icky! Get them off, Mama!" Rachel shrieks, momentarily distracted. She runs around me in a circle scrubbing her hands over her nose and cheeks.

My laughter almost causes me to fall on my bottom as she narrowly avoids a header with the back of the couch and a bookshelf. Finally, she races back up and grabs both of my cheeks between her still pudgy fingers. "You promise you'll come home soon?"

"Soon," I promise, though soon has been known to extend on more than one occasion. I can pray this time it won't. I really need to have a conversation with Rick about ending my time with Alliance. I can't do it anymore. I've dedicated so many years to rescuing people all over the world; I don't want to lose Rachel because I can't be here.

It's time to retire.

I've been thinking about this for more than six months. Sam has left the decision in my hands, reminding me I can set the terms of my retirement. "It can just be from active fieldwork, Iris. This way you can be home with Rachel. Then the team won't lose someone with your skill set."

But the problem isn't just Rachel. It's how divided I feel from Libby. With every moment my daughter grows up with this divide between me and her godmother, it forces the issue of how much I need to start rebuilding the bridge I tore down between us by lying with the sin of omission. *It's too bad she'll never know how much I advocated on her behalf for Cal to pull his head out of his ass.* My lips curve wryly over the amount of grief I shoveled at Cal from the time I officially became a member of his team. Obviously he wasn't affected by the amount of insubordination on the job or I'd have been fired a lot sooner for calling my boss a fuck on a regular basis for not telling his wife the truth about what it is we do. "I'm certain he'll be thrilled when I'm no longer around to give him hell."

Just then a pair of well-worn boots into my line of . I tip my head back and beam up at Sam as he offers me a hand. Rachel's now skipping around the vast space of our living room when he pulls me into his arms. "You decided?"

I nod. "It's too hard to leave her now, Sam. I'll sit down and talk specifics with both Cal and Rick when we're back, but I have to tell him today this is it. I can't leave Rachel anymore."

My husband's fingers trail beneath my hair to run up my back. "Whether it's right or wrong for the team doesn't matter. What matters is what's right for this family—you, me, and Rachel."

Before I can reply, the front door opens without warning. "Who's ready to spend the week with Nana?" Lukie calls out to Rachel.

Just like that, Rachel begins bawling. The three of us spend the next twenty minutes mopping up tears and making promises to the little girl in the room who has a hold of all our hearts. After she forlornly leaves with Sam's mother, he rubs his chin back and forth over the crown of my hair. "Just promise me something?"

"Anything. You know that."

"If I have to go away for the job, you won't make me promise to take you to Disney on Ice to make up for leaving," Sam begs.

My whole body begins to shake with suppressed laughter. "I won't but I might give that suggestion to Libby."

Sam whips me around in his arms and lays a hard kiss on my lips. "You are pure evil, sweetheart."

"You love it."

"I do." He rests his forehead against mine. For just a moment we drink in everything we hold dear—Rachel, family, home. Then we separate. Sam asks, "Are you ready?"

"Yes. Bags in the car."

"Then let's go. The sooner we're wheels up, the sooner we're back." He holds out his hand, which I take.

TWO HOURS LATER, I'm in my usual pre-departure mode of wanting to strangle Cal. "Well, maybe if your wife *knew* why you had to leave, Calhoun, she might be more understanding."

He opens his mouth to speak, but I instead face my husband who is tinkering on Cal's system to add in a live relay in the event we need more data in the field. "It's the same ole song and dance over here, babe."

Sam snickers before muttering abstractly, "You won't have to listen to it for much longer."

Something inside me relaxes at his words. "That's the truth."

Cal, not even paying attention to the two of us, blurts out, "There was something different today. It was like we'd finally connected in ways we haven't in a while."

"What do you want me to say, Cal? Congratulations?" I drawl.

His eyes narrow briefly before they crinkle at the corners. "Actually, I'm surprised you haven't. It's our sixth wedding anniversary."

My jaw falls open. Sam, pausing in his coding, laughs. "Well, we have multiple things to celebrate."

"Sam," I warn him. Cal in a good mood before a mission is a rarity, one the team has rarely enjoyed over the last few years.

"No, Iris. Tell him. I think you'll be surprised by his reaction."

"Tell me what?" Cal's brow furrows. It must be because he and Libby are back on track, but Cal's not demanding answers. He appears genuinely concerned.

Frantically, my head whips around to Sam. He mouths, "You're ready."

I am. I know I'm ready. It's time to step from working my job in the dark to living my life in the light. I study Cal's face closely when I announce, "I'm retiring."

For long moments, there's an almost eerie quiet in the room. Then he probes gently, "Rachel?"

I fumble for words. "Yes. It's hard . . . too hard. I can't leave my daughter anymore."

Sam speaks up. "It's the right decision for Iris, Cal."

My boss nods thoughtfully. "I can appreciate that. You're a family."

My mind is whirling with the craziness of this conversation. *Libby, what did you do to your husband in bed this morning?* I want to pick up the phone and ask her, at the very least taunt Cal with it, but something holds me back. Because an overwhelming empathy for the sadness I recognize for the first time in the back of Cal's eyes washes over me. It's an emotion I recognize because I'm leaving Alliance as a result of it. "It's becoming harder for you to leave her, isn't it?"

He reaches out and squeezes my shoulder. "Despite the numerous times you've given me crap, Iris, I love Libby. Leaving her side has never once been what I wanted to do. But like you and the others, we didn't have a choice."

I want to shake him and tell him he had a choice to let her in. Instead, feeling like maybe, after all these years, Cal finally appreciates the loneliness that's forced his wife to rebuild her walls, I murmur, "I can't believe we have to go today of all days." Hastily I add, in the event he turns from Dr. Jekyll into Mr. Hyde, "Not that I'm not excited, it's just . . ."

"I know." Cal's voice is exasperated. "The timing sucks."

Looking over my shoulder, Sam mouths, "I love you." Mouthing the Lakota version back to him, I try to get Cal's mind off Libby and back to my announcement about retiring. "It will be good not to leave Rachel all the time."

"She'll be thrilled one of you will be home all the time. Remember, I know Lukie."

Cal's dry words make me grin. I can't prevent the bubbly, "I'm so happy, Cal. So excited."

"You and me both, Iris." His face leans closer so I can absorb his next words into my soul. "Because I know with you here, you'll also protect Libby if anything happens. Won't you?"

Somehow, my lips curve into a smile that's a promise.

Then my heart stops.

Because that's when Cal brushes his lips gently against mine for half a heartbeat. In my estimation, it's a beat too long. But for the first time in over a decade of knowing him, I find myself on the direct receipt of a Calhoun Sullivan smile when he lifts his head. "Thank you."

Immediately, any peace between us is over when I gasp and immediately swipe the back of my hand across my lips. Cal's face turns affronted when I shout, "Are you crazy? What the hell was that kiss for?"

Cal rears back as if I slapped him. "What do you mean? Siblings kiss all the time."

Sam, who surged to his feet leaving his coding trance behind when he heard my shout, drops back into his chair with a roar of laughter. "What the hell makes you think that?"

"You, you jackass," Cal snarls.

My face twists as if I've swallowed something distasteful. "Trust me, Sam does not kiss Evie and Lisa on the cheek, let alone like that."

"He kisses Libby," Cal accuses.

I open my mouth to correct him on his misconception, but Sam begins chortling. "Did you seriously think I was kissing your wife on the lips all these years?"

Cal is clearly trying to hold his discomfort at bay when he realizes he made a miscalculation. "Well, yes. Twice. Every time you see her."

Sam saves his work before maneuvering out from around Cal's desk, beckoning me to join him. Eyeing Cal as if he's been taken over by an alien, I quickly move into my husband's arms begging, "Do you have any mouthwash?"

Cal sneers at that comment. Sam shakes his head. "Be nice. Cal made a mistake. Now, help me fix it."

"What? With a lobotomy? Cal just had his lips on mine!" I screech.

My husband places a finger over them to silence me. "If he meant it in any way other than what he said, he'd already be dead. Now, Cal," Sam twists his head and locks eyes with a chalk-faced Cal. "This is what you see when you watch me greet Libby."

Sam presses a quick kiss to the corner of my mouth and then the other side where Libby's dimples lie. Instinctively, I do the same to him.

Cal grumbles, "That was two . . ."

I drawl sarcastically. "Kisses on their dimples. Something they used to do as babies. Did you ever catch Nancy greeting Marcus and Winston like that?"

Cal swallows audibly before putting voice to his heart. "Everything I've learned about family, I've learned from watching Libby."

Okay, that was really sweet. I'll have to remember to tell that to Libby one day. Right now, I'm too busy accepting a kiss from my husband that wipes out the terrible feel of Cal's lips on mine.

I shiver in Sam's arms and thank the Lord Libby wasn't there to witness that disaster.

49

EIGHTEEN YEARS AGO FROM PRESENT DAY

Iris

"We've accepted the blame for other people's mistakes long enough. That ends now," Sam shouts at his mother. He lifts Rachel into his strong arms and turns to make his way to the door.

I don't immediately follow him. Instead, I stand in place and let the threat Lukie and Winston just leveled at us wash over me.

Not long after we first arrived to pick up our little girl, they invited us into the parlor. Stiffly, they proclaimed, "We'll be seeking full custody of Rachel since you can't seem to make the right decisions about her welfare in supporting . . . that man . . . through the trauma your cousin is experiencing."

The life I sacrificed to save those who couldn't save themselves meant nothing. All that mattered was that my best friend walked into Alliance at the worst possible time, when her emotionally devoid husband decided to express something beyond the woman he loves with everything inside his heart. Now, the Akin family—especially Libby—is convinced I've been committing adultery with Cal—a completely ridiculous notion to the three people who were actually in that room for the joke of a kiss.

We can't share what we were doing together or where we were going. We can't tell the truth or we risk the people we just rescued.

On the night we came home, eager to hold Rachel against our heart, we're immediately attacked not with sticks and stones but with clubs and boulders. Even though I don't share their blood, I thought after all this time I was accepted as a member of this family, that my opinion mattered. I'm conscious of every breath each of us takes in the room. I'm conscious of the fact I'm letting them sit there and judge me, the woman who loves their son. I give this once more chance, not for my sake but for my husband's. "I love Sam with everything in my heart, every part of my soul. What you're hearing is not true."

Winston starts to speak, but Lukie stops him. "Don't you dare call Libby a liar in this house. She brought you into this family long before Sam fell prey to your charms."

A dark cloud falls over my vision. I rely on my training not to give in to the agony pulsating through me. I have to be in control to think, not to react recklessly. Right now, only one person has that right and that's Libby. So, I remain as still as possible waiting for Winston's and Lukie's next moves. Only, they're too polite to throw me out and I'm just perverse enough to wait for them to force me to leave.

That is until I hear the only words that could make me give up my game. Rachel's voice echoes through the hall. "Mama! Let's go home. Daddy promised ice cream."

"I'm ready, ladybug," I call out. Lowering my voice, I taunt, "After all, since I'll be in town for the foreseeable future, there's no need for you to come back here." I direct the comment with unerring accuracy at Rachel's angry grandparents.

Winston flinches. Lukie's eyes narrow. Not giving them a chance to respond, I toss my hair and saunter out the door, closing it softly behind me.

"WHAT'S YOUR PLANS FOR TODAY?" Sam asks as he slips on his suit coat six months later. He frowns at me when I stride into our walk-in closet and come out with a suit and heels. "While it's possible my mother might try to drop by, I'm not certain you need to be that dressed up."

I smooth a hand up his chest after letting my shoes clatter to the floor with a thunk. "That's because Rachel and I don't plan on being here."

His arms wrap around me. "Where are you going?"

"Alliance."

The surprise on his face is natural since I've taken a temporary hiatus from work, citing personal reasons. This wasn't long after the night we picked up Rachel. Fortunately, Cal dispatched the papers with undue haste, likely because of his own hell since Libby walked out on him. The look on his face was that of a child when he asked, "We haven't lost you for good, have we? You're still going to be a part of this family?"

Sam's arm was around my shoulder when I met Cal's eyes head on and informed him, "I don't know."

As I turned to walk away, his frightened voice shouted, "We're not disabling your badge. Come see us!"

I've used it only a few times, like when I had to tell Cal his beloved wife, who was filing for divorce from him, had removed her wedding rings. I later told Sam, "I felt like I was kicking a puppy."

Sam, who was inspecting my jaw from the swing Libby landed on my cheek, said, "I don't fucking care. He needs to figure this shit out on his own. I refuse to let Cal's crap drag our lives down along with his."

Later that night he and Libby fought like never before when Sam told her she needed to talk to Cal. After defending me, standing at my front, back, side, Sam declared Libby unwilling to listen. "What you saw wasn't what it was. Please, Libby, stop being so stubborn and talk with Cal. For all our sakes."

Being curled closely to Sam, I heard her scathing response. "For all your sakes? You have a stake in this, Sam? Beyond the fact your wife was kissing my husband? No. You're supposed to be my family, my protector, someone who loves me unconditionally."

Sam retorted, "That's supposed to be your husband."

Tears leaked from my eyes when Libby drawled, "Well, look how well that turned out. He ended up with your wife. Must be a side effect of loving me."

After she hung up on him, Sam declared, "You are not to absorb this. This isn't your fault. Too many mistakes have been made, and none of them were preventable."

I open my mouth to release the ball of guilt I'm holding in a rush of furious words, but find the effort futile. Sam and I have disagreed far too much over Cal and Libby in the past. Right now, we're holding each other aboard a lifeboat made of bamboo and vine that's floating in a tropical storm. There's nothing we can do but support the decisions we each have made—past and present.

While I wasn't ready to confront my future then, now it's time for me to go into the office to negotiate the rest of my life. Sam just offers me the comfort of his strength while I pull together the words I need. "I took oaths I'm bound to for life. I made promises to myself and others. I did the right thing and hurt the wrong people."

"You never meant to," Sam defends me.

"No, I didn't. But I finally realized my reward is waiting for me with you, with Rachel. I pay for it by knowing there's no avoiding being persecuted for what I didn't do."

"Iris, she can't blame you forever."

"Can't she?" Before Sam can argue on my behalf, I lay my fingers across his lips. "She has every right to. When we lived together, I blathered on and on over umpteen bottles of wine about how communication so critical to a relationship, how a lack of it could kill it. Look at what we helped contribute to —albeit inadvertently."

"It's Cal who never opened up to his wife," Sam argues.

"But I chose not to speak. Even though I knew, I made the choice. Right now, if you were Libby, what's worse?" I press my lips against his chin before I move away to get dressed.

Sam doesn't reply.

"ARE you sure this is what you want, Iris?" Rick questions hours later. He's holding out a bottle of water he's just retrieved from his private refrigerator.

Instead of answering him, I gesture across his office to where Rachel is enthralled with the view and coloring quietly. "She's the most important thing in our lives, Rick. If something happened to one of us, it would be bad enough. But to both of us? We'd destroy the essence of that little girl." I accept the water and twist off the top, taking a long drink. "We both know with the new tech that Sam's testing, I could work from here and provide most of the services I do today."

"Most," Rick counters.

I tip my head in acknowledgment. "Most. We both know there's nothing better than on-site intel, but this is what I can offer."

His lips thin. "I rarely involve myself in the personal lives of my employees."

"Probably an excellent decision for your heartburn," I return.

He tips his bottle in my direction. "The better decision would be to stop drinking with Cal when we win a new contract."

Instinctively, my hand reaches up and touches my cheek at the mention of Cal's name. Emotionally, I can't do anything but associate his name with the last time I saw Libby. Then again, I refused to lie to her anymore. Seeing Rick's eyes narrow in on my fingers, I toss my hair and declare, "I can handle myself. The slap was worth it to see Libby's light begin to spark."

Rick leans forward to ask, "But at what cost, Iris?"

I turn my head so the only thing in my vision is Rachel. "As long as she's the only one who doesn't have to pay it."

"So, you're going to become this Stepford wife and mother?" Rick challenges.

My head whirls back in his direction before I snap, "No, if this doesn't work out, I'll find something else. I'll be Rachel's mother. But don't you think I've earned some peace?" A little voice inside me nags, *But will you be satisfied by it?*

Immediately contrite, he lifts his hands. "Absolutely. I just think you won't have to search very hard for work."

My head cants. "What are you thinking?"

Rick begins to lay out a job offer that would keep me at Alliance when he has international delegates who come into the office. He pledges, "Normal hours, Iris. I swear!"

I rise from my chair and hold out my hand to shake his. "Then draw up the contract."

"Mommy?" Rick and I both turn to where Rachel's sitting at the table. "I already have."

"You already have what, love bug?"

"A contract's a promise, right?" Rachel confirms.

"That's absolutely what it is, young lady." Rick strides over to the table and bends over my daughter's shoulder. His eyes widen fractionally. Then he bends over and whispers something in Rachel's ear. She giggles before carefully picking up a new crayon and adding to it. He nods succinctly. "Now it's perfect."

Suspiciously, I make my way over. "What are you two up to?"

"I'm good to sign this if you are, Iris." Rick gestures to my daughter's colorful handwriting.

I lean over to read it.

1. Mama will help with funny words.
2. She sleeps at home at night unless she REALLY can't. If that happens, Mr. Rick takes me out for ice cream.
3. Mama gets time off when she gets back to play with me. So does Daddy.
4. This makes everyone happy.

The End.

Rick, the giant marshmallow he is, murmurs, "She's going to change the world someday. I just hope I'm around to see it."

Huskily, I respond, "You'd better be."

"Anything else you want to add?" he offers.

"No." Because my precocious daughter has managed to sum up exactly what we all need. My chin lifting, I challenge him, "Are you ready to sign it?"

"Dam—"

I cough.

Rick corrects himself. "Darn tootin'. This is one of the finest negotiations I've ever had the pleasure of being in. Let me just call in Svetlana to witness it." He moves over to the phone while I explain to Rachel what's about to happen.

Rachel squeals. "Really? You're going to keep your promise?"

I brush the loose hair out of her eyes. "For you, bug, I'll always keep them."

50

IRIS

Present DAY

"I REMEMBER THAT DAY SO WELL." Rachel's voice is barely a whisper but it's loud enough for me to hear.

"When you were accepted into Columbia, I asked Rick for the original to have it framed. He was honored to give it to me. It was the first contract you ever negotiated and you wrote it for a three-star admiral. Not everyone will be able to say that in their career."

"Particularly the fact he signed it and upheld it for the remainder of the time you worked for Alliance."

"Yes." I leave it at that and wait. There's something else bothering Rachel. Her body position with her palms pressed against the glass is a sure sign she's processing everything I just told her.

Finally, her frustration erupts. "I still don't understand."

Sam and I don't say anything, not because I haven't tried but because this is something Rachel has to work out on her own. Behind us the door opens and closes, but none of us turn to acknowledge Erika reentering the room.

"I've spoken with both of you, with Uncle Cal, even with Aunt Libby and somehow it still feels ridiculous to me."

"We know," Sam acknowledges quietly.

"You raised me to tell the truth, to acknowledge wrongs when they're happening."

"We did," Sam agrees.

"Then how could you all have lied to Aunt Libby for so long?"

I'm grateful when Erika speaks up from behind us. "It's not quite that simple, Rachel. We've discussed it."

"Oh, give me a break, Erika," Rachel jeers contemptuously.

Surging to my feet, I recite the words I know by heart considering the number of times I've read and reread the documents since I was twenty-two. "Intending to be legally bound, I hereby accept the obligations contained in this agreement in consideration of my being granted access to classified information. I hereby acknowledge that I have received a security indoctrination concerning the nature and protection of classified information, including the procedures to be followed in ascertaining whether other persons to whom I contemplate disclosing this information have been approved for access to it, and that I understand these procedures."

Rachel starts to interrupt, but I hold up a hand. I continue to paraphrase the oath I've signed every two years. "I have been advised that the unauthorized disclosure, unauthorized retention, or negligent handling of classified information by me could cause damage or irreparable injury to the United States or could be used to advantage by a foreign nation. Unless and until I am released in writing by an authorized representative of the United States Government, I understand that all conditions and obligations imposed upon me by this apply during the time I am granted access to classified information, and at all times thereafter."

"So, that gives you a right to withhold information?" she shouts.

"No, that makes me legally bound to," I hurl back.

"That's bullshit."

"Why?"

"Because that's not how the real world lives," she declares confidently.

Sam begins to speak, but I reach for my purse. I pull out a folded article I printed out that's been in the pocket of my bag for some time. I read it aloud, "The President recognized a Medal of Honor winner posthumously two years after succumbing to injuries from the shrapnel due to a hand grenade. The soldier was killed in Baghdad after tossing their body onto a grenade thrown into the gunner's hatch. The action saved the lives of four. The award was presented to the nineteen-year-old soldier's parents." I let my words sink in for a moment before I say quietly, "You may not believe in them, but each of us took that same oath. The young soldier who died, your father, and me. We accepted this oath freely, without reservation. Even if it meant we could never tell our families what we were doing—then or now."

Sam picks up where my words leave off. "Contrary to what everyone believed at first, we encouraged Cal to get your Aunt Libby a level of clearance she needed so she could know the bare bones about what the three of us were doing. He refused."

I let out a growl recalling the frustration I felt. Rachel's head snaps in my direction, but I don't speak, electing to let Sam's calm wash bathe over us both.

He chooses his words carefully in an attempt to do just that. "You heard your mother; part of our oaths is we would not reveal to anyone information pertaining our actions on behalf of protecting our government against enemies, foreign or domestic."

"Even if it meant watching your family fall apart?" Both of us bob our heads up and down, acknowledging the side we chose to protect and the battering of waves we inadvertently set rolling by our actions—to do nothing when our family was in danger of breaking apart. Rachel cries, "How could you put your country before the people you love?"

I lift the article and skip to the bottom. "'Four people are alive because this soldier embodied our values and gave his life.'" I pin my daughter in place with a ferocious glare. "Do you think a kid who should be a year older than you wanted to die?"

Rachel's voice is small when she finally responds, "No."

"That's right. No. I damn well bet his parents didn't want him to either. What happened between your aunt and uncle had absolutely nothing to do with our jobs, Rachel."

"But Mama, if you all could have told her . . ."

"What would it have changed?" I ask her wearily. "The problems between Libby and Cal were always there. Their world imploded because they constructed their lives in a sandcastle. A fantasy. The first time a wave tested it, all the walls crumbled."

Sam reinforces my declaration. "Just like us, they took vows to love each other. It's how they implemented those vows that made the difference."

"Are you saying words are all that's held them together?"

"Don't knock vows, oaths, and promises. Sometimes holding onto them are all that carry you through. Even pride is a poor crutch when it's swept away from you." Flashbacks of the confrontations with our families swirl through my mind. On Sam's face, I recognize the miracle that we managed to survive when so many couples wouldn't.

He holds out his hand and I grip it quickly. My love, my lifeline. He's always been my anchor amid the uncertainties life has thrown our way. I find the strength to tell Rachel the truth stamped on his face. My lips part and the words come rushing out. "By the time we came home from that mission, your father and I were branded as cheaters—against Libby, the family, moral values. All kinds of threats were made. Including . . ." I swallow around the knot that formed in my throat.

Silence permeates the room until Erika prods me, "Including what, Iris?" It's something Sam and I told Erika in our individual sessions, but not something Rachel's aware of. It's something we hoped to keep from her considering how close she is with her grandparents.

This secret is the kind of nightmare no parent wants to hold. Eventually, Karma will circle back when she's least expected to unleash her fury in retribution—something we've all learned in the last eighteen months. My head drops, unable to be supported by the pressure bearing down upon my shoulders. This is it. The test I've been expecting. There's a danger in sharing this information. Will the work Erika's done with my daughter make her strong enough to understand the actions taken were all out of love? Love for her?

That's when a miracle occurs. I feel Rachel's hand pushing my hair back. She angles her face down. "Mama? Just say it."

I choke out, "They tried to take you from me. That's the part I left out of the story the first time you heard it. They threatened during that time to sue your father and me for custody. That didn't let up until after Josh spoke to them after we were aboard the ship to save Libby—after Rick gave him the go ahead to release a little bit of information about who we were."

When my eyes connect with hers, my knees weaken. In them, I recognize she already knew the truth. She's been waiting for me to purge this last bit of poison from my own soul so we can move on. Tears burn a trail down my face when I let go of Sam to reach for her. "My baby."

Rachel surges into my arms whispering, "Always. Always yours."

Hearing her say that to me starts to take the edge off the memories of that part of our past, I sniffle. Almost immediately, Sam's handing out tissues to us both.

51

EIGHTEEN YEARS AGO FROM PRESENT DAY —OCTOBER 22

Iris

"SOMETHING'S HAPPENED," I declare to Sam.

Sam looks up from the earpiece he's tuning to focus on me warily. "Define something. The last time 'something happened' and you came rushing in here, I was checking you over for bruises."

I wave my hand. I still want to contact Libby to give her lessons on how to hit someone without hurting herself, but Sam has flatly said, "No. No way. Let Cal teach her after he figures their shit out."

Fortunately, Cal might have found a way to do just that. After a long talk Rick directed us to have with Libby's brother, Josh now understands what really happened and—at a high level—what we do for a living.

I'm not certain what he said to Libby, his parents, or Lukie and Winston, but there was a tentative invitation from Sam's parents for dinner on our machine an hour ago which I relay to Sam. "Any time you want, Sam, Iris. We would love the chance to speak with you both and to see Rachel. We just . . . miss her so much."

It was hard for me to harden my heart against the plea in the older woman's message, but I will leave it up to him though I remind him, "The more people who realize that nothing has changed between us, the more people who will mention that to Libby. The better chance we have of breaking through."

Sam's jaw tics. Before he can say anything, a recognizable sound of two short beeps and a long one—Cal's personal distress signal—comes over the intercom. Since Cal's voice doesn't follow it, we take it for what it is—a summons to his office. Sam stands from behind his desk and walks around, his hand outstretched. I clasp it without hesitation as we make way for the door. "What assignment is this about? How does Cal know I'm here?"

"He doesn't."

I dig in my heels. "Then why am I coming with you?"

"Because lately the only time he uses it is when he has news about Libby. It isn't Cal who needs your support, it's me." Sam's tone is aggrieved.

With a light laugh, I get closer to Sam. "Poor baby. Now you might have an idea of what my life was like when Libby was pining for Cal during college."

Sam badges us into the elevator before using his fingerprints on the keyless panel to bring us up to the executive floor. Moments later, we burst into Cal's office to find him clutching his phone, oblivious to our presence. I close the door behind us while Cal hands his phone to Sam without a word.

Unabashedly, I peer over Sam's shoulder. What I see causes me to jerk back with a gasp. It's a picture of a sketch she drewp—I'd recognize her art anywhere. But it's the subject that has me reeling. Libby drew her impression of what she 'saw' the day Cal tried to act like a big brother for the first time in his life. I jerk the phone out of Sam's hands to get a better view of it. Purely as a woman, my heart breaks because I can feel the emotions Libby's been enduring—agony, suffering, and love. *Oh, Libby. I really wish you would have listened to me.* In the picture, in every stroke of Libby's hand, I can feel her love for Cal. Then I read what she wrote him and tears well up in my eyes. Even though she believes she's releasing him, she's chained by her love for him. The selflessness of my friend's heart overwhelms me and tears overflow. I gasp, "That's so beautiful."

Sam shoots Cal a confused look before he begins to comfort me. "Babe, she's letting him go."

"Because she loves him. God, are men that stupid? Libby loves Cal so deeply, she won't accept less than all of him. Since she figures she doesn't have it—not that it's true—she's setting him free so she can hold onto the memories." Lifting the phone again, my face contorts. "She's giving her blessing to your happiness, no matter what that is." Unable to say more, I bury my face deep into Sam's neck.

There's not a sound in the room but Cal's deep breathing. Then he flings out, "I don't care what anyone says, I will be waiting for my wife when she gets home. She's not going one more day without understanding it all."

Sam had been murmuring comforting words in my ear. They cut off abruptly when he lifts his head to address Cal. "Everything?" The hope in his voice is clear to me.

It must be to Cal as well who emphasizes, "Everything."

I feel the need to caution, "She figures you're already looking for the next possibility. Even with explanations, winning her back isn't going to be easy."

"Don't you understand? Without Libby, life has no possibility."

HOURS LATER, after finishing up with some translations needed for Interpol, I find Sam lounging in the common room. "Nothing happening?"

"Doesn't look like it."

"Have you made a decision about dinner with your family?" I ask pointedly.

His mouth opens to respond. Just as it does, an announcement comes across the television causing everyone—including me—to go static. "We interrupt this broadcast to bring you a special news bulletin."

"Saved by the bell." Sam leaps out of his chair.

Just as I'm about to unfurl my temper, Cal shouts, "Shut it, everyone! Let's see if we're going anywhere."

I still manage to hiss, "What is your problem?"

Sam growls, "I refuse to give them the chance to hurt you and I refuse to apologize for who we are. Where does that leave us?"

My heart thumps erratically against my breast bone. *With me helplessly in love with you.* But I don't get a chance to speak the words as the broadcaster's shaky voice sends chills down my spine. "The *Sea Force*, a luxury yacht that originated from Malaga, Spain four days ago, stopped in Funchal, Portugal for a day of excursions. Less than twelve hours after it departed the small island, an emergency distress signal was picked up by the USS *Lassen,* an Arleigh Burke class destroyer on maneuvers out of their home-port of Mayport, Florida. Only fifteen miles away, they quickly headed in the direction of the ship. Approximately five miles out, they received a communication. The *Sea Force* has been hijacked."

My mind stops listening at that point as I catch sight of Cal tearing out of the room without waiting to be called in by Rick. Every sense I have is on high alert. I inform Sam, "I'm calling your mother."

He scowls down at me. "We're going to talk about this now? Iris, with the way Cal took off it's likely . . ."

"You're going to need a translator," I conclude quietly. I have my cell phone in my hands when Sam lays his hand over mine.

"Are you sure? You've been home with Rachel for months," he reminds me.

I twist my head to the horror lining the broadcaster's face. The numbers flashing on the screen are unlike anything any of us have dealt with before—112 passengers and almost one hundred crew members. "Rachel will understand." I'm about to hit Send, but he stops me again.

"How can you be sure?"

A faint smile crosses my lips. "She wrote it into my contract with Rick. I have to sleep in my bed at night unless I really can't. If I explain it to her like that, she'll know, Sam."

He nods and removes his hand so I can call his mother to go pick up our daughter from the sitter. But before I can, a pale-faced Cal enters the room. "Sam, Iris. I need you both for ten minutes. The rest of you are on standby," he says before he turns and heads back down the hall toward a private conference room.

Once we're inside, he begins without preamble. "You both have the right to refuse this mission and there will be no repercussions. I, myself, will be going out to the *Lassen.*"

One day, years from now, I might forget the look on his face. God, I hope I do because it's filled with the kind of nightmarish horror one should never be witness to in real life. I tentatively reach for his arm. "Cal?"

Cal jerks away, like a wild animal. Sam slides me slightly behind him. "Cal, what is it? Just tell us. We can handle it."

He braces his hands on the table for a few seconds before he shakes his head. "No, you can't. You shouldn't have to."

"We're your friends," Sam counters.

He nods. "I know. That's why I should do this alone. That way if this mission goes to hell, the family won't . . ."

Sam and I say together, "The family?"

Cal curses roundly before he whispers her name almost soundlessly, "Libby."

Just her name. Nothing more.

But that's more than I need.

I round Sam and shove Cal so hard he stumbles. My voice cracks as I shout, "Libby? *Our* Libby? Is she on that ship? Is that what you're trying to say, you stupid asshole?"

Cal winces but doesn't deny it. "Yes."

"This is your fault, Cal."

"Iris," Sam warns.

"Don't you say a word, Samuel. It's because he couldn't tell her the damn truth. She wanted to give him everything of hers from the moment she met him. What did you give her in return, Calhoun?"

He stands there and takes everything I throw at him without saying a single word. It's Sam who has to wrap me up and growl in my ear, "Either you lock it down or *I* won't let you get on the bird that flies us out there. Do you understand me?"

I don't say a word.

Sam shakes me. "Do you? Because you can't do this now or Libby might die, Iris. Is that what you want?"

I shake my head, my eyes still locked to Cal's. The fury I've been holding back is being reined in only because Sam's right. We need Cal at his best to get Libby home. I shake my husband off with a jerk. "I'm going to arrange for childcare for my daughter. If that bird leaves without me, I'll just meet you there even if I have to swim to the *Lassen*."

I storm to the door when I hear Cal's voice behind me. "Iris? We'll all have it out when we get her back."

I lift my hand to acknowledge his statement on my way out the door to call Lukie. I can't say a word because if I do, I'll likely start crying. I don't have time for that.

Not now. Not when Libby's life is on the line.

52

EIGHTEEN YEARS AGO FROM PRESENT DAY—OCTOBER 23, 2300 HOURS GMT

SAMUEL

"SAM. TAKE A BREAK."

My head jerks away from the monitor I've been glued to for the last twelve hours. My eyes feel like sand has been ground into the corneas every time I blink but I can't—no, won't— stop. Not as long as I know there's one single person alive on the ship that's so close, I could run to her if I could walk on water. Which right now, I desperately wish I could. I jut my chin at the competent and lethal man standing in front of me. "Later."

"Five minutes won't make a difference," he argues, placing a cup of coffee at my elbow.

"Go bother someone else." But one side of my mouth quirks upward as I lift the coffee to my lips.

"I can't," Lieutenant Parker Thornton, SEAL team leader, says after thoughtful consideration.

Brow furrowing, I ask, "Why?"

"Because two-thirds of the team I'm relying on for comms so my team doesn't get killed is so focused on the life and death of a single woman, I have no reassurance whatsoever they are focused on the mission, such as it is."

I surge to my feet, the empty cup falling harmlessly to the deck. "Fuck you, Thorn. It's not my fault I'm handcuffed by your international jurisdiction."

"Hmm," is his only response.

"What the hell is that supposed to mean?"

"I've worked with you before, Sam. I don't recall you letting anyone or anything get in your way. What's holding you back?" he challenges.

The answer hovers between us without her name being spoken. He pushes away from my console. "The way I see it, the only person still managing to do her job is your wife."

I curse Thorn under my breath as he saunters away but the truth is, he's right. I know it, Cal knows it, and Thorn predicted this would happen the moment Cal admitted Libby was one of the hostages aboard the *Sea Force* when we boarded.

It was bad enough knowing Libby was on board to consider the state of her marriage. But the agony I'm feeling to get her off that boat is increasing minute by minute since Iris had translated what was happening to Libby physically on board the luxury yacht. It's affecting us all. Iris and I came upon Cal in the passageway curled in a ball—ashen and trembling, no sign of our unshakable leader in sight.

We're all teetering on a precipice knowing damn well what will push us over.

Thorn is about to leave the bridge when I call his name. He pauses, "Yes?"

I jump up from my chair and slam it into place. "Come with me."

I storm past the SEAL who would have no problem killing me with his thumbs tied behind his back. My insolence to such a man is unusual, so I'm not surprised by his laconic, "Sir, yes sir."

But he follows me below deck. After he listens while I explain why Cal, Iris, and I are ready to launch our own offensive against the *Sea Force*, the only words he manages are, "Holy hell."

I give him a grim smile. "That about sums it up. Now, can I get back to work?"

He nods absently as he calculates what I just told him and how it impacts his mission parameters when I know the Alliance team has only one—get Libby out alive.

Just as I'm about to cross over the bulkhead, he calls out, "Sam?"

I turn to partially face him. "Yeah?"

"Don't tell Cal I said this but fuck the jurisdiction. Get us eyes and ears and do it fast."

I feel like I'm choking when I try to acknowledge his words, but I manage a quick nod before heading back up to the bridge.

I HEAR Josh's voice on a network broadcast being played about the events occurring on the *Lassen* and Libby as I slide my way past another firewall. Cal and Thorn are talking quietly in front of the screen. "Until Libby changed the game, there's no way I would have said this was a K and R," Thorn murmurs to Cal. My ears perk up. A kidnap and rescue?

Cal must read my mind. "What do you mean?"

"Look at the profiles of everyone on that boat, Cal. By no means is Libby the wealthiest. What does that tell you?"

I tune Cal out as the command line I entered gives me back a different response than the previous thousand times I've tried it. "Ensign, take a look."

The young Navy officer leans over my shoulder. He breathes, "Hell yes, open up for Daddy."

I type the command sequence the cruise line assured me should have given me access to their bridge hours ago and pray. By some miracle, this time, it works.

With a whoop, I call out, "Cal! Check this out! We just got eyes into their bridge."

Cal stalks over and shoves aside the ensign. "Let me see." After scanning the screen, he shakily chastises me, "Took you long enough."

"Would have been easier if we could have forced the issue," The ensign drawls laconically. Cal whips his piercing stare at the Navy officer. "Don't get me started on international law. Bane of my existence."

"I just bet." Cal returns his focus to the screen in front of me. He demands, "Is there any way to get them any kind of word without getting them killed?"

I warn him, "I can try, but I can't leave it up long." I click a few keys on my smaller keyboard that I wired into the more powerful Navy mainframe. Within seconds, the screen around the room are replaced with scripts. I begin cursing, "Come on you little bastard, let me . . . no. That's not the one I want. Not that console. I don't want it near the reflection." I shout to anyone in the room who can answer, "What's the other fucking console number?"

"Seven!" is shouted back.

I open up a new script line and think about what equipment I know to be at console seven. Finally, it comes to me, the water recycling system. Backing out of the system I was in, I begin scripting a new code on the fly where every third line has actual English amid the coding, "US NAVY" "FRIENDLY" "TURN SHIPS CAMERAS ON." Pressing Enter, I transfer from my monitor back to the single camera I spent hours hacking into, praying these guys are as tired as I am at having a gun pointed at their head when there's no hope. "Come on, come on, do your checks," I mutter as the pale-faced officer at console seven just sits like a limp puppet.

"Why did you just ask him to do that, Sam?" The captain asks me.

"Because while I can hack into most of the locations, it's going to take too much time. If he gets the balls to help me out, then we'll have eyes everywhere," I say grimly. "It's our best chance to be able to plan the attack."

"You don't think they'll notice," Cal asks, terrified.

"I think if they would, they'd have their own guys in the chair, not the crew."

"Look!" Thorn calls out.

All our heads snap forward as the first officer, previously slumped down—defeated, snaps to attention. His eyes narrow at the man who whirled in his direction holding a gun aimed at his forehead. "We need to cycle some water before we overheat and become a target."

We all catch our breath because, according to what we've learned about the system, it automatically conducts these operations unless they're stopped—which they haven't been.

"Then do it!" The terrorist screams. "Just do it!"

"Aye, aye, sir." Without a glance at the monitor in front of him, his fingers begin flying across the keyboard demonstrating a proficiency I easily recognize from one hacker to another. The man in front of me has been waiting for his chance and now he has it.

Pixel by pixel, the screen in front of me changes. My shout reverberates around the room. "We're getting eyes!" Just that quickly, my heart hits the floor when the images become clearer. "Oh, God. No."

The chatter mingled with elation drowns out everyone but the captain's authoritative order. "Throw them up on screen."

My voice is hoarse. "Sir . . ."

"What are you waiting for, Sam? Just do it," he persists.

My fingers begin the dance on my end as the first officer slumps back in defeat. I'm not certain what he was waiting for—maybe for someone to acknowledge he did a good job. If I could take the risk of contacting him again, I would do it in an instant. But right now, I'm relaying the horror he's been living to every man and woman standing in the room with me.

We wanted to know how bad it was and now we know it's worse. Even as Cal whispers, "Have mercy on their souls." I lay my hand over the monitor of my laptop and whisper words of thanks for this small chance, praying Thorn and his men can rescue the brave man who risked a bullet so we can save so few.

Not so many.

53

EIGHTEEN YEARS AGO FROM PRESENT DAY—
OCTOBER 24, 0800 HOURS GMT

SAMUEL

IRIS'S HANDS slip over my shoulders in comfort. "It will be okay, Sam."

I can't begin to face her, let alone myself. The full implications of everything that's happened on the *Sea Force* are just starting to settle in my mind. My heart feels like it's going to explode, enduring the agony of what I unintentionally supported over the years.

Because of a vow to support a mission.

I manage to croak out, "I don't think I can do it anymore."

I feel Iris's arms slide around me. "Don't make any rash decisions, Sam."

I lay my hands on top of hers before my breath jerks out, "How do I live with myself? With what we saw?" What's left unsaid between us is *What Libby endured?*

We're standing on the deck of the *USS Lassen*, the wind lifting my hair back away from my face. I came out here after over thirty hours of trying to find a way to penetrate through the systems of the *Sea Force*. It will be a long time before I can sleep without the nightmares I witnessed. I say as much to my wife.

Iris presses her lips to my shoulder before she reminds me, "What we need to focus on is healing."

"Absolutely." Turning, I pull her tight against me. "Has the doc said how long until Libby's ready to travel?"

"When we fly back, we can take her with us. She'll have to be checked out at a hospital Stateside, but then she can return . . ." Iris hesitates.

"Where?"

"I was about to say home but where is that, Sam? Is it with Cal?" Her head twists away. "You didn't see the way he shoved through everyone to get to her, but I did."

I easily read the concern on her face. "You're worried."

"Of course I'm worried!" she snaps. "We're where we are with your family because he couldn't have a damn conversation with her and she took rightful exception to what she believed was her husband kissing another woman."

"It was you," I protest stubbornly.

"With their issues, that should have made it better?"

I'm about to devolve into the same argument we've had about Cal and Libby in the past when I realize today is the day that all ends. My dedication to a friend means nothing in comparison to the devotion I have to my wife. Her unrest with this whole situation has almost foreshadowed this tragedy between our respective best friends. It's past time I admit to myself I've been an accomplice to the pain Libby's been enduring. "You're right."

"Sam, I refuse to . . . what?"

"You're right." A brutal wave of emotion crashes over me for what I've done. "How could I defend Cal's behavior all this time?" I turn my head away

Iris cups my cheek. "Because it's impossible to accept your heroes are human."

Startled, my eyes lock with hers over her stunning insight. Scrubbing a weary hand over my face, I sigh, "Christ, Iris."

Her next words are humbling. "We surround ourselves with people we need to get ourselves through our everyday. Regretting your choice would make you a different man, Sam. You're the only man I could ever love." She steps back, her fingers trailing off my face slowly. "I'm going to see if Libby's awake. If she is, I need to apologize for my part in whatever part of her pain I've contributed to. Then I'll be able to face what happens next."

I watch her as she turns and walks through the bulkhead leading to the lower decks. I've witnessed my wife's bravery on umpteen missions where her life has been in danger, never when her heart has been threatened. A surge of pride unleashes inside me. *That's my Iris.* She's walking into the unknown, facing potential condemning words head-on to give someone else a modicum of peace.

I nod, my remorse easing as I realize that not all my heroes had feet of clay. After all, the one I worship the most taught me the most important lesson—that love can't exist without communication.

Slapping my hand on the railing, I head back inside to locate Cal. It's time he knows my opinion on his silence.

DAYS LATER, the chopper circles the landing field at Alliance. Aboard is the team we left with plus one additional passenger. Although Libby is sitting next to Cal and though there's an ease in the tension between them, she's studiously avoiding his touch.

I nudge Iris and jerk my chin in their direction. She draws a question mark on the back of my hand.

Shit. That isn't good.

Apparently, their discussion on board the *Lassen* didn't go quite as Cal hoped as Libby stated emphatically she'll be returning to Akin Hill after landing back in Charleston. "After that, who knows?" Her voice was as empty as her eyes.

As the chopper lines up to descend, something catches Libby's eye out the window, knocking the distance from her expression. She lowers her mic on her cans before nudging Cal and pointing to ask, "What's that?"

Cal leans across her body to see where her finger extends. Libby's face, previously vacant, fills with sorrow, regret, and levels of pain I can't begin to interpret. I know Iris has seen it because her fingers crush my own before she asks, "What do you see, Libs?"

"It looks like a crowd of people."

"Maybe the team from Alliance?" Iris wonders.

Cal shakes his head as the chopper descends easily. He sits back and reaches for Libby's hand. Much to my surprise, she doesn't jerk it away from her husband. He searches her eyes intently. "No. Libby, it's your family."

I grunt. "Excluding the people on this bird, our daughter, and Josh, I'm with the only family I care about."

Libby's eyes whip to mine. For just a moment, we're the two cousins who were closer than siblings. The last six months—hell, the last seven years—have been washed away and I finally understand what I lost when I backed Cal's decisions.

Trust. Until this moment, I refused to recognize what Iris has been saying all along—in the process of living our own lives and building our own family, someone who was already my family was drowning in despair. I unconsciously contributed to it. Libby doesn't deserve that and I need to correct any misconceptions about that before we get off this flight.

I lean forward and gently touch the side of Libby's bruised face. Like a startled doe, she eyes me warily. I lean over and press a kiss where both of her dimples should live. Then I whisper, "I love you, Libs, whatever you decide to do."

Tears pool in her eyes but her unbroken spirit declares, "I deserve happiness."

"Then whatever you need to find it, you have to just ask."

Cal growls in my ear to shut up, but it's not about facing the backlash of a man I respect anymore. It's about facing myself in the mirror. It's about shedding the ever present regret suffocating me since I knew Libby was on board that ship.

It's about finding the crest of the low wave and making my way to the surface just to find the ability to breathe.

The skids touch down and the crowd surges forward, including a stretcher, I note. After also spotting the medics, Iris drawls, "Sorry Libs. You owe me twenty."

Libby stands, unaided. "I will walk off this helicopter."

Cal snarls, "Why must you be so stubborn?"

"To erase what's been done to me. To regain some part of my independence. To show the world they didn't break me. Take your pick."

Cal wisely backs off. Iris is undeterred. "Let me and Sam go ahead of you, Libs. This way, if you start to stumble due to the pain meds, you can grab one of our shoulders."

Libby considers it while the rotors are cut off. Finally, she nods.

Right before we descend into Akin family chaos with Iris taking point.

HOURS LATER, we've made it home after leaving shell-shocked family members at the airstrip. Their looks of hostility drained as we passed through them when the admiral called to us for a debrief, but in the end, we stopped for only two people who called our names—Libby and Josh. Libby, despite her physical and emotional injuries, wrapped her arms around us and whispered a fervent "thank you" before she was whisked away to the hospital.

Josh, with his wife and daughter at his side, stepped forward and embraced each of us for long moments. "I'm eternally grateful." His simple words were overheard and caused a ripple among the remaining family members.

When a knock comes at our door, we both stiffen. Since Rachel is safely asleep upstairs, I'd just splashed a few fingers of bourbon into a glass. Iris, having just taken a sip of wine, frowns. "Are we expecting anyone?"

I set the glass down on the table next to me before getting to my feet. "No."

She rolls her eyes dramatically. "As long as it isn't Cal."

I scoff. "I suspect he's doing much the same thing we are right . . ." I don't finish my sentence because standing in front of me after I've flung open the door are my parents. Politely, I inquire, "Didn't we already thank you for taking care of Rachel at the airstrip?"

My mother shoves past me heading straight for Iris. I turn to follow her, but my father's hand stops me. "Let her, son. She needs to get this out."

Quivering with barely restrained anger, I follow at a more sedate pace to hear my mother begging Iris for forgiveness. ". . . was so wrong. I didn't realize the enormity of your jobs. What you do is just incredible!"

My wife calmly lifts her glass of wine to her lips and takes a sip before reminding my mother, "You believed I'd betray the man I love with another."

My mother starts to deny it, but Iris isn't accepting her prolific apology just then. Her face is emotionless which is better than her letting loose the restrained devastation building behind her eyes. "While you may mean every word you're saying, now is not the time."

That stops my mother in her tracks. "Excuse me?"

I move to align myself next to Iris, lending her my support if she needs it but, more importantly, demonstrating to my parents whose side I'm on. I inform them, "You have no idea what we've been through. Now is not a good time. Now is the time for us to regain our sense of selves."

"Son, we're trying to mend fences," my father tries.

"You have no right to come in with your needs, your wants, after we just came back from witnessing the atrocities we did. Libby's safe, but what about the others or do they not matter? Because each and every one of those bodies is going to be burned on my soul for the rest of my life," Iris shoots back.

That causes them to physically jolt— with revulsion? With shock? I can't tell and that unto itself leaves a bitter taste in my mouth. Lisa's words from long ago come back to haunt me. *"It likely hasn't escaped your notice how much of the family was built on impressions."* I step between my parents and my wife and end this farce once and for all. "We need time."

"Sam, more time? Really? We need to show a united front," my mother says firmly

I slide back and without hesitation my arm slips around my wife's waist. Pulling her back against my front, I inform them, "The united front you should have shown was believing me when I told you nothing had happened."

My fury escalates when her eyes flick to Iris briefly. "Who were we to doubt —Libby?"

"Who were you to doubt your own son?" Iris fires back, directing my mother's attention to her rather than me.

I press a kiss to the side of her head. "This is so like you."

"What is?"

"Just like you took the bullet for me that first mission, you'll stand in the way of any harm coming to me. Is it any wonder I love you as much as I do?"

Iris whirls around and grins. "You've loved me for a lot longer than that, Sam."

My lips curve up. "That's the truth." Just as I'm about to pull her into an embrace, I catch sight of my parents, who are as pale as statues. "You're still here?" I demand rudely.

"You took a bullet for our Sam?" my mother clarifies.

Iris nods. My father inhales sharply.

Neither of us could expect my mother's reaction. She squares her shoulders and proclaims, "I'll be having a word with Natalie about her daughter's unjust accusations."

"The hell you will!" Iris bellows. Everyone in the room, including me, turns their attention to her. "What Libby felt, what she continues to feel, is between her and Cal. She needs this family's support, not their derision."

My father immediately agrees. "Well said, Iris."

With that, I declare the discussion over. "We need time. We'll call you."

Accepting that's as far as I'm willing to bend, my parents slink out with a quiet goodnight to Iris. I turn out the overhead lights and lock the door after they leave.

Returning to the living room, I find Iris contemplating the photos littering our mantel. She lifts one down and stares at it intently. I wrap my arms around her and find myself face-to-face with Nonna. My chin jerks down into Iris's shoulder before I ask, "What do you think Nonna would have to say about all this?"

"Truth?"

"Always."

"Probably that not one of us is innocent and we're all transferring our guilty consciences back and forth." A tear slips from Iris's eye and lands on the glass covering the precious photo.

"You're likely right."

"Sam?"

"Yes, sweetheart?"

"Take me to bed. Make me forget about what I had to listen to on that ship." That's when my wife melts down in my arms.

Without a word, I pluck Nonna's picture from her hand and place it back on the mantel before scooping her up into my arms. Then I carry her down the hall to our room so we can affirm we're still alive amid the sea of death we just escaped from.

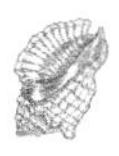

54

EIGHTEEN YEARS AGO FROM PRESENT DAY—
EARLY DECEMBER

Iris

"I SHOULD HAVE KNOWN you'd be the first to figure out where I was," Libby says as she opens the door, gesturing me inside. She glances around. "Are you certain you weren't followed?"

More than anything, I want to wrap my arms around Libby and never let her go, but I'm not certain she's ready for that. "No. I waited until Sam went to work before leaving to drive here. I called him to let him know I was being asked to consult for a university project."

Libby eyes me speculatively but doesn't say anything as she leads me into our former living room.

"It feels like yesterday," I confess. My eyes mist as memories fill my heart when I step inside the small space. Even though more years and emotional distance than I care to think about separate us from the young girls we were when we both lived here.

Libby joins me where I'm standing in the middle of the room absorbing all the changes, big and small. "I know. At first, I wasn't certain I would be able to handle staying here—especially on my own."

"I would have . . . ," I start.

"I know you would have. So would Josh, my mom, dad, anyone who loves me but I needed to do this to see if I could," she explains.

My heart relaxes a bit when I hear Libby categorize me with her loved ones, people who never let her down. "I never doubted you for a minute."

"I'm glad one of us didn't," she admits wryly. Gesturing me to the couch behind me, she takes a seat in an oversized armchair across from me.

Her gaze falls over my shoulder, her expression morphing into something I recognize from the faces of people I've helped escape during my missions. I just never expected to see it on my best friend's face. I blurt out, "I almost wish you would smack me."

Libby's jaw drops open as she snaps back into the moment. "Why on earth would you say something so insane?"

"Because I can't reach you where you go to. If you hit me again, at least I can keep you here."

A tear trickles down Libby's face. I panic, "God, I'm sorry. Please believe that if you don't believe anything else. From the bottom of my soul, I am so sorry."

She dashes it away. "For what? Living your life? Being honest with me however and whenever you could? How can I hold that against you?"

"Please believe me, I tried . . . Wait." I halt myself as her words penetrate. Cautiously, I ask, "Libby?"

"I know my name, Iris. The cheap-ass wine I used to drink while we were in school didn't kill that," Libby sasses.

I burst into tears because right here, right now, I have *my* Libby back after all this time, when I know I'm being granted absolution for all my sins of omission. Libby uncurls herself from her chair and joins me on the couch. Wrapping her arms around me, she lays her chin on my shoulder. "Look at me, Iris."

Immediately, I comply.

"The answers I need are from Cal, not from you. We can talk about anything—including therapy—but I will not discuss my husband."

The conviction behind her words is clear. But I give her an escape clause. "Are you sure there's nothing you want to ask about him? I'll answer what I can, Libby."

Her head tips to the side. She studies my face for long moments. I'm unsurprised when she asks me a question about Cal but shocked what it is. "Is my husband really this stupid? He hired you and Sam for a reason, I presume."

"One would assume," I answer caustically, not giving voice to the fact I agree with her wholeheartedly.

Libby muses, "I mean, I've been here a month. If he's your boss, I assume he's supposed to be some sort of hot shit at his job."

"Supposedly."

"He's way overpaid."

I open my mouth and close it before sliding backward out of Libby's arms laughing.

Libby declares, "That's what I thought. It's just like Nonna always used to say about men."

"'They exist so they already have two strikes against them?'"

"Exactly." We beam at one another. Libby holds out her hand to help me up and I accept it. When I'm sitting back up, she pulls me into her arms. "You're not the only one who has to apologize."

"Libby, no," I immediately protest. My best friend has been wounded far too much and I don't need it.

But Libby pulls back, shaking her head. "It's a part of my healing, so let me. Please?"

"Okay but know I don't need it."

"I do." Libby pushes to her feet and wanders to the glass doors leading to the backyard. "My therapist said this would be incredibly difficult because of the guilt and shame I feel."

I leap to my feet in fury. "Guilt? Shame? Over what? Libby, you're a survivor of an incredibly heinous attack, one that had the potential to end very differently . . ." I trail off in the event she wasn't in the right headspace to realize what was actually occurring around her on the *Sea Force*.

Libby's silence extends for long moments. Her hand rubs absentmindedly over her stomach where I know she took repeated kicks. "I know too well what was happening."

"I don't understand."

Her hand stills and presses in. Bewilderingly, she answers, "Because I didn't answer the phone before I left," as she stares out the window. Turning she faces me with an anguished face. "But that isn't the only reason. I've known and loved you longer than Cal, Iris. You're my sister in every way but blood and I allowed my insecurity about my marriage to come between us. You had the courage to approach me. I was hurting in unimaginable ways and I lashed out at you emotionally and physically. For that, I apologize."

I'm reeling. "Libby, I understood. I never blamed you for it."

Her lips curve. "No, likely you blamed Cal."

"Well, yes," I admit. Not without my own shame, I look away. "Ask. You're the one with the right to. Hell, by now the whole family has."

"I don't need to." Hearing those words has my eyes locking on hers. The Libby I know and love stares back at me before she responds, "I already know the answer."

"When?" I rasp, my heart beating in triple time. Maybe I needed to hear her confession after all.

Thoughtfully, she says, "For certain? The morning I left for Spain. Cal had just left me my new puppy—"

"I heard all about him from Josh. Apparently your niece's dolls are being trained to ride on his back."

Libby's smile brightens the dark place in my soul that's been withering away for the last six months. "I made a deal with my brother. I'd keep him as long as he's potty trained by the time I get home." Libby steps forward and brushes her fingers along my cheek where she slapped me. "I'm sorry, Iris. For this, for not believing in you. My head just couldn't refute the pain my heart was suffocating with. I wish it had."

"So do I. I wouldn't have had you suffer what you did for anything."

"No one should have." That's when Libby begins to sob.

For the first time in longer than I can remember, she lets me hold her when she does.

HOURS LATER, I place a call with Libby's blessing. "Hey."

"Shit," Sam curses. "I just burned my hand getting some mac 'n cheese out of the microwave. How are things going at the university? Do you think they're interested in hiring you?"

Since the phone's on speaker, I quirk a brow at Libby. She nods her approval. Taking a sip of wine, I admit, "Well, I'm not exactly where I said I would be."

He tells Rachel not to touch the plate, he'll be back in a minute. Stepping out of the kitchen, he demands, "Iris, are you okay?"

Libby sighs exasperatedly, "Yes, Sam. She's fine. I'm fine. We're having some girl time. She'll be home tomorrow. Do you think you can handle your daughter for one night?"

Sam shouts, "Libby! Holy hell!"

I warn my husband, "Do not find my phone, Sam. You are forbidden from using any technological means of tracking me to locate Libby for Cal."

"Oh, come on, sweetheart. He's getting pathetic."

"He's always pathetic," I snap.

"It's bleeding into work," Sam wheedles.

"Suck it up. If you had listened to me years ago . . . ," I begin, but I trail off when I realize Libby's shaking next to me. Fortunately, it's with laughter and not with tears.

She removes her hand from her mouth and lets the musical sound escape. "God, how did I not figure this out years ago? Y'all are terrible at keeping secrets."

I say indignantly, "I so am not."

Libby doesn't even bother answering. "Sam, I'm keeping your wife for the night. If you don't want me pissed at you for eternity, you won't track her."

"Libby, please at least let me tell Cal you sound better," he begs.

She considers his request. "That you can share."

I pick up the phone. "We'll call later before Rachel's bedtime."

"Okay. I love you, sweetheart.

"Čhaŋtéčhičiye, my love."

"Libby, it's good to hear your voice."

Pulling the spoon from her mouth, she warns him, "You and I are going to have words, Samuel."

"I know. For the first time in all our lives, I can honestly say I look forward to it." Then Sam disconnects the call.

Libby hands me the carton of Ben & Jerry's we've been eating out of while gorging on wine. "How long until he tells Cal?"

I snort. "Not even sixty seconds."

"He does have your child to feed," she points out.

"Won't even factor in. He knows he can pacify Rachel with ice cream. Cal's a bastard to work for," I share.

Libby opens her mouth to ask something when her phone pings with a text. I blatantly read it and am not the least bit surprised to find it's Cal. When I glance at Libby to gauge her reaction, her face softens momentarily before she tosses her phone to the side. "You'll never guess what I found the other night."

"What?"

"Let me go get it." She leaps up and runs into her old bedroom. A few moments later, she comes out holding a familiar purple journal.

"Oh. My. God." The spoon I was holding clatters to the floor. I jump to my feet and grab for it but Libby holds it out of reach. "Where the hell was it?"

"You hid it in the panel where the water main was in your closet, you ass. I had to get in there the other day when they were remodeling your shower to turn off the water."

"Give it to me," I demand.

"No. Not until I read this section to you. '*My heart beats differently when I'm around Sam Akin. But being the woman I am, will I be too difficult for him to love?*' The answer to that, my beautiful friend, has always been no. You're not too difficult for anyone to love."

I'm still trying to absorb her words when she hits me with more. "I remember what you said to me when you thought Sam might not want you because of your strength." Libby's eyes flick to the side.

I recall the conversation as easily as she does. The very journal she's clutching like a lifeline in her hand was the way she dragged me out of the doldrums after Sam left for his first assignment at Alliance; just before I left for DLI. "I do as well."

"What if the opposite is true?"

I tilt my head to the side. "What do you mean?"

"What if you're left wondering if you'll ever be enough because you're perceived as too weak?" The book in her hand shakes.

"You're not weak. You are one of the strongest people I know."

"How can you say that?"

"Because you stood tall when the waves tried to knock you to the ground. You fought for everything you have including your life. So don't ever try to take on someone else's mistakes." My voice breaks.

Libby closes the book and holds it out to me but I step past it and move into her arms, relishing the beating heart holding it out to me. I want to make her the vow that nothing will be put before her again, but I know I'd be lying. Life holds enough uncertainty that no one can make that kind of promise. Life can come between friends. It's in the reverence of how you treat the person the rest of the time that allows you to find your way home to one another.

"HOW IS SHE?" Sam demands the minute I come through the garage door the following afternoon. Before I can say a word, Sam swoops me up into his arms for an enormous hug. "More importantly, how are you?"

I think back to the emotional hurts Libby finally let go of in the wee hours of the morning. I give my husband the only answer I can. "She's healing."

"And you?" He brushes a wayward curl away from my cheek and leads me over to our kitchen table. "How are you?"

I sit down on his lap and rest my head against his shoulder. "There are times when I wish I could turn back time and make different choices. Losing Libby's respect, even for a short while, makes me wish I'd never joined Alliance in the first place."

Then Sam brings me back to our reality. "But what would have happened to her if we weren't there to help, Iris?"

"That's why I feel devastated, Sam."

"Because you know you made the right decision to join the team?" he guesses.

I shake my head. "No. I know I wouldn't have changed a thing because, in the worst of times, it meant being there for someone I love when they need me the most. Just like I've been there for you."

"Then what is it?"

"I just hate myself for deceiving her worse than her husband has. I feel like the largest hypocrite on the planet."

"You didn't have a choice," he argues softly.

I push out of his lap. Smoothing a lock of hair off his forehead, I whisper, "We all had a choice."

Then I turn and head to our room to shower away the feeling of filth coating my skin because my best friend apologized to me for what she perceived to be her truth.

55

IRIS

"THAT WHOLE EVENT changed all our lives," I quietly inform my daughter.

"Especially Aunt Libby's."

"Oh, without question, but it slapped the family hard as well." Sam wraps his arms around me where I'm perched on the arm of the couch next to him.

"Because Libby almost died?"

Sam shakes his head. "Because they had to look at themselves in the mirror and didn't much like what they saw." At Rachel's confused expression, he elaborates, "They had judged the three of us—Cal, your mother, and I—so wrongly."

"Yet in many ways, so right," I tack on brutally.

"Explain, Mama." Rachel drops down on the couch opposite me and Sam.

"The accusations flung at us were as simple as we lied down to how we were perverted bastards," I recount with a great deal of shame. Rachel appears ready to explode, so I hold up my hand. "If you take our jobs down to their basest level, we were liars, Rach. We lied to everyone but to our way of thinking there was honor in it."

"Is there honor in lies?" Rachel wonders aloud.

"That's an age-old question that field agents everywhere ask themselves when justifying their work," I admit softly. I chuckle softly, recalling some of the more creative ways I unveiled some critical intelligence. "I lied to people about being a waitress, a teacher, a military officer—"

"That one wasn't a lie, sweetheart. You were."

"Just not for their country, Sam," I counter before resuming my list. "A customs agent, a bartender, the list goes on. Did I hurt people with those lies? Some might say I did if I took actual money for them, which is why I never did. Some might say I could have unearthed the answers a different way. Maybe, but at what cost. I don't have any trouble laying my head on a pillow knowing I did my job and helped protect our assets around the globe."

"You keep saying assets, both of you. Does that mean money? Guns? People? What?"

Sam answers for us both, "Any of the above, depending on what was needed. There were times we had to intercede physically, but more often than not it was intelligence that was needed. Your mother's linguistics skills were particularly important."

"As was your ability to hack anything and everything once we were on-site," I remind him.

Sam shrugs modestly. "I still believe the human intelligence was just as good if not better."

I frown sharply. "I disagree. How would we ever have found located all those children if you hadn't . . ."

"Children!" Rachel exclaims, drawing our attention back to her.

I gather my wits. "Yes. Some of the most rewarding and most traumatizing missions we went on were kidnapping and rescue ones."

"Your uncle had a passion for reuniting missing children with their families." Sam smiles fondly. "He still does."

There's a stretch of silence where Sam plays with the ends of my hair. Rachel breaks it by saying, "Yes."

"Yes, what?" I ask.

"I was just answering my own question. There is honor in some lies. Some of them are necessary to bring about justice. People just abuse them, manipulate them for their own means," she adds harshly.

Sam replies gruffly, "Rachel, you're going to find people will lie, cheat, and steal if they think they can gain the upper hand. To keep it, they have to do it more. They wallow in the mud so often they will never come clean. We had to get dirty just long enough to expose them."

"When it was done, and the people we loved were safe, none of us had a problem with walking away."

"To do what you do now," Rachel presses.

"Yes," Sam says emphatically.

"Sort of." My husband flings a dirty look up at me. I ignore it and give Rachel the truth. "When you have the reputation your father and I have, sometimes you're called back in to assist when the situation is desperate."

"That's happened?"

I nod. "To both of us."

56
TWELVE YEARS AGO FROM PRESENT DAY

SAMUEL

"TELL ME MORE," I encourage Cal.

Rick lifts his glass in assent. "Go ahead."

Cal, Karl, Rick and I are kicked back after hours in Rick's spacious office as we contemplate the offer Cal received from an investigative firm based out of New York wanting to acquire Alliance under their umbrella.

Cal starts, "God, it was about five years ago or so, but you unearthed intel about a missing girl in Connecticut—Charlotte Collins?"

"Of course. There was a pattern to the kidnapper that no one saw because no data was shared between the FBI and the local police. Finally, the parents brought in an outside investigation agency . . ." I freeze mid-sentence. "That's who wants to acquire Alliance?"

"Hudson Investigations. I was approached that night—by one of the owners —for a job. I remember asking him how the hell I was supposed to know who he was." Cal reminisces.

Rick leans forward and places his tumbler down on his desk. "Let's be clear, Sam. They don't want to acquire the whole firm—just the parts that Cal and Karl own."

I'm dumbfounded. "Which is most of the agents and support staff. What does that leave you, Rick?"

He taps his fingers on his desk. “With a few options. I’ve had numerous offers for the building and grounds from the government.”

My gaze clashes with Rick’s. His face doesn’t give anything away. My voice is shakey when I manage, “You mean you wouldn’t be a part of this deal?” I’ve worked for Rick Yarborough since I graduated from college. Contemplating doing something else is unfathomable.

“That’s why we brought you in to discuss this, Sam,” Karl explains patiently.

“What do you mean?”

“I want out, Sam,” Rick declares bluntly.

There’s no way to hide the shock that rips through my system at his declaration. “For real?”

“It’s going to take a while for this to occur, but the assets of Alliance will be split.” He nods at Karl. “Karl handles personnel security better than anyone in the business.”

Cal takes over explaining. “Hudson has been around for years. Their primary offices are in New York and DC. Keene Marshall and Caleb Lockwood—co-founders of Hudson—along with another partner, Colby Hunt . . .”

I interject on a groan, “Please tell me he’s not a relation to Senator Hunt out of Virginia.” In my mind I can easily recall images of the elder statesman ranting about military spending.

Rick chimes in. “One and the same. Colby’s his grandson; I’ve known him since he was a little boy.” I immediately revise my opinion of both the cantankerous senator and his grandson as Rick continues, “Hudson needs the expansion to satisfy their government contracts. If Karl takes the position, he’ll take his part of his team and relocate to their DC offices with little to no turnover. Now, Cal . . .”

My head whips around to my friend to find him calmly sipping from his tumbler. Once he finishes, he wipes his lips against the back of his hand. “Libby and I want out. We need a new start without the memories of Charleston plaguing us every time we turn around. We’re heading to DC.”

Rick picks up where Cal left off. “That will mean cleared agents will go with Cal, helping to bone up the government contracts Hudson is involved with. Additionally, they want him head their missing children division—a role being filled by a Hudson agent looking to retire. Cal's ownership in Alliance will convert to a percentage of ownership at Hudson."

Where does that leave me? The question pops into my head but Cal answers before I can voice it. "Rick wants to sell you seven percent before the Hudson deal goes through, Sam."

Rick reaches inside his desk, pulls out a thick packet of papers, and tosses it at me. "It's about twenty million, Sam, but you'll double your investment once the acquisition goes through."

I snatch it as it comes skidding across the desk. "What makes you so certain about the return?"

"Because among the other things Hudson lists as an asset is ownership of a building in New York City's Rockefeller Center."

My fingers become numb and I almost drop the stack of papers. "An entire building?"

"That's just the beginning. They also own the property where their DC offices are located, right Karl?"

Karl swallows before agreeing. "Sam, the company is so far in the black their profit is close to ours and our contracts are one hundred percent military. They're so diversified the government stuff is a bonus."

I finger through the top sheet before asking the other man, "And you don't want more?"

Karl laughs. "Man, I'm going to Hudson long enough to train my replacements."

Cal intones dryly, "Never mind doubling your investment."

"That too. I've been doing this since I joined the Navy at eighteen, Sam. I'm ready to retire."

Rick jumps in. "For that matter, so am I. I'd like to see my people settled before I go."

One question tugs at me. "Would I be expected to move to DC?"

Cal jumps in. "No, Hudson headquarters is in New York."

My head swivels in Cal's direction. "Seriously?"

"No joke, Sam. They were explicit about who they want and where they want them to go from the executive team. I should also mention if Iris wants to work for them, they might be willing to negotiate your stake in the company for her return."

"When do they need an answer by?" My mind reels with the decision to be made. Not just by me, but Iris.

"Three days." My head snaps in Cal's direction. His smile is crooked. "They don't need the money by then, just a commitment."

I stand, clutching the stack of papers in front of me. "You all have given me something to think about."

Rick pushes to his feet. "Sam, if I didn't think it was a solid opportunity, I wouldn't have presented it to you."

I nod before walking out without a word. I want to head down to my office to dig up everything I can on Hudson Investigations before going home to discuss every aspect of this with Iris.

SPREAD out on our coffee table is the offer packet from Rick and every feasible piece of information I was able to dig up about the owners of Hudson Investigations: Caleb Lockwood, Keene Marshall, and Colby Hunt. My head hurts, likely from how hard I rolled my eyes after Iris exclaimed, "I know exactly who they are, Sam. Caleb Lockwood? Colby Hunt? Their spouses are constantly being featured in magazines."

"What on earth for?"

"They own Amaryllis Events." I must give my wife a blank look because she snaps her fingers several times. "You're a bright man, Sam. Put it together. Amaryllis Events? Most exclusive wedding planners on the East Coast? Maybe the US? I know for certain it means Amaryllis Designs. If this gives me an in to get an Emily Freeman original, I'm sold."

"Iris, think with your head, not your wardrobe," I plead.

She flops back against me on our overstuffed sofa before declaring, "You're no fun." I snort in response. She pushes, "What's holding you back?"

"You, Rachel, moving to New York, spending our entire combined savings to buy in, and probably a number of things I'm not thinking of yet." When my wife appears unfazed by my list, I groan, "You think I'm being an idiot."

"No, I think your concerns are valid."

"You do?"

"Certainly. But you're so focused on the negatives, you're forgetting about the positives."

"Which are?"

She begins to tick off, "You, me, and Rachel together. That doesn't change no matter where we are. We're blessed to have the money to spend to invest, Sam. We have enough in our Swiss bank accounts without touching the Akin trust. If we needed to, we could."

"We wanted to save that for Rachel," I protest.

"We will if those financials aren't inflated." Iris waves her arm out. She wraps it around me instead of letting it drop into her lap. "But you're forgetting something important."

I snuggle her close and inhale her intoxicating scent before asking, "What's that?"

"They want you, which means you hold the power in this negotiation. Put an addendum in the contract that indicates you'll move to New York for a year—no, make it two. And if we absolutely hate it at the end of two years, you reserve the right to work from another office or move back to Charleston."

"What about you? Do you want back in?"

She shakes her head. "The reasons I left Alliance are still there, Sam. I'll find a way to utilize my language skills, but now I want to be here for Rachel." She presses her lips against my chin. "For you." Another kiss where one of my dimples hides. "For us."

Her lips find mine. For long moments after, we forget about acquisitions or moving beyond what it takes to move from the couch to our bedroom.

57

TWELVE YEARS AGO FROM PRESENT DAY

Iris

While Rachel has a teacher workday, Libby and I openly discuss the potential move over coffee Rachel does her best to serve all her stuffed animals in the living room, I'm placing a second cup in front of Libby. "What does Cal have to say about it?"

Libby is thoughtful. "He was more worried about me and what it would mean for my business if he decided to take it. I have to say, that was a first. The last time we talked about him buying into Alliance, he presented it as *fait accompli*."

I snicker. "Which I'm certain you responded to so well."

Libby giggles. "I should tell you what I said to Cal."

I lean forward. "Oh, please share."

Soon we're laughing wildly when Libby recounts how Cal, in his dictator-like manner, laid out all the pros for his wife. I catch my breath long enough to check, "Your clearance came through, right?"

She nods hesitantly. I grin. "Good because this story is absolutely something you need to know."

For the first time, I share with someone not on the Alliance team the events of how Sam and I ended up married in Vegas. Libby spits her coffee out. "This can't be the truth. You and Sam got married at The Little White Wedding Chapel?"

"All because your husband was a complete asshole," I conclude.

"Why was that part of the mission classified?" she wonders.

"Because we were never supposed to be on that airstrip. Hell, it's not even supposed to exist. If it wasn't for that emergency landing though . . ." Before I can say anything else, Libby's standing and rushing around the table to give me an enormous hug. I return it just as tightly. "Libs? What's this for?"

"This is absolutely one of my cons for moving to DC. Now that I have you back—really have you back— I don't want to let you go." Her voice is muffled with tears.

"We're as close as an hour flight," I remind her, my voice breaking as I make promises. "We'll video chat every morning."

"We can we take vacations together—just us without the guys?" She lifts her tearstained face away from my shoulder.

"The guys can hold their breath until we get back," I reassure her.

She pulls back but doesn't let go of my hand. "We'll make this work."

"We will," I swear.

LATER THAT NIGHT, while shoving a bite of ziti in my mouth, I recount the story to Sam. I'm laughing so hard recalling Libby's reaction over where we got married that I don't notice how still he gets until I realize he's not joining my moment of hysterics. Leaning back in my chair, I ask, "What's wrong?"

"I need to report this breach." His voice is completely monotone.

"What breach? Sam?" His green eyes are hard as they stare into mine. "What? That I told Libby where we got married?"

"No, that you told her the story about the base. She wasn't cleared to know that." Sam reaches for his phone.

I slap my hand on top of his to stop him. "I can't believe you're serious. She's cleared, Sam."

"But that base is completely need to know, Iris. Libby didn't have a need to know," he counters.

I shove myself to my feet. "She doesn't know where it is."

He pushes to his. "She knows it's within driving distance of Vegas."

"That could be hundreds of miles," I counter.

"You said we got to Vegas after dark," he challenges.

"Sam, that's any time after eight p.m.," I shout. He picks up his phone and flips it end over end. "God, if you're serious, you better be ready to report yourself."

He stills. "What the hell do you mean?"

"Because you still come home from work and share more information with me than I should know about the inner workings of Alliance," I fling out.

He dismisses that. "Your clearance is still active."

I slide the knife in. "But do I have a need to know?"

He stills. Driving my point home, I recount the story of how Cal informed Libby of buying into Alliance.

"That's all he could do back then," Sam starts.

"God, did you learn nothing from what happened to us? There are ways of communicating without it being a breach of national security," I shout.

"Something you obviously forgot about during your coffee this afternoon," he throws out acidly.

Ignoring what's left of dinner, I storm out of the room. I grab my keys and purse and fling open the garage door. Sam follows me. "Where are you going?"

"The one place I know I can get some answers."

"Libby and Cal's? He'll likely be having more of a meltdown than me."

"No."

"Then where?"

I don't bother to respond. Unlike Libby, I don't care if Sam tracks my phone. If he does, he'll realize I'm going to confess my own sins to the only person who matters.

I CROSS my ankles atop the familiar conference room table after I'm done telling Rick what happened. Much like I expected, he's laughing in remembrance of the early days when we all started and bickering was a daily part of our lives. I finger the visitor badge around my neck. "I won't be cut out solely because I no longer work for the team."

"Hudson wants you too," he says, reiterating what Sam already told me.

"I might consider the odd job here and there, but right now I'm now faced with my husband drawing lines between us where there were none before. I've never been in the position Libby was."

"Ah, now we get to the crux of the matter."

"The fact Sam was ready to report me because I shared my wedding story is inconceivable."

"You know what some would say, Iris," Rick reprimands me.

"That if I don't like the rules to get the hell out. Fine." My feet slam to the floor, and I'm just about to fly to the door when Rick's words stop me.

"Or change the game." He gets to his feet and walks over to his desk. "This offer came to us for you today. I was going to give you a call tomorrow."

I recognize the emblem blazing across the tamper-proof envelope as well as the markings indicating it's for my eyes only. "What is this?" I ask Rick cautiously.

"Do you want to slip into that room over there and find out?" Rick points to the personal SCIF off his office

I nod, still staring down at the envelope that bears the unmistakable emblem of a pair of olive tree branches and a map of the world. I stride away and ensure I'm sealed inside the vault before I tear it open.

And receive the job offer of a lifetime.

OVER AN HOUR LATER, I've resealed the information into a new tamper-evident envelope and am pulling into my driveway. As the garage

door clangs upward, Sam's standing in the entranceway to the house as I pull in. For long moments after I kill the ignition, I sit there, unable to move my hands off the steering wheel as the overwhelming ramifications of the offer fully sink in.

Me? They want me to translate for the UN's General Assembly? The level of degrees required even to meet the basic qualifications is outrageous, so I never entertained the thought. I'd burst out of Rick's personal SCIF, demanding to know if he pulled a few strings.

That's when he read to me a slice of the letter of commendation written by the captain of the USS Lassen. "'In one of the most intense combat situations I've been in throughout my military career, one with numerous civilian lives at stake, the pivotal moment came from the Alliance linguistics expert. If she hadn't been able to ascertain the exact translation of the terrorists, I have little doubt there would have been no survivors on board. Her devotion, drive, and conscientious efforts achieved results. Despite knowing she was motivated as much by personal concerns as professional ones, she showed resilience when faced with insurmountable challenges.' Once this hit your file, Iris, I've had intel agencies worldwide demanding your services."

Still gripping the envelope bearing the UN seal, I murmured, "Yet you chose to pass this one along."

Rick pulled out a familiar folder with crayon markings from his desk. "I have a notarized contract that demands you be home each night. I think this might be the perfect position for you to be able to do just that."

I pressed my lips together and nodded before I handed him back the sealed envelope to file until I could formulate a proper response. "I need to talk to Sam."

"I'd expect nothing less. Circling back around to why you came here tonight, tell your husband to come to me with any questions about what you can or can't share."

"Thank you, sir."

"And Iris?" I paused. Rick's smile is bittersweet. "I'm going to miss you all."

"No, you're not. You're just going to pester us more than ever," I informed him confidently.

His laughter followed me down the hall.

Now that I'm safely inside my garage, I finally understand Sam's emotional outburst. It wasn't a regression, but a habit. He wasn't angry, but scared. It's because this isn't just the end of Alliance, but the end of the only life we've known for so long.

His knock on the window startles me. Opening the door, I see his handsome face twisted with regret. The first words out of his mouth are an apology. "I overreacted. I'm sorry."

"I understand." *Boy, do I ever.*

We stand in our garage, in full view of any nosy neighbors, swaying back and forth in each other's arms. He murmurs into my hair, "You were there so long, I was afraid you weren't coming back from seeing Rick."

I'm not even surprised he tracked my phone. I pull back and say, "We had a lot to talk about."

His lips quirk. "How much am I going to get chewed out tomorrow?"

"I don't know," I tell him honestly.

"You mean I wasn't your main topic of conversation?" Sam's smiling as he brushes his nose against mine.

"Oh, you were. Then Rick railroaded me."

His brows draw together. I continue, "Nothing is going to be the same."

"What do you mean?"

I drag Sam to the doorway and slap the button to close the garage door. "Let's just say it takes away another concern of yours about New York."

"It does?"

Thinking of the job offer awaiting me, my voice is filled with wonder. "Oh yeah. The best part is, I can be home at least as often as you will be."

58

SAMUEL

"THEN WE MOVED TO NEW YORK," Rachel concludes.

"Not without a host of family drama," I admit.

"Would you mind explaining that more completely, Sam?" Erika prods.

I do my best to do that without alienating my daughter from her family in Charleston. "You have an incredible bond with my mother, Rachel."

"Not to mention that you're the oldest grandchild of your generation, sweetheart. At the time, you were the only grandchild of your generation," Iris interjects.

"So, what? Was I supposed to be groomed to take over Akin Timbers?" When neither Iris nor I speak, Rachel's face screws up with a sneer. "Oh, please. Give me a break."

"Nonna did," I remind her.

"Get real, Dad. It's a new world, and I'm sure as hell not moving back to Charleston to run a furniture company and timber mill. Send Bishop when he's old enough. He's the one who loves making stuff out of wood when we fly home for vacation."

Iris holds out her hand without looking at me. I fish out my wallet and slap a twenty into it. Rachel is aghast. "You bet on your children?"

Iris stretches out her legs, showing off her new heels. "How do you think I saved up enough money for these babies? You both have been good to my shoe collection over the years."

Rachel chokes on her own breath, trying to regain her voice. Finally she manages to say with more than a note of haughtiness, "I should get to wear them, Mama, since I helped pay for them."

Iris fingers the twenty in contemplation before dropping it into her handbag. "You wish."

"Mama!"

"These shoes cost as much as your textbooks for this semester. The last pair I loaned you I know damn well I never received back. What collateral are you going to give me? The new computer your father built for you?" Iris demands.

Rachel's face is so shocked at the idea of turning over her brand new baby, she immediately forgets about the shoes. "What did you mean the family blew a gasket?"

"When you run a computer process, what do you do?" I ask my oldest child.

"At a high level?" At my nod, she starts, "First, the process has to be created. It can be done off-line on a secondary hard drive, CD, or USB, but it must be loaded into the main memory. After that, there has to be a scheduler that assigns it a waiting state."

"Then what?" I prod.

"Then while it's waiting, the scheduler has to load a context switch—which is loading a process into the processor. That modifies the state from waiting to running. If a process is in running state, it waits for a file, an event, something, or it's moved back to blocked but essentially, once the process finishes executing, it terminates."

"Let me break this down for you. The family has been operating in the same process over and over for generations, but we modified the event context switch load by announcing we—and not just your mother and me, but Libby and Cal—were picking up stakes and moving."

"So, what operations did they try to terminate, Dad?" Rachel demands.

Iris says, "That's a moot point, darling."

"Is it? You and Dad were castigated over and over. I'd like to know how often you shielded me."

Erika chooses then to interject, "Iris, Sam?"

Iris lays her hand over mine. "It's up to you. It's never meant anything to me; you know that."

I lift her hand to my mouth. "I know."

Rachel pieces it together without us saying a word. Furiously she spits, "The Akin Trust? They threatened to withhold it if you moved because of your job?"

Iris leans forward and clasps our daughter's hand. "Just from your father and me. His portion—"

"Our portion," I growl.

Iris rolls her eyes. "Whatever. The portion earmarked for your father was petitioned to be withheld because we decided to move you away."

"That is such bullshit!" Rachel yells.

"That's what your father thought at first," Iris concedes.

"Then your mother made me realize something."

"What's that?" Erika pushes when Rachel doesn't.

"That money means nothing when your happiness is ruled by it."

"So you gave up your inheritance, Dad?" Rachel's shocked.

"Gave it up? No, darling, that's not how it worked because if they did that to us, they had to do the same to Libby's portion," Iris says smugly.

"Then what happened?" Rachel asks.

"Libby and I petitioned to have the distribution clause modified." I think about the brilliant argument we presented before the Akin board and my lips curve upward.

"And that was?"

"Now, excluding education or medical purposes, any withdrawal or removal has to be reviewed and approved by the board."

"Why was that so important to the family?" Rachel holds her breath for the answer.

"Because Nonna's house, even though it was willed to Libby, is still part of the trust. Your father inherited property through the trust at Akin Hill because Nonna thought we might build a home there eventually. Imagine the uproar if either he or Libby decided to sell that property to buy homes out of state?"

Dawning comprehension lights Rachel's face. I take over where Iris left off. "The family needed the reassurance, Rachel. None of us needed the capital to start our lives away from Charleston."

"To the family, it was your father and Libby's respect for everything Nonna devoted so much of her life to preserving—the Akin family legacy," Iris concludes.

"What if you needed the money?" Rachel persists.

Iris's smile is wicked. "Well, then they should all remember your father keeps evidence of everything he's ever hacked."

I roll my eyes. "It was good practice at the time. I never thought I'd need those drives."

"Uh-huh." I'm not certain which one made the sound since both of the women I love disregard my explanation. Their identical smiles are beaming at me.

My cheeks turn warm under their regard. "It wasn't that big of a deal."

"No, Sam. Not that big of a deal," Iris drawls.

"Yeah, Dad. I mean, every operative and safe house worldwide had the potential of being exposed until you fixed it."

There's a crash as a cup lands on the floor near Erika's desk. She croaks, "That was you?"

I don't get a chance to respond because Rachel proudly declares, "Yep. That was my dad."

Erika comes around and stands in front of me and Iris. "My husband was working in the office that was compromised initially. Thank you for what you did, Sam." Then she holds out her hand.

Taking it, I feel the burden of an exoneration and accolades—neither of which I felt I deserved—begin to lift from my chest.

CHAPTER 58

59

SIX YEARS AGO FROM PRESENT DAY - APRIL 26 0857 EST

SAMUEL

I HAVE the ankle of one leg balanced on the knee of the other, admiring the view out of Caleb Lockwood's office window while he and the other primary investors in Hudson Investigations review the quarterly earnings report. With humor, I toss my copy on the table and ask the assorted men, "Just tell me two things."

Colby Hunt, who runs our Norwalk office, grins at me across the table. "What's that?"

"Can I get brand new hardware for my lab and can I buy my wife the diamond earrings I saw for her in the window of Cartier? She killed it translating during the Security Council meeting between Egypt, Ghana, and Great Britain."

Cal and Keene Marshall—who despite being a founder of the firm often acts as Hudson's lawyer—are cracking up through the teleconference I established with our DC outlet. Keene scoffs, "No to the first. Absolutely to the second. I loved the dirty look she shot the other translator when he tried to question what she was saying to the Secretary-General."

A surge of pride so fierce flows through me as I begin to quote my wife as she was captured on C-SPAN. " 'Much to my disgust, your use of the feminine possessive was inaccurate in that last translation, Mr. Osei. It is not only women who are subject to these atrocities, but the men in your country as well. Unless you deliberately meant to provide misinformation to His Excellency?'"

Keene's smirk blows into a full-blown grin. "As I said, buy your wife the diamonds."

I let out a beleaguered sigh. "But I can't have a toy too? So unfair."

"Sam, the toys you want to buy will cost upward of ten million," Caleb explains patiently, as he draws the quarterly results and the proposed budget in front of him again.

"It will be worth it," I declare stubbornly just as Cal excuses himself to take a call in his office that's attached to the conference room he and Keene are sitting in.

"I'm sure it will, but . . ." An eerie ping we all recognize comes out of the speaker. Caleb leans forward and demands, "Keene? What's going on?"

"No idea. Cal just locked us down. Sullivan?" Keene bellows.

"Tell them to turn on the news!" Cal shouts.

Colby fumbles with the remote. A familiar banner pops up declaring another Ransomware attack. "Sam, I swear if it's our network that just got hacked. . ." Caleb begins.

I punch him in the arm but Cal just shushes us. The very next image we see has my breath escaping my lungs in a whoosh.

The phone ringing in Caleb's office without his admin announcing the caller prompts Cal to say, "I think you should answer that."

Suddenly, Caleb's the one who's locking us down.

"AGENTS WILL BE happy to escort Mr. Akin to Washington," the director of an internationally recognizable agency offers.

"I can make my own way to DC. You worry about turning off every damn system you can preserve in your office," I argue.

"Sam's right, Director. Hudson has a private jet at its disposal. Tell us what airfield we can land at and we'll get him to DC within the next two hours."

"We need him here sooner than that."

"You wasted time by going to the media before picking up the phone. You can give me twenty minutes to go home and say goodbye to my family for the foreseeable future," I snap.

"Ms. Akin and your daughter can be placed in suitable accommodations for the duration. . ." the director begins.

"I agree to have my wife and daughter watched by agents due to the national security risk, but I refuse to have their lives upended because someone from the government clicked on the wrong file."

"I disagree with your assessment, Mr. Akin."

"Disagree all you like; I'll prove it when I get there." I disconnect the call before turning back to the men I nominally report to. "Is this room secure?"

Colby pulls out a device to scramble the signal despite the fact the office is supposed to be as secure as any locked-down facility. "Tell us what you need."

"Twenty minutes in our condo." My mind is whirling with the implications of what might be happening right now to the intelligence agents embedded all over the world.

"Colby, get him out of here," Caleb snaps as he snatches the phone.

"What are you doing?" I demand.

"Calling your wife. She has about ten minutes to meet you there." Caleb then presses a button to release the lockdown.

Sprinting for the door, I find Colby fast on my heels.

As soon as we hit the garage, I pull out my phone and text Iris. *Head home.*

Her text comes back almost immediately. Sam, is everything all right? I'm supposed to translate in twenty minutes.

I respond with one word. *No.*

60

SIX YEARS AGO FROM PRESENT DAY - APRIL 26 0922 EST

SAMUEL

I'M waist deep inside the crawl space behind Iris's closet by the time she gets home. Her clothes are shoved haphazardly to the side as I try to wiggle my shoulders inside the door to reach the box of our college memorabilia. "Fuck," I swear.

"Sam? What the hell is going on?" Her voice is muffled.

Wiggling out, I meet her panicked eyes. I know Colby's pacing our living room. Without a word, I drag her into my office and engage the sound-proofing I use when Rachel decides to have a dance party and I need to focus on coding. "It's not as good as a SCIF, but it's all we have."

"You're scaring the hell out of me," she warns.

"Did you hear about the latest Ransomware attack?" I ask her urgently.

"Yes. Of course. They said it was a think tank in DC . . ." Her voice trails off as I begin shaking my head urgently. "Who?"

I lean over and whisper the name of the agency in her ear. Her hands come up and slap my chest. "No. That's impossible."

"Nothing is impossible."

"Then why are you here? Why aren't you on your way there?"

I wrap my arms around her before dropping my head against hers. My lips brush her ear, and I say, "Remember our interviews at Alliance?"

She stills beneath my arms. "Yes."

"I recreated it that night when I got back to my parents."

"You never got caught?"

I shake my head.

"Did it create a hole?"

I pull back and scowl down at my wife. "Give me some credit."

"Then what's wrong?"

I let out the breath I'm holding. "If things go tits up, I may hold the only key to accessing the agency's server files dating back that far if I can't restore them."

Her hand flies up and covers her mouth. "Sam. They'll know."

"I'm well aware of that."

"Back then, we were protected by Alliance. Now, they can prosecute you." Her voice is shrill.

I push a lock of her hair out of the way to cup her chin. "I'm aware of that, but Iris, American lives are at stake. We took a vow."

Tears trickle down her face right before she face-plants into my chest. "What do you need from me?"

"This." I lower my head and press my lips against my wife's. I steal minutes I don't have to pour every emotion I feel into this kiss so Iris understands how much I love her, have always loved her. When our lips finally part, I whisper the words, "I love you, sweetheart."

"*Čhaŋtéčhičiye,* my love." She pulls back and between one heartbeat and the next sets aside everything to get the job done. "Now, what are you looking for?"

I give myself a mental reminder to kick Cal's ass when I see him for failing to recognize all those years ago that Iris would refuse to let anything stand in her way of completing a mission. *Even me,* I think wryly. "I need to find the box we packed of our mementos from Athens."

She turns and walks straight over to the door. After I disengage the soundproofing, we hurry back to the room. Iris makes it to the closet before I do.

Kicking off her heels, she wedges herself into the crawl space. Within seconds, she's passing out two boxes. "This is all we packed, Sam."

I tear open the first box and find hundreds of pictures—mainly of her and Libby. I mutter, "I wish I had the time to go through these." I quickly set it aside, tear the tape off the second, and find exactly what I'm looking for.

A bag full of thumb drives.

I surge to my feet and kiss Iris hard. "Whatever I don't need, I'll send back with Colby," I say before making our way out of the closet.

Trailing me on bare feet, Iris calls my name. I whirl around just in time to catch something flying at my head. I snatch it with one hand and find myself clutching a positive pregnancy test. "In case they throw you into the big house, I wanted you to know. Better make certain that doesn't happen. I can't raise two of your children on my own." Her voice warbles.

I drop the bag at my feet and surge directly back into Iris's arms. Catching her, I swing her around, unseeing due to the moisture filling my eyes. "I promise, I'm coming home to you—to all of you."

Iris squeezes me just a moment longer before she lets me loose. "Then get out of here and fix their shit so you can come back to me."

I nod and place my wife gently back on her feet. At the doorway, I bend down to pick up the bag of drives and pause, absorbing the impact of this moment. "This life I've had with you is everything I could have ever dreamed of. I knew how much you loved me with every touch, every kiss, and every time you stood at my back or protected my front. But there's never been a time I knew you loved me more than each time you told me you were carrying my child. I love him or her as much as I love Rachel. I'm not going to fail. We're going to ride this wave forever."

Her hand flies to her mouth to subdue her cries. But Iris composes herself before striding forward to grip my hand. "I'll walk you to the door."

With the bravery centuries of loved ones have demonstrated for their beloveds going off to battle, Iris stands there until she's the last thing I see when the elevator doors close between us.

THE HUDSON JET lands sixty-six minutes later at an undisclosed airfield. I peer out the window and notice a small caravan of vehicles nested off to the side of the airstrip. Quickly sliding the drives I don't need back into the bag, I toss them into Colby's waiting hands. "Make certain Iris gets those back after this is all over."

Colby's eyes are flat when he catches it. "I sincerely hope you mean after you're picked back up in a few days."

The plane rolls to a stop. As the flight attendant unlatches the door, I stand and hold out a hand. "You and me both."

Colby hesitates a moment before gripping mine firmly. "Do what you have to, Sam. I'll get Keene working on protecting you legally."

Doors open and bodies begin to slide out. I recognize Cal immediately and am grateful that I'll have him near at the end of my career—and possibly my freedom. "Don't."

"Sam," Colby starts, but I'm already bounding down the plane's steps ready to live up to the code I swore by years ago. Unfortunately to the people whose asses I'm about to save, just being in possession of the thumb drives in my pocket is enough to sentence me to a jail term, even though it may save them from something much worse—complete exposure of their deepest secrets to the world. It won't matter to them that I performed the acts well before taking my first oath to protect the United States from foreign and domestic enemies.

Right now, anyone in possession of this capability should rightfully be considered an threat.

Cal's face has a myriad of emotions flickering across it when he pulls me in close for a slap on the back. "It's been too long."

I can't help but smile despite the severity of the reason we're standing in front of one another. "We were just on a video conference this morning."

He turns and we both make our way over to the vehicles. "It just isn't the same. Keene isn't as good at calming me down."

"What do you mean?" But before Cal can answer, a door opens and a familiar broad-shouldered man slides out of the front seat, looking for all intents and purposes like he's going to split the seams of his suit jacket. My feet stop moving and my thoughts scatter. Words stutter out of my mouth, "Crap. . .shit. . . no. Thorn is here?" The last time I saw him, he fought Cal tooth and nail over the tactics we were about to employ to rescue any survivors on board the *Sea Force*.

"Welcome to my nightmare. I can't seem to keep away from him. I just want to know what I'm being punished for this time," Cal drawls sardonically as we approach the dark-haired man.

Parker "Thorn" Thornton hangs up his cell phone before holding out a hand. "Sam, I wish it was under better circumstances."

"Why the hell are the SEALs involved with a DoD hack?" I demand hotly.

"The SEALs aren't." Thorn smirks. Cal tilts his head skyward, likely praying for patience which is something I'm used to him frequently doing when the two of them were thrown together for past ops.

My stomach churns violently. There's only one answer that makes sense, and if it's the one I think it is, I should have delayed my arrival by making love to my wife one last time. Because there's no way "by-the-book" Parker Thornton will ever let me see the light of day again. I manage to choke out, "You work for the agency now?"

He jerks up his chin. "Assistant director. Now, let's get you to the war room, Sam."

I turn to Cal without acknowledging Thorn. "Are you coming with?"

Cal shakes his head. "This is code word classified, Sam. From here on out, you're on your own." He clasps my shoulder and squeezes, infusing me with years of leadership, camaraderie, and confidence. "You can do this."

I grip his arm back. After a few long seconds, I break away and follow Thorn to the waiting SUV he emerged from, knowing I have to succeed.

Or go to jail trying.

61

SIX YEARS AGO FROM PRESENT DAY - APRIL 26 1042 EST

SAMUEL

I'M FINGERING the drives in my pocket like talismen. At the same time, I'm being briefed by a three-star general in an underground space large enough to hold fifty or so of the highest ranking technology savants in the United States government.

Over and over I keep rubbing the drive as time ticks down. I'm not surprised nothing registered on the drive when it was swept. After all, I used the technology named after my wife—technology I built close to twenty years ago—to partition a portion of each drive so it's not recognizable. It was determined to be clean by the gunny on duty. "Here you are, Mr. Akin. Once the drives enter the space, you are aware they are not permitted to leave."

I managed to not shudder as I pocketed the drives. "I'm well aware of the protocols."

His face registered his exhaustion. "I'm not certain what three blank drives will do to help us at this point, but whatever you need, sir. Just let us know."

If he only knew.

My long-ago senior project combined with my intuitive talent for hacking permitted me to get past the supposedly impenetrable firewalls of this institution when I was interviewing at Alliance many years ago. That was a test system. The men and women in this room are hoping because I successfully managed it once, I can do it again.

Little does anyone but Iris know, I did it twice. By doing so, I have the means to restore close to four million endpoint devices and five hundred cloud initiatives resting in my pocket. The question is, do I lay my cards on the table now or do I try to reverse engineer the malware giving the United States an advantage over the cyber security threats plaguing its national security on a daily basis?

The answer is taken out of my hands when General Peavey declares, "We need to know as much about the perpetrators as possible, people."

I narrow my eyes at the screen with the countdown clock before raising my hand. The general's black eyes flick over to me. "Akin? You have a question?"

"With the amount of time left—" The clock ticks down to one hundred and seven hours. "—do we have enough time to be ferreting out that information?"

The general's fist slams down on the table. "I will know who dared to strike out at this country in such a manner."

"At what cost, sir? American assets? American lives? At what point do I stop trying to launch a counterattack and begin trying to protect the lives of the people who are already in danger?"

Thorn, whose face had been blank, flicks a look of respect in my direction.

General Peavey's chest heaves a huge sigh. "I'm afraid those assets may already be compromised."

There's a low murmur around the table. Thorn shoves to his feet and fires out hotly, "We don't leave them behind to be slaughtered, General."

I recognize his SEAL training kicking in. Obviously Peavey does as well. "We won't here, Thornton. Not if it's possible to avoid an international incident." He glances over his shoulder and watches the time slip away like sand in an hourglass. "You have until the final day, Akin. Coordinate what you need." With that, the officious man strides from the room with his aides following.

Everyone's eyes swivel toward me. I can feel the weight of Thorn's as I make my way to the front of the room. With my back to everyone, I throw my analysis up on the screen before announcing, "We have to assume every DoD system is compromised."

Immediately, the room goes ballistic behind me. "That's not what Peavey said, Akin!" an analyst named Drake shouts.

I wait for the noise to die down before stating without hesitation, "Look at the malware pattern. Anytime something is modified from the baseline directory, new reports about more systems being infected come in. You want to contain this, then that means shutting down every system immediately."

Thorn studies the pattern and comes to the same conclusion I do. "The only areas not infected are radio comms, satellites, the nuclear warheads."

"Exactly. But the codes for the football are due to be changed when?"

A White House aide swallows hard. "Soon. I can't disclose specifics."

"Don't let them be changed. If they are, they're compromised," Thorn orders.

The aide scrambles out of the room to contact his superiors.

Silence descends on the room as the weight of the assignment descends on us all. "We have two objectives—reverse engineer the virus and protect the boundaries of the United States. Now, let's get to work."

Everyone scrambles to log in to the secure host network I created earlier. Before I can make my way back around to my seat, Thorn approaches. His eyes bore into mine. "I know you can do this, Sam."

I bark out a rough sound. "What makes you so certain?"

"Because you pulled off a miracle of your own when a family member's life was at stake. They don't know who they're up against." Thorn jerks up his chin before striding out of the room.

You're wrong, Thorn. I do have a personal stake in this—my own freedom. With that last thought, I make my way over to my desk and begin the arduous process of stripping apart encrypted lines of code while still secreting away the files hidden on the drives in my pocket.

62

SIX YEARS AGO FROM PRESENT DAY - APRIL 28 1146 EST

Iris

"Iris, let me fly up to help you while Sam's at his symposium," Libby begs.

"It's okay, Libs. We'll be just fine." Rachel pokes her head out of her room when she hears me on the phone with her godmother. I put my hand on the phone to muffle my words. "Not now, baby. You can talk with Aunt Libby in a few."

"Okay, Mama." Rachel's door slams, adding more pain to the headache building behind my eyes. Fortunately, she can amuse herself while her mother has a nervous breakdown pacing the floors back and forth.

"You don't sound fine. You sound like you're ready to kick someone's ass," Libby probes cautiously.

That's because I'm petrified that I will never see my husband again. Barely managing to hold the words back, I do what I swore I never would do ever again—lie to my best friend. "I'm good. I'm just frustrated that Sam forgot to put this on the family calendar the week I'm in chambers, so I'm running around like mad."

Caleb Lockwood nods approvingly from where he's sitting in my living room as I pace back and forth across the Turkish rug I acquired on one of the many times we went to Africa. He mouths, "Keep going."

So, I do. "Anyway, by the time you'd get here and settled, Sam should be back." *I pray to God that he's going to be back.*

Reluctantly, Libby agrees. "If you're sure."

"Positive, Libs. If anything happens, you know I'll call you." Because I'll be a devastated basket case that after all we sacrificed, something Sam did years ago came back to bite him in the ass.

"All right. Keep me posted. I can be there in a couple of hours. Love you, Iris."

"Love you too." I disconnect the call before devoting my full attention to Sam's business partner. "What's the countdown now?"

He flicks his watch up. "Seventy-four hours."

"Still nothing?"

"No. You would have heard as quickly as I would. Possibly sooner with the contacts you have on the Security Council." He gestures to the television I've had running non-stop since Sam left a day and a half ago.

"Do we need to be worried about Rachel being in danger?" I ask him bluntly.

In all the years I worked as a field agent, I learned to read people and nothing in Caleb's posture alarms me. "No."

"Then why are you here?"

"Because you need someone who knows what's going on that you can talk with. All our wives have been in the same position when we've worked cases of this magnitude, Iris."

"And one of you sits with each of them?" I cock a brow in amazement.

"Sam and Cal are the first partners we've had outside of family, so yes." He gives me a lopsided grin that relaxes me somewhat.

"Why do I get the feeling I—we—are a bit different from your family?"

He gives me an assessing once-over. "Only by profession. In your hearts, which is where it really counts, you and Sam are just like them. I don't say that about many individuals—men or women."

Managing to swallow down the ball of emotion that wells in my throat, I push out, "Thanks Caleb. That means a lot coming from you."

"He's the best at what he does, Iris."

But will he be prosecuted for it? The fear the kiss I shared with my husband —the man who's held my heart in his hands since I was eighteen years old— was quite possibly the last makes me shudder. "He'd better be." Snatching up my phone from where it's resting on an end table, I shoot Sam another text though I know he can't receive it. He needs to know only one thing right now.

Čhaŋtéčhičiye, my love.

"IRIS, there's no point in you bothering to come in," Chu, the tech lead for my office, groans in my ear the next morning. "All communications with the DoD pipeline have been disabled. We're trying to determine why. It appears to be some kind of outage on their end."

Holy hell. The hopelessness I feel from knowing what is actually happening and the fear that crashes over me is overwhelming. "Have you notified other team members?"

"Absolutely."

"Page me if something changes," I conclude. I whirl around and face a concerned Keene Marshall who has just flown in from DC. He reaches over and turns on a device to block any and all transmissions that may be aimed at our condo. Once the device is humming, I announce, "If Sam shut down the external communication pipelines from the DoD, this is enormous. He's going to end up using the drives."

"You don't know that for certain, Iris."

I shoot him a filthy glare. "I know my husband."

Keene leans forward and braces his elbows on his knees, his green eyes boring into mine. "I'm already preparing a defense for him."

I brace against the back of the sofa and hiss, "Keene, you know as well as I do just being in possession of those drives is enough to raise questions about his loyalty to the United States. It doesn't matter to them that they were created when he was back in college; he attested to the fact he wasn't illegally attempting to access computer systems for his clearance."

Keene's head drops into his hands. "So, our only option is clemency."

My laughter is just shy of hysterical. "You've heard the same press conferences I have. You know damn well to avoid having egg on their face for such a disaster, they'll hang Sam out to dry as one of the perpetrators if he can't point the finger explicitly at a group. Clemency? A pardon? We'll be lucky if he gets out of Leavenworth in time to see this baby graduate from college!" I slap my hand over my stomach. I had to explain my condition to Keene earlier when he threatened to call a doctor after I raced off to the powder room to relieve myself of the small amount of lunch I was able to consume.

"Calm down, Iris. Going hysterical won't help anything," Keene snaps.

"No, but it makes me feel better!"

Suddenly Keene smirks. "I know. I was briefed that I'd have to put up with a lot of your shit when I arrived and not to take it personally."

At his words, my emotions just snap. I storm over to my cell and snatch it up. Punching in Cal's number, I put the call on speaker and wait for him to answer. The minute he says, "Hey. Any news?" I cut loose.

"I've waited almost twenty years to tell you what I think of you, you sanctimonious prick."

"Whoa, Mount Iris. Slow down. What's wrong?" Cal's taken aback. Ever since he and Libby repaired their marriage, he and I have been on great terms. But nobody gives a random stranger advice on how to handle me. Not even my husband. At the reminder of Sam, I bellow, "All those years you tried to keep us apart on missions. What was the goddamn point, Cal?"

His silence doesn't answer my question, so I keep going. "Now? Now, the clock's counting down and I can't save him. I don't have the skills to be in the room. I can't rescue him from whatever is going to happen. I can't step in front of the bullet for him."

"I know," he says, trying to console me.

"How dare you fucking give your bosses advice on how to handle me? *Vas tu future!*"

There's a pregnant pause before I hear Libby's sympathetic voice pouring from the speaker. "Did calling Cal a fuck help you feel better?"

That's when I burst into tears. I sniffle, "Not even the slightest bit."

"Does knowing I know help?"

"Yes. Without question."

"Good. Now, stop treating me like Cal used to and give me an update on what's going on with Sam," Libby demands.

I shoot Keene a quick glance. He nods before informing me loftily, "That's what I was doing this morning—reading Libby in. Just an FYI, she's the one who told me how to handle you best."

All the muscles in my body turn to pudding. I collapse onto the couch, take Libby off speaker, and immediately begin sharing my burden with my best friend. Less than ten minutes into our call, Keene and Cal are making arrangements for her to fly to New York.

Because as she so eloquently put it, "Shut up, Iris. That's what Sam would want."

63

SIX YEARS AGO FROM PRESENT DAY - APRIL 29 0738 EST

SAMUEL

I'D DO anything at this moment to slow time down.

Fingering the devices in my pocket, little pieces of my childhood burst through the lines of code I've been scrolling through for the last few days. I wanted nothing more than to grow up, to make my own decisions, maybe even to run away from the responsibilities of being an Akin. After doing that, I unleashed a tide of love that threatens to drown me every single day. Briefly, my eyes drift shut and Iris's face appears before mine. I don't dare call her, though I have the option to. If I do, I'll crumble. I know it as sure as I know my own name. And I can't. This isn't about how much I love her, this is about saving lives—those who served, those in the field, and those who are training to uphold the same oaths we vowed to protect.

When you're young, forever is nebulous. But when your forever is being counted down on a wall, it takes on a whole new meaning. Forever can't possibly be long enough.

Eternity would never be long enough for me to love Iris.

The clock clicks down to twenty-five hours and nineteen minutes. As requested, the team identified the source of the cyberattack— not the Iranians, who immediately accepted blame, but a narrow splinter group operating out of Russia. Thorn has already reported this to his superiors.

All that's left is to eliminate the virus itself and pray my family can move on after I put into motion what I'm about to do.

Striding over to Thorn's terminal where he's on the phone with God only knows who, I demand, "I need one of the infected laptops and a hub." My fingers are rubbing the three drives in my pocket over and over.

Tailsmen or a jail sentence? I guess I'll find out soon enough.

Thorn stumbles in his hushed conversation before proclaiming, "I'll call you back." Lifting his body from the chair, he pushes to his full height. Bracing his fists on the desk, he pins me with his eyes before demanding, "Why?"

Wearily, I guardedly say, "Don't ask until I know if it works." Turning from him, I hear him snatch up the phone and bark out orders.

Thirty precious minutes later, one of the original laptops is carried in by the sergeant-at-arms, sealed in a protected evidence bag. He additionally carries a USB hub—the make and model I specified that will be compatible with both my drives and this hardware. The box is open, so I know it's been checked thoroughly by the security teams stationed between the front entrance and where I'm sitting.

I yell out, "Save everything and shut down your terminals." Amid protests, I cut everyone off at the knees. "We're out of time. We need to start trying to recover data before it's lost."

Waiting until the last system is off-line, I order Thorn, "Turn off all wireless and hardwire internet access to the room."

His forehead wrinkles in confusion. "Then how the hell are you going to get that"—he nods down at the laptop I'm removing from the evidence bag—"back online?"

"You'll see. In the meanwhile, I don't want to open any more holes." No more than I did when I was twenty-two and lacked the terror I do at this very moment. Piece by piece, I begin the process of setting up: first the hub, then the drives.

"What the hell are those, Sam?" Thorn points to the drives.

"Ask me after this works." Thorn's eyes narrow, but he doesn't say anything else.

Finally, I plug in the laptop to give it some juice, uncertain of the battery life. Praying like hell this works, I turn on the computer.

"What the fuck are you doing, Sam?" Thorn shouts.

Ignoring his outburst, I quickly punch in a series of keys to take me out of the operating system boot up and into a command line prompt. My fingers whisper across the keys as I activate the hidden partition of the first drive. I hold my breath while waiting for the prompt.

```
> Continue, Sam . . .
```

Thorn is eerily silent behind me as I run the hidden scripts behind the second drive. The drives the agency security said were clean as they ran them through their scans. Thorn leans over to murmur, "What are you doing?"

"Shut the fuck up right now," I snarl as I wait for the second prompt.

```
> Almost there, Sam . . .
```

"One more. Come on, let this work," I beg. Fingers fly as I type in an unrecognizable cadence of characters. It may appear to be letters and numbers on my keyboard, but that's not what appears on the screen. I'm lost in translating the minefields and prompts I coded in just in case someone ever got a hold of these drives because in the wrong hands, they're catastrophic.

```
> Access granted.
```

I breathe a sigh of relief and begin repairing the operating system of the agency computer in front of me. The room is deathly still as I quarantine the virus before plugging a CD-ROM into my hub so I can offload the specific file for analysis.

Then I destroy every trace of it from the root files of the infected system.

Unplugging the drive, I reboot the computer and hold my breath. When a normal boot screen appears, I call out, "Horton, turn on the internet at my terminal only."

The access engineer turns on my access and I plug in an Ethernet cable into the machine. Flicking out a wrist, I ask Thorn, "Want to give it a try?"

He quickly steps up and logs in with the test account we prepared. His eyes widen when not only is he allowed in, but after a few moments of testing, he can get to the files and folders that were previously locked down. "You did it."

An enormous war whoop goes up around the room. My head drops into my hands. I knew I could, but at what cost? A hand clamps down on my arm. I know it's Thorn's without having to move a muscle. The hair next to my ear raises as he hisses, "First, you're going to repair as much of this shit as you can, then we're going to have a little chat. Agreed?"

I lift my head and meet his furious eyes. Piercing Thorn with a stare I'm sure holds a lot of reluctance with some defiance tossed in, I reply in the only way I can. "Sir, yes sir."

He drops my arm and orders, "Start with the cloud servers," before stalking away.

Using the now clean computer, I easily log in to the cloud server environment and begin to run the scripts one at a time to eliminate the threat. As time drips away, and I feel Thorn's fury mounting, I can't help but wonder how he will neutralize the threat I pose to the government I've always protected.

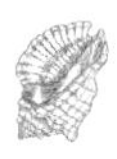

64

SIX YEARS AGO FROM PRESENT DAY - APRIL 29 1342 EST

SAMUEL

AFTER RESTORING the infected servers back to capacity and as many of the machines as I could at individual agencies to get them operational, Thorn demanded I begin documenting the process of how I restored the systems. "You're not being let out of this room until you do."

The first thing I did was send someone off for as many unencrypted USB keys as they could find. "Nothing special," I warned the gunny who appeared at the door. Frazzled, I babble, "I'm talking about decent . . ."

"Mr. Akin, why don't you just write down what you want and let me know if substitutes work," the man orders me dryly.

"Right. Good idea." So, I tried to hold a pencil to do just that but found my hands were shaking too hard.

The older man, recognizing my fatigue, began to take notes. An hour later, when he came back with a box of the very drives I requested, I swore, "I could kiss you right now."

He warily took a step back. "I might have to punch you, sir."

"As my wife would me." Recalling Iris's lips on mine, I want hers to be the last kiss I feel as I leave this earth. Which, considering the furious looks I keep intercepting from Thorn, might very well be the case. I heft the box to my station and begin documenting the procedures as I copy each of the three drives.

Another six hours later, I've made at least six sets for each division as well as written up very technical instructions on how to bypass the partition I put up on each of the drives. That's when Thorn loses his patience. "Now, we talk." Before I can agree or disagree, he informs the room, "The rest of you, take a set of Sam's instructions and three sets of each drive and get back to your agencies and offices. Get that garbage off your systems so we can go back to work."

The next few moments are spent accepting accolades from the other software giants in the room. "Way to go, Sam" "Great job" "Wish I had your skills, man." Handshakes and back slaps accompanied each one. Until the last person filed out with a way of restoring national security to our nation, Thorn was strung tighter than a tightrope.

Finally, it's just Thorn and me facing one another. I'm prepared for anything, including him outright beating the hell out of me. His question is simple and direct. "Why wait, Sam? You could have stopped this days ago." He drags his chair to the center of the room, gesturing for me to do the same.

"Because you all didn't just want a fix. You wanted to know the who and the why. You would never have had those answers if I just wiped out the virus," I tell him truthfully.

He accepts my response before his next words cause hope to deflate in my chest. "I can't forget what happened in here."

I square my shoulders and tilt my head in deference. "I know."

He leans forward and claps me on the shoulder. "I'm glad you understand." Whirling around, Thorn presses a button on his desk, one I haven't paid much attention to in the last few days.

A voice comes on the line. "Yes, sir?"

"White House Situation Room. On the screen, please, Scott," Thorn commands before he disconnects the open line.

I begin coughing on the simple act of inhaling air. Immediately, I comb my fingers through my hair I'm certain is sticking up on end and begin straightening my shirt to something more presentable. "Christ, Thorn. How about giving a guy a heads up?"

That's when I fully understand why he and Cal used to clash on missions. He counters, "Like you gave me one?" just before the enormous screen in front of us switches from a red clock to a camera where a cadre of men and women are seated around a table. I recognize the president, the vice president, the secretary of state, the national security adviser, the director for counterterrorism for the National Security Council, the chair of the Joint Chiefs of Staff, and the director of the agency Thorn works for. There are other individuals in the room I know I've seen on television from Iris obsessively watching C-SPAN, but I can't pick them out. That might be due to a lack of sleep or utter terror.

Either way, I'm on my feet a half a second before Thorn begins addressing the room. "Madam President, Mr. Vice President, the attack has been successfully blocked."

I'm taken aback by the euphoric cry that rises up in the Situation Room. Somehow, I always imagined these people to be more restrained in their enthusiasm. Thorn waits for the chatter to die down a bit before he announces, "I'd like to introduce Samuel Akin, who works for one of our government contractors. He's the individual who was able to stop the virus."

The president stands before she directs her comments to me. "Mr. Akin, on behalf of a very grateful nation, I—we— thank you."

"You're welcome, ma'am. It was my honor to assist in whatever way I could." Even if it means life behind bars, it was worth it. I recognize the same fatigue and relief on each of these individuals' faces as I feel dragging down the skin of my own.

"Based on the briefing Agent Thornton has provided to us, I am aware this has taken you away from your family. We'll try to return you to them as soon as we can."

My heart skips a beat. I don't dare let my eyes stray from her face. "They understood, ma'am."

"Regardless, we'll have you back in New York tonight," she reiterates firmly.

Tonight! My heart explodes with joy over the last word in her sentence. Then Thorn's boss takes a moment to personally thank me and my legs almost give out. "Sam, we appreciate the assistance. Thorn informs us you offered your services for such situations in the future?"

Now, I hazard a glance at the man at my side. His smile says, "Gotcha," without a word being said. Swallowing hard, I address the man on the screen. "Of course, sir. I only hope I can produce the same results."

"As do we. Thorn, we'll connect later for a full debrief."

"Certainly, sir. Madam President?"

The weary woman cracks a smile. "Go back to work, Agent Thornton. Make sure Mr. Akin is bound for home this evening." She makes a throat slash and the Situation Room disappears.

The moment the red light disappears from our camera, I remark, "I know that so easily could have been an order to say, 'Off with his head.'"

Thorn bellows out a laugh. "Not quite that easily, Sam."

"So, what does this mean? Do I have to move to DC?" I cringe at the idea of informing Iris we're moving again after she found a career that challenges her as much as Alliance had but on a completely different level.

"Actually, no. I need some eyes and ears in the New York area. You up for that?" Thorn begins outlining the kind of technical snooping he might require.

I can live with his terms. In fact, I can more than live with them. "Just this and I don't get prosecuted for having hacked the DoD nearly twenty years ago?"

"Just this and we forget those drives weren't created in this room." Thorn holds out a hand to shake.

I consider the ramifications of what Thorn signed me up for. How can I say no when it will give me a taste of the old life of Alliance too? I take his hand firmly. "You have yourself a deal."

"Like that was in question? You must mistake me for Cal," he scoffs before asking. "How much longer do you need?"

"Another few hours?"

Thorn nods and goes over to pick up the receiver on his desk. I wheel my chair back to my workstation and begin copying more sets of drives with the instructions to packet them together. That's when the phone on my desk begins to ring.

"It's Iris. You may want to answer it. I'm stepping out for a quick break." It's a measure of the trust the man has in me. He's not only letting me talk with my wife, but he's also leaving me alone with the ability to hack back into the DoD.

Choked up, I lift the receiver. "Hey sweetheart."

Just like Iris, she gets right to what she wants to know. "Was Thorn telling the truth? Is it over?"

I nod before realizing she can't see through the phone. "It is. I'll be home tonight."

When Iris begins to cry, I'm suddenly grateful to Thorn in a way I never experienced— even after he and his team rescued Libby all those years ago. Because this time, it's my woman he helped save from the uncertainty of going through life without love.

Whatever he asks for isn't big enough, I think fiercely as I try to soothe my wife's tattered emotions.

65

IRIS

RACHEL GRINS AT SAM. "I remember your name appearing in the paper. It was really annoying, Dad."

I poke her in the ribs. "That wasn't what you were saying when you were making eyes at the bodyguards Caleb and Keene insisted take you to school."

Rachel's cheeks flame a fiery red before her eyes turn downcast. "That was back when I thought I had good taste when it came to men."

"Don't worry about your taste. Remember what we've talked about; relationships are built on love and communication. They only work if both are in play. Any man who won't give you that isn't worthy of you," I state firmly.

Sam's cheeks redden with temper, likely recalling what helped facilitate our daughter's breakdown last year, contributing to our need for family counseling. But Rachel doesn't regress. Instead, she asks him another question. "So has Uncle Parker ever collected on the debt he thinks you owe him?"

Simultaneously, I begin laughing as Sam coughs, likely as hard as he did that day when Thorn so calmly asked for the White House Situation Room. I can't look at my husband—not even to give him a look to support him as he muddles through this answer—or I'll burst out with something as inappropriate as, *Do you mean this week?*

Sam fumbles for an answer. His "Umm . . . well, you see . . ." covers for *What can I say to our daughter?* Unlike me, who would have had Thorn sign a document years ago dictating the where, when, how, and why he could call upon my services, Sam feels it's his duty—or penance—to continue answering Thorn's summonses.

Then Rachel's laugh, so reminiscent of mine at that same age, tumbles out. "Don't worry, Dad. Your face says it all. You feel indebted to him."

Sam readily agrees. "I do. I'd do anything to help him after he gave me back the most important things in my life."

"Us?" Rachel questions, already knowing the answers.

"Yes."

We all contemplate the definitiveness of Sam's response when Rachel muses, "Despite everything that went down, I'll concede I occasionally miss my escort to and from school. I learned a lot from some of those guys."

Rachel and I laugh while Sam grumbles about slapping a muzzle on some of the Hudson Investigations bodyguards. She throws a little of her old sass at him when she drawls, "Don't worry, Dad. I was too young to admire more than just their minds. Then."

"Stop," Sam pleads, but he's joking. If there's a man on the planet who has ever been grateful to hear such talk, it's Sam because it means his daughter is healing from the events over the last eighteen months. Our family crisis was the last burden that sent her flying over the edge, as we found out. I broach the topic carefully. "How do you feel now versus eighteen months ago?"

Rachel considers her words carefully. "More aware and infinitely more cautious."

It's Erika who probes, "Can you explain that, Rachel?"

"I feel like before all this happened, I was protected in a bubble. I knew awful things happened in the world, but not to the people I loved. I was sheltered but confident. I thought I knew everything there was to know about love when I knew nothing at all." Her eyes meet mine, then drift over to her father's. "It turns out the very definition of love has been sitting right in front of me."

Despite the confidence her words portray, and the emotional pride I have, some of her words disturb me. "Rachel, you weren't sheltered."

Her laugh hints at the pain and agony she suffered. "Please, Mama. I was. I'm not ashamed I was. Being raised as a member of this family was a blessing I will never take for granted. But until I lost that connection with all you, I never wondered who I really was or what I could do on my own if I had to. I didn't know what to feel, waking up on my own without an identity of being an Akin."

"Being an Akin doesn't define who you are," Sam points out.

"True. The last months, I've been so confused about who I was until you let me meet the true you—both of you. Then fear set in. Who was I? Was I just been flitting through life coasting on my family name?" She shifts and points to me. "You were Iris Cunningham long before you became Iris Akin. You never lost the strength and courage I hope like hell I inherited. And you, Dad? You may have always been an Akin, but you forged your own path. Maybe this happened to show me I need that to be complete."

My pride in my daughter wars with my maternal need to slide her back into an even more protected bubble. Still, I need to ensure nothing lies between us any longer that can cause bitterness and hurt. "Rachel, there are always going to be secrets of one kind or another due to the nature of our jobs."

"I understand that now," she affirms.

"Our world came crashing down around us because you found a box of Aunt Libby's old things in Nonna's attic," I remind her quietly as Sam strokes my hair.

Rachel holds onto my hand so tightly that the circulation might cut off, but I don't care. She's sitting here listening instead of turning away which is all that matters. "I'm so sorry, Mama."

"Good heavens. For what, baby?"

"Because I should have listened all those months ago when you, Dad, Aunt Libby, and Uncle Cal wanted to sit me down and explain. Instead, I lost it." Rachel yanks her hand away from mine before lifting both hands and burying her face into them.

"No, Rachel. There's no need to apologize. Too many things were happening in your life," Sam protests.

"Dad, stop making excuses." she cries weakly.

"Rachel Elizabeth Akin, you'd know it if we were making excuses." My words are a whip cracking in the room, which she needs. Sam needs to acknowledge our girl is stronger than he comprehends and it's time to start treating her like it. Months of therapy don't diminish that, in fact it's done nothing more than strengthen the core of steel I've always known is there.

She lifts her stricken face. All I want is to pull her into my arms, but she needs to get the words out so they don't fester deep inside. "Yes, it was too much. Knowing I'd just been hacked—me!— and some piece of shit stole my tuition money, then getting back to my dorm after dealing with the financial office only to find . . . ," she sputters over her ex-boyfriend's name— "*Aiden* laughing over my mess. The things he said? I was so humiliated to find I was nothing more to him than . . ."

Erika pipes in over our daughter's sputtering. "A dalliance?"

"Exactly. No, worse. An opportunity. I gave him every part of me, and he used me for what? To look get in tight with the crew who hacked me? To cozy up with that . . . bitch? God, I wanted to die."

Sam tightens his arms around me because if there's one thing I can't share it's what happened to the young man Rachel's spitting fire about. "*What he's a part of is classified, Iris. As much as she's hurting, you can't tell Rachel anything about what I've shared with you about Aiden,*" he warned me. Something we're both all too familiar with.

Rachel has no idea of the web of decit she was swept into. It all started by falling for Aiden when she met him at the campus bookstore. As I observe the tension in her body, I know it's not over. Knowing my daughter, I suspect one day she's going to find all about Aiden on her own. After all, she's determined to help the world in her own distinctive style.

Just like me.

Only the languages she speaks fluently are the same as her father.

Rachel continues, "Then I flew to Akin Hill to get some perspective, needing time alone, and when I stumbled across Aunt Libby's drawing in the attic . . . I just lost it."

That's when her tears well over. I wrench out of Sam's grip to hold out my arms. She falls into them gratefully. After a long while, she tries to pull back. "I'm certain your jacket is ruined."

I snort, "I couldn't care less. Nothing is more important than you, Rachel. We'd give up everything and anyone to protect you. Don't you know that by now?"

Her eyes scan my face and then Sam's as he leans over my shoulder to wrap his arms around us. "Yeah. I do."

She leans forward to rest her head against my heart, healing wounds that she inadvertently opened eighteen months ago with a phone call I thought I'd never survive the aftereffects of.

66

EIGHTEEN MONTHS AGO FROM PRESENT DAY

Iris

"How could you?" Rachel hisses at me over the phone.

"Well, hello to you," I drawl. I've just been dropped off outside Rockefeller Center where I plan on joining my husband for lunch. I'm thrilled we each have a large enough hole in our schedules that we can sneak in a lunch date. The older we get, the busier we seem to become as we both take off in our individual professions. Narrowly missing running into a family who stopped to gawk at the gold statue of Prometheus, I press my hand to my ear to make certain I didn't disconnect the call before prompting my daughter, "Rachel? How could I what?"

"You kissed Cal?" Three words laden with accusations and betrayal. I stop short, ignoring the frustrated cursing that explodes behind me.

"How . . ." I barely get one word out before Rachel jumps all over me.

"How did I find out? What does that matter?"

"It matters very much." I try to regulate my voice, keeping my words calm.

"Explain what? That you're nothing but a liar? A fake? Did you sleep with him?"

I press my hand hard against my stomach as our daughter hurls vicious accusations at me. *Keep it together,* I warn myself. "Watch yourself, Rachel. You have no idea what you're talking about."

There's a sneer in Rachel's voice when she taunts, "How many other men have there been over the years? I mean, is Bishop even Dad's? There's such a huge age gap between us."

The skyscrapers towering over head begin to close in on me as my vision narrows to pinpoints of darkness. I finally manage, "Rachel, I love your father. What on earth is making you say such horrid things?"

"I'll make it easy for you, Mama. Check your phone."

"Don't hang up," I warn her.

She laughs, the bitter sound twisting my stomach muscles tighter. "I wouldn't dream of it."

My phone pings with an incoming text. I open it. My first words are a soft, "Oh, Libby." In my hand is a snapshot of the long ago picture Libby drew of Cal when he first tried to show me brotherly affection. My lips curve upward when I realize how far we've all come from that moment—that Sam and I and Cal and Libby have the kind of marriages that are unbreakable.

With a mother's intuition, I put together the fact she's looking at this picture Libby drew but she's reliving what happened so recently in her past with her boyfriend, Aiden. I begin, "What you're seeing has to do with what happened to you."

She scoffs. "Don't you try to pawn off you kissing Cal on what Aiden did to me. All it shows me is there's no one I can trust."

I try to get through despite the bodies that keep shoving past me. I want to follow them and race into the Hudson building, but I know once I enter the elevator, I'll lose Rachel. "You don't understand, Rachel. Aunt Libby misunderstood. Everything's fine."

"How dare you say her name?"

"Because you don't understand. It's not what it seems!" I want to smash the phone holding the image that finally made Cal pull his head out of his ass. "We've all moved on."

Rachel's laugh is so filled with bitterness, it's like being transported in time to reliving the moments again with Libby. I hurriedly explain, "Cal made a mistake. It was a moment of nothing, a mistake. It literally meant nothing." But even I can hear my own desperation because I know it almost meant the end of everything. Then. "Rachel, please let me explain."

"Does it matter? I never want to speak to you ever again. I told you the other day on the phone I was done with people lying to me. You supported me cutting them out of my life. Great job, Mother. That now includes you." With that declaration, Rachel disconnects the call in my ear.

I remain frozen in place, the phone still held up to my ear for an indeterminate amount of time. I'm jolted from the ghosts we all buried when my cell vibrates in my hand. I manage to unlock my muscles long enough to twist my head to see who it is. I immediately answer.

Before he can say a word, I tell Sam, "Rachel called."

His warm, honeyed voice teases, "I wondered if I was being stood up."

"Sam, she knows."

"What? That we're going to lunch?"

Normally, his teasing confusion would make me smile but the panic surging through me has my voice borderline hysterical when I growl, "She knows about you and me . . ."

I interrupt his seductive, "I hope so," when I shout over him, "No, Sam! She knows what happened! Somehow she found the picture Libby drew about what happened with Cal!"

There's a long silence on the other end of the line before, "I'll try to call her. Explain."

I tip my head back, tears welling in my eyes. Sam is in the building in front of me, just a few floors up. Right now, it feels like a million miles away. Like something is trying to drag me away from the anchor of his strength. "She hung up on me," I whisper.

"She'll understand," he soothes.

Will she? I question. People judged me harshly for what they didn't understand. Sam, the only person who was there in the room, never wavered. He knew exactly what happened and tried his best to protect me from the backlash.

To have Rachel being the one holding the whip is more than I can bear.

"Come inside, Iris. I'm waiting for you," he murmurs in my ear before disconnecting.

Taking a few deep breaths, I manage to put one foot in front of the other. The path I chose long ago put me right in the arms of Sam Akin, the only man I've ever loved.

The only man I ever will.

Now, how do we make certain Rachel understands that?

67
EIGHTEEN MONTHS AGO FROM PRESENT DAY

SAMUEL

As MY WIFE stumbles into my lab after being cleared into the space, there's no trace of the cool, confident woman who's meant to be in the office of the secretary-general of the United Nations performing top secret-level translation work at the bequest of the president this afternoon.

Iris is everything no one assumed she'd be when she became a mother—frantic, terrified, and radiating so much love it's a wonder I'm not knocked clear across the room with the force of power she's exuding. Sliding from behind my desk, I don't beat around the bush. That's not how my wife prefers to handle the blows life has thrown at her. Though these are the words I never would want to say to her, she needs to know what we're dealing with. "She hung up on me, too."

Iris crumbles before me. I rush forward, catching her up in my arms. Murmuring against her hair, "Together, we'll make this right."

"How, Sam? How do we get a do-over for our past?" She lifts her tear-streaked cheek from my chest.

"We can't, but we can explain what really happened." *Again,* I add silently. I drag my knuckles over the smoothness of her face and brush away her tears. "It isn't *our* past, Iris."

"Yes, Sam, it is." With that, she pushes out of my arms and begins to pace. Her heels begin a back and forth staccato on the tiles as she mutters under her breath in multiple languages. I have to smother my grin as I'm certain she's questioning the parentage of the person who allowed our daughter to find something about the misunderstanding that occurred between Cal and Libby so long ago without context. Or giving us the opportunity to gentle her into the conversation now that she's old enough to understand a woman's emotions.

And be hurt by them.

I remind her, "You are the strongest woman I've ever known. Your heart is without equal."

That stops her pacing. Her sharp eyes meet mine. In precious seconds I recall vividly how I yanked Libby aside the first day I met Iris when she and my cousin were moving into their college dorm room.

"Is she Russian?" I hiss, trying to place the features of the exotic beauty laughing with my aunt and uncle .

Libby laughs, "No, but she speaks it."

"What?" I exclaim.

"I know. Crazy, right? But Iris consumes languages the way you eat Nonna's coconut cake," Libby teases me.

Just the memory of that cake has my stomach rumbling in hunger. "Cruel." I try to bring the conversation around to her new roommate. "So, uh, what else do you know about Iris?"

Libby glares at me before declaring, "That she's half Irish, half Lakota, speaks as many languages as you code, and you're not going to mess around with her because she'd likely kick your ass." With that, Libby flounces off, leaving me wondering if Iris told her to give me that warning.

One of the things I've learned since we started dating over thirty years ago is time is sacred. We would never have lost as much as we did but for lack of communication. I clear my throat before continuing, "I mean it, Iris. I fell in love with your heart, not just your mind and body. Long after we're back in South Carolina sitting on our porch swing holding hands, I'll . . . Umph!" I catch my breath as her body crashes into mine.

Then I'm too busy holding on to my sobbing wife. "Christ, Sam."

With those words, my heart settles even while our worlds careen out of control. I squeeze her tighter. "I love you too, I always will." I bury my head in her neck and just breathe in the scent of the woman who loved me for who I was, accepted when I needed to be a different man, and loved me just the same.

My cell begins to ring. Since I've assigned rings to every family member, both of us freeze when we hear The Clash—Cal's ring. Slipping my phone from my pocket, I put it on speaker. Immediately, I inform him. "Iris can hear you."

His voice is ragged. "Libby and I just got a call from Rachel. Did you . . . ?"

I pull Iris tighter into my embrace. "No. Do you have any idea what happened?"

"Libs is a wreck. She said the picture was in a box of stuff she stored at Nonna's."

I exchange a look of horror with Iris. She emits a choked sob. Carefully, I explain, "Cal, Rachel is down at the estate. My mother invited her over after everything that happened with her getting hacked, then Aiden."

"Fucking hell," he bites off. I hear Libby's voice. Cal murmurs to her in an aside before declaring, "We have to make this right, Sam." His voice holds a note of desperation. His and Libby's love for Rachel is as strong as it is for their own children as they're her godparents. Then he passes along a message. "Iris, Libby asked for you to call her. She wants you to know she's here for you. Always."

The sob that erupts from Iris almost causes one to spill from my own lips. She promises, "I'll . . . I'll call her later, Cal."

"Good." With that, he hangs up.

I brush my hand over the mane of black curls she has twisted up. Without apology, I unclip her hair and begin massaging her head. She lets out a small moan as her eyes drift shut. "The idea is not to be comatose while I'm at work, Sam."

I pause in my ministrations. "Are you sure you're up to it?"

Her eyes flick open in irritation. "Keep massaging and let me determine what I'm up to. After all, who was shot at and still managed . . ."

I kiss her before she can remind me of the time a bullet grazed the top of her shoulder and she still managed to pull a gun on the boss she had yet to meet yet. When I let her up for air, I murmur against her lips, "Good times."

She shakes her head as she steps back and holds out her hand for her hair clip. "Not as good as being your wife and the mother of your children has been, Sam. Nothing has been as good as those moments." Tears fill her eyes briefly before she blinks them away.

I step forward and grip her arm. "You'll have more of them."

Vulnerable in a way few see her, she whispers, "Are you sure?"

"You said it the moment she was born, 'I'll do anything for you, little one,'" I remind her. "We will. We'll get through this, love."

Iris's eyes sweep over my face before she nods. "Anything, Sam."

68
IRIS

"THE EXPRESSION on both your faces was so intimate, Mama. How was Aunt Libby able to capture that unless she felt it?" Rachel whispers.

"By the time she drew that picture, Libby felt betrayed—no, she was betrayed, just not in the way she believed she was." I capture Rachel's gaze. "Like you were."

"Yes," she acknowledges.

At that moment, I offer thanks for the miracle being granted to me. My daughter, who refused to speak to us because in her mind's eye all she felt was her own heart's betrayal. I cling to my daughter's hand tightly as I try to explain. "After years of therapy, that drawing represents something completely different to Libby."

"What's that?"

"Never take a single day of love for granted. You're never guaranteed tomorrow."

Rachel's voice cracks. "She needs that reminder of that time in her life? Of all yours?"

"Yes," Sam replies.

Erika pipes in. "We've spoken of this, Rachel. Survivors of traumatic experiences find their sense of self through increasing ability to be resilient to tangible and sensory experiences. If that image was aligned to your aunt's trauma . . ."

"Then she kept it to remind her not to lose herself again," Rachel concludes.

"Exactly." Erika types a few notes before using her mouse to click a couple of times. Pressing a button, her monitor disappears beneath her desk before she asks Rachel directly, "How do you feel about opening your heart up again? Perhaps dating?"

Rachel's expression is so appalled and frightened, my chest constricts. Love is messy enough without adding the element of fear to it. I gently prod her. "What you have to remember, Rachel, is that when you open yourself to taking the fall, you're both out on that ledge together. It's a leap of faith. No one's love story is perfect."

"Yours comes close," Rachel disagrees.

"That's because you didn't live it. If you heard nothing else during our sessions, realize nothing about love is flawless." Standing, I move closer to her and kneel, impressing upon her the importance of my words. "At the beginning, I likely oversimplified it believing if I had your father in my life, I'd have it all. That wasn't true. Without knowing who I was—me, Iris Cunningham—before we ever went on our second date? Refusing to budge on the important issues—the really critical ones in our relationship? That's what builds faith and trust, the kind that keeps you going when the rest of the world is shoving its way in—whether that's family or a skanky news magazine."

Rachel nods in agreement, so I continue, "Your father inspires my heart, makes it bigger and more complete. From the first time we met to right now, he's made me fall in love with him a million times."

"And likely infuriated your mother just as many," Sam quips.

I shoot him a withering glare before returning my focus to Rachel, who has brightened considerably. I remind her, "Love is like the changing tides. The highs and lows will happen, just like the sun rises and sets. It's who you choose to navigate the seas with that matters."

"I'll remember that, Mama." Her face twists toward Sam, who shrugs helplessly.

"I still vote for letting me run every guy you date. It would give me peace of mind if nothing else," Sam jokes.

I yell, "Sam!" at the same moment Rachel shouts, "Dad!" Giving me hope that she will dip her toe back into the dating pool eventually.

She just needs time.

Rising from my knees, I scoot her over to cuddle next to her in the oversized chair. "What other questions do you have, Erika?"

Rachel gives her therapist her full attention. I wrap my arm around her shoulders and hold on—just because I can.

"Do you still feel embarrassed about the hack?" Erika asks pointedly.

Rachel rolls her eyes. "Well, duh."

"Rachel," Sam warns her. "We've been over this."

"Dad, I'm your daughter through and through. I was upset, didn't pay attention to my email. I clicked on a link I shouldn't have and lost *three hundred thousand dollars*!" Rachel's head falls back against my shoulder. Her eyes close and her body shudders over the loss of such an enormous sum of money.

Her guilt is something only Sam can absolve her of. He clucks his tongue. "Would now be the time to tell you that you're going to work for me for the summer?"

Her body stills. One eye opens. "I am?"

"Yes. I'm docking your entire salary." After private discussions with Erika about how to help Rachel move forward, the three of us came to the conclusion only actual compensation for losing such an egregious amount in a field she plans on specializing in would ever allow Rachel to move past this.

She groans. "Great. It will take me ten years to pay you back."

Quietly, I inform her, "Less than two years, providing you work full time."

Her head almost collides with my chin. "What do you mean, two? How much money do you get paid, Dad?"

I bump her hips and admonish her, "Don't ask that. It's rude."

"Mama, but I owe . . ." Then my daughter's mind seems to clear and she smacks her hands to her face. "Federal deposit insurance."

"It wasn't a hack against you, Rachel, but against the bank," I inform her, finally able to share the news Sam told me last week.

"What?" she squawks. At my nod, she glares at Sam who just shrugs modestly. "Let me guess? Dad proved it didn't just affect us, so *voila*! Most of the money was returned. I still gave them the in though."

"Which is why you'll be helping teach people at Hudson the same lessons while you're still in school. Free of charge. Enjoy the most hated part of my job," he reminds her with glee in his tone. I can't hold back my chuckle at how much father and daughter are alike.

"Yes, sir," she grumbles, but her voice holds a note of laughter, something I'll never take for granted again.

My heart is ready to burst but there's just one more concern weighing us down. Erika clears her throat. "About your family? Your Aunt Libby and Uncle Cal? Do you feel differently about them?"

Rachel's body stiffens. Sitting so close to her, I can feel the tenseness that whips through her. I prod, "You've heard us revisit a number of emotions today, sweetheart. Do you have any lingering feelings you need to get out?" I hear Sam draw in a breath swiftly as he holds it while waiting for her answer.

"I do have one question, Mama," Rachel begins.

"What's that?" I rub her arm gently, mentally bracing for anything.

"Can Uncle Cal please stop calling you Mount Iris? You were fairly restrained with how you handled the family, including him, if you ask me." Her hand reaches for mine and grips it with the same burning intensity I know lives inside me.

I can't stop the grin that leaps to my face. "Likely not. Besides, it was your father who gave him the idea for that nickname."

"What? Dad!" Rachel is horrified.

Sam just shakes his head before he launches into the story which involved Cal courting Libby, a Brendan Blake concert, and my reaction when I found out.

Mount Iris, indeed.

I listen to the other people in the room giggle and think, *Who needs Brendan Blake when I have Sam Akin?* Not me. That's for certain.

SAMUEL

AFTER PICKING Bishop up at school, the four of us head to Teterboro Airport just in time to catch the Hudson jet that has touched down. Caleb offered it to us for the weekend when he heard about Iris's and my plans to surprise the kids with a weekend at home.

As we move as a group across the tarmac, one of Hudson's youngest agents holds the door for us. Thankfully, Rachel doesn't notice him as she passes by because she's too busy chattering with her mother. He opens his mouth to call out to her when I shoot him a withering glare intended to freeze his vocal cords permanently. I linger back from my family and inform him, "You screwed up royally, kid. You don't need me to tell you what I know for damn certain your boss already did." Keene verbally fileted Aiden's ass within minutes of yanking him to the office for an emergency meeting about the undercover assignment he was working on—finding the hacker group at Columbia. "Do you realize all the people you just pissed off by proving you're no better than the people we're trying to help get arrest? What were you thinking using Rachel Aiken like that? No, don't speak, Aiden. You're lucky we need the intel you're bringing in or you'd be gone." I still feel an urge to find Keene and kiss him when I recall how he stood up for my little girl.

Like right now.

Aiden flinches imperceptibly, whether at my words now or the reminder—I don't care.

I drive my point home. "You didn't have to humiliate her to get the job done. Heard you busted the hackers last week. Thanks for getting my money back. Now go away."

"Sam," he starts but I don't want to hear it. I've spent so much time being angry and afraid I just want to enjoy the brief respite of joy I've been given. "If, and that's a huge if, she chooses to ever speak to you again be ready to beg. Her mother will insist upon it. Frankly, so will I."

The dark-haired man opens his mouth to continue to debate the issue when I decide I've had enough. I whirl around and force him against the glass doors with my forearm at his throat. "Don't. I've stayed out of it professionally but she's my daughter. Be grateful I'm leaving you still standing when you contributed to almost breaking her. Nothing you can say right now helps you get what you want." Which I damn well know is my daughter.

He taps my arm for me to ease up. Releasing a slow breath, I step back. Aiden twists his neck from side to side, his eyes never moving from his target. It's a simple matter of following his line of sight to find his gaze has never left Rachel as she climbs the steps to the jet, still laughing with her mother. All he asks is, "She's better?"

As gently as I can, I tell him, "That's no longer your concern," before I jog to catch up with my son who is waiting for me at the base of the stairs before we climb the steps so we can fly back to Charleston.

With a quick stopover to pick up the rest of our family.

LESS THAN AN HOUR LATER, the pilot advises us to buckle our seatbelts as we descend into Washington, DC's National Airport to pick up the rest of our guests. Rachel's eyes grow wide with delight, much to Iris's and my unspoken relief. "Libby, Cal, and the kids are coming too?"

"This will be the true definition of a party plane," Bishop jokes.

Iris reaches over and ruffles his hair affectionately. "You only wish. Do you think you and Jax can keep it down to a reasonable decibel? We know you both will be excited to see each other again, but the rest of us don't need to hear 'whoosh' and 'swish' as you recreate every scene from Fortnite."

He scowls at his mother just as the steps descend. A few moments later, a man bounds onto the plane, but it isn't Cal.

The blood in my veins chills even as Rachel cries out, "Uncle Parker! Are you coming with us to Charleston?"

He rewards her with an enormous hug, shaking Bishop's hand, even pressing a kiss to Iris's cheek before approaching me with his hand outstretched. "Sam. I heard you were on your way here."

I unbuckle my seatbelt and offer my own before replying sardonically, "Aren't you lucky?"

"Immensely." I'm taken aback by the relief present in Thorn's voice. He calls out to my family, "I'm borrowing Dad for just a minute. Be right back."

Imagine his shock when Rachel calls out, "Uncle Parker, I hear you tend to keep my father when you 'borrow' him. I'd like him back so we can leave on time, please."

Thorn throws Iris a glare—which she is completely immune to its potency—while she's screeching with laughter. Instead, he turns it on me as he accuses, "You've been telling stories."

"I only wish they were made up," I grumble as I follow him off the plane so we can speak outside without being overheard. Once we're a few steps clear of the plane, I hold up my hand. "I'm getting back on that plane and I'm flying to Charleston."

Thorn studies the plane intently before transitioning into the man who has become a close family friend as well as an indirect line of work. "Rachel's doing better?"

"Much," I emphasize. Although Thorn's a pain in my ass on most days, the man has a heart of solid gold for the people he cares about. Softening, I remind him, "You could have just called to check."

"I know." Then he drops a bomb that I can't hide my reaction to. "*Qəza* is missing. Last I heard from her was two days ago."

I fall back a step in shock. As one of the few people on the planet who knows the true identity of Thorn's field agent, *Qəza*, I know her safety is paramount to an ongoing murder investigation. Having voiced my concern about working with someone so young in the past, I know for a fact Thorn personally trained her in everything except the computer skills she acquired as easily as breathing. If she's missing . . . "What do you need me to do?" I ask without hesitation.

Thorn passes me a thumb drive. "Everything I know is on there."

"I'll get to work on it as soon as I get the family settled," I vow.

He shakes his head before correcting me, "As soon as you celebrate having your daughter back, Sam. I know it's been a difficult eighteen months for you."

I'm about to respond when a door behind him opens and Cal, Libby, and their brood come toward us. Cal's face immediately settles into a friendly scowl while Libby's brightens. She holds out her hands to greet Thorn. "Are you and B joining us?"

He shakes his head after bestowing a kiss on her cheek. "Unfortunately, I have to run. I just dropped by to say hello." *Not to mention shake my world on its axis.* The thought must be clear as day on my face because Cal's scowl turns ferocious behind his wife's head.

"That's so lovely," Libby enthuses.

I clear my throat. "We need to board so we don't miss our takeoff window."

Thorn holds out his calloused hand. "Thanks, Sam." Years of working together amid layers of subterfuge don't diminish his enthusiasm when he says, "Hope you have a terrific trip. Say hello to your family for me."

"Of course." I try to reassure him with one last chin lift before leading my cousin and her family to the plane.

HOURS LATER, after bunking down at Nonna's old house under the same roof as Libby, Cal, and their brood, Iris demands answers about Thorn and what happened with Aiden before we boarded the plane in New York. She hisses, "What the hell was he thinking?

"Which one of them are you referring to, sweetheart?"

"Either, both. They had to interrupt our weekend—this weekend—with their crap?" She begins pacing back and forth around the room as steam rises.

I simply wait for the eruption. Because if I know my wife the way I do, it won't be long.

Iris shouts, "*Zasranec*!" Calling both men assholes.

Promptly, there's a knock on our door. Iris scrambles to answer it.

Rachel is on the other side, her lips pressed together tightly.

Iris demands, "Sweetheart, what's wrong?"

She doesn't answer Iris but instead leans around her to address both of us. "I just want you to know I love you. I've been mulling over Erika's question. If I decide to try for love again, it's because of both of you and the love you've always given to me, shown me. Being back here with our family in Nonna's home reminded me of that." After hugging her mother swiftly, our daughter disappears across the hall into her own room.

"Sam," Iris calls urgently.

I'm behind Iris in an instant. Without her having to explain it, my heart thumps in recognition when I see the same thing she does through the enormous window—the moon shining down over the water of the Cooper River while the tide changes.

Exactly what we hoped we'd be celebrating this weekend as a family.

A flood tide.

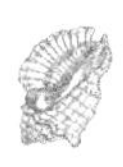

EPILOGUE

ELEVEN YEARS LATER

Iris

I've just slipped into the black sheath with the cowl neck when I feel a presence behind me. I declare huskily, "We don't have time for what's on your mind. You'd just better pray traffic isn't that bad to get across town."

I know very well what's on my husband's mind since he kept me in bed far longer than we should have been today of all days.

Sam's hands slide over my back, causing a shiver to race up my spine. "It's impossible to believe you have two grown children, Iris. You're as devastating to my senses now as you were the first day I met you."

I outright laugh. "Would that be before you blew me off for close to four years?"

Sam ducks his head and takes a nip of my earlobe. "Of course."

I twist my head to the side and find his lips waiting for me. Taking them in a long satisfying kiss, I murmur, "*Čhaŋtéčhičiye,* Sam."

His forehead lowers to mine. "And I, you, Iris." After an emotionally charged silence, he breaks it by informing me, "I have something for you."

I pull my head back slightly as his hand dips into his pocket. As he slips out a distinctive blue bag, I remind him, "It's not my day."

"No, but moments like this would never have happened without you. What was it you said to me? Ah, yes. Life isn't about the high or low tides. It's made up of moments of the flood—the transitions in between. Maybe when you wear this, you'll know that without you by my side, I would have experienced none of it—especially where you simply flooded my life with love." He upends the bag so the delicate chain falls into his hand.

A sparkle of aqua blue catches my eye through the tears that threaten the makeup I applied earlier. "Sam, we're here because of *us*." I emphasize the last word.

He corrects me as he shakes out the chain. "No, Iris, we're here because you demanded we work through issues with one another, and then later as a family. Never once did you give up on any of us, not from the moment we two became an us through the best and worst of times." Holding my eyes, he reaches around my neck and hooks the choker around my neck.

Immediately, my hand reaches for it as I press the lingering heartbeat from where his hands touched me into my skin. He leans down and nuzzles his nose against mine before murmuring, "There isn't a single moment I'd change because it brought me to right here, right now, with you."

By this point, I'm a wreck as tears course down my face. Even if he never gave me the necklace that now graces my throat, his words are the kind of gift that is everlasting. He just articulated perfectly why we endured every high and low. To be together.

Our flood tide. That's what our life's been about. It's the moments in between where our adrenaline wasn't soaring or crashing but fueled by our every day. God willing, we'll have a lot more of those.

Sprinkled with some more incredible memories, of course.

I tip my head back and press my lips to his. His arm slides easily around my waist. Mentally, I do the calculation. *If we really drive fast . . .*

That's my last coherent thought until I scramble to find my panties and shoes. Sam's laughing at me as I hop on one foot as I slip into the other. I huff, "We can't be late, today of all days!"

"We won't be. I promise."

"SHE'S LATE," I fume to Sam.

"We were almost late," he reminds me.

"That's different."

"Why?"

I have absolutely no good answer, so I turn my back to him, enjoying the way his laughter calms my already jumbling nerves. This isn't just any day. It's my baby's graduation day. As we've learned as a family, any type of graduation is something to be celebrated together.

He checks his watch for the fifth time in the last ten minutes. "She'll make it."

No sooner do the words come out of Sam's mouth than I catch sight of her long curls flying behind her as she bounds down the stairs in a pair of high-heeled shoes taller than any I've ever sported. I mutter to Sam, "She's taking the aisle so fast, I swear she's going to wipe out."

Sam's chuckling when Rachel slams to a stop at our row, narrowly avoiding tumbling down the deep stairway. Her eyes are sparkling with excitement when she passes by the other family members before she drops down into the reserved seat next to us. Immediately she launches into an explanation about why she almost missed the processional. "There was a breakdown on the train. I ran the last couple of blocks."

I glance downward, impressed despite myself. "In those?"

She nudges my knee with hers. "Come on, Mama. Get real. I took them off. It must have looked like I was chasing after someone."

Sam grumbles, "Not the first time that's happened."

It wouldn't be the first time our intrepid daughter squared off her seemingly delicate shoulders and got the job done. Years ago, after we shared some of the more intimate details of who and what we were, the results changed Rachel. She ripped off the mask she'd been hiding behind and bloomed.

Using her intuitive understanding of languages plus the hard work she dedicated to emulating her father's success with computers, Rachel found her true talents lie with code breaking. After years of her intel proving substantial payoffs, she convinced the powers that be at Hudson Investigations to put her in the field instead of spending her life behind the scenes. Now, she's on the front lines working directly for Cal in the missing children division, spearheading an elite cadre of agents who slip in and out to rescue high value targets

The last time we had dinner with Cal and Libby, he playfully drawled, "I never thought I'd say this but I'm grateful you got married and had Rachel. She's the best operative I ever worked with. I only had to endure the two of you to get her."

Fortunately Libby hit him before I could leap over the table and choke him, a pleasure that's still been denied to me all these years.

Sam slips an arm around my shoulder before addressing our oldest child. "How long are you in town, honey?"

"Well, funny you should mention that. I'll know more after the meeting I have tomorrow with Cal, Keene." She hesitates before adding, "And Aiden."

Just hearing the name of the agent who broke my baby's heart long ago sends all my maternal antennae on high alert. Just as I'm about to interrogate Rachel, the lights flicker on and off. Sam grips my shoulder. "Let's table this conversation for later. They're about to begin."

All of us shift, turning toward the back doors where Bishop will soon appear —proudly marching in the lead of his high school graduating class despite being a year younger than most. The doors open and everyone surges to their feet. The moment he appears looking just like Sam, my heart flies back to the first time I met Sam when he was just a few moments older than Bishop is now.

Like he can read my thoughts as if they're written on my face, Sam leans forward and whispers in my ear, "It feels like yesterday, not over thirty years ago."

We take our seats as Bishop, the salutatorian, the head of school, and the administration make their way to the stage. I cross one leg over the other and begin swinging it with anticipation I'm not accustomed to. Bishop wouldn't let us read his speech before he got up to make it. Our little boy is growing up, I think wistfully.

Next to me, Sam appears to be engrossed in the speech being made by the head of the board of education, but I know better. His posture is just like I used to see on so many missions, ready to leap into action. It calms me to know he's just as anxious for our son as I am. Reaching over, I cover his fingers with my own. His jewel-colored eyes fly to mine. A half-smile to acknowledge his behavior. Then he opens his mouth just as the principal announces, "Giving this year's valedictorian speech, Bishop Akin."

His fingers tighten around mine. Blindly, I reach for Rachel's hand. She squeezes my hand as her brother strides with a young man's self-confidence to the microphone.

"Students, families, teachers, Head of School Finaldi, and our esteemed board of education, welcome. We endeavored to fill our memories during the last four years with unforgettable moments. As we lived them, perhaps we were too involved in our every day to appreciate them. Having been asked to offer a retrospection of them, I fear I cannot do so for anyone else but myself because the highs and lows we each lived are sacred to each individual.

"In fact, they somewhat resemble the waves of the ocean. That ocean is our future the minute we walk out of these doors.

"I'd like to invite all the graduating class and, all those who supported us to reach this milestone, to close their eyes. Take a deep breath. Imagine your perfect ocean. Think about the soft ripples, the soothing sounds, even the sun warming the epipelagic zone. Peaceful, right?

"Okay. Now wake up and face your future. Nothing is as serene as what you just pictured.

"There will be perfect days and there are going to be storms. We will be forced to stand strong as we plant ourselves in the shallows as crashing waves break against us. Whether you fear them or are thrilled by them, substantial moments in your life are about to occur. You've been given the building blocks to put your mark in the sand by families, friends, and teachers. You've learned how to handle the extremes.

"But what about the time in between?

"The time in between, often forgot between the highs and lows, is called a flood tide. Don't know what a flood tide is? Well, for me, it's peace. It's the time I know I made it through until the next battle, where the pain will go away and healing can come. The high tide isn't battering you, nor are you pleading for a second chance on the low tide's ripple. It's the calm you dreamed of just a few short moments ago.

"Growing up with a family whose roots are deep in the heart of the low country of Charleston, South Carolina, you quickly learn about how tides can change. It's possible that after today, people in your life may change. You may never get this chance ever again. So, with that, I'd like to invite the graduates to stand."

I'm ripped from my shock over Bishop's graduation speech when his fellow graduates clammer to their feet. "We may have spent four years being Dolphins, but we're about to be cut loose into a brand new ocean. When the waves drag you under, come back here. Be proud of who you are in this moment, standing in front of the people who are just as inspired by you as you are of them. Hold your head high remembering the hard work it took to get to this moment. Then when things get rough, reach for the lessons you learned in your school—in this ocean. There's no time limit on the lessons you learned from your family, friends, or here at Delford.

"Come home often. I plan to.

"Congratulations to everyone sitting here today. While supporting each other, and providing each other inspiration, we did it.

"Together, we found our flood tide.

"Before I turn the microphone over to Teresa, I just have to say—Mom, Dad, Rach? *Čhaŋtéčhičiye*." With that, our son steps back, but it's far too late for my makeup which I can feel melting down my face. He seems to pinpoint us in the audience and flings his small tribe of well-wishers an enormous smile. Now, if I could just stop sobbing long enough to signal we heard him.

That's when Sam leans over to whisper, "God, he totally knows how to play you."

"I wonder where he gets that from?" I manage. Then I eye Sam's jacket before rubbing my face against it. "Better. Much better."

Sam bursts out laughing, prompting Cal, Libby, their kids, Lukie, Winston, as well as Libby's parents to send withering glances in his direction—everyone who came to witness Bishop graduate from high school. Except Rachel.

My daughter just leans over and whispers in my ear, "*Čhaŋtéčhičiye*, Mama. Always. Forever. As long as there are waves in the ocean."

Now there's no stopping the tears that fall. Not that I even try.

Love's worth crying a flood of tears over.

THE END

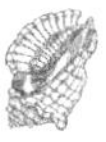

RIPPLE EFFECT

Have you read Libby and Cal Sullivan's emotionally charged path to happily ever after? Read an exclusive excerpt ahead and then buy Ripple Effect on ALL platforms!

✔ Amazon Universal ~ https://geni.us/QtjEx

✔ Nook ~ https://geni.us/TDaw8N

✔ Apple Books ~ https://geni.us/2YxhZZ

✔ Kobo ~ https://geni.us/U3dX

✔ Google Books ~ https://geni.us/Fn0O5D

PRESENT DAY
ELIZABETH

I've tried to leave this part of my life behind so many times. Over and over, I'm dragged back to rehash the memories of the worst days I've ever endured. *How many times can I do it before I say no more?* I think wearily. I'm proud to say I've moved on. It took years for me to get to where I am right now.

My husband, recognizing the tension whipping through my body, offers with complete seriousness, "We can leave."

I snicker. "'Cause that will go over well." I rub my hands up and down my arms, trying to warm myself.

He turns me to face him, and my slight baby bump brushes against his muscular abs. "Like I give a damn about that. Especially now." His hand drops to caress my stomach tenderly.

I reach up and cup his cheek. Smoothing my hand back and forth over the bristles that tickle the inside of my palm, I murmur, "You need to shave."

"I ran out of time. This gorgeous pregnant woman had her way with me this morning. I was a wreck when she was done." His smile, the very first thing I noticed about him, makes my stomach flutter. Then again, maybe that's our baby kicking. Either way, I'm flooded with gratitude.

Now.

"I didn't notice you complaining," I tease.

He gives me a look rife with disbelief. "I may be called many things, but I hope I've grown out of my idiot stage."

Brushing my lips against his, I whisper, "I occasionally have to check. It took you a little longer than the average male."

Just as my husband's about to retaliate with some smart-ass comment, a door opens behind us. "Mrs. Sullivan? Dr. Powell is ready for you."

Cal doesn't let me go right away. "I'm right here, Libby. I've got you."

"I know." And I do; he's more than shown me that.

Concern flashes over his face. He opens his mouth but closes it just as quickly.

"What is it?" I ask. I don't have a lot of time before I need to be on the other side of that door.

Crushing me to him, he whispers directly in my ear, "You had a nightmare last night."

Surprised, I lean back in his strong arms. "I did?"

He nods solemnly. "And I know today's going to make things worse." The tick in his jaw betrays his calm demeanor.

Knowing I'm putting the schedule at risk, I wrap my arms around him and hold him as hard as I can. Cal buries his head in my neck. "Even if they try to get to me in dreams, there's nothing for you to be afraid of."

"Why's that?" His voice is raw with remembered pain.

I search his tired eyes, which I can now see reflect his lack of sleep. Probably because he was standing guard over his family. Kissing him briefly, I pull out of his warm embrace and make my way to the door. I pause there and look back. "Because just like the first time I woke from my nightmare, you were there for me."

"I always will be. No matter what."

Without another word, I follow the young intern down the hall. Another person greets us before saying, "I'll take Mrs. Sullivan from here. How are you today?"

I smile and nod, but inside I'm screeching in maniacal laughter. Is anyone ever ready to have their emotions dissected like they're a frog in science class?

It takes another few minutes before I'm settled facing Dr. Powell. "It's a pleasure to see you again, Mrs. Sullivan."

"Libby, please," I correct him. I can't do this if we're going to stand on formality.

"Libby," he returns. "We left off yesterday talking about your background; you're an interior designer in the Washington, DC, area, correct?"

Smoothing a hand over my stomach, I nod. "Yes. A little less than four years ago now, my husband's company was bought out. We decided to relocate with the new owners."

"How does it feel to be back in Charleston?"

My eyes drift out the window overlooking the harbor. Sunlight glistens off the water. I shudder.

"Is strange an acceptable answer?"

"It is."

"Then let's go with that." The laugh I receive is appreciated, so I begin to relax.

Maybe it's too soon to do that.

"Libby, I can't help but notice you're expecting. "

"It's getting harder and harder for me to miss too," I joke, earning another chuckle.

"Is your family excited?"

"Beyond belief." I smooth a hand over my stomach, pulling my dress tighter.

"After everything you've been through, it must feel like a miracle," Dr. Powell says gently.

"Yes." I don't elaborate more because I suspect he will.

And I'm right.

"We're here for a reason, today, Libby. And this miracle is a perfect conclusion to it. I hate to take you back..."

"You don't have to," I tease. "We can just talk about how I plan on decorating the nursery."

He smiles. There's an edge of determination covered by a layer of sympathy to it that I abhor—not that I'd let him see. I don't need the sympathy; the families of the people who didn't survive do.

What I need is peace.

"I'd like to go back, Libby."

I shake my head, still wearing a smile. "What's the good in that?" For me, for Cal, for any of us?

"Context." Dr. Powell's words come back at me so succinctly, I want to roll my eyes, but I can hear Cal's voice in my head telling me to calm my sass.

Reaching for the unopened bottle of juice on the table next to me, I twist the cap off and take a small sip. Just a small one. I still can't consume liquids any faster than a tiny drink at a time. "How far back would you like to go?"

Flipping through the notes on his lap, he lifts off his glasses before asking, "What made you decide to take a trip on your own on the luxury cruise liner, *Sea Force*?"

Even knowing the question was coming, my heart sinks because I know of all the subsequent questions that are going to follow.

Cal was wrong. I was wrong. To keep raking this over the coals punishes more than just us.

Taking a deep breath, I admit, "Because I was certain my marriage was over."

After all, when a communication breakdown occurs in most marriages, there's always a ripple effect. But when it occurs on the international stage, and it involves a coordinated military rescue, well, the ripples are the size of a tsunami.

Plucking at my dress, a dress I chose to wear because it has sunflowers scattered on it, I remember the days leading up to when Cal gave them to me for the first time. It was right at the end of college, and every day seemed as beautiful outside as this one.

1

FIFTEEN YEARS AGO FROM PRESENT DAY

Elizabeth

Calhoun Sullivan. Just thinking his name sends tingles through my body the likes of which I've never understood.

It all started a few months ago when after months of being in his class, my cousin Sam brought Cal out to dinner when he met up with me at the local diner on campus. "Libs, Cal," he introduced us before dropping into the seat next to me.

When our hands touched for the first time, a frisson ran up my spine. My body locked as I met his brown eyes beneath furrowed brows. It was in complete contrast to the abrupt "Libby" he gave me before sitting.

Sam and Cal began talking—no, debating—about politics in earnest that night. Tuning their words out, I instead listened to the lazy cadence of both of their voices, wondering exactly how quickly I could manage to escape without being rude. Finally, I shifted uncomfortably in my seat. "Don't take this the wrong way—" I offered them both a smile. "—but I have an exam to prepare for tomorrow."

"Crap, Libs. I was going to..." Sam was utterly contrite as he was going to help me study.

Pushing at his shoulder gently, I grabbed my bag and slid out of the seat. "Nothing to apologize for. You're not always going to be there for me to lean on."

A flash of something crossed Sam's face. "No, but I'm here now."

Leaning upward, I brushed my lips across his cheek. "And after I pass this test, you can take me out to make it up to me." Looking over my shoulder, I tossed a "Nice to meet you" to Cal with a smile.

He didn't say anything. His dark head just tipped in my direction with a murmured "Libby."

That was the first time I saw Cal, but it wasn't the last. Over the next few weeks, Cal would accompany Sam to our weekly dinners. Then, as I was not so subtly trying to play matchmaker between my cousin and my roommate, Cal would be at dinners, on hikes, around concerts. It became obvious to me that my cousin, who didn't have many close friends growing up, had found someone he trusted and liked in Cal.

And if I fell in love just a little more every moment I had to spend in his presence, well, that became my problem.

We've laughed, joked, teased each other for months. As friends, we've argued current events, talked about sports, and made plans with no indication he's ever seen me as anything more than what I am—Sam's cousin. So, it's my fault if I lie in my bed late at night dreaming of what it would be like to have his dark caress on my skin. It's not like he's helping himself to a smorgasbord of undergraduates. As much as I might want him to with this undergrad, I think glumly.

It doesn't matter—it's never going to happen. At least, there's nothing giving me any sort of hope it will.

Shifting, I lift a glass of less-than-stellar wine to my lips. At least now that I'm old enough to drink, I can drown the agony of the rumors of how he fucks like the end of the world is coming before he rolls out of whatever bed he's in.

I smile into my glass before an elbow to my ribs almost causes me to upend the entire thing. "You rang?" I ask my best friend, Iris Cunningham, drolly.

"Is it just me, or is Sam taking on more and more of Cal's behavior traits?" Iris has had a crush on my cousin since the day she met him, not that it's stopped her from dating half of the male population on campus.

I, on the other hand, took one look at Cal and felt like time stood still. When we're all together—which is more and more of late—I feel like it's my mission to make the somber-faced man crack a smile. I've yet to succeed, but hey, at least Iris appreciates my efforts as she normally collapses on Sam howling. I still have time, I think determinedly, as there's still a few weeks before I graduate and head home to Charleston.

Turning to answer Iris, I ask, "Do you mean the man-whoring?"

Iris grins. "Your cousin has a way to go for that," she teases, inadvertently sending a swift pain in the region of my stomach. Pushing my wine aside, knowing I'll be ill if I drink any more of it, I ask, "Elaborate, please."

"Look at them." She tips her head to the side. Glancing over her shoulder, she continues. "They're a pair of matched emo bookends holding up the collective honeypot of campus."

I burst into gales of laughter. "Lord, deliver me," I wheeze out. My drawl is more pronounced than it normally is.

The devil that dances in Iris's eyes is more wicked than normal. "You know you're going to miss every second we're not doing just this."

"Too true, darling." I lift my glass to toast the best part of my college experience when I feel a mysterious pull from the far side of the room. Allowing my eyes to flicker in that direction, they clash with Cal's. This time there's something different about them.

They're crinkled around the corners, and one side is hitched up. He's not looking down at the woman he'll likely take home later, I think with my heart pounding. He's watching me. And whether it's wishful thinking or not, he lifts his beer in my direction to toast me.

Without thinking, I send a beaming smile in his direction. Taking a deep breath, I lift the glass to my lips and manage to swallow a little more of the lighter fluid they pass off as wine.

"What was that all about?" Iris demands. She starts to turn around, but I stop her by pinching her. Hard.

"I...I'm not really sure," I admit.

"What do you mean?"

"One minute, I'm laughing with you and the next, Cal's..." I don't get to finish my sentence because Iris has whipped around.

Cal's gone and so's the cute blonde. I'm not shocked neither by their departure nor by my feelings of disappointment. Iris prompts, "Cal was?"

"Nothing. It's nothing." I wave my hand to indicate the subject's closed, but I didn't take into account the subject sliding into the booth next to me. Iris's eyes bug out.

What the hell's happening here? Am I asleep and this is a beautiful dream? Surreptitiously, I pinch my arm. Nope. I'm awake.

"Hey, Libby. Iris. You both seem to be having quite the evening over here." Cal's dark voice sends every nerve ending on red alert.

"Well, you know us, Cal. We know how to enjoy ourselves." As soon as the words pass her lips, Iris looks like she got goose-egged herself when Sam slides into the booth on her side.

He smiles easily at me. "Cousin, do you know what to do with the trouble sitting next to you?"

"Who says I plan on doing anything?" I drawl, earning a loud guffaw from Sam and Iris.

Cal just looks thoughtful.

"I have big news," Sam announces.

"Oh, what's that?" I lean forward eagerly. Although I have an older brother, Sam and I being mere months apart in age, we were raised practically as twins.

"I got a job," he announces proudly.

A thrilled gasp escapes my lips. Suddenly, I'm shoving at Cal. "Get out of my way," I demand. "I need to congratulate him."

"Don't you want to hear what it is?" Cal asks with a bemused expression.

I'm still shoving at his shoulder even as I contemplate climbing over the table. "It doesn't matter. Look at him." I beam when I do. "He's so happy right now, he's lighting up the room."

Cal hesitates for just a second, murmuring, "I think that's you who's doing that, Libby." But he slides out of the booth so I can make my way over to Sam to hug him.

"I am so, so proud of you. Was it that government contractor you were telling me about? The one with offices overseas? Confederation?"

Sam chuckles as he squeezes the breath out of me. When did the scrawny boy who used to fish while I read on the banks of the Cooper River grow up? I bury my head against his shoulder to avoid those memories right now, knowing we'll never have those carefree days again. "Alliance, and yes. That's the one."

"When will you tell the family?" He lets me go. I turn to slide back into the booth only to be startled. Cal's been standing waiting patiently for us to finish. Slipping past him, I sit back down.

It must be my imagination that he slides a little closer when he sits back down himself.

"I wanted to tell you first. I'll call Mom and Dad sometime tomorrow," Sam tells me.

"Good." I flash a grin at him. "I want to be able to tell my parents I knew before they did."

Sam leans over and tweaks my nose. "What about you? Are you still heading back to Charleston after graduation?"

I nod. I've known what I've wanted for my life since the first day I ever entered Stafford Antiques with Nonna. Miss Julie gave me cookies and a tour of her store, telling me where all the beautiful treasures were from. And I imagined if I had all the money in the world, where I would put them in my house. It wasn't long after, I began to redecorate first my room, then my parents' home, and eventually Nonna's home on the estate with an emphasis on our family heirlooms.

"I've been waiting for this moment since I was six, Sam." We both exchange grins at the truth of my statement. "It's time."

"Time? Time for what?" Cal's demanding question forces me to turn toward him.

I shrug before picking up my drink. Wrinkling my nose, I attempt another sip. "I'm a dual major, fine arts and business. I've got plans of my own."

Pursing his lips at my nonanswer, Cal plucks my drink out of my hand—my drink! Taking a swallow, he mutters, "You need to be drinking better than this."

I shrug. "It's what I can afford." At least on a student budget, which I'm determined to live on while I'm here.

"I can afford better." Flagging down a waitress, he orders me a glass of wine —the brand I would normally drink at home. Before she can escape, he asks Sam and Iris, "Anything else?"

Iris holds up her almost empty beer. "I'll take another."

Sam shakes his head. "I'm driving."

"That will do it, then. Thanks." Cal dismisses the harried woman before turning his not-insubstantial attention back to me.

I'm stunned and a little taken aback. "I was okay with what I had."

Flicking a stray hair away from my face, he shrugs as if it's no big deal. Then again, to him, it probably isn't, I remind myself. He brings us back around to what we were discussing as he polishes off the dredges of the drink I'd been nursing. "So, a dual major? That's impressive. Do you already have a job lined up back in Charleston?"

I duck my head. It's not something I share with a lot of people. "Less of a job, more of a dream."

"I like the idea of you having dreams, Libby." My head snaps up. An arc of something different moves between us. We're butting up against a line I stopped daring to toe up against.

Then I know I'm not imagining the brief flit of a smile that crosses his lips after the new wine is put down in between us and he takes a sip before I can even reach for it. Handing it to me, his voice drops as he says, "Much better. It tastes like something the sun actually kissed versus something it killed."

The comment is so outrageous, I toss my hair back and laugh. When I finish, Cal's still smiling. I reach for the wine and declare flippantly, "You should smile more. You're incredibly handsome when you do."

Even though Cal's smile fades—a terrible shame—the words he whispers in my ear will make me remember that smile forever. "Since you're going to be leaving soon, I suppose it's safe to tell you the only time I ever think about smiling is when I'm around you."

He sits back and rests an arm over the back of the booth, leaving me frozen in place.

Why would he say that to me? Why now when we've got less than two weeks left until I leave?

Picking up the wine, I take a long drink and hate that he's right. It does taste like liquid sunlight. And I'll never be able to drink it again without thinking of him.

2

FIFTEEN YEARS AGO FROM PRESENT DAY

CALHOUN

LIBBY AKIN IS CAUSING me to lose sleep and not in a way that gives me any sort of satisfaction.

I roll over and punch my pillow in the off-campus apartment I live in, unable to stop thinking of her mahogany-brown hair and gem-colored eyes. While I'm recovering from a few injuries I sustained on my last assignment, I was sent here to scout out and recruit candidates for Alliance. Both of our time here is almost over.

It's why I haven't touched her the way I've been dying to.

But God, what I wouldn't give to have her beautiful smile warm the cold dark parts of me. It's impossible not to know when she's in the vicinity, and that's not simply when I'm around her cousin. All I have to do is walk out the political science building where a former Alliance employee contacted the Admiral six months ago about a few potential recruits and wham! I know she's there when her laughter peals out above the melee of students.

When she touches me, even if it's in the most innocent of ways, my skin tingles. My heart rate starts to accelerate faster than if I've just clocked five miles. And my cock? It's harder than if one of the women I've fucked since I've been here has lavished attention on it for hours.

Because it's just Libby. And the truth is she's the only thing I've ever wanted in a life where I've been given nothing.

Rolling onto my back, I make out the whirring blades of the ceiling fan in the dark. At least this assignment comes with a bed, I think ruefully. The last one involved sleeping bags and sand for much longer than I enjoyed. Rubbing the heel of one calloused foot up my leg to feel the scar, I remember the blisters I suffered as the fine sand of the Middle Eastern desert found its way into my combat boots. Pain in the ass. Sand doesn't come out of anything. I'm certain I was still shitting it when the Admiral told me I was coming here; I ate so much of it. But it was worth it. We managed to rescue the Bahraini ambassador's son without starting an international incident.

At twenty-eight, I've done more than I ever expected to do in this life. I've visited more countries on the map than most people have heard of, many of which I couldn't even identify in my youth growing up in a foster home after my mother decided she'd had enough of motherhood after three short days and abandoned me in a gas station in nowheresville Georgia.

While my resume officially reads I'm a member of the National Guard, the reality is I've worked for Alliance since my junior year of college. At the beginning, I interned for the Charleston-based company doing nothing but admin work. It was one of our former team leaders who noticed me staying late and studying mission reports with hungry eyes. "That mission was completed FUBARed," he drawled. "See anything you would have done differently, Cal?"

My guard was up, because I was uncertain if I was in trouble for reviewing the materials. But I was cleared to read them. After all, part of my job was to make certain they ended up in the right hands. But still, I answered honestly. "Your point man gave away your position, whether he intended to or not. You need to rework your signal process," I told him bluntly.

He acknowledged my feedback with a brisk nod before walking out the door without another word. I was certain I was fucked the next day when I was called into Ret. Admiral Richard Yarborough's office. Yarborough, the owner of Alliance, was and is not a man to fuck with. A former SEAL, he was taken out due to a shot to the leg that shattered his kneecap. Unwilling to sit on the sidelines, he brought together a coalition of the best civilians to operate with permission of the government to go where they can't due to negotiated treaties and peace agreements.

Alliance has never been limited by such boundaries.

"So, I hear I have a mole, Sullivan?"

"What...what do you mean, sir?" I stuttered. He spun his chair around to face me.

"Byers called me last night and said you spotted what he didn't. The signals were compromised—we could have lost brave men and women out there." He gestures to a chair in front of his mammoth desk. "Please sit."

I did, not because he asked me, but because my legs were so filled with jelly, I was afraid I was going to fall down. "Maybe it's because I'm removed from it all," I offered.

He snorted. "Bullshit, son. It's because you have an aptitude for this business. Now, have you ever heard of OCS?"

My face paled. "Is that another company?" Alliance was the only family I knew. I didn't want to leave.

"Officer Candidate School, Cal. We're going to get you in as soon as you graduate. Then"—Yarborough's eyes gleamed with unholy amusement—"we're going to get you out."

I finished college at twenty, OCS by the time I was twenty-one. And by the time I was twenty-three, there was an "accident" that required a medical discharge requiring me to be released out of my five-year commitment to the Navy. At least that's what Yarborough arranged.

Since then, I've traveled the world anywhere Alliance has sent me—including my current assignment on this college campus. Here, the "professor" became the student in so many ways, and I begin to wonder if Yarborough didn't arrange for that knife to slice into me. Before, I never understood when we'd try to rescue families with the guarantee of asylum, they would elect to live in the bowels of poverty. "You no understand. Wife gone." Then they'd turn away, asking only for the food and medical supplies we'd readily offer to leave when we were willing to offer them so much more. I witnessed people crying over loved ones, and while I felt compassion, I never understood their heartbreak.

Not until a smile more powerful than the sun started lighting the dark corners of my heart.

For the first time, I understood why men would break allegiance, disregard political survival, and beg for mercy. But I know better than to reach out for it. After all, as Yarborough once said, "Peace is a facade we convince our families of so they can sleep at night. Right, Sullivan?"

My laconic "I don't have a family" earned me a slap on the back. It might be the first and last time being an orphan was a bonus. Forget about the years of looking at the door every time there was a knock wondering if it was someone coming to claim me—as if I meant something to someone.

For once meaning nothing to anyone seemed a bonus when Yarborough said, "Good. Then there's nothing anyone can hold over you."

Rolling to my side, I realize it was a mistake to touch the silk of Libby's hair tonight. Now, I'll never forget what the strands felt like between my fingers. Angry, I grab my phone, determined to find a way to forget her.

But even as my finger hovers over the buttons, I find myself going to my photos. Flipping through, I find a picture I snapped of Libby when she was sitting on the walls of the quad. Someone had just dropped a pile of leaves over her head. Instead of being angry and seeking retaliation, something I likely would have done, she reached down and threw them up in the air again with a laugh. God, her beauty hurts my heart. Her smile is the kind that would bring me to my knees if I'd met her in a different life.

"Somehow you're always seeking the sun. It's too bad I live in the shadows." Closing the phone, I toss it onto the nightstand, determined to get some sleep.

I need to be up early for a run with our newest recruit tomorrow at 0500.

* * *

"You're a sadistic bitch, Cal," Sam pants next to me. He's running in wingtips per today's instructions. I have little doubt his feet are going to be blistered later.

I smirk, my breathing easy as we take another hill. No one's up this early to hear his suffering. "What if you had to run for your life, Sam? You're not always going to be in running sneakers and compression socks."

"That's not why you suck," he mutters.

I'm unperturbed when I ask, "Not that I care, but curiosity has me now. Why am I a sadist?"

"A sadistic bitch," he corrects. I'm pleased to see his breathing has evened out. He doesn't answer me for a few as our shoes slap along the old gravel road I chose specifically for its rough terrain. "It's because you make this look so easy," he says.

I jolt to a stop, so of course Sam does too. "Sam," I reply carefully. "I've been doing this for seven years, three of those in the military. You're coming straight into Alliance because you're a fucking genius with a computer. We just don't want you to end up dead in the process of working out in the field."

"I know. That would piss Libby and our family off to no end."

Shaking my head, I begin running again with Sam keeping pace. "You're the oddest person I've ever recruited."

"Yeah, but I bet I'm the only one who has a family member you've got the hots for," he says cheerfully.

And I trip. Fortunately, I catch myself before I go down on the sharp stones lining the trail. "Jesus Christ," I growl.

Sam laughs at me. "So, what are you going to do about it?"

"Nothing."

Disappointment etches his face. "Why not?"

Rubbing the back of my neck, I glare at him. "Because it's not a good decision."

"Hmm." Sam stretches.

Smart man, I think approvingly as I begin to do the same. But the silence that stretches out between us starts to annoy me. "What?" I finally ask.

"I never took you for a coward," he says offhandedly.

My muscles all lock. "Excuse me?"

He backs away. "Now, Cal, I just meant in terms of matters of this. You're a badass."

Fucking right I am. "Better run, Sam. If I catch up, there's going to be hell to pay," I warn him in a lethal voice.

He takes off in a sprint.

I take a moment to rub my hand over my chest where the shot he landed aimed true. I am a coward when it comes to Libby Akin. I want her so damn much, I'm afraid of what will happen when I have to leave.

And I always do. There's always more risk, another mission, another life to protect.

I just wish I could take a piece of her with me.

Jogging after Sam, I see him a few hundred yards ahead with his head between his legs. When he sees me, he straightens before sprinting away. Even though I hadn't planned on educating him on evasive techniques this morning, it looks like Sam's about to get a small lesson in it.

EVERY SUNDAY since I started working here last semester, there's been a local farmer's market in town. Normally, I go first thing in the morning so I can beat the students who end up coming down later in the day. But now that I'm training Sam, I don't make it until 10:30. I race through, picking up fresh fruit and vegetables for the week, before I make my way for the exit.

I freeze in place when I see Libby. Juggling my packages, I manage to get my phone out and snap a picture of her surrounded by flowers. It may be my imagination, but she laughs at something the elderly woman says, and the sunflowers seem to reach for her. "Beautiful," I murmur aloud.

Libby accepts a bouquet of purple flowers wrapped in cellophane with another smile before turning her back and walking away. In her arms she's also managing a cake box with a carefully wrapped present on top.

Dialing quickly, I hear, "Didn't you torture me enough this morning?" growled by Sam in my ear.

"Is it a special occasion for Libby?" I ask without answering him.

"Not that I know of." He sounds confused.

"Birthday, anniversary of an important date? I can find out, but I'd prefer you think."

"It's not her birthday, Cal. That's October 1st."

I commit the date to my memory and then ask, "Then why is she carrying a cake, a bouquet of flowers, and..."

With a yelp, Sam yells, "What kind of flowers?"

"I don't know. They were purple."

"They were irises, Cal. It's Iris's birthday! Shit, I can't walk, and I need to go to her birthday dinner at Libby's."

"Go take a shower. I'll pick up some flowers for you to bring to her and drop them by with some Tiger Balm." His relieved sigh worries me a bit. "Are you going to be able to let her go?" Sam's growing feelings for Libby's best friend are starting to concern me.

"Let her go? I don't have to. You tagged her to be recruited as well. Remember, one of your colleagues is training her" is all he says before he hangs up the phone.

Huh. I forgot we don't have a no-fraternization policy. But now I'll have to do some deeper digging on Ms. Iris Cunningham when I get back to my apartment to make certain recruiting them both isn't going to be a colossal mistake. In the meanwhile, I approach the same flower vendor Libby just vacated. "Hello. I need a bouquet of flowers for a birthday."

"Seems to be the specialty of the day." The woman smiles. "Do you know what kind of flowers?"

"Something unique but lovely." The woman nods before turning away. Soon, she presents me with a bouquet that Sam will be proud to give Iris. I'm pulling out my card to pay when suddenly I ask, "Can you also make me up a bouquet of sunflowers?"

I must be crazy. That's the only way to explain it.

"Of course. Give me just one more moment." Soon, I have a gorgeous bunch of sunflowers in my arms. A smile spreads across the woman's face as she runs my card through. "They're such a happy flower."

"Hmm?" I'm too busy looking at the bright cheerful flowers in my arms. In their own way, it's like holding a piece of Libby.

"Sunflowers. They symbolize adoration, loyalty, and longevity, but overall they just make people happy," I'm informed.

A little stunned, I scrawl my name on the receipt and pocket the card. "That they do." But my mind is on Libby, not the flowers. "Thank you."

"Anytime."

ACKNOWLEDGMENTS

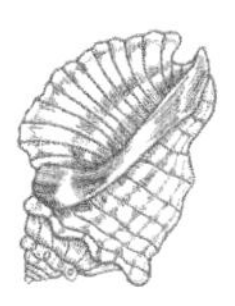

To my husband, Nathan, we've had so many highs and lows, I know we're both grateful for the in betweens. Regardless of where we are on the tide, I love you.

To my son, my little code ninja. Thank you for making me a mother. You are worth anything.

Mom, growing up, I may have lived in shark-infested waters, but you helped me navigate them to become the woman I am today. Thank you for always doing your best to protect me. XOXO

Jen, tides ebb and flow but one thing is constant—we're in the same ocean together. I love you.

My Meows, maybe I was inspired by Caymans. Just a little bit. I love you all so much and can't wait for our trip in November.

For my colleagues, you inspire me everyday. AR, JG, ND^2, and so many others, your continuous support means the world.

To the Happily Editing Anns, thank you for your incredible skill and flexibility! I just wish I could send you some Beach Road Chicken.

To Missy Borucki, working together is never dull. After all, there was absolutely nothing going on in our lives when you read this. LOL. XOXO

To Holly Malgeri. My twin, holy timeline, holy word count. I LOVES YOU!

To my amazing cover designer Deborah Bradseth of Tugboat Design, This whole series has my head spinning! XOXO

To Gel, at Tempting Illustrations, absolutely stunning.

To the team at Foreword PR, thank you for making us shine. Alissa, thank you for saving me so many times!

Linda Russell, you know my stance on this. In the end I need to be able to say I'm proud of the writer I am and what I've done. Thank you for helping me with both. I love you, lady!

To Amy Rhodes, Kristin Lira, and Dawn Hurst, thank you for your early input into Iris and Sam's story. Your generosity and time made Flood Tide even better.

To the amazing people in Tracey's Tribe, MUAH!

To all of the bloggers and readers who take the time to read my books, thank you from the bottom of my heart. I am overwhelmed by your emails, your comments, and reviews. Thank you for your continuous support.

XOXO

ABOUT THE AUTHOR

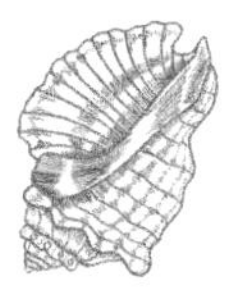

Tracey Jerald knew she was meant to be a writer when she would rewrite the ending of books in her head when she was a young girl growing up in southern Connecticut. It wasn't long before she was typing alternate endings and extended epilogues "just for fun".

After college in Florida, where she obtained a degree in Criminal Justice, Tracey traded the world of law and order for IT. Her work for a world-wide internet startup transferred her to Northern Virginia where she met her husband in what many call their own happily ever after. They have one son.

When she's not busy with her family or writing, Tracey can be found in her home in north Florida drinking coffee, reading, training for a runDisney event, or feeding her addiction to HGTV.

Connect with her on her website (https://www.traceyjerald.com/) for all social media links, bonus scenes, and upcoming news.

Made in the USA
Middletown, DE
28 June 2022